SETTEMBRE

23 MARTEDI, ss. Cosma e D, 270-95

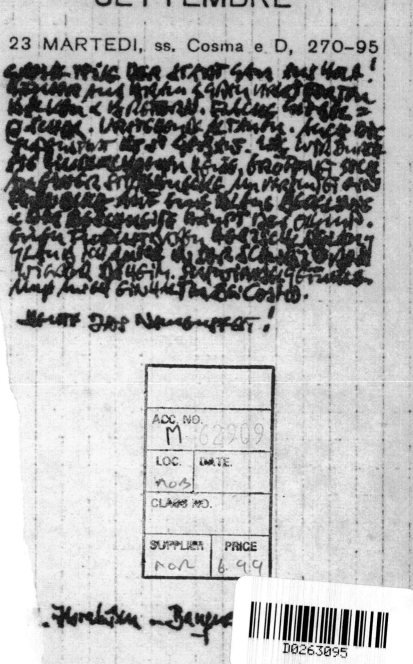

THE EMIGRANTS

"An unconsoling masterpiece . . . It is exquisitely written and exquisitely translated . . . a true work of art"

CAROLE ANGIER, *Spectator*

"The delicate accumulation of vanishing details of four slowly diminishing lives hints at the vast amount of life that has been irrevocably lost and forgotten. This is one of those books that is so good that its sadness is paradoxically enlivening against all the odds"
A. S. BYATT, *Times Literary Supplement*

"A sober delicate account of displacement, and a classic of its kind. Modest and remote, it resurrects older standards of behaviour, making most contemporary writing seem brash and immature. No book has pleased me more this year"

ANITA BROOKNER, *Spectator*

"*The Emigrants* is the most extraordinary, thrilling new book I've read this year . . . indeed, for several years. It is like nothing I've ever read . . . A book of excruciating sobriety and warmth and a magical concreteness of observation . . . I know of no book which conveys more about that complex fate, being a European at the end of European civilization. I know of few books written in our time but this is one which attains the sublime"

SUSAN SONTAG, *Times Literary Supplement*

"This profoundly moving book . . . is a sustained elegy for a vanished Jewish culture, and for those who were, and are, forever displaced . . . It gives a vivid, and heart-rending, picture of a way of life that can never return" PAUL BAILEY, *Daily Telegraph*

"It is like a Kaddish spoken softly by a very civilized man weighted with sadness and alive with love of what is and what was"

MICHAEL HULSE, the translator

W. G. SEBALD was born in Wertach im Allgäu, Germany, in 1944. He studied German language and literature in Freiburg, French-speaking Switzerland and Manchester. In 1966 he took up a position as an assistant lecturer at the University of Manchester, and settled in England in 1970. He has taught at the University of East Anglia since that date, becoming Professor of European Literature in 1987, and from 1989 to 1994 he was the first Director of the British Centre for Literary Translation at UEA. In addition to the present work, which won the Berlin Literature Prize, the Literatur Nord Prize and the Johannes Bobrowski Medal, W. G. Sebald is the author of two other works of fiction: *Schwindel. Gefühle* (1990) and *Die Ringe des Saturn*, which will be published by Harvill with the title *The Rings of Saturn*.

MICHAEL HULSE has translated Goethe's *The Sorrows of Young Werther* and Jakob Wassermann's *Caspar Hauser* (both for Penguin), as well as contemporary German writing by Luise Rinser, Botho Strauss and Elfriede Jelinek. An award-winning poet, he is the author of *Eating Strawberries in the Necropolis* (Harvill, 1991).

W. G. Sebald

THE EMIGRANTS

*Translated from the German
by Michael Hulse*

THE HARVILL PRESS
LONDON

First published as *Die Ausgewanderten* by
Vito von Eichborn GmbH & Co. Verlag KG, Frankfurt am Main, 1993

First published in Great Britain in 1996 by The Harvill Press, 84 Thornhill Road, London N1 1RD

This edition first published in 1997 by The Harvill Press

2 4 6 8 9 7 5 3 1

Copyright © Vito von Eichborn GmbH & Co. Verlag KG, Frankfurt am Main, 1993

English translation copyright © The Harvill Press, 1996

W. G. Sebald asserts the moral right to be identified as the author of this work

The publication of this work is supported by Inter Nationes, Bonn

A CIP catalogue record for this title is available from the British Library

ISBN 1 86046 349 5

Designed and typeset in Adobe Garamond at
Libanus Press, Marlborough, Wiltshire

Printed and bound in Great Britain by Mackays of Chatham

Half title illustration: from Ambros Adelwarth's diary (see p. 132)

CONTENTS

DR HENRY SELWYN

*And the last remnants
memory destroys*

At the end of September 1970, shortly before I took up my position in Norwich, I drove out to Hingham with Clara in search of somewhere to live. For some 25 kilometres the road runs amidst fields and hedgerows, beneath spreading oak trees, past a few scattered hamlets, till at length Hingham appears, its asymmetrical gables, church tower and treetops barely rising above the flatland. The market place, broad and lined with silent façades, was deserted, but still it did not take us long to find the house the agents had described. One of the largest in the village, it stood a short distance from the church with its grassy graveyard, Scots pines and yews, up a quiet side street. The house was hidden behind a two-metre wall and a thick shrubbery of hollies and Portuguese laurel. We walked down the gentle slope of the broad driveway and across the evenly gravelled forecourt. To the right, beyond the stables and outbuildings, a stand of beeches rose high into the clear autumn sky, its rookery deserted in the early afternoon, the nests dark patches in a canopy of foliage that was only occasionally disturbed. The front of the large, neoclassical house was overgrown with Virginia creeper. The door was painted black and on it was a brass knocker in the shape of a fish. We knocked several times, but there was no sign of life inside the house. We stepped back a little. The sash windows, each divided into twelves panes, glinted blindly, seeming to be made of dark mirror glass. The house gave the impression that no one lived there. And I recalled the château in the Charente that I had once visited from Angoulême. In front of it, two crazy brothers – one a parliamentarian, the other an architect – had built a replica of the façade of the palace of Versailles, an utterly pointless counterfeit, though one which made a powerful impression from a distance. The windows of that house had been just as gleaming and blind as those of the house we now stood before. Doubtless we should have driven on without accomplishing a thing, if we had not summoned up the nerve, exchanging one of those swift glances, to at least take a look at the garden. Warily we walked round the house. On the north side, where the brickwork was green with damp and variegated ivy partly covered the walls, a mossy path led past the servants' entrance, past a woodshed, on through deep shadows, to emerge, as if upon a stage, onto a terrace with a stone balustrade overlooking a broad, square lawn bordered by flower beds, shrubs and trees. Beyond the lawn, to the west, the grounds opened out into a park landscape studded with lone lime trees, elms and holm oaks, and beyond that lay the gentle undulations of arable land and the white mountains of cloud on the horizon. In silence we gazed at this view, which drew the eye into the distance as it fell and rose in stages, and we looked for a long time, supposing ourselves quite alone, till we noticed a motionless figure lying in the shade cast on the lawn by a lofty cedar in the southwest corner of the garden. It was an old man, his head propped on his arm, and he seemed altogether absorbed in contemplation of the patch of earth immediately before his eyes. We crossed the lawn towards him, every step wonderfully light on the grass. Not till we were almost upon him, though, did he notice us. He stood up, not without a certain embarrassment. Though he was tall and broad-shouldered, he seemed quite stocky, even short. Perhaps this impression came from the way he had of looking, head bowed, over the top of his gold-rimmed reading glasses, a habit which had given him a stooped, almost supplicatory posture. His white hair was combed back, but a few stray wisps kept falling across his strikingly high forehead. I was counting the blades of grass, he said, by way of apology for his absentmindedness. It's a sort of pastime of mine. Rather irritating, I am afraid. He swept back one of his white strands of hair. His movements seemed at once awkward and yet perfectly poised; and there was a similar courtesy, of a style that had long since fallen into disuse, in the way he introduced himself as Dr Henry Selwyn. No doubt, he continued, we had come about the flat. As far as he could say, it had not yet been let, but we should have to wait for Mrs Selwyn's return, since she was the owner of the house and he merely a dweller in the garden, a kind of ornamental hermit. In the course of the conversation that followed these opening remarks, we strolled along the iron railings that marked off the garden from open parkland. We stopped for a moment. Three heavy greys were rounding a little clump of alders, snorting and throwing up clods of turf as they trotted. They took up an expectant position at our side, and Dr Selwyn fed them from his trouser pocket, stroking their muzzles as he did so. I have put them out to grass, he said. I bought them at an auction last year for a few pounds. Otherwise they would doubtless have gone straight to the knacker's yard. They're called Herschel, Humphrey and Hippolytus. I know nothing about their earlier life, but when I bought them they were in a sorry state. Their coats were infested with lice, their eyes were dim, and their hooves were cracked right through from standing in a wet field. But now, said Dr Selwyn, they've made something of a recovery, and they might still have a year or so ahead of them. With that he took his leave of the horses, which were plainly very fond of him, and strolled on with us towards the remoter parts of the garden, pausing now and then and becoming more expansive and circumstantial in his talk. Through the shrubbery on the south side of the lawn, a path led to a walk lined with hazels, where grey squirrels were up to their mischief in the canopy of branches overhead. The

ground was thickly strewn with empty nutshells, and autumn crocuses took the weak light that penetrated the dry, rustling leaves. The hazel walk led to a tennis court bounded by a whitewashed brick wall. Tennis, said Dr Selwyn, used to be my great passion. But now the court has fallen into disrepair, like so much else around here. It's not only the kitchen garden, he continued, indicating the tumble-down Victorian greenhouses and overgrown espaliers, that's on its last legs after years of neglect. More and more, he said, he sensed that

Nature itself was groaning and collapsing beneath the burden we placed upon it. True, the garden, which had originally been meant to supply a large household, and had indeed, by dint of skill and diligence, provided fruit and vegetables for the table throughout the entire year, was still, despite the neglect, producing so much that he had far more than he needed for his own requirements, which admittedly were becoming increasingly modest. Leaving the once well-tended garden to its own devices did have the incidental advantage, said Dr Selwyn, that the things that still grew there, or which he had sown or planted more or less haphazardly, possessed a flavour that he himself found quite exceptionally delicate. We walked between beds of asparagus with the tufts of green at shoulder height, rows of massive artichoke plants, and on to a small group of apple trees, on which there were an abundance of red and yellow apples. Dr Selwyn placed a dozen of these fairy-tale apples, which really did taste better than any I have eaten since, on a rhubarb leaf, and gave them to Clara, remarking that the variety was aptly named Beauty of Bath.

Two days after this first meeting with Dr Selwyn we moved in to Prior's Gate. The previous evening, Mrs Selwyn had shown us the rooms, on the first floor of the east wing, furnished in an idiosyncratic fashion but otherwise pleasant and spacious. We had immediately been very taken with the prospect of spending a few months there, since the view from the high windows across the garden, the park and the massed cloud in the sky was more than ample recompense for the gloomy interior. One only needed to look out, and the gigantic and startlingly ugly sideboard ceased to exist, the mustard yellow paintwork in the kitchen vanished, and the turquoise refrigerator, gas-powered and possibly not without its dangers, seemed to dissolve into nowhere, as if by a miracle. Elli Selwyn was a factory owner's daughter, from Biel in Switzerland, and we soon realized that she had an excellent head for business. She gave us permission to make modest alterations in the flat, to suit our taste. Once the bathroom (which was in an annexe on cast-iron columns and accessible only via a footbridge) had been painted white, she even came up to approve our handiwork. The unfamiliar look prompted her to make the cryptic comment that the bathroom, which had always reminded her of an old-fashioned hothouse, now reminded her of a freshly painted dovecote, an observation that has stuck in my mind to this day as an annihilating verdict on the way we lead our life, though I have not been able to make any change in it. But that is beside the point. Our access to the flat was either by an iron staircase, now painted white as well, that rose from the courtyard to the bathroom footbridge, or (on the ground floor) through a double door into a wide corridor, the walls of which, just below the ceiling, were festooned with a complicated bell-pull system for the summoning of servants. From that passageway one could look into the dark kitchen, where at any hour of the day a female personage of indeterminable age would always be busy at the sink. Elaine, as she was called, wore her hair shorn high up the nape, as the inmates of asylums do. Her facial expressions and movements gave a distraught impression, her lips were always wet, and she was invariably wearing her long grey apron that reached down to her ankles. What work Elaine was doing in the kitchen, day in, day out, remained a mystery to Clara and myself; to the best of our knowledge, no meal, with one single exception, was ever cooked there. Across the corridor, about a foot above the stone floor, there was a door in the wall. Through it, one entered a dark stairwell; and on every floor hidden passageways branched off, running behind walls in such a way that the servants, ceaselessly hurrying to and fro laden with coal scuttles, baskets of firewood, cleaning materials, bed linen and tea trays, never had to cross the paths of their betters. Often I tried to imagine what went on inside the heads of people who led their lives knowing that, behind the walls of the rooms they were in, the shadows of the servants were perpetually flitting past. I fancied they ought to have been afraid of those ghostly creatures who, for scant wages, dealt with the tedious tasks that had to be performed daily. The main access to our rooms was via this rear staircase, at the bottommost level of which, incidentally, was the invariably locked door of Elaine's quarters. This too made us feel somewhat uneasy. Only once did I manage to snatch a glance, and saw that her small room was full of countless dolls, meticulously dressed, most of them wearing something on their heads, standing or sitting around or lying on the bed where Elaine herself slept – if, that is, she ever slept at all, and did not spend the entire night crooning softly as she played with her dolls. On Sundays and holidays we occasionally saw Elaine leaving the house in her Salvation Army uniform. She was often met by a little girl who would then walk beside her, one trusting hand in hers. It took a while for us to grow used to Elaine. What we found particularly unsettling was her intermittent habit, when she was in the kitchen, of breaking into strange, apparently unmotivated, whinnying laughter that would penetrate to the first floor. What was more, Elaine, ourselves excepted, was the sole occupant of the immense house who was always there. Mrs Selwyn was frequently away on her travels for weeks at a time, or was about her business, seeing to the numerous flats she let in town and in nearby villages. As long as the weather permitted, Dr Selwyn liked to be out of doors, and especially in a flint-built hermitage in a remote corner of the garden, which he called his folly and which he had furnished with the essentials. But one morning just a week or so after we had moved in, I saw him standing at an open window of one of his rooms on the west side of the house. He had his spectacles on and was wearing a tartan dressing gown and a white neckerchief.

He was aiming a gun with two inordinately long barrels up into the blue. When at last he fired the shot, after what seemed to me an eternity, the report fell upon the gardens with a shattering crash. Dr Selwyn later explained that he had been finding out whether the gun, which was meant for hunting big game and which he had bought many years ago as a young man, was still  in working order after decades of disuse in his dressing room. During that time, as far as he could remember, it had been cleaned and checked over only a couple of times. He told me he had bought the gun when he went to India to take up his first position as a surgeon. At that time, having such a gun was considered obligatory for a man of his caste. He had gone hunting with it only once, though, and had even neglected to put it to inaugural use on that occasion, as he ought to have. So now he had been wondering if the piece still worked, and had established that the recoil alone was enough to kill one.

Otherwise, as I have said, Dr Selwyn was scarcely ever in the house. He lived in his hermitage, giving his entire attention, as he occasionally told me, to thoughts which on the one hand grew vaguer day by day, and, on the other, grew more precise and unambiguous. During our stay in the house he had a visitor only once. It was in the spring, I think, about the end of April, and Elli happened to be away in

Switzerland. One morning Dr Selwyn came up to tell us that he had invited a friend with whom he had been close for many years to dinner and, if it was convenient, he would be delighted if we could make their twosome a *petit comité*. We went down shortly before eight. A fire was blazing against the distinct chill of evening in the vast hearth of the drawing room, which was furnished with a number of four-seater settees and cumbersome armchairs. High on the walls mirrors with blind patches were hung, multiplying the flickering of the firelight and reflecting shifting images. Dr Selwyn was wearing a tie and a tweed jacket with leather patches at the elbows. His friend Edwin Elliott, whom he introduced to us as a well-known botanist and entomologist, was a man of a much slighter build than Dr Selwyn himself, and, while the latter inclined to stoop, he carried himself erect. He too was wearing a tweed jacket. His shirt collar was too large for his scrawny, wrinkled neck, which emerged from it accordion-style, like the neck of certain birds or of a tortoise; his head was small, seeming faintly prehistoric, some kind of throwback; his eyes, though, shone with sheer wonderful life. At first we talked about my work and our plans for the next year or so, and of the impressions we had, coming from mountainous parts, of England, and particularly of the flat expanse of the county of Norfolk. Dusk fell. Dr Selwyn stood up and, with some ceremony, preceded us into the dining room next door. On the oak table, at which thirty people could have been seated with no difficulty, stood two silver candelabra. Places were set for Dr Selwyn and Edwin at the head and foot of the table, and for Clara and me on the long side facing the windows. By now it was almost dark inside the house, and outside, too, the greenery was thickening with deep, blue shadows. The light of the west still lay on the horizon, though, with mountains of cloud whose snowy formations reminded me of the loftiest alpine massifs, as the night descended. Elaine pushed in a serving trolley equipped with hotplates, some kind of patented design dating from the Thirties. She was wearing her grey full-length apron and went about her work in a silence which she broke only once or twice to mutter something to herself. She lit the candles and shuffled out, as she had come in, without a word. We served ourselves, passing the dishes along the table to one another. The first course consisted of a few pieces of green asparagus covered with marinated leaves of young spinach. The main course was broccoli spears in butter and new potatoes boiled with mint leaves. Dr Selwyn told us that he grew his earlies in the sandy soil of one of the old glasshouses, where they reached the size of walnuts by mid April. The meal was concluded with creamed stewed rhubarb sprinkled with Demarara sugar. Thus almost everything was from the neglected garden. Before we had finished, Edwin turned our conversation to Switzerland, perhaps thinking that Dr Selwyn and I would both have something to say on the subject. And Dr Selwyn did indeed, after a certain hesitation, start to tell us of his stay in Berne shortly before the First World War. In the summer of 1913 (he began), he had completed his medical studies in Cambridge, and had forthwith left for Berne, intending to further his training there. In the event, things had turned out differently, and he had spent most of his time in the Bernese Oberland, taking more and more to mountain climbing. He spent weeks on end in Meiringen, and Oberaar in particular, where he met an alpine guide by the name of Johannes Naegeli, then aged sixty-five, of whom, from the beginning, he was very fond. He went everywhere with Naegeli – up the Zinggenstock, the Scheuchzerhorn and the Rosenhorn, the Lauteraarhorn, the Schreckhorn and the Ewigschneehorn – and never in his life, neither before nor later, did he feel as good as he did then, in the company of that man. When war broke out and I returned to England and was called up, Dr Selwyn said, nothing felt as hard, as I realize now looking back, as saying goodbye to Johannes Naegeli. Even the separation from Elli, whom I had met at Christmas in Berne and married after the war, did not cause me remotely as much pain as the separation from Naegeli. I can still see him standing at the station at Meiringen, waving. But I may

only be imagining it, Dr Selwyn went on in a lower tone, to himself, since Elli has come to seem a stranger to me over the years, whereas Naegeli seems closer whenever he comes to my mind, despite the fact that I never saw him again after that farewell in Meiringen. Not long after mobilization, Naegeli went missing on his way from the Oberaar cabin to Oberaar itself. It was assumed that he had fallen into a crevasse in the Aare glacier. The news reached me in one of the first letters I received when I was in uniform, living in barracks, and it plunged me into a deep depression that nearly led to my being discharged. It was as if I was buried under snow and ice. But this is an old story, said Dr Selwyn after a lengthy pause. We ought really, he said, turning to Edwin, to show our guests the pictures we took on our last visit to Crete. We returned to the drawing room. The logs were glowing in the dark. Dr Selwyn tugged a bell-pull to the right of the fire-place, and almost instantly, as if she had been waiting in the passage for the signal, Elaine pushed in a trolley with a slide projector on it. The large ormolu clock on the mantelpiece and the Meissen figurines, a shepherd and shepherdess and a colourfully clad Moor rolling his eyes, were moved aside, and the wooden-framed screen Elaine had brought in was put up in front of the mirror. The low whirr of the projector began, and the dust in the room, normally invisible, glittered and danced in the beam of light by way of a prelude to the pictures themselves. Their journey to Crete had been made in the springtime. The landscape of the island seemed veiled in bright green as it lay before us. Once or twice, Edwin was to be seen with his field glasses and a container for botanical specimens, or Dr Selwyn in knee-length shorts, with a shoulder bag and butterfly net. One of the shots resembled, even in detail, a photograph of Nabokov in the mountains above Gstaad that I had clipped from a Swiss magazine a few days before.

Strangely enough, both Edwin and Dr Selwyn made a distinctly youthful impression in the pictures they showed us, though at the time they made the trip, exactly ten years earlier, they were already in their late sixties. I sensed that, for both of them, this return of their past selves was an occasion for some emotion. But it may be that it merely seemed that way to me because neither Edwin nor Dr Selwyn was willing or able to make any remark concerning these pictures, whereas they did comment on the many others showing the springtime flora of the island, and all manner of winged and creeping creatures. Whilst their images were on screen, trembling slightly, there was almost total silence in the room. In the last of the pictures we saw the expanse of the Lasithi plateau outspread before us, taken from the heights of one of the northern passes. The shot must have been taken around midday, since the sun was shining into our line of vision. To the south, lofty Mount Spathi, two thousand metres high, towered above the plateau, like a mirage beyond the flood of light. The fields of potatoes and vegetables across the broad valley floor, the orchards and clumps of other trees, and the untilled land, were awash with green upon green, studded with the hundreds of white sails of wind pumps. We sat looking at this picture for a long time in silence too, so long that the glass in the slide shattered and a dark crack fissured across the screen. That view of the Lasithi plateau, held so long till it shattered, made a deep impression on me at the time, yet it later vanished from my mind almost completely. It was not until a few years afterwards that it returned to me, in a London cinema, as I followed a conversation between Kaspar Hauser and his teacher, Daumer, in the kitchen garden at Daumer's home. Kaspar, to the delight of his mentor, was distinguishing for the first time between dream and reality, beginning his account with the words: I was in a dream, and in my dream I saw the Caucasus. The camera then moved from right to left, in a sweeping arc, offering a panoramic view of a plateau ringed by mountains, a plateau with a distinctly Indian look to it, with pagoda-like towers and temples with strange triangular façades amidst the green undergrowth and woodland: follies, in a pulsing dazzle of light, that kept reminding me of the sails of those wind pumps of Lasithi, which in reality I have still not seen to this day.

We moved out of Prior's Gate in mid May 1971. Clara had bought a house one afternoon on the spur of the moment. At first we missed the view, but instead we had the green and grey lancets of two willows at our windows, and even on days when there was no breeze at all they were almost never at rest. The trees were scarcely fifteen metres from the house, and the movement of the leaves seemed so close that at times, when one looked out, one felt a part of it. At fairly regular intervals Dr Selwyn called on us in our as yet almost totally empty house, bringing vegetables and herbs from his garden – yellow and blue beans, carefully scrubbed potatoes, artichokes, chives, sage, chervil and dill. On one of these visits, Clara being away in town, Dr Selwyn and I had a long talk prompted by his asking whether I was ever homesick. I could not think of any adequate reply, but Dr Selwyn, after a pause for thought, confessed (no other word will do) that in recent years he had been beset with homesickness more and more. When I asked where it was that he felt drawn back to, he told me that at the age of seven he had left a village near Grodno in Lithuania with his family. In the late autumn of 1899, his parents, his sisters Gita and Raja, and his Uncle Shani Feldhendler, had ridden to Grodno on a cart that belonged to Aaron Wald the coachman. For years the images of that exodus had been gone from his memory, but recently, he said, they had been returning once again and making their presence felt. I can still see the teacher who taught the children in the *cheder*, where I had been going for two years by then, placing his hand on my parting; I can still see the empty rooms of our house. I see myself sitting topmost on the cart, see the horse's crupper, the vast brown earth, the geese with their outstretched necks in the farmyard mires and the waiting room at Grodno station, overheated by a free-standing railed-off stove, the families of emigrants lying around it. I see the telegraph wires rising and falling past the train window, the façades of the Riga houses, the ship in the docks and the dark corner on deck where we did our best to make ourselves at home in such confined circumstances. The high seas, the trail of smoke, the distant greyness, the lifting and falling of the ship, the fear and hope within us, all of it (Dr Selwyn told me) I can now live through again, as if it were only yesterday. After about a week, far sooner than we had reckoned, we reached our destination. We entered a broad river estuary. Everywhere there were freighters, large and small. Beyond the banks, the land stretched out flat. All the emigrants had gathered on deck and were waiting for the Statue of Liberty to appear out of the drifting mist, since every one of them had booked a passage to Americum, as we called it. When we disembarked we were still in no doubt whatsoever that beneath our feet was the soil of the New World, of the Promised City of New York. But in fact, as we learnt some time later to our dismay (the ship having long since cast off again), we had gone ashore in London. Most of the emigrants, of necessity, adjusted to the situation, but some, in the teeth of all the evidence to the contrary, persisted for a long time in the belief that they were in America. So

I grew up in London, in a basement flat in Whitechapel, in Goulston Street. My father, who was a lens-grinder, used the money he had brought with him to buy a partnership in an optician's business that belonged to a fellow countryman from Grodno by the name of Tosia Feigelis. I went to primary school in Whitechapel and learnt English as if in a dream, because I lapped up, for sheer love, every word from the lips of my beautiful young teacher, Lisa Owen. On my way home from school I would repeat everything she had said that day, over and over, thinking of her as I did so. It was that same beautiful teacher, said Dr Selwyn, who put me in for the Merchant Taylors' School entrance examination. She seemed to take it for granted that I would win one of the scholarships that were available every year to pupils from less well-off homes. And as it turned out I did satisfy her hopes of me; as my Uncle Shani often remarked, the light in the kitchen of our two-room flat in Whitechapel, where I sat up far into the night after my sisters and parents had long since gone to bed, was never off. I learnt and read everything that came my way, and cleared the greatest of obstacles with growing ease. By the end of my school years, when I finished top of my year in the exams, it felt as if I had come a tremendous way. My confidence was at its peak, and in a kind of second confirmation I changed my first name Hersch into Henry, and my surname Seweryn to Selwyn. Oddly enough, I then found that as I began my medical studies (at Cambridge, again with the help of a scholarship) my ability to learn seemed to have slackened, though my examination results were among the best. You already know how things went on from there, said Dr Selwyn: the year in Switzerland, the war, my first year serving in India, and marriage to Elli, from whom

I concealed my true background for a long time. In the Twenties and Thirties we lived in grand style; you have seen for yourself what is left of it. A good deal of Elli's fortune was used up that way. True, I had a practice in town, and was a hospital surgeon, but my income alone would never have permitted us such a life style. In the summer months we would motor right across Europe. Next to tennis, said Dr Selwyn, motoring was my great passion in those days. The cars are all still in the garage, and they may be worth something by now. But I have never been able to bring myself to sell anything, except perhaps, at one point, my soul. People have told me repeatedly that I haven't the slightest sense of money. I didn't even have the foresight, he said, to provide for my old age by paying into a pension scheme. That is why I am now practically a pauper. Elli, on the other hand, has made good use of the not inconsiderable remainder of her fortune, and now she must no doubt be a wealthy woman. I still don't know for sure what made us drift apart, the money or revealing the secret of my origins, or simply the decline of love. The years of the second war, and the decades after, were a blinding, bad time for me, about which I could not say a thing even if I wanted to. In 1960, when I had to give up my practice and my patients, I severed my last ties with what they call the real world. Since then, almost my only companions have been plants and animals. Somehow or other I seem to get on well with them, said Dr Selwyn with an inscrutable smile, and, rising, he made a gesture that was most unusual for him. He offered me his hand in farewell.

After that call, Dr Selwyn's visits to us became fewer and further between. The last time we saw him was the day he brought Clara a bunch of white roses with twines of honeysuckle, shortly before we left for a holiday in France. A few weeks after, late that summer, he took his own life with a bullet from his heavy hunting rifle. He had sat on the edge of his bed (we learnt on our return from France) with the gun between his legs, placed the muzzle of the rifle at his jaw, and then, for the first time since he bought the gun before

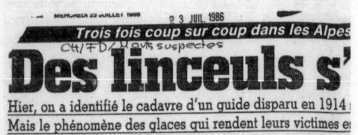

MERCREDI 23 JUILLET 1986
2 3 JUIL. 1986

Trois fois coup sur coup dans les Alpes

CH/FD/Morts suspectes

Des linceuls s'

Hier, on a identifié le cadavre d'un guide disparu en 1914
Mais le phénomène des glaces qui rendent leurs victimes e

Septante-deux ans après sa mort, le corps du guide bernois Johannes Naegeli a été libéré de son linceul de glace.

PAR Véronique TISSIÈRES

Hier, on apprenait en effet que la dépouille découverte jeudi dernier sur le glacier supérieur de l'Aar était celle de cet homme de Wittingen (près de Meiringen) dont on avait perdu la trace depuis ces jours d'été 1914, où il resta

seul à la cabane du CAS. Âgé, à l'époque de 66 ans, il est probable qu'il tenta de regagner la plaine par le glacier ; il n'y parvint jamais et toutes recherches entreprises à l'époque demeurèrent sans résultats.

Coïncidence ? Quelque jours avant la découverte de la dépouille du guide bernois, le corps d'un fantassin de l'armée austro-hongroise, victime de la Première Guerre mondiale, émergeait du Giogo Lungo (Dolomites). Début juillet, enfin, la Vallée Blanche rendait le cadavre d'une de ses victimes...

Trois cas recensés dans le massif alpin au cours des quinze premiers

jours de juillet ! C'est beaucoup, c'... même tout à fait exceptionnel, car restitution de corps par les glacie contrairement à ce que pourraient te ser supposer les exemples ci-dess reste un phénomène rare. « Rare m cyclique, précise-t-on au service secours en haute montagne de la pol valaisanne. Il ne faut en effet pas p dre de vue que ces restitutions so étroitement liées au mouvement c masses de glace. Certaines années, glaciers du canton livrent deux vic mes presque coup sur coup, puis pl rien pendant longtemps. »

Ce fut le cas l'an dernier. Le co d'une jeune femme, disparue qua ans auparavant, fut retrouvé à la su face du glacier de Breney (val Bagnes). Peu après, le Théodule ren

L'hist

Film, légendes, la rest
l'imagination. Mais il

C'était en 1937. Fin août, la son terminée, le gardien de cabane Bertol (au-dessus d'Aro quitta la petite bâtisse pour la lée. Il n'y arriva jamais. Des rech ches furent entreprises, en vain.

Qu'était-il devenu ? Les lang allèrent bon train dans la région. lisse, on parle d'une escapade Italie. D'autant plus qu'il n'avait disparu seul, mais avec la cai contenant les recettes du refu Pas une grosse somme, de q toutefois recommencer une n velle vie ailleurs.

Sept ans plus tard, un gu repéra, émergeant de la masse glacier, une main tenant fermem

☐ LE GLACIER DE L'AAR.
Qui vient de rendre un guide décédé en 1914.

departing for India, had fired a shot with intent to kill. When we received the news, I had no great difficulty in overcoming the initial shock. But certain things, as I am increasingly becoming aware, have a way of returning unexpectedly, often after a lengthy absence. In late July 1986 I was in Switzerland for a few days. On the morning of the 23rd I took the train from Zurich to Lausanne. As the train slowed to cross the Aare bridge, approaching Berne, I gazed way beyond the city to the mountains of the Oberland. At that point, as I recall, or perhaps merely imagine, the memory of Dr Selwyn returned to me for the first time in a long while. Three quarters of an hour later, not wanting to miss the landscape around Lake Geneva, which never fails to astound me as it opens out, I was just laying aside a Lausanne paper I'd bought in Zurich when my eye was caught by a report that said the remains of the Bernese alpine guide Johannes Naegeli, missing since summer 1914, had been released by the Oberaar glacier, seventy-two years later. And so they are ever returning to us, the dead. At times they come back from the ice more than seven decades later and are found at the edge of the moraine, a few polished bones and a pair of hobnailed boots.

PAUL BEREYTER

There is mist that no eye can dispel

In January 1984, the news reached me from S that on the evening of the 30th of December, a week after his seventy-fourth birthday, Paul Bereyter, who had been my teacher at primary school, had put an end to his life. A short distance from S, where the railway track curves out of a willow copse into the open fields, he had lain himself down in front of a train. The obituary in the local paper was headed "Grief at the Loss of a Popular Teacher" and there was no mention of the fact that Paul Bereyter had died of his own free will, or through a self-destructive compulsion. It spoke merely of the dead man's services to education, his dedicated care for his pupils, far beyond the call of duty, his great love of music, his astonishing inventiveness, and of much else in the same vein. Almost by way of an aside, the obituary added, with no further explanation, that during the Third Reich Paul Bereyter had been prevented from practising his chosen profession. It was this curiously unconnected, inconsequential statement, as much as the violent manner of his death, which led me in the years that followed to think more and more about Paul Bereyter, until, in the end, I had to get beyond my own very fond memories of him and discover the story I did not know. My investigations took me back to S, which I had visited less and less since leaving school. I soon learned that, right up to his death, Paul Bereyter had rented rooms there, in a house built in 1970 on the land that had once been Dagobert Lerchenmüller's nursery and market garden, but he had seldom lived there, and it was thought that he was mostly abroad, no one quite knew where. His continual absence from the town, and his increasingly odd behaviour, which had first become apparent a few years before his retirement, gave him the reputation of an eccentric. This reputation, regardless of his undoubted pedagogic ability, had clung to Paul Bereyter for some considerable time, and had, as far as his death was concerned, confirmed the belief among the people of S (amidst whom Paul Bereyter had grown up and, albeit it with certain interruptions, always lived) that things had happened as they were bound to happen. The few conversations I had in S with people who had known Paul Bereyter were not very revealing, and the only thing that seemed remarkable was that no one called him Paul Bereyter or even Bereyter the teacher. Instead, he was invariably referred to simply as Paul, giving me the impression that in the eyes of his contemporaries he had never really grown up. I was reminded then of how we had only ever spoken of him as Paul at school, not without respect but rather as one might refer to an exemplary older brother, and in a way this implied that he was one of us, or that we belonged together. This, as I have come to realize, was merely a fabrication of our minds, because, even though Paul knew and understood us, we, for our part, had little idea of what he was or what went on inside him. And so, belatedly, I tried to get closer to him, to imagine what his life was like in that spacious apartment on the top floor of Lerchenmüller's old house, which had once stood where the present block of flats is now, amidst an array of green vegetable patches and colourful flower beds, in the gardens where Paul often helped out of an afternoon. I imagined him lying in the open air on his balcony where he would often sleep in the summer, his face canopied by the hosts of the stars. I imagined him skating in winter, alone on the fish ponds at Moosbach; and I imagined him stretched out on the track. As I pictured him, he had taken off his spectacles and put them on the ballast stones by his side. The gleaming bands of steel, the crossbars of the sleepers, the spruce trees on the hillside above the village of Altstädten, the arc of the mountains he knew so well, were a blur before his short-sighted eyes, smudged out in the gathering dusk. At the last, as the thunderous sound approached, all he saw was a darkening greyness and, in the midst of it, needle-sharp, the snow-white silhouettes of three mountains: the Kratzer, the Trettach and the Himmelsschrofen. Such endeavours to imagine his life and death did not, as I had to admit, bring me any closer to Paul, except at best for brief emotional moments of the kind that seemed presumptuous to me. It is in order to avoid this sort of wrongful trespass that I have written down what I know of Paul Bereyter.

In December 1952 my family moved from the village of W to the small town of S, 19 kilometres away. The journey – during which I gazed out of the cab of Alpenvogel's wine-red furniture van at the endless lines of trees along the roadsides, thickly frosted over and appearing before us out of the lightless morning mist – seemed like a voyage halfway round the world, though it will have lasted an hour at the very most. When at length we trundled across the Ach bridge into S, at that time no more than a small market town of perhaps nine thousand souls, I was overcome by a powerful feeling that a new life filled with the bustle of cities would be starting for us there. The blue enamel street names, the huge clock in front of the old railway station, and what seemed to me then the truly magnificent façade of the Wittelsbacher Hof Hotel, were all, I felt, unmistakable signs of a new beginning. It was, I thought, particularly auspicious that the rows of houses were interrupted here and there by patches of waste land on which stood ruined buildings, for ever since I had once visited Munich I had felt nothing to be so unambiguously linked to the word *city* as the presence of heaps of rubble, fire-scorched walls, and the gaps of windows through which one could see the vacant air.

On the afternoon that we arrived, the temperature plummeted. A snow blizzard set in that continued for the rest of the day and eased off to an even, calm snowfall only towards the night. When I went to the school in S for the first time the following morning, the snow lay so thick that I felt a kind of exhilaration at the sight of it. The class I joined was the third grade, which was taught by Paul Bereyter. There I stood, in my dark green pullover with the leaping stag on it, in front of fifty-one fellow pupils, all staring at me with the greatest possible curiosity, and, as if from a great distance, I heard Paul say that I had arrived at precisely the right moment, since he had been telling the story of the stag's leap only the day before, and now the image of the leaping stag, worked into the fabric of my pullover, could be copied onto the blackboard. He asked me to take off the pullover and take a seat in the back row beside Fritz Binswanger for the time being, while he, using my picture of a leaping stag, would show us how an image could be broken down into numerous tiny pieces – small crosses, squares or dots – or else assembled from these. In no time I was bent over my exercise book, beside Fritz, copying the leaping stag from the blackboard onto my grid-marked paper. Fritz too, who (as I soon learnt) was repeating his third grade year, was taking visible pains over his effort, yet his progress was infinitely slow. Even when those who had started late were long finished, he still had little more than a dozen crosses on his page. We exchanged silent glances, and I rapidly completed his fragmentary piece of work. From that day on, in the almost two years that we sat next to each other, I did most of his arithmetic, his writing and his drawing exercises. It was very easy to do, and to do seamlessly, as it were, chiefly because Fritz and I had the self-same, incorrigibly sloppy handwriting (as Paul repeatedly observed, shaking his head), with the one difference that Fritz could not write quickly and I could not write slowly. Paul had no objection to our working together; indeed, to encourage us further he hung the case of cockchafers on the wall beside our desk. It had a deep frame and was half-filled with soil. In it, as well as a pair of cockchafers labelled Melolontha vulgaris in the old German hand, there were a clutch of eggs, a pupa and a larva, and, in the upper portion, cockchafers were hatching, flying, and eating the leaves of apple trees. That case, demonstrating the mysterious metamorphosis of the cockchafer, inspired Fritz and me in the late spring to an intensive study of the whole nature of cockchafers, including anatomical examination and culminating in the cooking and eating of a cockchafer stew. Fritz, in fact, who came from a large family of farm labourers at Schwarzenbach and, as far as was known, had never had a real father, took the liveliest interest in anything connected with food, its preparation, and the eating of it. Every day he would expatiate in great detail on the quality of the sandwiches I brought with me and shared with him, and on our way home from school we would always stop to look in the window of Turra's delicatessen, or to look at the display at Einsiedler's exotic fruit emporium, where the main attraction was a dark green trout aquarium with air bubbling up through the water. On one occasion when we had been standing for a long time outside Einsiedler's, from the shadowy interior of which a pleasant coolness wafted out that September noon, old Einsiedler himself appeared in the doorway and made each of us a present of a white butterpear. This constituted a veritable miracle, not only because the fruits were such splendid rarities but chiefly because Einsiedler was widely known to be of a choleric disposition, a man who despised nothing so much as serving the few customers he still had. It was while he was eating the white butterpear that Fritz confided to me that he planned to be a chef; and he did indeed become a chef, one who could be said without exaggeration to enjoy international renown. He perfected his culinary skills at the Grand Hotel Dolder in Zurich and the Victoria Jungfrau in Interlaken, and was subsequently as much in demand in New York as in Madrid or London. It was when he was in London that we met again, one April morning in 1984, in the reading room of the British Museum, where I was researching the history of Bering's Alaska expedition and Fritz was studying eighteenth-century French cookbooks. By chance we were sitting just one aisle apart, and when we both happened to look up from our work at the same moment we immediately recognized each other despite the quarter century that had passed. In the cafeteria we told each other the stories of our lives, and talked for a long time about Paul, of whom Fritz mainly recalled that he had never once seen him eat.

In our classroom, the plan of which we had to draw to scale in our exercise books, there were twenty-six desks screwed fast to the oiled floorboards.

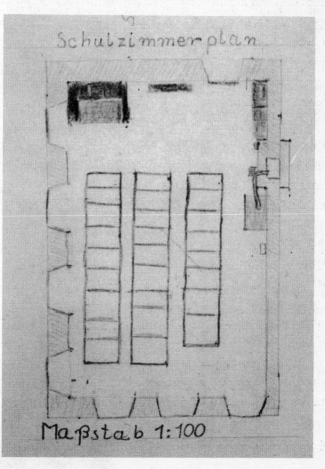

From the raised teacher's desk, behind which the crucifix hung on the wall, one could look down on the pupils' heads, but I cannot remember Paul ever occupying that elevated position. If he was not at the blackboard or at the cracked oilcloth map of the world, he would walk down the rows of desks, or lean, arms folded, against the cupboard beside the green tiled stove. His favourite place, though, was by one of the south-facing windows let into deep bays in the wall. Outside those windows, from amidst the branches of the old apple orchard at Frey's distillery, starlings' nesting boxes on long wooden poles reached into the sky, which was bounded in the distance by the jagged line of the Lech valley Alps, white with snow for almost the entire school year. The teacher who preceded Paul, Hormayr, who had been feared for his pitiless regime and would have offenders kneel for hours on sharp-edged blocks of wood, had had the windows half whitewashed so that the children could not see out. The first thing Paul did when he took up the job in 1946 was to remove the whitewash, painstakingly scratching it away with a razor blade, a task which was, in truth, not urgent, since Paul was in any case in the habit of opening the windows wide, even when the weather was bad, indeed even in the harshest cold of winter, being firmly convinced that lack of oxygen impaired the capacity to think. What he liked most, then, was to stand in one of the window bays towards the head of the room, half facing the class and half turned to look out, his face at a slightly upturned angle with the sunlight glinting on his glasses; and from that position on the periphery he would talk across to us. In well-structured sentences, he spoke without any touch of dialect but with a slight impediment of speech or timbre, as if the sound were coming not from the larynx but from somewhere near the heart. This sometimes gave one the feeling that it was all being powered by clock-work inside him and Paul in his entirety was a mechanical human made of tin and other metal parts, and might be put out of operation for ever by the smallest functional hitch. He would run his left hand through his hair as he spoke, so that it stood on end, dramatically emphasizing what he said. Not infrequently he would also take out his handkerchief, and, in anger at what he considered (perhaps not unjustly) our wilful stupidity, bite on it. After bizarre turns of this kind he would always take off his glasses and stand unseeing and defenceless in the midst of the class, breathing on the lenses and polish-ing them with such assiduity that it seemed he was glad not to have to see us for a while.

Paul's teaching did include the curriculum then laid down for primary schools: the multiplication tables, basic arithmetic, German and Latin handwriting, nature study, the history and customs of our valley, singing, and what was known as physical education. Religious studies, however, were not taught by Paul himself; instead, once a week, we first had Catechist Meier (spelt e-i), who lisped, and then Beneficiary Meyer (spelt e-y), who spoke in a booming voice, to teach us the meaning of sin and confession, the creed, the church calendar, the seven deadly sins, and more of a similar kind. Paul, who was rumoured to be a free-thinker, something I long found incomprehensible, always contrived to avoid Meier-with-an-i or Meyer-with-a-y both at the beginning and at the end of their religion lessons, for there was plainly nothing he found quite so repellent as Catholic sanctimo-niousness. And when he returned to the classroom after these lessons to find an Advent altar chalked on the blackboard in purple, or a red and yellow monstrance, or other such things, he would instantly rub out the offending works of art with a conspicuous vigour and thoroughness. Always before our religion lessons, Paul would always top up to the brim the holy water stoup, embellished with a flaming Sacred Heart, that was fixed by the door, using (I often saw him do it) the watering can with which he normally watered the geraniums. Because of this, the Beneficiary never managed to put the holy water bottle he always carried in his shiny black pigskin briefcase to use. He did not dare simply to tip out the water from the brimful stoup, and so, in his endeavour to account for the seemingly inexhaustible Sacred Heart, he was torn between his suspicion that systematic malice was involved and the intermittent hope that this was a sign from a Higher Place, perhaps indeed a miracle. Most assuredly, though, both the Beneficiary and the Catechist considered Paul a lost soul, for we were called upon more than once to pray for our teacher to convert to the true faith. Paul's aversion to the Church of Rome was far more than a mere question of principle, though; he genuinely had a horror of God's vicars and the mothball smell they gave off. He not only did not attend church on Sundays, but purposely left town, going as far as he could into the mountains, where he no longer heard the bells. If the weather was not good he would spend his Sunday mornings together with Colo the cobbler, who was a philosopher and a downright atheist who took the Lord's day, if he was not playing chess with Paul, as the occasion to work on pamphlets and tracts against the one True Church. Once (I now remember) I witnessed a moment when Paul's aversion to hypocrisy of any description won an incontestable victory over the forbearance with which he generally endured the intellectual infirmities of the world he lived in. In the class above me there was a pupil by the name of Ewald Reise who had fallen completely under the Catechist's influence and displayed a degree of overdone piety – it would not be unfair to say, ostentatiously – quite incredible in a ten-year-old. Even at this tender age, Ewald Reise already looked like a fully-fledged chaplain. He was the only boy in the whole school who wore a coat, complete with a purple scarf folded over at his chest and held in place with a large safety pin. Reise, whose head was never uncovered (even in the heat of summer he wore a straw hat or a light linen cap), struck Paul so powerfully as an example of the stupidity, both inbred and wilfully acquired, that he so detested, that one day when the boy forgot to doff his hat to him in the street Paul removed the hat for him, clipped his ear, and then replaced the hat on Reise's head with the rebuke that even a prospective chaplain should greet his teacher with politeness when they met.

Paul spent at least a quarter of all his lessons on teaching us things that were not on the syllabus. He taught us the rudiments of algebra, and his enthusiasm for natural history once led him (to the horror of his neighbours) to boil the flesh off a dead fox he had found in the woods, in an old preserving pan on his kitchen stove, so that he would then be able to reassemble the skeleton with us in school. We never read the text books that were intended for third and fourth years at primary school, as Paul found them ridiculous and hypocritical; instead, our reading was almost exclusively the *Rheinische Hausfreund*, a collection of tales for the home, sixty copies of which Paul had procured, I suspect at his own expense. Many of the stories in it, such as the one about a decapitation performed in secret, made the most vivid impression on me, and those impressions have not faded to this day; more than anything else (why, I cannot say) I clearly recall the words said by the passing pilgrim to the woman who kept the Baselstab Inn: When I return, I shall bring you a sacred cockleshell from the Strand at Askalon, or a rose from Jericho. – At least once a week, Paul taught us French. He began with the simple observation that he had once lived in France, that people there spoke French, that he knew how to do it, and that we could easily do it too, if we wished. One May morning we sat outside in the school yard, and on that fresh bright day we easily grasped what *un beau jour* meant, and that a chestnut tree in blossom might just as well be called *un chataignier en fleurs*. Indeed, Paul's teaching was altogether the most lucid, in general, that one could imagine. On principle he placed the greatest value on taking us out of the school building whenever the opportunity arose and observing as much as we could around the town – the electric power station with the transformer plant, the smelting furnaces and the steam-powered forge at the iron foundry, the basketware workshops, and the cheese dairy. We visited the mash room at the brewery, and the malt house, where the silence was so total that none of us dared to say a word. And one day we visited Corradi the gunsmith, who had been practising his trade in S for close on sixty years. Corradi invariably wore a green eyeshade and, whenever the light that came through his workshop window permitted, he would be bent over the complicated locks of old fire-arms which no one but himself, far and wide, could repair. When he had succeeded in fixing a lock, he would go out into the front garden with the gun and fire a few rounds into the air for sheer pleasure, to mark the end of the job.

What Paul termed his "object lessons" took us, in the course of time, to all of the nearby locations that were of interest for one reason or another and could be reached on foot within about two hours. We visited Fluhenstein Castle, explored the Starzlach Gorge, went to the conduit house above Hofen and the powder magazine where the Veterans' Association kept their ceremonial cannon, on the hill where the stations of the cross led up to the Calvary Chapel. We were more than a little surprised when, after various preliminary studies that took several weeks, we succeeded in finding the derelict tunnel of the brown coal mine on the Straussberg, which had been abandoned after the First

World War, with what was left of the cable railway that had transported the coal from the mouth of the tunnel to the station at Altstädten below. Not all our excursions, however, were made with a specific purpose. On particularly fine days we often simply went out into the fields, to go on with our botany or sometimes, under a botanical pretext, simply to idle the time away. On these occasions, usually in early summer, the son of Wohlfahrt the barber and undertaker would frequently join us. Known to everyone as Mangold, and reckoned to be not quite right in the head, he was of uncertain age and of a childlike disposition. It made him deliriously happy, a gangling fellow among school-children not yet into adolescence, to tell us on which day of the week any past or future date we cared to name would fall – despite the fact that he was otherwise incapable of solving the simplest mathematical problem. If, say, one told Mangold that one was born on the 18th of May, 1944, he would shoot back without a moment's hesitation that that was a Thursday. And if one tried difficult questions on him, such as the Pope's or King Ludwig's date of birth, again he could say what day of the week it was, in a flash. Paul, who excelled at mental arithmetic and was a first-rate mathematician, tried for years to fathom Mangold's secret, setting him complicated tests, asking questions, and going to a variety of other lengths. As far as I am aware, though, neither he nor anyone else ever worked it out, because Mangold hardly understood the questions he was asked. That aside, Paul, like Mangold and the rest of us, clearly enjoyed our outings into the country-side. Wearing his windcheater, or simply in shirtsleeves, he would walk ahead of us with his face slightly upturned, taking those long and springy steps that were so characteristic, the very image (as I realize only now as I look back) of the German *Wandervogel* hiking movement, which must have had a lasting influence on him from his youth. Paul was in the habit of whistling continuously as he walked across the fields. He was an amazingly good whistler; the sound he produced was marvellously rich, exactly like a flute's. And even when he was climbing a mountain, he would with apparent ease whistle whole runs and ties in connected sequence, not just anything, but fine, thoroughly composed passages and melodies that none of us had ever heard before, and which infallibly gave a wrench to my heart whenever, years later, I rediscovered them in a Bellini opera or Brahms sonata. When we rested on the way, Paul would take his clarinet, which he carried with him without fail in an old cotton stocking, and play various pieces, chiefly slow movements, from the classical repertoire, with which I was then completely unfamiliar. Apart from these music lessons at which we were merely required to provide an audience, we would learn a new song at least once a fortnight, the contemplative again being given preference over the merry. "Zu Strassburg auf der Schanz, da fing mein Trauern an", "Auf den Bergen die Burgen", "Im Krug zum grünen Kranze" or "Wir gleiten hinunter das Ufer entlang" were the kinds of songs we learnt. But I did not grasp the true meaning that music had for Paul till the extremely talented son of Brandeis the organist, who was already studying at the conservatoire, came to our singing lesson (at Paul's instigation, I assume) and played on his violin to an audience of peasant boys (for that is what we were, almost without exception). Paul, who was standing by the window as usual, far from being able to hide the emotion that young Brandeis's playing produced in him, had to remove his glasses because his eyes had filled with tears. As I remember it, he even turned away in order to conceal from us the sob that rose in him. It was not only

music, though, that affected Paul in this way; indeed, at any
time – in the middle of a lesson, at break, or on one of our
outings – he might stop or sit down somewhere, alone and
apart from us all, as if he, who was always in good spirits
and seemed so cheerful, was in fact desolation itself.

It was not until I was able to fit my own fragmentary
recollections into what Lucy Landau told me that I was
able to understand that desolation even in part. It was Lucy
Landau, as I found out in the course of my enquiries in S,
who had arranged for Paul to be buried in the churchyard
there. She lived at Yverdon, and it was there, on a summer's
day in the second year after Paul died, a day I recall as
curiously soundless, that I paid her the first of several visits.
She began by telling me that at the age of seven, together with
her father, who was an art historian and a widower, she had
left her home town of Frankfurt. The modest lakeside villa
in which she lived had been built by a chocolate manufacturer
at the turn of the century, for his old age. Mme Landau's
father had bought it in the summer of 1933 despite the fact
that the purchase, as Mme Landau put it, ate up almost his
whole fortune, with the result that she spent her entire childhood and the war years that followed in a house well-nigh
unfurnished. Living in those empty rooms had never struck
her as a deprivation, though; rather, it had seemed, in a way
not easy to describe, to be a special favour or distinction
conferred upon her by a happy turn of events. For instance,
she remembered her eighth birthday very clearly. Her father
had spread a white paper cloth on a table on the terrace, and
there she and Ernest, her new school friend, had sat at dinner
while her father, wearing a black waistcoat and with a napkin
over his forearm, had played the waiter, to rare perfection.

At that time, the empty house with its wide-open windows and the trees about it softly swaying was her backdrop for a magical theatre show. And then, Mme Landau continued, bonfire after bonfire began to burn along the lakeside as far as St Aubin and beyond, and she was completely convinced that all of it was being done purely for her, in honour of her birthday. Ernest, said Mme Landau with a smile that was meant for him, across the years that had intervened, Ernest knew of course that the bonfires that glowed brightly in the darkness all around were burning because it was Swiss National Day, but he most tactfully forbore to spoil my bliss with explanations of any kind. Indeed, the discretion of Ernest, who was the youngest of a large family, has always remained exemplary to my way of thinking, and no one ever equalled him, with the possible exception of Paul, whom I unfortunately met far too late – in summer 1971 at Salins-les-Bains in the French Jura.

A lengthy silence followed this disclosure before Mme Landau added that she had been reading Nabokov's auto-biography on a park bench on the Promenade des Cordeliers when Paul, after walking by her twice, commented on her reading, with a courtesy that bordered on the extravagant. From then on, all that afternoon and throughout the weeks that followed, he had made the most appealing conversation, in his somewhat old-fashioned but absolutely correct French. He had explained to her at the outset, by way of introduction, as it were, that he had come to Salins-les-Bains, which he knew of old, because what he referred to as his condition had been deteriorating in recent years to the point where his claustrophobia made him unable to teach and he saw his pupils, although he had always felt affection for them (he stressed this), as contemptible and repulsive creatures, the very sight of whom had prompted an utterly groundless violence in him on more than one occasion. Paul did his best to conceal his distress and the fear of insanity that came out in confessions of this kind. Thus, Mme Landau said, he had told her, only a few days after they had met, with an irony that made everything seem light and unimportant, of his recent attempt to take his own life. He described this episode as an embarrassment of the first order which he was loath to recall but about which he felt obliged to tell her so that she would know all that was needful concerning the strange companion at whose side she was so kind as to be walking about summery Salins. Le pauvre Paul, said Mme Landau, lost in thought, and then, looking across at me once more, observed that in her long life she had known quite a number of men – closely, she emphasized, a mocking expression on her face – all of whom, in one way or another, had been enamoured of themselves. Every one of these gentlemen, whose names, mercifully, she had mostly forgotten, had, in the end, proved to be an insensitive boor, whereas Paul, who was almost consumed by the loneliness within him, was the most considerate and entertaining companion one could wish for. The two of them, said Mme Landau, took delightful walks in Salins, and made excursions out of town. They visited the thermal baths and the salt galleries together, and spent whole afternoons up at Fort Belin. They gazed down from the bridges into the green water of the Furieuse, telling each other stories as they stood there. They went to the house at Arbois where Pasteur grew up, and in Arc-et-Senans they had seen the saltern buildings which in the eighteenth century had been constructed as an ideal model for factory, town and society; on this occasion,

Paul, in a conjecture she felt to be most daring, had linked the bourgeois concept of Utopia and order, as expressed in the designs and buildings of Nicolas Ledoux, with the progressive destruction of natural life. She was surprised, as she talked about it now, said Mme Landau, at how clear the images that she had supposed buried beneath grief at the loss of Paul still were to her. Clearest of all, though, were the memories of their outing – a somewhat laborious business despite the chair lift – up Montrond, from the summit of which she had gazed down for an eternity at Lake Geneva and the surrounding country, which looked considerably reduced in size, as if intended for a model railway. The tiny features below, taken together with the gentle mass of Montblanc towering above them, the Vanoise glacier almost invisible in the shimmering distance, and the Alpine panorama that occupied half the horizon, had for the first time in her life awoken in her a sense of the contrarieties that are in our longings.

On a later visit to the Villa Bonlieu, when I enquired further about Paul's apparent familiarity with the French Jura and the area around Salins from an earlier time in his life, which Mme Landau had intimated, I learnt that in the period from autumn 1935 to early 1939 he had first been for a short while in Besançon and had then taught as house tutor to a family by the name of Passagrain in Dôle. As if in explanation of this fact, not at first glance compatible with the circumstances of a German primary school teacher in the Thirties, Mme Landau put before me a large album which contained photographs documenting not only the period in question but indeed, a few gaps aside, almost the whole of Paul Bereyter's life, with notes penned in his own hand. Again and again, from front to back and from back to front, I leafed through the album that afternoon, and since then I have returned to it time and again, because, looking at the pictures in it, it truly seemed to me, and still does, as if the dead were coming back, or as if we were on the point of joining them. The earliest photographs told the story of a happy childhood in the Bereyter family home in Blumenstrasse, right next to Lerchenmüller's nursery garden, and frequently showed Paul with his cat or with a rooster that was evidently completely domesticated. The years in a country boarding school followed, scarcely any less happy than the years of childhood that had gone before, and then Paul's entry into teacher training college at Lauingen, which he referred to as

the teacher processing factory in his gloss. Mme Landau observed that Paul had submitted to this training, which followed the most narrow-minded of guidelines and was dictated by a morbid Catholicism, only because he wanted to teach children at whatever cost – even if it meant enduring training of that kind. Only because he was so absolute and unconditional an idealist had he been able to survive his time at Lauingen without his soul being harmed in any way. In 1934 to 1935, Paul, then aged twenty-four, did his probation year at the primary school in S, teaching, as I learnt to my amazement, in the very classroom where a good fifteen years later he taught a pack of children scarcely distinguishable

from those pictured here, a class that included myself. The summer of 1935, which followed his probation year, was one of the finest times of all (as the photographs and Mme Landau's comments made clear) in the life of prospective primary school teacher Paul Bereyter. That summer, Helen Hollaender from Vienna spent several weeks in S. Helen,

who was a month or so older, spent that time at the Bereyter home, a fact which is glossed in the album with a double exclamation mark, while her mother put up at Pension Luitpold for the duration. Helen, so Mme Landau believed, came as a veritable revelation to Paul; for if these pictures can be trusted, she said, Helen Hollaender was an independent-spirited, clever woman, and furthermore her waters ran deep. And in those waters Paul liked to see his own reflection.

And now, continued Mme Landau, just think: early that September, Helen returned with her mother to Vienna, and Paul took up his first teaching post in the remote village of W. There, before he had had the time to do more than remember the children's names, he was served official notice that it would not be possible for him to remain as a teacher, because of the new laws, with which he was no doubt familiar. The wonderful future he had dreamt of that summer collapsed without a sound like the proverbial house of cards. All his prospects blurred. For the first time, he experienced that insuperable sense of defeat that was so often to beset him in later times and which, finally, he could not shake off. At the end of October, said Mme Landau, drawing to a close for the time being, Paul travelled via Basle to Besançon, where he took a position as a house tutor that had been found for him through a business associate of his father. How wretched he must have felt at that time is apparent in a small photograph taken one Sunday afternoon, which shows Paul on the left, a Paul who had plunged within a month

from happiness to misfortune, and was so terribly thin that he seems almost to have reached a physical vanishing point. Mme Landau could not tell me exactly what became of Helen Hollaender. Paul had preserved a resolute silence on the subject, possibly because he was plagued by a sense of having failed her or let her down. As far as Mme Landau had been able to discover, there could be little doubt that Helen and her mother had been deported, in one of those special trains that left Vienna at dawn, probably to Theresienstadt in the first instance.

Gradually, Paul Bereyter's life began to emerge from the background. Mme Landau was not in the least surprised that I was unaware, despite the fact that I came from S and knew what the town was like, that old Bereyter was what was termed half Jewish, and Paul, in consequence, only three quarters an Aryan. Do you know, she said on one of my visits to Yverdon, the systematic thoroughness with which these people kept silent in the years after the war, kept their secrets, and even, I sometimes think, really did forget, is nothing more than the other side of the perfidious way in which Schöferle, who ran a coffee house in S, informed Paul's mother Thekla, who had been on stage for some time in Nuremberg, that the presence of a lady who was married to a half Jew might be embarrassing to his respectable clientele, and begged to request her, with respect of course, not to take her afternoon coffee at his house any more. I do not find it surprising, said Mme Landau, not in the slightest, that you were unaware of the meanness and treachery that a family like the Bereyters were exposed to in a miserable hole such as S then was, and such as it still is despite all the so-called progress; it does not surprise me at all, since that is inherent in the logic of the whole wretched sequence of events.

In an effort to resume a more factual tone after the little outburst she had permitted herself, Mme Landau told me that Paul's father, a man of refinement and inclined to melancholy, came from Gunzenhausen in Franconia, where Paul's grandfather Amschel Bereyter had a junk shop and had married his Christian maid, who had grown very fond of him after a few years of service in his house. At that time Amschel was already past fifty, while Rosina was still in her mid twenties. Their marriage, which was naturally a rather quiet one, produced only one child, Theodor, the father of Paul. After an apprenticeship in Augsburg as a salesman, Theodor was employed for a lengthy spell in a Nuremberg department store, working his way up to the higher echelons, before moving to S in 1900 to open an emporium with capital saved partly from his earnings and partly borrowed. He sold everything in the emporium, from coffee to collar studs, camisoles to cuckoo clocks, candied sugar to collapsible top hats. Paul once described that wonderful emporium to her in detail, said Mme Landau, when he was in hospital in Berne in 1975, his eyes bandaged after an operation for cataracts. He said that he could see things then with the greatest clarity, as one sees them in dreams, things he had not thought he still had within him. In his childhood, everything in the emporium seemed far too high up for him, doubtless because he himself was small, but also because the shelves reached all the four metres up to the ceiling. The light in the emporium, coming through the small transom windows let into the tops of the display window backboards, was dim even on the brightest of days, and it must have seemed all the murkier to him as a child, Paul had said, as he moved on his tricycle, mostly on the lowest level, through the ravines between tables, boxes and counters, amidst a variety of smells – mothballs and lily-of-the-valley soap were always the most pungent, while felted wool and loden cloth assailed the nose only in wet weather, herrings and linseed oil in hot. For hours on end, Paul had said, deeply moved by his own memories, he had ridden in those days past the dark rows of bolts of material, the gleaming leather boots, the preserve jars, the galvanized watering cans, the whip stand, and the case that had seemed especially magical to him, in which rolls of Gütermann's sewing thread were neatly arrayed behind little glass windows, in every colour of the rainbow. The emporium staff consisted of Frommknecht, the clerk and accountant, one of whose shoulders was permanently raised higher from years of bending over correspondence and the endless figures and calculations; old Fräulein Steinbeiss, who flitted about all day long with a cloth and a feather duster; and the two attendants, Hermann Müller and Heinrich Müller (no relation, as they incessantly insisted), who stood on either side of the monumental cash register, invariably wearing waistcoats and sleeve bands, and treated customers with the condescension that comes naturally, as it were, to those who occupy a higher station in life. Paul's father Theo Bereyter, though, whenever he, the emporium proprietor himself, came down to the shop for an hour or so (as he did every day) in his frock coat or a pin-striped suit and spats, would take up a position between the two potted palms, which would be either inside or outside the swing door depending on the weather, and would escort every single customer into the emporium with the most respectful courtesy, regardless of whether it was the neediest resident from the old people's home across the road or the opulent wife of Hastreiter, the brewery owner, and then see them out again with his compliments.

The emporium, Mme Landau added, being the only large store in the town and indeed in the entire district, by all accounts ensured a good middle class standard of living for the Bereyter family, and even one or two extravagances, as is evident (said Mme Landau) from the mere fact that Theodor drove a Dürkopp in the Twenties, attracting excited interest

as far afield as the Tyrol, Ulm or Lake Constance, as Paul liked
to recall. Theodor Bereyter died on Palm Sunday, 1936; this
too I heard from Mme Landau, who must have talked endlessly to Paul about these things, as I came to realize more
clearly with every visit. The cause of death was given as heart
failure, but in fact, as Mme Landau emphasized, he had died
from the fury and fear that had been consuming him ever
since, precisely two years before his death, the Jewish families,
resident in his home town of Gunzenhausen for generations,
had been the target of violent attacks. The emporium owner,
escorted only by his wife and those in his employ, was buried
before Easter in a remote corner, reserved for suicides and
people of no denomination, behind a low wall in the churchyard at S. It is worth mentioning in this connection, said
Mme Landau, that although the emporium, which passed
to the widow, Thekla, could not be "Aryanized" after Theodor
Bereyter's death, the family nonetheless had to sell it for

next to nothing to Alfons Kienzle, a livestock and real estate agent who had recently set up as a respectable businessman. After this dubious transaction Thekla Bereyter fell into a depression and died within a few weeks.

All of these occurrences, Mme Landau said, Paul followed from afar without being able to intervene. On the one hand, when the bad news reached him it was always already too late to do anything, and, on the other, his powers of decision had been in some way impaired, making it impossible for him to think even as far as a single day ahead. For this reason, Mme Landau explained, Paul for a long time had only a partial grasp of what had happened in S in 1935 and 1936, and did not care to correct his patchy knowledge of the past. It was only in the last decade of his life, which he largely spent in Yverdon, that reconstructing those events became important to him, indeed vital, said Mme Landau. Although he was losing his sight, he spent many days in archives, making endless notes – on the events in Gunzenhausen, for instance, on that Palm Sunday of 1934, years before what became known as the Kristallnacht, when the windows of Jewish homes were smashed and the Jews themselves were hauled out of their hiding places in cellars and dragged through the streets. What horrified Paul was not only the coarse offences and the violence of those Palm Sunday incidents in Gunzenhausen, not only the death of seventy-five-year-old Ahron Rosenfeld, who was stabbed, or of thirty-year-old Siegfried Rosenau, who was hanged from a railing; it was not only these things, said Mme Landau, that horrified Paul, but also, nearly as deeply, a newspaper article he came across, reporting with *Schadenfreude* that the schoolchildren of Gunzenhausen had helped themselves to a free bazaar in the town the following morning, taking several weeks' supply of hair slides, chocolate cigarettes, coloured pencils, fizz powder and many other things from the wrecked shops.

What I was least able to understand in Paul's story, after all that, was the fact that in early 1939 – be it because the position of a German tutor in France in times that were growing more difficult was no longer tenable, or out of blind rage or even a sort of perversion – he went back to Germany, to the capital of the Reich, to Berlin, a city with which he was quite unfamiliar. There he took an office job at a garage in Oranienburg, and a few months later he was called up; those who were only three-quarter Aryans were apparently included in the muster. He served, if that is the word, for six years, in the motorized artillery, variously stationed in the Greater German homeland and in the several countries that were occupied. He was in Poland, Belgium, France, the Balkans, Russia and the Mediterranean, and doubtless saw more than

any heart or eye can bear. The seasons and the years came and went. A Walloon autumn was followed by an unending white winter near Berdichev, spring in the Departement Haute-Saône, summer on the coast of Dalmatia or in Romania, and always, as Paul wrote under this photograph,

one was, as the crow flies, about 2,000 km away – but from where? – and day by day, hour by hour, with every beat of the pulse, one lost more and more of one's qualities, became less comprehensible to oneself, increasingly abstract.

Paul's return to Germany in 1939 was an aberration, said Mme Landau, as was his return to S after the war, and to his teaching life in a place where he had been shown the door. Of course, she added, I understand why he was drawn back to school. He was quite simply born to teach children – a veritable Melammed, who could start from nothing and hold the most inspiring of lessons, as you yourself have described to me. And furthermore, as a good teacher he would have believed that one could consider those twelve wretched years over and done with, and simply turn the page and begin afresh. But that is no more than half the explanation, at most. What moved and perhaps even forced Paul to return, in 1939 and in 1945, was the fact that he was a German to the marrow, profoundly attached to his native land in the foothills of the Alps, and even to that miserable place S as well, which in fact he loathed and, deep within himself, of that I am quite sure, said Mme Landau, would have been pleased to see destroyed and obliterated, together with the townspeople, whom he found so utterly repugnant. Paul, said Mme Landau, could not abide the new flat that he was more or less forced to move into shortly before he retired, when the wonderful old Lerchenmüller house was pulled down to make way for a hideous block of flats; but even so, remarkably, in all of those last twelve years that he was living here in Yverdon he could never bring himself to give up that flat. Quite the contrary, in fact: he would make a special journey to S several times a year especially to see that all was in order, as he put it. Whenever he returned from one of those expeditions, which generally took just two days, he would always be in the gloomiest of spirits, and in his childishly appealing way he would rue the fact that, to his own detriment, he had once again ignored my urgent advice not to go there any more.

Here in Bonlieu, Mme Landau told me on another occasion, Paul spent a lot of time gardening, which I think he loved more than anything else. After we had left Salins and our decision had been taken that from now on he would live in Bonlieu, he asked me if he might take the garden in hand, which at that time was fairly neglected. And Paul really did transform the garden, in a quite spectacular manner. The young trees, the flowers, the plants and climbers, the shady ivy beds, the rhododendrons, the roses, the shrubs and perennials – they all grew, not a bare patch anywhere. Every afternoon, weather permitting, said Mme Landau, Paul was busy in the garden. But sometimes he would simply sit for a while, gazing at the greenery that burgeoned all around him. The doctor who had operated on his cataracts had advised him that peaceful spells spent simply looking at the leaves would protect and improve his eyesight. Not, of course, that Paul took any notice whatsoever of the doctor's orders at night, said Mme Landau. His light was always on till the small hours. He read and read – Altenberg, Trakl, Wittgenstein, Friedell, Hasenclever, Toller, Tucholsky, Klaus Mann, Ossietzky, Benjamin, Koestler and Zweig: almost all of them writers who had taken their own lives or had been close to doing so. He copied out passages into notebooks which give a good idea of how much the lives of these particular authors interested him. Paul copied out hundreds of pages, mostly in Gabelsberg shorthand because otherwise he would not have been able to write fast enough, and time and again one comes across stories of suicide. It seemed to me, said

Mme Landau, handing me the black oilcloth books, as if
Paul had been gathering evidence, the mounting weight of

which, as his investigations proceeded, finally convinced him
that he belonged to the exiles and not to the people of S.

In early 1982, the condition of Paul's eyes began to
deteriorate. Soon all he could see were fragmented or
shattered images. No second operation was going to be

possible; Paul bore the fact with equanimity, said Mme Landau, and always looked back with immense gratitude to the eight years of light that the Berne operation had afforded him. If he paused to consider, Paul had said to her shortly after being given an extremely unfavourable prognosis, that as a child he had already been troubled with little dark patches and pearldrop shapes before his eyes, and had always been afraid that he would go blind at any time, then it was amazing, really, that his eyes had done him such good service for quite so long. The fact was, said Mme Landau, that Paul's whole manner at that time was extraordinarily composed as he contemplated the mouse-grey (his word) prospect before him. He realized then that the world he was about to enter might be a more confined one than that he had hitherto lived in, but he also believed there would be a certain sense of ease. I offered to read Paul the whole of Pestalozzi, said Mme Landau, to which he replied that for that he would gladly sacrifice his eyesight, and I should start right away, for preference, perhaps, with *The Evening Hour of a Hermit*. It was some time in the autumn, during one such reading hour, said Mme Landau, that Paul, without any preamble, informed me that there was now no reason to keep the flat in S and he proposed to give it up. Not long after Christmas we went to S to see to it. Since I had not set foot in the new Germany, I had misgivings as I looked forward to the journey. No snow had fallen, there was no sign anywhere of any winter tourism, and when we got out at S I felt as if we had arrived at the end of the world, and experienced so uncanny a premonition that I should have liked most of all to turn back on the spot. Paul's flat was cold and dusty and full of the past. For two or three days we busied ourselves in it aimlessly. On the third day a spell of mild *föhn* weather set in, quite unusual for the time of year. The pine forests were black on the mountainsides, the windows gleamed like lead, and the sky was so low and dark, one expected ink to run out of it any moment. The pain in my temples was so dreadful that I had to lie down, and I well remember that, when the aspirin Paul had given me gradually began to take effect, two strange, sinister patches began to move behind my eyelids, furtively. It was not till dusk that I woke; though on that day it was as early as three. Paul had covered me with a blanket, but he himself was nowhere to be seen. As I stood, irresolute in the hall, I noticed that Paul's windcheater was missing, which, as he had happened to mention that morning, had been hanging there for almost forty years. I knew at that moment that Paul had gone out, wearing that jacket, and that I would never see him alive again. So, in a way, I was ready when the doorbell rang soon after. It was only the manner in which he died, a death so inconceivable to me, that robbed me of my self-control at first; yet, as I soon realized, it was for Paul a perfectly logical step. Railways had always meant a great deal to him – perhaps he felt they were headed for death. Timetables and directories, all the logistics of railways, had at times become an obsession with him, as his flat in S showed. I can still see the Märklin model railway he had laid out on a deal table in the spare north-facing room: to me it is the very image and symbol of Paul's German tragedy. When Mme Landau said this, I thought of the stations, tracks, goods depots and signal boxes that Paul had so often drawn on the blackboard and which we had to copy into our exercise books as carefully as we could. It is hard, said Mme Landau, when I told her about those railway lessons, in the end it is hard to know what it is that

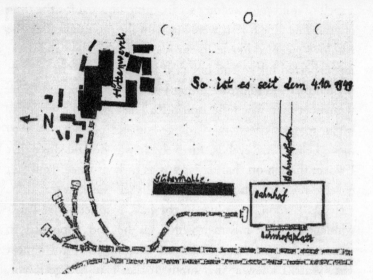

someone dies of. Yes, it is very hard, said Mme Landau, one really doesn't know. All those years that he was here in Yverdon I had no notion that Paul had found his fate already systematically laid out for him in the railways, as it were. Only once, obliquely, did he talk about his passion for railways, more as one talks of a quaint interest that belongs to the past. On that occasion, said Mme Landau, Paul told me that as a child he had once spent his summer holidays in Lindau, and had watched from the shore every day as the trains trundled across from the mainland to the island and from the island to the mainland. The white clouds of steam in the blue air, the passengers waving from the windows, the reflection in the water – this spectacle, repeated at intervals, so absorbed him that he never once appeared on time at the dinner table all that holiday, a lapse that his aunt responded to with a shake of the head that grew more resigned every time, and his uncle with the comment that he would end up on the railways.

When Paul told me this perfectly harmless holiday story, said Mme Landau, I could not possibly ascribe the importance to it that it now seems to have, though even then there was something about that last turn of phrase that made me uneasy. I suppose I did not immediately see the innocent meaning of Paul's uncle's expression, *end up on the railways*, and it struck me as darkly foreboding. The disquiet I experienced because of that momentary failure to see what was meant – I now sometimes feel that at that moment I beheld an image of death – lasted only a very short time, and passed over me like the shadow of a bird in flight.

AMBROS ADELWARTH

*My field of corn is
but a crop of tears*

I have barely any recollection of my own of Great-Uncle Adelwarth. As far as I can say with any certainty, I saw him only once, in the summer of 1951. That was when the Americans, Uncle Kasimir with Lina and Flossie, Aunt Fini with Theo and the little twins, and Aunt Theres, who was unmarried, came to stay with us in W for several weeks, either all together or one after the other. On one occasion during that time, the in-laws from Kempten and Lechbruck – emigrants, as is well known, tend to seek out their own kind – came to W for a few days, and it was at the resulting reunion of almost sixty members of the family that I saw my Great-Uncle Adelwarth, for the first (and, I believe, the last) time. Naturally, in the great upheaval caused by the visitors, in our own household and indeed throughout the whole village, since rooms had to be found elsewhere, he made no more impression on me at first than any of the others; but when he was called upon, as the eldest of the emigrants and their forefather, as it were, to address the gathered clan, that Sunday afternoon when we sat for coffee at the long trestle tables in the village hall, my attention was inevitably drawn to him as he rose and tapped his glass with a small spoon. Uncle Adelwarth was not particularly tall, but he was nonetheless a most distinguished presence who confirmed and enhanced the self-esteem of all who were there, as the general murmur of approval made clear – even though, as I, at the age of seven, immediately realized (in contrast to the adults, who were caught up in their own preconceptions), they seemed out-classed compared with this man. Although I do not remember what Uncle Adelwarth said in his rather formal address, I do recall being deeply impressed by the fact that his apparently effortless German was entirely free of any trace of our home dialect and that he used words and turns of phrase the meanings of which I could only guess at. After this, for me, truly memorable appearance, Uncle Adelwarth vanished from my sight for good when he left for Immenstadt on the mail bus the following day, and from there journeyed onward by rail to Switzerland. Not even in my thoughts did he remain present, and of his death two years later, let alone its circumstances, I knew nothing throughout my childhood, probably because the sudden end of Uncle Theo, who was felled by a stroke one morning while reading the paper, placed Aunt Fini and the twins in an extremely difficult situation, a turn of events which must have eclipsed the demise of an elderly relative who lived on his own. Moreover, Aunt Fini, whose closeness to him put her in the best position to tell us how things had been with Uncle Adelwarth, now found herself obliged (she wrote) to work night and day to see herself and the twins through, for which reason, understandably, she was the first to stop coming over from America for the summer months. Kasimir visited less and less often also, and only Aunt Theres came with any kind of regularity, for one thing because, being single, she was in by far the best position to do so, and for another because she was incurably homesick her whole life long. Three weeks after she arrived, on every visit, she would still be weeping with the joy of reunion, and three weeks before she left she would again be weeping with the pain of separation. If her stay with us was longer than six weeks, there would be a becalmed period in the middle that she would mostly fill with needlework; but if her stay was shorter there were times when one really did not know whether she was in tears because she was at home at long last or because she was already dreading having to leave again. Her last visit was a complete disaster. She wept in silence, at breakfast and at dinner, out walking in the fields or shopping for the Hummel figurines she doted on, doing crosswords or gazing out of the window. When we accompanied her to Munich, she sat streaming tears between us children in the back of Schreck the taxi driver's new Opel Kapitän as the roadside trees sped past us in the light of dawn, from Kempten to Kaufbeuren and from Kaufbeuren to Buchloe; and later I watched from the spectators' terrace as she walked towards the silvery aeroplane, with her hatboxes, across the tarmac at Riem airport, sobbing repeatedly and drying her eyes with a handkerchief. Without looking back once, she went up the steps and vanished through the dark opening into the belly of the aircraft – for ever, as one might say. For a while her weekly letters still reached us (invariably beginning: My dear ones at home, how are you? I am fine!) but then the correspondence, which had been kept up without fail for almost thirty years, broke off, as I noticed when the dollar bills that were regularly enclosed for me stopped coming. It was in the midst of carnival season that my mother put a death notice in the local paper, to the effect that our dear sister, sister-in-law and aunt had departed this life in New York following a short but bravely borne illness. All this prompted the talk again about Uncle Theo's far too early death, but not, as I well remember, of Uncle Adelwarth, who, like Theo, had died a few years or so before.

Our relatives' summer visits were probably the initial reason why I imagined, as I grew up, that I too would one day go to live in America. More important, though, to my dream of America was the different kind of everyday life displayed by the occupying forces stationed in our town. The local people found their moral conduct in general – to judge by comments sometimes whispered, sometimes spoken out loud – unbecoming in a victorious nation. They let the houses they had requisitioned go to ruin, put no window boxes on the balconies, and had wire-mesh fly screens in the windows instead of curtains. The womenfolk went about in trousers and dropped their lipstick-stained cigarette butts in the street, the men put their feet up on the table, the children left their bikes out in the garden overnight, and as for those negroes, no one knew what to make of them. It was precisely this kind of disparaging remark that strengthened my desire to see the one foreign country of which I had any idea at all. In the evenings, but particularly during the endless lessons at school, I pictured every detail of my future in America. This period of my imaginary Americanization, during which I crisscrossed the entire United States, now on horseback, now in a dark brown Oldsmobile, peaked between my sixteenth and seventeenth years in my attempt to perfect the mental and physical attitudes of a Hemingway hero, a venture in mimicry that was doomed to failure for various reasons that can easily be imagined. Subsequently my American dreams gradually faded away, and once they had reached vanishing point they were presently supplanted by an aversion to all things American. This aversion became so deeply rooted in me during my years as a student that soon nothing could have seemed more absurd to me than the idea that I might ever travel to America except under compulsion. Even so, I did eventually fly to Newark on the 2nd of January 1981. This change of heart was prompted by a photograph album of my mother's which had come into my hands a few months earlier and which contained pictures quite new to me of our relatives who had emigrated during the Weimar years. The longer I studied the photographs, the more urgently I sensed a growing need to learn more about the lives of the people in them. The photograph that follows here, for example, was taken in the Bronx

in March 1939. Lina is sitting on the far left, next to Kasimir. On the far right is Aunt Theres. I do not know who the other people on the sofa are, except for the little girl wearing glasses.

That's Flossie, who later became a secretary in Tucson, Arizona, and learnt to belly dance when she was in her fifties. The oil painting on the wall shows our village of W. As far as I have been able to discover, no one now knows the whereabouts of that picture. Not even Uncle Kasimir, who brought it with him to New York rolled up in a cardboard tube, as a farewell gift from his parents, knows where it can have got to.

So on that 2nd of January, a dark and dreary day, I drove south from Newark airport on the New Jersey turnpike in the direction of Lakehurst, where Aunt Fini and Uncle Kasimir, after they moved away from the Bronx and Mamaroneck in the mid Seventies, had each bought a bungalow in a so-called retirement community amidst the blueberry fields. Right outside the airport perimeter I came within an inch of driving off the road when a Jumbo rose ponderously into the air above a truly mountainous heap of garbage, like some creature from prehistoric times. It was trailing a greyish black veil of vapour, and for a moment it was as if it had spread its wings. Then I drove on into flat country, where for the entire length of the Garden State Parkway there was nothing but stunted trees, fields overgrown with heather, and deserted wooden houses, partly boarded up, with tumble-down cabins and chicken runs all around. There, Uncle Kasimir told me later, millions of hens were kept up to the postwar years, laying millions upon millions of eggs for the New York market till new methods of poultry-keeping made the business unprofitable and the smallholders and their birds disappeared. Shortly after nightfall, taking a side road that ran off from the Parkway for several kilometres through a kind of marshland, I reached the old peoples' town called Cedar Glen West. Despite the immense territory covered by this community, and despite the fact that the bungalow condominiums were indistinguishable from each other, and, furthermore, that almost identical glowing Father Christmases were standing in every front garden, I found Aunt Fini's house without difficulty, since everything at Cedar Glen West is laid out in a strictly geometrical pattern.

Aunt Fini had made *Maultaschen* for me. She sat at the table with me and urged me to help myself whilst she ate nothing, as old women often do when they cook for a younger relative who has come to visit. My aunt spoke about the past, sometimes covering the left side of her face, where she had had a bad neuralgia for weeks, with one hand. From time to time she would dry the tears that pain or her memories brought to her eyes. She told me of Theo's untimely death, and the years that followed, when she often had to work sixteen hours or more a day, and went on to tell me about Aunt Theres, and how, before she died, she had walked around for months as if she were a stranger to the place. At times, in the summer light, she had looked like a saint, in her white twill gloves which she had worn for years on account of her eczema. Perhaps, said Aunt Fini, Theres really was a saint. At all events she shouldered her share of troubles. Even as a schoolchild she was told by the catechist that she was a tearful sort, and come to think of it, said Aunt Fini, Theres really did seem to be crying most of her life. She had never known her without a wet handkerchief in her hand. And, of course, she was always giving everything away: all she earned, and whatever came her way as the keeper of the millionaire Wallerstein's household. As true as I'm sitting here, said Aunt Fini, Theres died a poor woman. Kasimir, and particularly Lina, doubted it, but the fact was that she left nothing but her collection of almost a hundred Hummel figurines, her wardrobe (which was splendid, mind you) and large quantities of paste jewellery – just enough, all told, to cover the cost of the funeral.

Theres, Kasimir and I, said Aunt Fini as we leafed through her photo album, emigrated from W at the end of

the Twenties. First, I took ship with Theres at Bremerhaven on the 6th of September 1927. Theres was twenty-three and I was twenty-one, and both of us were wearing bonnets. Kasimir followed from Hamburg in summer 1929, a few weeks before Black Friday. He had trained as a tinsmith, and was just as unable to find work as I was, as a teacher, or Theres, as a sempstress. I had graduated from the Institute at Wettenhausen the previous year, and from autumn 1926 I had worked as an unpaid teaching assistant at the primary school in W. This is a photograph taken at that time. We were on an outing to Falkenstein. The pupils all stood in the back of the

lorry, while I sat in the driver's cab with a teacher named Fuchsluger, who was one of the very first National Socialists, and Benedikt Tannheimer, who was the landlord of the Adler and the owner of the lorry. The child right at the back, with a cross marked over her head, is your mother,

Rosa. I remember, said Aunt Fini, that a month or so later, two days before I embarked, I went to Klosterwald with her, and saw her to her boarding school. At that time, I think, Rosa had a great deal of anxiety to contend with, given that her leaving home coincided so unhappily with her siblings' departure for another life overseas, for at Christmas she wrote a letter to us in New York in which she said she felt fearful when she lay awake in the dormitory at night. I tried to console her by saying she still had Kasimir, but then Kasimir left for America too, when Rosa was just fifteen. That's the way it always is, said Aunt Fini thoughtfully: one thing after another. Theres and I, at any rate, she continued after a while, had a comparatively easy time of it when we arrived in New York. Uncle Adelwarth, a brother of our mother, who had gone to America before the First World War and had been employed only in the best of houses since then, was able to find us positions immediately, thanks to his many connections. I became a governess with the Seligmans in Port Washington, and Theres a lady's maid to Mrs Wallerstein, who was about the same age and whose husband, who came from somewhere near Ulm, had made a considerable fortune with a number of brewing patents, a fortune that went on growing as the years went by.

Uncle Adelwarth, whom you probably do not remember any more, said Aunt Fini, as if a quite new and altogether more significant story were now beginning, was a man of rare distinction. He was born at Gopprechts near Kempten in 1886, the youngest of eight children, all of them girls except for him. His mother died, probably of exhaustion, when Uncle Adelwarth, who was given the name Ambros, was not yet two years old. After her death, the eldest daughter,

Kreszenz, who cannot have been more than seventeen at the time, had to run the household and play the role of mother as best she could, while their father the innkeeper sat with his customers, which was all he knew how to do. Like the other siblings, Ambros had to give Zenzi a hand quite early on, and at five he was already being sent to the weekly market at Immenstadt, together with Minnie, who was not much older, to sell the chanterelles and cranberries they had gathered the day before. Well into the autumn, said Aunt Fini, the two youngest of the Adelwarth children sometimes did nothing for weeks on end but bring home basketfuls of rosehips; they would cut them open, then dig out the hairy seeds with the tip of a spoon, and, after leaving them in a washtub for a few days to draw moisture, put the red flesh of the hips through the press. If one thinks now of the circumstances in which Ambros grew up, said Aunt Fini, one inevitably concludes that he never really had a childhood. When he was only thirteen he left home and went to Lindau, where he worked in the kitchens of the Bairischer Hof till he had enough for the rail fare to Lausanne, the beauties of which he had once heard enthusiastically praised at the inn in Gopprechts by a travelling watchmaker. Why, I shall never know, said Aunt Fini, but in my mind's eye I always see Ambros crossing Lake Constance from Lindau by steamer, in the moonlight, although that can scarcely have been how it was in reality. One thing is certain: that within a few days of leaving his homeland for good, Ambros, who was then fourteen at the outside, was working as an *apprenti garçon* in room service at the Grand Hôtel Eden in Montreux, probably thanks to his unusually appealing but nonetheless self-controlled nature. At least I think it was the Eden, said Aunt Fini, because, in one of the postcard albums that Uncle Adelwarth left, the world-famous hotel is on one of the opening pages, with its awnings lowered over the windows against the afternoon sun. During his apprenticeship in Montreux, Aunt Fini continued, after she had fetched the album from one of her bedroom drawers and opened it up before me, Ambros was

653 Montreux - Hôtel Eden et le Mont Cubli

not only initiated into all the secrets of hotel life, but also learnt French to perfection, or rather, he absorbed it; he had the special gift of acquiring a foreign language, without apparent effort and without any teaching aids, within a year or two, solely by making certain adjustments (as he once explained to me) to his inner self. Along with very accomplished New York English he also spoke a most elegant French and an extremely dignified German, which astounded me the most, since he could hardly have had it from Gopprechts. Furthermore, Aunt Fini recalled, he had a far from elementary knowledge of Japanese, as I once discovered by chance when we were shopping together at Sacks' and he came to the rescue of a Japanese gentleman who knew no English and was embroiled in some unpleasantness.

Once his Swiss apprentice years were over, Ambros went to London, with excellent recommendations and testimonials, where he took a job at the Savoy Hotel in the Strand in the autumn of 1905, again in room service. It was in his London period that the mysterious episode of the lady from Shanghai occurred. All I know of her is that she had a taste for brown kid gloves; although Uncle Adelwarth did make occasional references later to what he had experienced with this lady (she marked the beginning of my career in misfortune, he once said), I never managed to find out the true facts of the matter. I assume that the lady from Shanghai – whom I always associated, doubtless absurdly, with Mata Hari – often stayed at the Savoy, and that Ambros, who was now about twenty, had contact with her professionally, if one can put it like that. It was the same with the counsellor from the Japanese legation whom he accompanied – in 1907, if I am not mistaken – on a journey by ship and rail via Copenhagen, Riga, St Petersburg, and Moscow, right across Siberia, to Japan, where the unmarried gentleman had a wonderful house set in a lake, near Kyoto. Ambros spent almost two years, partly as valet and partly as the counsellor's guest, in that floating and well-nigh empty house, and as far as I am aware he felt happier there than he had been anywhere else until then. Once, at Mamaroneck, said Aunt Fini, Uncle Adelwarth spent all of one afternoon telling me about his time in Japan. But I no longer remember exactly what he told me. Something about paper walls, I think, about archery, and a good deal about evergreen laurel, myrtle and wild camellia. And I remember something about

an old hollow camphor tree which supposedly had room for fifteen people inside it, a story of a decapitation, and the call of the Japanese cuckoo, said Aunt Fini, her eyes half closed, *hototogisu*, which he could imitate so well.

After morning coffee on the second day of my stay at Cedar Glen West, I went over to Uncle Kasimir. It was about half past ten when I sat down at the kitchen table with him. Lina was already busy at the stove. My uncle had produced two glasses and poured out the gentian brandy I had brought. In those days, he began, once I had managed to steer the talk to the subject of emigration, people like us simply had no chance in Germany. Only once, when I had finished my tinsmith apprenticeship in Altenstadt, did I get work, in '28, when they were putting a new copper roof on the synagogue in Augsburg. The Jews of Augsburg had donated the old copper roof for the war effort during the First World War,

and it wasn't till '28 that they had the money they needed for a new roof. This is me, said Uncle Kasimir, pushing across the table a framed postcard-size photograph he had taken down from the wall – at the far right, from where you're looking. But after that job there was nothing again for weeks, and one of my mates, Josef Wohlfahrt, who still felt confident about things when we were at work up on the synagogue roof, later hanged himself in despair. Fini wrote enthusiastic letters from her new homeland, so it was no wonder that I finally decided to follow my sisters to America. Of the rail journey across Germany I remember nothing, except that everything seemed unfamiliar and incomprehensible to me – the country we passed through, the huge railway stations and cities, the Rhineland and the vast flatlands up north – most probably because I had never been beyond the Allgäu and the Lechfeld region. But I do still see the offices of Norddeutscher Lloyd in Bremerhaven quite clearly in front of me. The passengers with little money were obliged to wait there till they could embark. I particularly remember the many different kinds of head-gear the emigrants wore: hoods and caps, winter and summer hats, shawls and kerchiefs, and then the peaked caps of the shipping line's stewards and the customs officers, and the bowler hats of the brokers and agents. On the walls hung large oil pictures of the ocean liners of the Lloyd fleet. Every one of them was cleaving a course full steam ahead, the bow rearing up out of the waves, conveying a sense of an unstoppable force driving onward. Above the door through which we finally left was a circular clock with Roman numerals, and over the clock, in ornate lettering, was the motto *Mein Feld ist die Welt.*

Aunt Lina was pushing boiled potatoes through a press onto a floured pastryboard, and Uncle Kasimir, pouring me another gentian, went on to describe his crossing in the teeth of the February storms. The way the waves rose up from the deep and came rolling on was terrifying, he said. Even as a child I used to be horrified when the frog pond was frozen over, and we played curling on the ice, and I would suddenly think of the darkness under my feet. And now, nothing but black water all around, day in, day out, and the ship always seeming to be in the selfsame place. Most of my fellow travellers were sea-sick. Exhausted they lay in their berths, their eyes glassy or half closed. Others squatted on the floor, stood leaning for hours against a wall, or tottered along the passageways like sleepwalkers. For a full week, I too felt like death. I did not begin to feel better until we cleared the Narrows into Upper Bay. I sat on a bench on deck. The ship had already slowed. I felt a light breeze on my forehead, and as we approached the waterfront Manhattan rose higher and higher before us out of the sunshot morning mists.

My sisters, who were waiting for me on the quayside,

were not able to be of much help, nor could Uncle Adelwarth find anything for me, because I was no use as a gardener or cook or servant. On the day after my arrival I rented a back room that looked out on a narrow air shaft, from Mrs Risa Litwak in Bayard Street on the Lower East Side. Mrs Litwak, whose husband had died the year before, spent the whole day cooking and cleaning, or if she wasn't cooking and cleaning she was making paper flowers or sewing all night for her children or for other people, or as a supply sempstress for some business or other. Sometimes she played on a pianola very pretty songs that I seemed to know from somewhere. Until the First World War, the Bowery and the whole Lower East Side were the districts where the immigrants chiefly came to live. More than a hundred thousand Jews arrived there every year, moving into the cramped, dingy apartments in the five- or six-storey tenement blocks. The so-called parlour, which faced the street, was the only room that had two windows, and the fire escape ran past one of them. In the autumn, the Jews would build their sukkahs on the fire escape landings, and in summer, when the heat hung motionless in the city streets for weeks and life was unbearable indoors, hundreds and thousands of people would sleep outside, up in the airy heights, or even on the roofs or side-walks or the little fenced-off patches of grass on Delancey Street and in Seward Park. The whole of the Lower East Side was one huge dormitory. Even so, the immigrants were full of hope in those days, and I myself was by no means despondent when I started to look for a job at the end of February '28. And before the week was out I already had my place at a workbench, at the Seckler & Margarethen Soda and Seltzers Works near the sliproad up to Brooklyn Bridge. There I made stainless-steel boilers and vats of various sizes, and old Seckler, who was a Jew from Brünn (I never did find out who Margarethen was), sold most of them as "catering equipment" to illicit distilleries where the concern was far less about the asking price than about doing business with the utmost discretion. Seckler, who for some reason took a liking to me, said that the sale of these steel vats and all the rest of the plant

vital to the distilleries had developed as a side-line almost by itself, without his doing anything to encourage it, alongside the main business of the soda and seltzers works, and so he simply did not have the heart to cut it back. Seckler always praised my work, but he was reluctant to pay, and gave a poor wage. At least with me, he would say, you are on the first rung of the ladder. And then one day, it was a few weeks after Passover, he called me in to his office, leaned back in his chair, and said: Have you got a head for heights? If you have, you can go over to the new Yeshiva, they need metalworkers like you. And he gave me the address – 500 West 187th Street, corner Amsterdam Avenue. The very next day I was up on the top of the tower, just as I had been on the Augsburg Synagogue, only much higher, helping to rivet copper bands that were almost six metres wide onto the cupola that crowned the building, which looked like a cross between a railway station and an oriental palace. After that, I worked a lot on the tops of skyscrapers, which they went

on building until the early Thirties in New York, despite the Depression. I put the copper hoods on the General Electric Building, and from '29 to '30 we spent a year on the sheet-steel work on the summit of the Chrysler Building, which was unbelievably difficult on account of the curvatures and slopes. Since all my acrobatics were done two or three hundred metres above the ground, I naturally made a lot of money, but I spent it as fast as I earned it. And then I broke my wrist skating in Central Park and had no work till '34. And then we moved to the Bronx, and life up in the dizzy heights came to an end.

After lunch, Uncle Kasimir became visibly restless and paced to and fro, and at length he said: I have got to get out of the house! – to which Aunt Lina, who was washing up, replied: What a day to go for a drive! One might indeed have thought that night was falling, so low and inky black was the sky. The streets were deserted. We passed very few other cars on the road. It took us almost an hour to cover the thirty kilometres to the Atlantic, because Uncle Kasimir drove more slowly than I have ever known anyone drive on an open stretch of road. He sat angled up against the wheel, steering with his left hand and telling tales of the heyday of Prohibition. Occasionally he would take a glance ahead to check that we were still in the right lane. The Italians did most of the business, he said. All along the coast, in places like Leonardo, Atlantic Highlands, Little Silver, Ocean Grove, Neptune City, Belmar and Lake Como, they built summer palaces for their families and villas for their women and usually a church as well and a little house for a chaplain. Uncle slowed down even more and wound his window down. This is Toms River, he said, there's no one here in the winter. In the harbour, sailboats lay pushed up together like a frightened flock, rigging rattling. Two seagulls perched on top of a coffee shop built to look like a gingerbread house. The Buyright Store, the Pizza Parlour and the Hamburger Heaven were closed, and the private homes were locked up and shuttered too. The wind blew sand across the road and under the wooden sidewalks. The dunes, said Uncle, are invading the town. If people didn't keep coming in the summer, this would all be buried in a few years. From Toms River the road ran down to Barnegat Bay and across Pelican Island to the eighty-kilometre spit of land that stretches along the coast of New Jersey and is nowhere more than a kilometre or so wide. We parked the car and walked along the beach, with a biting northeasterly at our backs. I'm afraid I don't know much about Ambros Adelwarth, said Uncle Kasimir. When I arrived in New York he was already over forty, and in the early days, and later too, I hardly saw him more than once or twice a year. As far as his legendary past was concerned, of course there were rumours, but all I know for certain is that Ambros was major-domo and butler with the Solomons, who had an estate at Rocky Point, at the furthermost tip of Long Island, surrounded by water on

three sides. The Solomons – with the Seligmanns, the Loebs, the Kuhns, the Speyers and the Wormsers – were amongst the wealthiest of the Jewish banking families in New York. Before Ambros became the Solomons' butler he was valet and travelling companion to Cosmo, the Solomons' son, who was a few years younger than himself and was notorious in New York society for his extravagance and his eternal escapades. On one occasion, for instance, they said he had tried to ride a horse up the stairs in the lobby of The Breakers Hotel in Palm Beach. But I know stories like that only from hearsay. Fini, who became a sort of confidante for Ambros towards the end, sometimes hinted that there was something tragic about the relationship between Ambros and the Solomons' son. And, as far as I know, young Solomon really was destroyed by some mental illness in the mid Twenties. As for Uncle Adelwarth, all I can say is that I always felt sorry for him, because he could never, his whole life long, permit anything to ruffle his composure. Of course, said Uncle Kasimir, he was of the other persuasion, as anyone could see, even if the family always ignored or glossed over the fact. Perhaps some of them never realized. The older Uncle Adelwarth grew, the more hollowed-out he seemed to me, and the last time I saw him, in the house at Mamaroneck that the Solomons had left him, so finely furnished, it was as if his clothes were holding him together. As I said, Fini looked after him till the end. She'll be able to give you a better idea of what he was like. Uncle Kasimir stopped and stood gazing out at the ocean. This is the edge of the darkness, he said. And in truth it seemed as if the mainland were submerged behind us and as if there were nothing above the watery waste but this narrow strip of sand running up to the north and down towards the south.

I often come out here, said Uncle Kasimir, it makes me feel that I am a long way away, though I never quite know from where. Then he took a camera out of his large-check jacket and took this picture, a print of which he sent me two years later, probably when he had finally shot the whole film, together with his gold pocket watch.

Aunt Fini was sitting in her armchair in the dark living room when I went in to her that evening. Only the glow of the street lights was on her face. The aches have eased off, she said, the pain is almost over. At first I thought I was only imagining that it was getting better, so slow was the improvement. And once I was almost without pain, I thought: if you move now, it'll start again. So I just stayed sitting here. I've been sitting here all afternoon. I couldn't say whether I mightn't have nodded off now and then. I think I was lost in my thoughts most of the time. My aunt switched on the little reading lamp but kept her eyes closed. I went out into the kitchen and made her two soft-boiled eggs, toast, and peppermint tea. When I took the tray in to her I turned the conversation back to Uncle Adelwarth. About two years after he arrived in America, said Aunt Fini, dunking a soldier into one of the eggs, Ambros took a position with the Solomons on Long Island. What happened to the counsellor at the Japanese legation, I can't remember now. At all events, Uncle quickly made his way at the Solomons'. Within an amazingly short time, old Samuel Solomon, who was very impressed by the unfailing sureness of Ambros in all things, offered him the position of personal attendant to his son, to watch over him, since he believed, not without reason, that great dangers lay in his path. There is no doubt that Cosmo Solomon, whom I never had the opportunity to meet, was inclined to eccentricity. He was extremely gifted, and a very promising student of engineering, but gave up his studies to build flying machines in an old factory in Hackensack. At the same time, mind you, he spent a lot of time at places like Saratoga Springs and Palm Beach, for one thing because he was an excellent polo player, for another because he could blow huge sums of money at luxury hotels like the Breakers, the Poinciana or the American Adelphi, which at that time, so Uncle Adelwarth once told me, was plainly the main thing as far as he was concerned. Old Solomon was worried by the dissipated life his son was leading, and felt it had no future. When he tried to cut back his allowance, which in point of fact had been unlimited, Cosmo hit upon the idea of opening up a source of income that would never dry up, by playing the casinos of Europe during the summer months. In June 1911, with Ambros as his friend and guide, he went to France for the first time, and promptly won considerable sums at Evian on Lake Geneva and then at Monte Carlo, in the Salle

Schmidt. Uncle Adelwarth once told me that Cosmo would become strangely detached when he was playing roulette. At first, Ambros would think he was concentrating on calculations of probability, till one day Cosmo told him that at such times he actually was in a trance of some kind, trying to decipher the right number as it appeared for a fraction of a second from out of mists that were ordinarily impenetrable, whereupon, without the slightest hesitation, and as it were still in a dream, he would place his bet, either *en plein* or *à cheval.* Cosmo claimed that this condition of total withdrawal from normal life was dangerous, and it was the task of Ambros to watch over him as one would over a sleeping child. Of course I do not know what was really going on, said Aunt Fini, but one thing is certain: at Evian and Monte Carlo, the two of them made such a killing that Cosmo was able to buy an aeroplane from Deutsch de la Meurthe, the French industrialist. He flew it in the Quinzaine d'Aviation de la Baie de Seine at Deauville that August, and was by far the most daring of them all at looping the loop. Cosmo was in Deauville with Ambros in the summer of 1912 and 1913 also, and caught the imagination of society, not just with his astounding luck at roulette and his daredevil acrobatics on the polo field but chiefly, I'm certain, by the fact that he turned down every invitation he received to tea, dinner or such like, and never went out or ate with anyone but Ambros, whom he always treated as an equal. Incidentally, said Aunt Fini, in Uncle Adelwarth's postcard album there is a picture that shows Cosmo with a trophy presented by an aristocratic lady – the Comtesse de FitzJames, if I remember rightly – after a match at the Clairefontaine Hippodrome, probably a charity event. It is the only photograph of Cosmo Solomon

that I possess. There are relatively few photos of Ambros, too, probably because, like Cosmo, he was very shy, despite his familiarity with the ways of the world. In the summer of 1913,

Aunt Fini continued, a new casino was opened at Deauville, and during the first few weeks people were seized by so frenetic a gambling fever that all the roulette and baccarat tables, and what they call the *petits chevaux*, were constantly occupied by players, and besieged by more who wanted to play. One well-known *joueuse* called Marthe Hanau supposedly masterminded the hysteria. I remember clearly, said Aunt Fini, that Uncle Adelwarth once called her a notorious *filibustière*, who had been a thorn in the flesh of the casino management for years but was now coaxing the gamblers to the tables on their behalf and at their behest. Apart from the machinations of Marthe Hanau, it was the overexcited atmosphere, which had been quite changed by the ostentatious luxury of the new casino, that was responsible for the unparalleled rise in the earnings of the Deauville Bank that summer of 1913, in Uncle Adelwarth's view. As for Cosmo, in the summer of 1913 he held even more aloof than in previous years from a social whirl that was growing ever headier, and would play only late in the evening, in the inner sanctum, the Salle de la Cuvette. Only gentlemen in dinner jackets were admitted to the *privé*, where the atmosphere that prevailed was always, as Uncle Adelwarth put it, most ominous – small wonder, said Aunt Fini, if you consider that whole fortunes, family properties, real estate and the achievements of lifetimes were not infrequently gambled away within hours. At the start of the season, Cosmo's luck was often changeable, but towards the end it would surpass even his own expectations. Eyes half closed, he would win time after time, pausing only when Ambros brought him a *consommé* or *café au lait*. Two evenings in a row, so Uncle Adelwarth told me, Cosmo cleaned out the bank and runners had to fetch more money, said Aunt Fini; and then on the third evening, when he broke the bank again, Cosmo won so much that Ambros was busy till dawn counting the money and packing it into a steamer trunk. After spending the summer in Deauville, Cosmo and Ambros travelled via Paris and Venice to Constantinople and Jerusalem. I cannot tell you anything of what happened on that journey, said Aunt Fini, because Uncle Adelwarth would never answer questions about it. But there is a photo of him in Arab

costume, taken when they were in Jerusalem, and, said Aunt Fini, I have a kind of diary too, in tiny writing, that Ambros kept. For a long time I had quite forgotten about it, but, strange to say, I tried only recently to decipher it. With my poor eyes, though, I could not make out much more of it than the odd word; perhaps you should give it a try.

With long pauses, during which she often seemed very far away and lost, Aunt Fini told me, on my last day at Cedar Glen West, of the end of Cosmo Solomon and the later years of my Great-Uncle Ambros Adelwarth. Shortly after the two globetrotters returned from the Holy Land, as Aunt Fini put it, the war broke out in Europe. The more it raged, and the more we learnt of the extent of the devastation, the less Cosmo was able to regain a footing in the unchanged daily life of America. He became a stranger to his former friends, he abandoned his apartment in New York City, and even out on Long Island he soon withdrew entirely to his own quarters and at length to a secluded garden house known as the summer villa. Aunt Fini said that one of the Solomons' old gardeners once told her that in those days Cosmo would often be steeped in melancholy all day, and then at night would pace to and fro in the unheated summer villa, groaning softly. Wildly agitated, he would string out words that bore some relation to the fighting, and as he uttered these words of war he would apparently beat his forehead with his hand, as if he were vexed at his own incomprehension or were trying to learn what he said by heart. Frequently he would be so beside himself that he no longer even recognized Ambros. And yet he claimed that he could see clearly, in his own head, what was happening in Europe: the inferno, the dying, the rotting bodies lying in the sun in open fields. Once he even took to

cudgelling the rats he saw running through the trenches.
When the war ended, Cosmo's condition temporarily
improved. He went back to designing flying machines, drew
up a scheme for a tower house on the coast of Maine, took to
playing the cello again, studied maps and ocean charts, and
discussed with Ambros the various travels he planned. To the
best of my knowledge, they made only one of these journeys,
in the early summer of 1923, when the two of them went to
Heliopolis. One or two pictures have survived from that visit
to Egypt: one shows a *kafeneion* in Alexandria called the
Paradeissos, one the San Stefano casino at Ramleh, and one
the casino at Heliopolis. Their visit to Egypt seems to have

been made at rather short notice, said Aunt Fini, and from
what Uncle Adelwarth told me it was an attempt to regain

the past, an attempt that appears to have failed in every respect. The start of Cosmo's second serious nervous breakdown appears to have been connected with a German film about a gambler that was screened in New York at the time, which Cosmo described as a labyrinth devised to imprison him and drive him mad, with all its mirror reversals. He was particularly disturbed by an episode towards the end of the film in which a one-armed showman and hypnotist by the name of Sandor Weltmann induced a sort of collective hallucination in his audience. From the depths of the stage (as Cosmo repeatedly described it to Ambros) the mirage image of an oasis appeared. A caravan emerged onto the stage from a grove of palms, crossed the stage, went down into the auditorium, passed amongst the spectators, who were craning round in amazement, and vanished as mysteriously as it had appeared. The terrible thing was (Cosmo insisted) that he himself had somehow gone from the hall together with the caravan, and now could no longer tell where he was. One day, not long after, Aunt Fini continued, Cosmo really did disappear. I do not know where they searched for him, or for how long, but know that Ambros finally found him two or three days later on the top floor of the house, in one of the nursery rooms that had been locked for years. He was standing on a stool, his arms hanging down motionless, staring out at the sea where every now and then, very slowly, steamers passed by, bound for Boston or Halifax. When Ambros asked why he had gone up there, Cosmo said he had wanted to see how his brother was. But he never did have a brother, according to Uncle Adelwarth. Soon after, when Cosmo's condition had improved to some extent, Ambros accompanied him to Banff in the Canadian Rockies, for

the good air, on the advice of the doctors. They spent the
whole summer at the famous Banff Springs Hotel. Cosmo
was then like a well-behaved child with no interest in
anything and Ambros was fully occupied by his work and his
increasing concern for his charge. In mid October the snows
began. Cosmo spent many an hour looking out of the tower
window at the vast pine forests all around and the snow
swirling down from the impenetrable heights. He would hold
his rolled-up handkerchief clenched in his fist and bite into it
repeatedly out of desperation. When darkness fell he would
lie down on the floor, draw his legs up to his chest and hide
his face in his hands. It was in that state that Ambros had to
take him home and, a week later, deliver him to the Samaria
Sanatorium at Ithaca, New York, where that same year,
without saying a word or moving a muscle, he faded away.

These things happened more than half a century ago,
said Aunt Fini. At that time I was at the Institute in Wettenhausen and knew nothing of Cosmo Solomon, nor of our
mother's brother who had emigrated from Gopprechts. It was
a long time before I learnt anything of Uncle Adelwarth's

earlier days, even after I arrived in New York, and despite the
fact that I was always in touch with him. After Cosmo's death,
he became butler in the house at Rocky Point. From 1930 to
1950 I regularly drove out to Long Island, either alone or with
Theo, as an extra help when big occasions were being
prepared, or simply to visit. In those days, Uncle Adelwarth
had more than half a dozen servants under him, not counting
the gardeners and chauffeurs. His work took all his time and
energy. Looking back, you might say that Ambros Adelwarth
the private man had ceased to exist, that nothing was left but
his shell of decorum. I could not possibly have imagined him
in his shirtsleeves, or in stockinged feet without his half-
boots, which were unfailingly polished till they shone, and it
was always a mystery to me when, or if, he ever slept, or
simply rested a little. At that time he had no interest in talking
about the past at all. All that mattered to him was that the
hours and days in the Solomons' household should pass
without any disruption, and that the interests and ways of old
Solomon should not conflict with those of the second Mrs
Solomon. From about the time he was thirty-five, said Aunt
Fini, this became particularly difficult for Uncle Adelwarth,
given that old Solomon had announced one day, without
preamble, that he would no longer be present at any dinners
or gatherings whatsoever, that he would no longer have
anything at all to do with the outside world, and that he was
going to devote himself entirely to growing orchids, whereas
the second Mrs Solomon, who was a good twenty years
younger than him, was known far beyond New York for
her weekend parties, for which guests generally arrived on
Friday afternoons. So on the one hand Uncle Adelwarth
was increasingly kept busy looking after old Solomon, who

practically lived in his hothouses, and on the other he was fully occupied in pre-empting the second Mrs Solomon's characteristic liking for tasteless indiscretions. Presumably the demands made by these twofold duties wore him down more, in the long term, than he admitted to himself, especially during the war years, when old Solomon, scandalized by the stories that still reached him in his seclusion, took to spending most of his time sitting wrapped in a travelling rug in an overheated glasshouse amidst the pendulous air-roots of his South American plants, uttering scarcely a syllable beyond the bare essentials, while Margo Solomon persisted in holding court. But when old Solomon died in his wheelchair in the early months of 1947, said Aunt Fini, something curious happened: now it was Margo who, having ignored her husband for nearly ten years, could hardly be persuaded to leave her room. Almost all the staff were discharged. Uncle Adelwarth's principal duty was now to look after the house, which was well-nigh deserted and largely draped with white dust-sheets. That was when Uncle Adelwarth began, now and again, to recount to me incidents from his past life. Even the least of his reminiscences, which he fetched up very slowly from depths that were evidently unfathomable, was of astounding precision, so that, listening to him, I gradually became convinced that Uncle Adelwarth had an infallible memory, but that, at the same time, he scarcely allowed himself access to it. For that reason, telling stories was as much a torment to him as an attempt at self-liberation. He was at once saving himself, in some way, and mercilessly destroying himself. As if to distract me from her last words, Aunt Fini picked up one of the albums from the side table. This, she said, opening it and passing it over to me, is Uncle

Adelwarth as he was then. As you can see, I am on the left with Theo, and on the right, sitting beside Uncle, is his sister Balbina, who was just then visiting America for the first time. That was in May 1950. A few months after the picture was taken, Margo Solomon died of the complications of Banti's disease. Rocky Point passed to various beneficiaries and was sold off, together with all the furniture and effects, at an auction that lasted several days. Uncle Adelwarth was sorely affected by the dispersal, and a few weeks later he moved into

the house at Mamaroneck that old Solomon had made over
to him before he died. There is a picture of the living room on
one of the next pages, said Aunt Fini. The whole house was
always very neat and tidy, down to the last detail, like the
room in this photograph. Often it seemed to me as if Uncle

Adelwarth was expecting a stranger to call at any moment.
But no one ever did. Who would, said Aunt Fini. So I went
over to Mamaroneck at least twice a week. Usually I sat in the
blue armchair when I visited, and Uncle sat at his bureau, at
a slight angle, as if he were about to write something or other.
And from there he would tell me stories and many a strange
tale. At times I thought the things he said he had witnessed,
such as beheadings in Japan, were so improbable that I
supposed he was suffering from Korsakov's syndrome: as you
may know, said Aunt Fini, it is an illness which causes lost
memories to be replaced by fantastic inventions. At any rate,
the more Uncle Adelwarth told his stories, the more desolate

he became. After Christmas '52 he fell into such a deep depression that, although he plainly felt a great need to talk about his life, he could no longer shape a single sentence, nor utter a single word, or any sound at all. He would sit at his bureau, turned a little to one side, one hand on the desktop pad, the other in his lap, staring steadily at the floor. If I talked to him about family matters, about Theo or the twins or the new Oldsmobile with the white-walled tyres, I could never tell if he were listening or not. If I tried to coax him out into the garden, he wouldn't react, and he refused to consult a doctor, too. One morning when I went out to Mamaroneck, Uncle Adelwarth was gone. In the mirror of the hall stand he had stuck a visiting card with a message for me, and I have carried it with me ever since. Have gone to Ithaca. Yours

> *Have gone to Ithaca.*
>
> Ambrose Adelwarth
> 123 Lebanon Drive
> Mamaroneck
> New York
>
> *Yours ever - Ambrose.*

ever – Ambrose. It was a while before I understood what he meant by Ithaca. Needless to say, I drove over to Ithaca as often as I could in the weeks and months that followed. Ithaca is in a beautiful part of the country. All around there are forests and gorges through which the water rushes down towards the lake. The sanatorium, which was run by a Professor Fahnstock, was in grounds that looked like a park. I still remember, said Aunt Fini, standing with Uncle Adelwarth by his window one crystal-clear Indian Summer morning. The air was coming in from outside and we were looking over the almost motionless trees towards a meadow that reminded me of the Altach marsh when a middle-aged man appeared, holding a white net on a pole in front of him and occasionally taking curious jumps. Uncle Adelwarth stared straight ahead, but he registered my bewilderment all the same, and said: It's the butterfly man, you know. He comes round here quite often. I thought I caught an undertone of mockery in the words, and so took them as a sign of the improvement that Professor Fahnstock felt had been effected by the electroconvulsive therapy. Later in the autumn, though, the extent of the harm that had been done to Uncle's spirit and body was becoming clearer. He grew thinner and thinner, his hands, which used to be so calm, trembled, his face became lopsided, and his left eye moved restlessly. The last time I visited Uncle Adelwarth was in November. When it was time for me to leave, he insisted on seeing me to my car. And for that purpose he specially put on his *paletot* with the black velvet collar, and his Homburg. I still see him standing there in the driveway, said Aunt Fini, in that heavy overcoat, looking very frail and unsteady.

The morning I left Cedar Glen West was icy and dark. Exactly as she had described Uncle Adelwarth the day before, Aunt Fini now stood on the pavement in front of her bungalow, in a dark winter coat that was too heavy for her, waving a handkerchief after me. As I drove off I could see her in the mirror, with clouds of white exhaust about her, growing smaller and smaller; and, as I recall that mirror image, I find myself thinking how strange it is that no one since then has waved a handkerchief after me in farewell. In the few days I still had in New York I began making my notes on the inconsolable Aunt Theres, and about Uncle Kasimir on the roof of the Augsburg Synagogue. But my thoughts kept returning to Ambros Adelwarth in particular, and whether I ought not to see the sanatorium at Ithaca which he had entered voluntarily in his sixty-seventh year and where he had subsequently perished. At the time, true, the idea remained a mere thought, either because I did not want to waste my air ticket back to London or because I was wary of looking more closely into the matter. It was not until the early summer of 1984 that I finally went to Ithaca, having meanwhile taken great pains to decipher Uncle Adelwarth's travel notes of 1913 and having concluded that, if I intended to go to Ithaca, I ought not to defer it any longer. So I flew once more to New York and drove northwest along Highway 17 the same day, in a hired car, past various sprawling townships which, though some of their names were familiar, all seemed to be in the middle of nowhere. Monroe, Monticello, Middletown, Wurtsboro, Wawarsing, Colchester and Cadosia, Deposit, Delhi, Neversink and Niniveh – I felt as if I and the car I sat in were being guided by remote control through an outsize toyland where the place names had been picked at random by some invisible giant child, from the ruins of another world long since abandoned. It was as if the car had a will of its own on the broad highway. As all vehicles moved at almost the same speed, overtaking, when it occurred at all, went so slowly that I began to feel like a travelling companion of my neighbour in the next lane as I inched my way forward. At one point, for instance, I drove in the company of a black family for a good half hour. They waved and smiled repeatedly to show that I already had a place in their hearts, as a friend of the family, as it were, and when they parted from me in a broad curve at the Hurleyville exit – the children pulling clownish faces out of the rear window – I felt deserted and desolate for a time. The countryside began to look more uninhabited too. The road crossed a great plateau, with hills and undulations to the right, rising to mountains of some height towards the northerly horizon. Just as the winter days I had spent in America three years before had been dark and colourless, so now the earth's surface, a patchwork of greens, was flooded with light. In the long since abandoned pastures stretching towards the mountains grew clumps of oaks and alders; rectilinear plantations of spruces alternated with irregular stands of birches and aspens, the countless trembling leaves of which had opened only a week or so before; and even on the dark, distant slopes, where pine forests covered the mountainsides, the pale green of larches lit by the evening sun gleamed here and there in the background. When I saw those seemingly uninhabited highlands, I remembered the longing for faraway places that I had known when I bent over my atlas as a pupil at the monastery school, and how often I had travelled, in my thoughts, across the states of America, which I could recite by heart in alphabetical order. In the course of a geography lesson that lasted very nearly an eternity – outside, the early morning blue was still untouched by noonday brightness – I had once explored the regions I was now driving through, as well as the Adirondacks further to the north, which Uncle Kasimir had told me looked just like home. I still remember searching the map with a magnifying glass for the source of the Hudson River, and getting lost in a map square with a great many mountains and lakes. Certain place names such as Sabattis, Gabriels, Hawkeye, Amber Lake, Lake Lila and Lake Tear-in-the-Clouds have remained indelibly in my memory ever since.

At Owego, where I had to turn off the State Highway, I took a break and sat till almost nine in a roadside café, occasionally jotting down a word or two but mostly staring out absent-mindedly through the panoramic windows at the endless traffic and the western sky, still streaked with orange, flamingo pink and gold long after the sun had set. And so it was already late in the evening when I arrived in Ithaca. For maybe half an hour I drove around the town and its suburbs, to get my bearings, before pulling up at a guesthouse in a side street, silent and lit up in its dark garden, like the "Empire des Lumières" in which no one has ever set foot. A path curved from the pavement and ended in a flight of stone steps at the front door, where a shrub stretched out horizontal branches bearing white blossom. In the lamplight I thought for a moment that they were covered with snow. Everyone was plainly already asleep, and it was some time before an aged porter emerged from the depths of the house. He was so doubled over that he cannot have been able to see more than the lower half of anyone standing in front of him. Because of this handicap, no doubt, he had already taken a quick glance at the latecomer outside the glazed door before he crossed the hall, a glance that was the more penetrating for being brief. Without a word he escorted me up a fine mahogany staircase to the top floor, where he showed me to a spacious room over-looking the back garden. I put down my bag, opened one of the high windows, and looked out into the heaving shadows of a cypress that soared up from the depths. The air was filled with its scent and with an unceasing rushing sound, made not by the wind in the trees, as I supposed at first, but by the

Ithaca Falls, which were a short distance away, though invisible from my window. Before I arrived in the town it had been impossible to imagine that in the Lake Cayuga region more than a hundred such falls have been tumbling into the deep-carved gorges and valleys ever since the Ice Age. I lay down and immediately fell into a deep sleep, exhausted by the long journey. The powdery veils that rose silently from the roar of the Falls drifted into my sleep like white curtains blown into a room black with night. The next morning I searched the telephone books in vain for the Samaria Sanatorium or the Professor Fahnstock mentioned by Aunt Fini. Nor was I any more successful when I called on a psychiatric practice, and when I asked the blue-rinsed lady at reception she visibly paled with horror at the words *private mental home*. As I was leaving the hotel to make enquiries in town, I met the crooked porter in the front garden, coming up the path with a broom. He listened to my request for information most attentively and then, leaning on his broom, thought in silence for a good minute. Fahnstock, he exclaimed at length, so loudly that he might have been talking to a deaf person, Fahnstock died in the Fifties. Of a stroke, if I am not mistaken. And in a few words that came with a rattle from his constricted chest he went on to tell me that Fahnstock had had a successor, one Dr Abramsky, though Abramsky had not taken any more patients into the sanatorium since the late Sixties. What he did nowadays in that old place on his own, said the porter, turning abruptly to go, no one knew. And from the door he called after me: I have heard say he's become a beekeeper.

The old porter's information enabled me to find the sanatorium without difficulty that afternoon. A long drive

swept through a park that must have covered almost a
hundred acres and led up to a villa built entirely of wood.
With its covered verandahs and balconies it resembled a
Russian dacha, or one of those immense pinewood lodges
stuffed with trophies that Austrian archdukes and princes
built all over their hunting grounds in Styria and the Tyrol in
the late nineteenth century, to accommodate their aristocratic
guests and the accredited barons of industry. So clear were the
signs of decay, so singularly did the window panes flash in the
sunlight, that I did not dare go any closer, and instead began
by looking around the park, where conifers of almost every
kind – Lebanese cedars, mountain hemlocks, Douglas firs,
larches, Arolla and Monterey pines, and feathery swamp
cypresses – had all grown to their full size. Some of the cedars
and larches were forty metres tall, and one of the hemlocks
must have been fifty. There were woodland meadows between
the trees where bluebells, white cardamines and yellow goats-
beard grew side by side. In other parts of the park there were
many different ferns, and the new greenery of dwarf Japanese
maples, lit up by rays of sunlight, swayed over the fallen leaves
underfoot. I had been strolling around the arboretum for
almost an hour when I came upon Dr Abramsky busy fitting
out new beehives outside his apiary. He was a stocky man
close to sixty, and wore threadbare trousers. From the right
pocket of his patched-up jacket protruded a goose wing, such
as might once have been used as a hand brush. What struck
one immediately about Dr Abramsky was his shock of thick,
flaming red hair that stood on end as if he were in a state of
the greatest anxiety; it reminded me of the Pentecostal
tongues of fire over the heads of the disciples, depicted in my
first catechism. Quite unperturbed by my appearance out of

nowhere, Dr Abramsky pulled up a wicker chair for me and, going on with his work on the beehives, listened to my story. When I had finished he put his tools aside and began to talk himself. I never knew Cosmo Solomon, he said, but I did know your great-uncle, since I started here in 1949 at the age of thirty-one, as Fahnstock's assistant. I remember the Adelwarth case so clearly for a special reason. He came at the beginning of a complete change in my thinking, one that led me, in the decade following Fahnstock's death, to cut back my psychiatric practice more and more, and eventually to give it up altogether. Since mid May 1969 – I shall soon have been retired for fifteen years – I have spent my life out of doors here, in the boathouse or the apiary, depending on the weather, and I no longer concern myself with what goes on in the so-called real world. No doubt I am now, in some sense, mad; but, as you may know, these things are merely a question of perspective. You will have seen that the Samaria is now deserted. Giving it up was the step I had to take in order to free myself from any involvement in life. I do not expect anyone can really imagine the pain and wretchedness once stored up in this extravagant timber palace, and I hope all this misfortune will gradually melt away now as it falls apart. For a while Dr Abramsky said nothing, and merely gazed out into the distance. It is true, he said at length, that Ambrose Adelwarth was not committed into our care by any relative, but came to us of his own free will. Why he came here remained a mystery to me for a long time, and he never talked about it. Fahnstock diagnosed profound senile depression with a tendency to cataleptic seizures, though this was contradicted by the fact that Ambrose showed no sign at all of neglecting his person, as patients in that condition usually do. Quite the contrary, he attached the greatest importance to his appearance. I only ever saw him in a three-piece suit and wearing a flawlessly knotted bow tie. Nonetheless, even when he was simply standing at the window looking out he always gave the impression of being filled with some appalling grief. I do not think, said Dr Abramsky, that I have ever met a more melancholy person than your great-uncle; every casual utterance, every gesture, his entire deportment (he held himself erect until the end), was tantamount to a constant pleading for leave of absence. At meals – to which he always came, since he remained absolute in matters of courtesy even in his darkest times – he still helped himself, but what he actually ate was no more than the symbolic offerings that were once placed on the graves of the dead. It was also remarkable how readily Ambrose submitted to shock treatment, which in the early Fifties, as I understood only later, really came close to torture or martyrdom. Other patients often had to be frogmarched to the treatment room, said Dr Abramsky, but Ambrose would always be sitting on the stool outside the door at the appointed hour, leaning his head against the wall, eyes closed, waiting for what was in store for him.

In response to my request, Dr Abramsky described shock treatment in greater detail. At the start of my career in psychiatry, he said, I was of the opinion that electrotherapy was a humane and effective form of treatment. As students we had been taught – and Fahnstock, in his stories about clinical practice, had repeatedly described in graphic terms – how in the old days, when pseudo-epileptic fits were induced by injecting insulin, patients would be convulsed for minutes, seemingly on the point of death, their faces contorted and blue. Compared with this approach, the introduction of electric shock treatment, which could be dispensed with greater precision and stopped immediately if the patient's reaction was extreme, constituted a considerable step forward. In our view, it seemed completely legitimate once sedatives and muscle relaxants began to be used in the early Fifties, to avoid the worst of the incidental injuries, such as dislocated shoulders or jaws, broken teeth, or other fractures. Given these broad improvements in shock therapy, Fahnstock, dismissing my (alas) none too forceful objections with his characteristic lordliness, adopted what was known as the block method, a course of treatment advocated by the German psychiatrist Braunmühl, which not infrequently involved more than a hundred electric shocks at intervals of only a very few days. This would have been about six months before Ambrose joined us. Needless to say, when treatment was so frequent, there could be no question of proper documentation or assessment of the therapy; and that was what happened with your great-uncle too. Besides, said Dr Abramsky, all of the material on file – the case histories and the medical records Fahnstock kept on a daily basis, albeit in a distinctly cursory fashion – have probably long since been eaten by the mice. They took over the madhouse when it was closed and have been multiplying without cease ever since; at all events, on nights when there is no wind blowing I can hear a constant scurrying and rustling in the dried-out shell of the building, and at times, when a full moon rises beyond the trees, I imagine I can hear the pathetic song of a thousand tiny upraised throats. Nowadays I place all my hope in the mice, and in the woodworm and deathwatch beetles. The sanatorium is creaking, and in places already caving in, and sooner or later they will bring about its collapse. I have a recurring dream of that collapse, said Dr Abramsky, gazing at the palm of his left hand as he spoke. I see the sanatorium on its lofty rise, see everything simultaneously, the building as a whole and also the minutest detail; and I know that the woodwork, the roof beams, door posts and panelling, the floorboards and staircases, the rails and banisters, the lintels and ledges, have already been hollowed out under the surface, and that at any moment, as soon as the chosen one amongst the blind armies of beetles dispatches the very last, scarcely material resistance with its jaws, the entire lot will come down. And that is precisely what does happen in my dream, before my very eyes, infinitely slowly, and a great yellowish cloud billows out and disperses, and where the sanatorium once stood there is merely a heap of powder-fine wood dust, like pollen. Dr Abramsky's voice had grown softer as he spoke, but now, pausing first to review (as I supposed) the imaginary spectacle once more before his mind's eye, he returned to reality. Fahnstock, he resumed, had been trained in neurology at an asylum in Lemberg, immediately before the First World War: at a time, that is, when psychiatry was primarily concerned with subduing those in its custody, and keeping them in safe detention. For that reason he was naturally inclined to interpret the recurrent desolation and apathy of sick patients exposed to continued shock therapy, their growing inability to concentrate, their sluggishness of mind, their muted voices, and even cases when patients entirely ceased to speak, as signs of successful therapy. So to his mind the docility of Ambrose was a result of the new treatment. Ambrose was one of the first of our patients to undergo a series of shocks, over a period of weeks and months; but that docility, as I was already beginning to suspect, was in fact due simply to your great-uncle's longing for an extinction as total and irreversible as possible of his capacity to think and remember.

Once again Dr Abramsky fell silent for a lengthy spell, occasionally scrutinizing the lines on his left hand. I believe, he then went on, looking up at me, I believe it was Fahnstock's unmistakably Austrian intonation that predisposed me towards him at first. He reminded me of my father, who was from Kolomea and, like Fahnstock, came from Galicia to the west after the dissolution of the Habsburg empire. Fahnstock tried to re-establish himself in his home town, Linz, whilst my father tried to start up in the liquor trade in Vienna, but both fell foul of circumstances, the one in Linz and the other in Vienna's Leopoldstadt. In early 1921 my father emigrated to America, and Fahnstock must have arrived in New York during the summer months, where he soon resumed his career in psychiatry. In 1925, following two years at the state hospital in Albany, he took up a position at Samaria, a newly established private sanatorium. At about the same time, my father died when a boiler exploded in a soda factory on the Lower East Side. After the accident, his body was found in a partly poached state. When I was growing up in Brooklyn I missed him very much. Even in the face of the greatest adversity he was confident; my mother, by contrast, seemed only a shadow after his death. I now think that, when I myself began as an assistant at the Samaria, I was uncritically on Fahnstock's side because much about him recalled my father. But when Fahnstock began to believe, towards the end of his career, that he had discovered a psychiatric miracle cure in the block or annihilation method, and when he, who had never had the slightest scientific ambition, increasingly became caught up in a kind of experimental mania and even planned to publish a paper about Ambrose, then, and only then, did it dawn on me that his fanatical interest as well as my own vacillation were, in the end, merely proof of our appalling ignorance and corruptibility.

It was almost evening. Dr Abramsky led me back through the arboretum to the drive. He was holding the white goose wing, and from time to time pointed the way ahead with it. Towards the end, he said as we walked, your great-uncle suffered progressive paralysis of the joints and limbs, probably caused by the shock therapy. After a while he had the greatest difficulty with everyday tasks. He took almost the whole day to get dressed. Simply to fasten his cufflinks and his bow tie took him hours. And he was hardly finished dressing but it was time to undress again. What was more, he was having constant trouble with his eyesight, and suffered from bad headaches, and so he often wore a green eyeshade – like someone who works in a gambling saloon. When I went to see him in his room on the last day of his life, because he had failed to appear for treatment for the first time, he was standing at the window, wearing the eyeshade, gazing out at the marshlands beyond the park. Oddly, he had put on armlets made of some satin-like material, such as he might have worn when he used to polish the silver. When I asked why he had not appeared at the appointed time, he replied (I remember his words exactly): It must have slipped my mind whilst I was waiting for the butterfly man. After he had made this enigmatic remark, Ambrose accompanied me without delay, down to the treatment room where Fahnstock was waiting, and submitted to all the preparations without the least resistance, as he always did. I see him lying before me, said Dr Abramsky, the electrodes on his temples, the rubber bit between his teeth, buckled into the canvas wraps that were riveted to the treatment table like a man shrouded for burial at sea. The session proceeded without incident. Fahnstock's prognosis was distinctly optimistic. But I could see from Ambrose's face that he was now destroyed, all but a vestige of him. When he came round from the anaesthetic, his eyes, which were now strangely glassy and fixed, clouded over, and a sigh that I can hear to this day rose from his breast. An orderly took him back to his room, and when I went there early the following morning, troubled by my conscience, I found him lying on his bed, in patent-leather boots, wearing full uniform, so to speak. Dr Abramsky walked the rest of the way beside me in silence. Nor did he say a word in farewell, but described a gentle arc with the goose wing in the darkening air.

In mid September 1991, when I travelled from England to Deauville during a dreadful drought, the season was long over, and even the Festival du Cinéma Américain, with which they tried to extend the more lucrative summer months a little, had come to its end. I cannot say whether I was expecting Deauville to have something special to offer – some remnant of the past, green avenues, beach promenades, or even a stylish or scandalous clientèle; whatever my notions may have been, it was immediately apparent that the once legendary resort, like everywhere else that one visits now, regardless of the country or continent, was hopelessly run down and ruined by traffic, shops and boutiques, and the insatiable urge for destruction. The villas built in the latter half of the nineteenth century, neo-Gothic castles with turrets and battlements, Swiss chalets, and even mock-oriental residences, were almost without exception a picture of neglect and desolation. If one pauses for a while before one of these seemingly unoccupied houses, as I did a number of times on my first morning walk through the streets of Deauville, one of the closed window shutters on the *parterre* or *bel étage* or the top floor, strange to relate, will open slightly, and a hand will appear and shake out a duster, fearfully slowly, so that soon one inevitably concludes that the whole of Deauville consists of gloomy interiors where womenfolk, condemned to perpetual invisibility and eternal dusting, move soundlessly about, waiting for the moment when they can signal with their dusters to some passer-by who has happened to stop outside their prison and stand gazing up. Almost everything, in fact, was shut, both in Deauville and across the river in Trouville – the Musée Montebello, the town archives in the town hall, the library (which I had planned to look around in), and even the children's day nursery *de l'enfant Jésus*, established through the generosity of

the long-deceased Madame la Baronne d'Erlanger, as I was informed by a commemorative plaque placed on the façade of the building by the grateful citizens of Deauville. Nor was the Grand Hôtel des Roches Noires open any more, a gigantic brick palace where American multimillionaires, English aristocrats, French high financiers and German industrialists basked in each other's company at the turn of the century. The Roches Noires, as far as I was able to

discover, had closed its doors in the Fifties or Sixties and was converted into apartments, though only those that had a sea view sold well. Now what was once the most luxurious hotel on the coast of Normandy is a monumental monstrosity half sunk in the sand. Most of the flats have long been empty, their owners having departed this life. But there are still some indestructible ladies who come every summer and haunt the immense edifice. They pull the white dustsheets off the furniture for a few weeks and at night, silent on their biers, they lie in the empty midst of it. They wander along the broad passageways, cross the huge reception rooms, climb and descend the echoing stairs, carefully placing one foot before the other, and in the early mornings they walk their ulcerous poodles and pekes on the promenade. In contrast to the Roches Noires, which is gradually falling down, the Hôtel Normandy at the other end of Trouville-Deauville, completed in 1912, is still an establishment of the finest class. Built around a number of courtyards in half-timber that looks at

once outsize and miniature, it is frequented nowadays almost exclusively by the Japanese, who are steered through the minutely prescribed daily programme by the hotel staff with an exquisite but also, as I observed, ice-cold courtesy verging on the indignant. And indeed, at the Normandy one felt one was not so much in a celebrated hotel of international standing as in a gastronomic pavilion built by the French for a world fair somewhere near Osaka, and I for one should not have been surprised in the slightest if I had walked out of the Normandy to find next to it another incongruous fantasy in the Balinese or Tyrolean style. Every three days the Japanese at the Normandy were exchanged for a new contingent of their countrymen, who, as one hotel guest explained to me, were brought direct, in air-conditioned coaches, from Charles de Gaulle airport to Deauville, the third call (after Las Vegas and Atlantic City) in a global gambling tour that took them on, back to Tokyo, via Vienna, Budapest and Macao. In Deauville, every morning at ten, they would troop over to the new casino, which was built at the same time as the Normandy, where they would play the machines till lunchtime, in arcades dense with flashing, kaleidoscopic lights and tootling garlands of sound. The afternoons and evenings were also spent at the machines, to which, with stoical faces, they sacrificed whole handfuls of coins; and like children on a spree they were delighted when at last a payout tinkled forth from the box. I never saw any of them at the roulette table. As midnight approached, only a few dubious clients from the provinces would be playing there, shady lawyers, estate agents or car dealers with their mistresses, trying to out-manoeuvre Fortune, who stood before them in the person of a stocky croupier clad inappropriately in the livery of a circus attendant in the big top. The roulette table, screened off with jade-green glass *paravents*, was in a recently refurbished inner hall – not, in other words, where players had gambled at Deauville in former times. I knew that in those days the gaming hall was much larger. Then there had been two rows of roulette and baccarat tables as well as tables where one could bet on little horses that kept running round and round in circles. Chandeliers of Venetian glass hung from the stuccoed ceiling, and through a dozen eight-metre-high half-rounded windows one looked out onto a terrace where the most exotic of personages would be gathered, in couples or groups; and beyond the balustrade, in the light that fell from the casino, one could see the white sands and, far out, the ocean-going yachts and small steamers, lit up and riding at anchor, beaming their Aldis lamps into the night sky, and little boats moving to and fro like slow glow-worms between them and the coast. When I first set foot in the casino at Deauville, the old gaming hall was filled with the last glimmer of evening light. Tables had been laid for a good hundred people, for a wedding banquet or some anniversary celebration. The rays of the setting sun were caught by the glasses and glinted on the silver drums of the band that was just beginning to rehearse for their gig. The instrumentalists were curly-haired and no longer the youngest. The songs they played dated from the Sixties, songs I heard countless times in the Union bar in Manchester. *It is the evening of the day.* The vocalist, a blonde girl with a voice still distinctly child-like, breathed passionately into the microphone, which she held up close to her lips with both hands. She was singing in English, though with a pronounced French accent. *It is the evening of the day, I sit and watch the children play.* At times, when she could not remember the proper words, her singing would become an ethereal hum. I sat down in one of the white lacquer chairs. The music filled the whole room. Pink puffy clouds right up to the golden arabesques of the ceiling stucco. "A whiter shade of pale."

Later that night, in my hotel room, I listened to the sound of the sea. I dreamt I was crossing the Atlantic in a *paquebot* whose deck superstructure looked exactly like the Hôtel Normandy. I was standing at the rail as we entered Le Havre at dawn. The foghorn boomed three times and the immense ship trembled beneath my feet. From Le Havre to Deauville I took the train. In my compartment there was a woman wearing a feathered hat, with a large variety of hatboxes. She was smoking a large Havanna cigar, and gazed tauntingly across at me through the blue haze from time to time. But I did not know how to address her, and in my embarrassment I sat staring at the white kid gloves, with their many tiny buttons, that lay beside her on the upholstered seat. Once I had reached Deauville I took a fly to the Hôtel des Roches Noires. The streets were inordinately busy: coaches and carriages of every kind, cars, handcarts, bicycles, errand boys, delivery men and *flâneurs* wove their seemingly aimless way. It was as if all pandemonium had broken loose. The hotel was hopelessly overbooked. Crowds of people were jostling at the reception desk. It was just before the start of the racing season, and everyone was determined to lodge at one of the best addresses, whatever the cost. Those who were staying at the Roches Noires hired sofas or armchairs to sleep on in the reading room or the salon; the staff were evacuated from their attic quarters to the cellar; the gentlemen ceded their beds to the ladies and lay where they could, in the foyer or the corridors, the window bays or landings, and on the billiard tables. By paying a horrendous bribe I secured a bunk in a lumber room, high on the wall like a luggage rack. Only when I was too fatigued to go on did I climb up into it and sleep for an hour or so. The rest of the time I was looking for Cosmo and Ambros night and day. Now and then I thought I saw them disappear into an entry or a lift or turn a street corner. Or else I really did see them, taking tea out in the courtyard, or in the hall leafing through the latest papers, which were brought early every morning at breakneck speed from Paris to Deauville by Gabriel the chauffeur. They were silent, as the dead usually are when they appear in our dreams, and seemed somewhat downcast and dejected. Generally, in fact, they behaved as if their altered condition, so to speak, were a terrible family secret not to be revealed under any circumstances. If I approached them, they dissolved before my very eyes, leaving behind them nothing but the vacant space they had occupied. Whenever I caught sight of them, I contented myself with observing them from a distance. Wherever I happened upon them it was as if they constituted a point of stillness in the ceaseless bustle. It seemed as though the whole world had gathered there in Deauville for the summer of 1913. I saw the Comtesse de Montgomery, the Comtesse de FitzJames, Baronne d'Erlanger and the Marquise de Massa, the Rothschilds, the Deutsch de la Meurthes, the Koechlins and Bürgels, the Peugeots, the Wormses and the Hennessys, the Isvolskys and the Orlovs, artistes of both sexes, fast women like Réjane and Reichenberg, Greek shipping tycoons, Mexican petroleum magnates and cotton planters from Louisiana. The *Trouville Gazette* reported that a veritable wave of the exotic had broken upon Deauville that year: *des musulmans moldo-valaques, des brahmanes hindous et toutes les variétés de Cafres, de Papous, de Niam-Niams et de Bachibouzouks importés en Europe avec leurs danses simiesques et leurs instruments sauvages.* Things were happening round the clock. At the first big race of the season, at La Touque hippodrome, I heard an English gossip columnist say: It actually seems as though people have learnt to sleep on the hoof. It's their glazed look that gives them away. Touch them, and they keel over. Dead tired myself, I stood on the grandstand of the hippodrome. The grass track around the polo field was bordered by long rows of poplars. Through my binoculars I could see their leaves turning in the breeze, silvery grey. The crowd was growing by the minute. Soon there was one vast sea of hats swelling below me, the white egret feathers cresting them like crowns of foam on waves that ebb darkly away. The loveliest of the young ladies appeared last of all, the yearlings of the season, as it were, wearing lace dresses through which their silken undergarments gleamed in Nile green, crevette, or absinthe blue. In no time at all they were surrounded by men in black, the most raffish of whom raised their top hats aloft on their canes. When the race was already due to have started, the Maharajah of Kashmir arrived in his Rolls, which was gold-plated within, and behind him a second limousine from which an incredibly obese lady alighted and was led to her seat by two ancient grooms. Immediately above her, I suddenly realized, were sitting Cosmo Solomon and Ambros. Ambros was wearing a buff linen suit and a black-lacquered Spanish straw hat on his head. But Cosmo was clad in a thick fleeced coat, despite the cloudless midsummer weather, and an aviator's cap from which his blond curls escaped. His right arm, resting on the back of Ambros's seat, was motionless, and motionless they both gazed into the distance. Otherwise, as I now recall, my dreams in Deauville were filled with constant whisperings of the rumours that were in circulation concerning Cosmo and Ambros. On one occasion I saw the two young men sitting late in the evening in the Normandy's vast dining hall at a small table of their own, placed especially for them in the centre of the room, apart from all the rest. On a silver platter between them, occasionally making slow movements, lay a lobster, gleaming a wonderful pink in the muted atmosphere. Ambros was steadily taking the lobster apart, with great skill, placing little morsels before Cosmo, who ate them like a well brought up child. The diners swayed as if there were a light swell, and only the women's glittering earrings and necklaces and the gentlemen's white shirt-fronts were to be seen. Nonetheless, I sensed that everyone kept their eyes on the two lobster eaters, whom I heard variously described as master and man, two friends, relatives, or even brothers. Endlessly the pros and cons of all these theories were advanced, and the discussions filled the hall with a low murmur, even long after the table for two had been cleared and the first light of dawn was at the windows. No doubt it was above all the eccentricity of Cosmo, combined with the impeccable manners of Ambros, that had aroused the curiosity of the Deauville summer guests. And their curiosity naturally grew, and the suspicions that were voiced waxed more audacious, the more the two friends contented themselves with each other's company, turning down the invitations that were extended to them daily. The astounding eloquence of Ambros, which contrasted so strikingly with Cosmo's seemingly total lack of words, also prompted speculation. Moreover, Cosmo's aerobatics and escapades on the polo field afforded a continual talking point, and the interest people took in the curious Americans reached its climax when Cosmo's unparalleled streak of luck began, in the *séparée* of the casino. Word of it spread through Deauville like wildfire. On top of the whispers already in circulation there was now added the rumour of fraud, or crooked dealing; and talk – on that evening in the dining room, too – never tired of suggesting that Ambros, who did not sit at the roulette table himself, but was always standing immediately behind Cosmo, possessed the mysterious powers of a *magnetiseur*. Indeed, he was so unfathomable that I felt that he could be compared only to the Austrian countess, a *femme au passé obscur* who held court in the somewhat remoter corners of my Deauville dream world. Exceptionally delicately built, and indeed almost transparent, she wore grey or brown moiré silk dresses, and would be besieged at any time of the day or night by a horde of admirers of either sex. No one knew her real name (there was no such person as Gräfin Dembowski in Vienna), nor could anyone estimate her age or say if she were married or not, or a widow. I first noticed Gräfin Dembowski when she did something that no woman had dared to do before her: she removed her white sun hat on the terrace of the casino and laid it on the balustrade beside her. And I saw her for the last time when, awakened from my Deauville dream, I went to the window of my hotel room. Morning was breaking. The beach still merged colourless into the sea, the sea into the sky. And there she was, in the pale but growing light of daybreak, on the deserted Promenade des Planches. Dressed in the most tasteless of styles and appallingly made up, there she came, with a white Angora rabbit lolloping along on a lead. She was also attended by a clubman in acid green livery, who would stoop down whenever the rabbit refused to go on and feed it a little of the enormous cauliflower he held in his crook'd left arm.

On the desk in front of me is the agenda book that belonged to Ambros, which Aunt Fini gave me on my winter visit to Cedar Glen West. It is a pocket diary for the year 1913, bound in soft burgundy leather and measuring about twelve centimetres by eight. Ambros must have bought it in Milan, because that is where his entries begin, on the 20th of August: Palace H, 3 pm, Signora M. Evening, Teatro S. Martino, Corso V. Em. *I tre Emisferi*. Deciphering his tiny handwriting, which not infrequently moved to and fro between several

languages, was an arduous task, one I should probably never have accomplished if those words committed to paper almost eighty years before had not, as it were, opened up of their own accord. The entries gradually become more detailed, and it appears that, at the end of August, Ambros and Cosmo left from Venice for Greece and Constantinople, in a steam yacht. Early morning (it says), myself on deck for a long time, looking astern. The lights of the city receding into the distance under a veil of rain. The islands in the lagoon like shadows. *Mal du pays. Le navigateur écrit son journal à la vue de la terre qui s'éloigne.* The following day he writes: Off the Croatian coast. Cosmo very restless. A beautiful sky. Treeless mountains. The clouds built high. As good as dark at three in the afternoon. Bad weather. We strike our sails. Seven in the evening, the storm full force. Waves breaking on the deck. The Austrian captain has lit an oil lamp before the picture of Our Lady in his cabin. He is kneeling on the floor, praying. In Italian, strange to say, for the poor lost seamen *sepolti in questo sacro mare.* The stormy night is followed by a windless day. Steam up, steadily southward. I put things back in order. In the failing light ahead, pearly grey on the line of the horizon, an island. Cosmo stands fore like a pilot. Calls the name Fano to a sailor. Sísiorsí, the sailor shouts, and, pointing ahead, he repeats, louder: Fano! Fano! Later, low on the already darkened island, I see a fire. There are fishermen on the beach. One of them waves a burning piece of wood. We pass them, and a few hours later enter the harbour of Kassiopé on the north coast of Kérkyra. Next morning the most fearful racket on board. Repairing damage to the engine. Ashore with Cosmo. Up to the ruins of the fortifications. A holm oak growing right out of the castle. We lie beneath the canopy of leaves as in an arbour. Below, they are hammering away at the boiler. A day out of time. At night we sleep on deck. The singing of crickets. Woken by a breeze on my brow. Across the straits, beyond the blue-black mountains of Albania, day is breaking, its glowing flame blazing across the lightless world. And at the same time two white ocean-going yachts trailing white smoke cross the scene, so slowly it is as if they were being pulled across a stage inch by inch. One would hardly think they were moving, but at length they are gone, into the wings of Cape Varvara with its dark green forests, over which hangs the thin sickle of the crescent moon. – 6th September: From Kérkyra via Ithaca and Patras into the Gulf of Corinth. At Itéa decided to send the boat on ahead and travel overland to Athens. Now in the hills at Delphi, the night already very cool. We lay down to sleep two hours ago, wrapped in our coats. Our saddles serve as pillows. The horses stand heads bowed beneath the laurel tree, the leaves of which rustle softly like tiny sheets of metal. Above us the Milky Way (where the Gods pass, says Cosmo), so resplendent that I can write this by its light. If I look straight up I can see the Swan and Cassiopeia. They are the same stars I saw above the Alps as a child and later above the Japanese house in its lake, above the Pacific, and out over Long Island Sound. I can scarcely believe I am the same person, and in Greece. But now and then the fragrance of juniper wafts across to us, so it is surely so.

After these nocturnal entries, the next of any length was written on the day they arrived in Constantinople. Yesterday morning left Piraeus, Ambros recorded on the 15th of September. Somewhat the worse for wear, he wrote, after the laborious overland journey. Calm voyage. Resting for hours under the awning on deck. Never seen water as blue. Truly ultramarine. This morning through the Dardanelles. Great flocks of cormorants. In the early afternoon, far ahead, the capital of the Orient appeared, like a mirage at first, then the green of trees and the colourful jostling houses gradually becoming more distinct. The masts of ships, crowding and swaying gently in a breeze, and the minarets, seeming to sway a little as well. – The Trieste captain paid, we take rooms at the Pera Palas for the time being. We enter the lobby as afternoon tea is being served. Cosmo writes in the register: *Frères Solomon, New York, en route pour la Chine. Pera*, the reception clerk tells me when I enquire, *pera* means beyond. Beyond Stamboul. Mellow orchestral music drifts through the foyer. Behind the drawn tulle curtains of the ballroom glide the shadows of dancing couples. *Quand l'amour meurt*, sings a woman, her voice meandering eerily. The stairs and rooms magnificent. Carpeted landscapes beneath high ceilings. Immense tubs in the bathrooms. From the balcony, a view across the Golden Horn. Evening falls. We watch the dark descending from the outlying hills upon the low roofs, rising from the depths of the city atop the lead-grey cupolas of the mosques till at length it reaches to the tips of the minarets, which gleam especially brightly one last time before the light goes. – At this point, Ambros's entries continue regardless of the dates in his diary. No one, he writes, could conceive of such a city. So many different kinds of buildings, so many different greens. The crowns of pines high aloft. Acacias, cork oaks, sycamores, eucalypts, junipers, laurels, a paradise of trees, shady slopes and groves with tumbling streams and springs. Every walk full of surprises, and indeed of alarm. The prospects change like the scenes in a play. One street lined with palatial buildings ends at a ravine. You go to a theatre and a door in the foyer opens into a copse; another time, you turn down a gloomy back street that narrows and narrows till you think you are trapped, whereupon you take one last desperate turn round a corner and find yourself suddenly gazing from a vantage point across the vastest of panoramas. You climb a bare hillside forever and find yourself once more in a shady valley, enter a house gate and are in the street, drift with the bustle in the bazaar and are suddenly amidst gravestones. For, like Death itself, the cemeteries of Constantinople are in the midst of life. For every one who departs this life, they say, a cypress is planted. In their dense branches the turtle doves nest. When night falls they stop cooing and partake of the silence of the dead. Once the silence descends, the bats come out and flit along their ways. Cosmo claims he can hear every one of their cries. – Whole districts of the city built entirely of wood. Houses of brown and grey weatherworn boards and planks, with flat-topped saddleback roofs and balconies. The Jewish quarter is built the same way. Walking through it today, we turn a corner and unexpectedly have a distant view of a blue line of mountains and the snowy summit of Olympus. For one awful heartbeat I imagine myself in Switzerland or at home again . . .

Have found a house out of the city, at Eyüp. It is next to the old village mosque, at the head of a square where three roads meet. In the middle of the paved square, with its pollard plane trees, the circular white marble basin of a fountain. Many people from the country pause here on their way to the city. Peasants with baskets of vegetables, charcoal burners, gypsies, tightrope walkers and bear trainers. I am surprised to see hardly a single wagon or any other vehicle. Everyone goes on

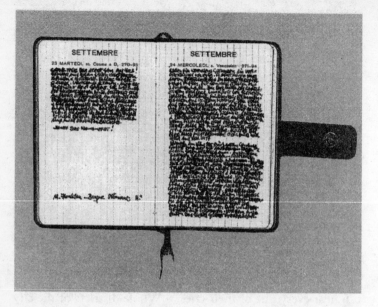

foot, or at best on a beast of burden. As if the wheel had not
yet been invented. Or are we no longer a part of time? What
meaning has a date like the 24th of September?? – Behind the
house is a garden, or rather a kind of yard with a fig and a
pomegranate tree. Herbs also grow there – rosemary, sage,
myrtle, balm. Laudanum. One enters by the blue-painted
door at the rear. The hall is broad and stone-flagged and
newly whitewashed. The walls like snow. The rooms are
almost bare of fittings, and make an empty, deserted impression. Cosmo claims we have rented a ghost house. Wooden
steps lead up to a rooftop terrace shaded by an ancient vine.
Next door, on the gallery of the minaret, a dwarfish muezzin
appears. He is so close that we can see the features of his face.
Before crying out the prayer, he calls a greeting across to us. –
Under the rooftop vine, the first evening meal in our house.
Below on the Golden Horn we can see thousands of boats

crossing to and fro, and further to the right the city of Istanbul stretches to the horizon. Mounds of cloud above it, flame-red, copper and purple, lit by the setting sun. Near daybreak we hear a sound that fills the air, such as we have never heard before, a sound like the whispering of a far-off multitude gathered in the open in a field or on a mountainside. We go up to the roof and see a moving baldachin, a pattern of black and white canopied overhead as far as the eye can see. Countless storks, migrating south. Later in the morning we still talk about them in a coffee house on the shore of the Horn. We are sitting on an open balcony at some height, on show like two saints. Tall schooners pass by, at no distance at all. One can feel the swathes of air as they go. In stormy weather, the proprietor says, their booms sometimes smash a window or knock plants off ledges. – 17th October: behind with my notes, less through the demands of life than through idleness. Yesterday an excursion in a Turkish boat, down the Golden Horn and then along the right, Asian bank of the Bosphorus. We leave the outer parts of the city behind. Forested crags, embankments with evergreens. Here and there, lone villas and white summerhouses. Cosmo proves a good sailor. At one point we are surrounded by I do not know how many dolphins. There must have been hundreds, if not thousands. Like a great herd of swine they ploughed the waves with their muzzles and circled us time and again before finally plunging head over tail away. In the deep coves, the branches bent down low to the eddying waters. We slipped through beneath the trees and, with just a few pulls on the oars, entered a harbour surrounded by strangely silent houses. Two men were squatting on the quay playing dice. Otherwise there was not a soul about. We entered the little mosque by the gate. In an alcove in the half-light within sat a young man studying the Koran. His lids were half closed, his lips were murmuring softly. His body was rocking to and fro. In the middle of the hall a husbandman was saying his afternoon prayers. Again and again he touched his forehead to the floor and remained bowed down for what seemed to me an eternity. The soles of his feet gleamed in the straggling light that entered through the doorway. At length he stood up, first casting a deferential glance to right and left, over his shoulders – to greet his guardian angels, who stand behind him, said Cosmo. We turned to go, from the half-dark of the mosque into the sand-white brightness of the harbour square. As we crossed it, both shading our dazzled eyes like desert travellers, a grey pigeon about the size of a full-grown cockerel tottered clumsily ahead of us, leading us to an alley where we came across a dervish aged about twelve. He was wearing a

very wide gown that reached to the ground and a close-fitting jacket made, like the gown, of the finest linen. The boy, who was extraordinarily beautiful, was wearing a high brimless camel-hair toque on his head. I spoke to him in Turkish, but he only looked at us without a word. On the return, our boat seemed to glide of itself along the dark green overhung crags. The sun had set, the water was a shadowy plain, but higher up a light still moved here and there. Cosmo, at the tiller, says he wants to come out shortly once again, with a photographer, to take a souvenir photograph of the boy dervish . . .

On the 26th of October Ambros writes: Collected the photographs of the white boy from the studio today. Later, made enquiries at the Chemins de Fer Orientaux and the Banque Ottomane concerning our onward journey. Also bought a Turkish costume for Cosmo and one for myself. Spent the evening with timetables, maps and Karl Baedeker's handbook.

The route they took from Constantinople can be followed fairly closely from the diary notes, despite the fact that they are farther apart now, and at times stop altogether.

They must have crossed the whole of Turkey by rail, down to Adana, and gone on from there to Aleppo and Beirut, and seem to have spent the best part of a fortnight in the Lebanon, for it is not till the 21st of November that "passage to Jaffa" is entered. The day they arrived in Jaffa, through an agent at Franks Hotel, Dr Immanuel Benzinger, they hired two horses at a cost of 15 francs each for the twelve-hour ride up from the coast to Jerusalem. The luggage went ahead by rail. Early on the morning of the 25th, Cosmo and Ambros were on their way through the orange groves and on, in a southeasterly direction, across the plain of Sharon and towards the mountains of Judaea. Through the Holy Land, writes Ambros, often far off the track. The rocks all around radiantly white in the light. For long stretches not a tree, not a shrub, scarcely so much as a meagre clump of weeds. Cosmo very taciturn. Darkened sky. Great clouds of dust rolling through the air. Terrible desolation and emptiness. Late in the afternoon it cleared once more. A rosy glow lay upon the valley, and through an opening in the mountainous terrain we could see the promised city in the distance – a ruined and broken mass of rocks, the Queen of the desert . . . An hour after nightfall we ride into the courtyard of the Hotel Kaminitz on the Jaffa Road. The maître d'hôtel, a pomaded little Frenchman, is utterly astounded, indeed *scandalisé*, to see these dust-caked new arrivals, and shakes his head as he studies our entry in the register. Not until I ask him to see that our horses are properly looked after does he recall his duties, whereupon he deals with everything as fast as he is able. The rooms are furnished in a most peculiar manner. One cannot say what period or part of the world one is in. View to one side across domed stone rooftops. In the white moonlight they resemble a frozen sea. Deep weariness, sleep till well into the morning. Numerous dreams with strange voices and shouts. At noontime a deathly silence, broken only by the eternal crowing of cocks. – Today (it reads two days later) a first walk through the city and into the outer districts. All in all, a frightful impression. Vendors of souvenirs and devotional objects in almost every building. They crouch in the gloom of their shops amidst hundreds of olivewood carvings and junk decorated with mother-of-pearl. From the end of the month the faithful will be coming to buy, hordes of them, ten or fifteen thousand Christian pilgrims from all around the world. The more recent buildings of an ugliness hard to describe. Large quantities of filth in the streets. *On marche sur des merdes!!!* Pulverized limestone ankle-deep in places. The few plants which have survived the drought that has lasted since May are covered in this powdery meal as if by a blight. *Une malédiction semble planer sur la ville.* Decay, nothing but decay, marasmus and emptiness. Not a sign of any business or industry. All we passed were a tallow-and-soap factory and a bone-and-hide works. Next to this, in a wide square, the knacker's yard. In the middle a big hole. Coagulated blood, heaps of entrails, blackish-brown tripes, dried and scorched by the sun . . . Otherwise one church after another, monasteries, religious and philanthropic establishments of every kind and denomination. On the northerly side are the Russian cathedral, the Russian Men's and Women's hospice, the French Hôpital de St Louis, the Jewish Home for the Blind, the Church and Hospice of St Augustine, the German school, the German Orphanage, the German Asylum for the Deaf and Dumb, the School of the London Mission to the Jews, the Abyssinian Church, the Anglican Church, College

and Bishop's House, the Dominican Friary, the Seminary and
Basilica of St Stephen, the Rothschild Girls' Institute, the
Alliance Israélite College of Commerce, the Church of Notre
Dame de France, and, beside the pool of Bethesda, the
Monastery of St Anne; on the Mount of Olives are the
Russian Tower, the Church of the Assumption, the French
Church of Pater Noster, the Carmelite nunnery, the building
that houses the Empress Augusta Victoria Foundation,
the Russian Orthodox Church of Mary Magdalene, and the

Church of Agony; to the south and west are the Armenian
Orthodox Monastery of Mount Zion, the Protestant School,
the Sisters of St Vincent, the Hospice of the Knights of St
John, the Convent of the Sisters of St Clare, the Montefiore
Hospice and the Moravian Lepers' Home. In the centre of the
city there are the Church and Residence of the Latin
Patriarch, the Dome of the Rock, the School of the Frères de
la Doctrine Chrétienne, the school and printing works of the
Franciscan Brotherhood, the Coptic Monastery, the German

Hospice, the German Protestant Church of the Redeemer, the United Armenian Church of the Spasm (as it is called), the Couvent des Soeurs de Zion, the Austrian Hospital, the Monastery and Seminary of the Algerian Mission Brotherhood, the Church of Sant'Anna, the Jewish Hospice, the Ashkenazy and Sephardic Synagogues, and the Church of the Holy Sepulchre, below the portal of which a misshapen little man with a cucumber of a nose offered us his services as a guide through the intricacies of the aisles and transepts, chapels, shrines and altars. He was wearing a bright yellow frock coat which to my mind dated far back into the last century, and his crooked legs were clad in what had once been a dragoon's breeches, with sky-blue piping. Taking tiny steps, always half turned to us, he danced ahead and talked nonstop in a language he probably thought to be German or English but which was in fact of his own invention and to me, at all events, quite incomprehensible. Whenever his eye fell on me I felt as despised and cold as a stray dog. Later, too, outside the Church of the Holy Sepulchre, a continuing feeling of oppressiveness and misery. No matter which direction we went in, we always came up at one of the steep ravines that crisscross the city, falling away to the valleys. By now the ravines have largely been filled with the rubbish of a thousand years, and everywhere liquid waste flows openly into them. As a result, the water of numerous springs has become undrinkable. The erstwhile pools of Siloam are no more than foul puddles and cesspits, a morass from which the miasma rises that causes epidemics to rage here almost every summer. Cosmo says repeatedly that he is utterly horrified by the city.

On the 27th of November Ambros notes that he has been to Raad's Photographic Studio in the Jaffa Road and has had his picture taken, at Cosmo's wish, in his new striped Arab robe. In the afternoon (he continues) out of the city to the Mount of Olives. We pass a withered vineyard. The soil beneath the black vines rust-coloured, exhausted and scorched. Scarcely a wild olive tree, a thorn bush, or a little hyssop. On the crest of the Mount of Olives runs a riding track. Beyond the valley of Jehoshaphat, where at the end of time, it is said, the entire human race will gather in the flesh, the silent city rises from the white limestone with its domes, towers and ruins. Over the rooftops not a sound, not a trace of smoke, nothing. Nowhere, as far as the eye can see, is there any sign of life, not an animal scurrying by, or even the smallest bird in flight. *On dirait que c'est la terre maudite . . .* On the other side, what must be more than three thousand feet below, the Jordan and part of the Dead Sea. The air is so bright, so thin and so clear that without thinking one might reach out a hand to touch the tamarisks down there on the river bank. Never before had we been washed in such a flood of light! A little further on, we found a place to rest in a mountain hollow where a stunted box tree and a few wormwood shrubs grow. We leant against the rock wall for a long time, feeling how everything gradually faded . . . In the evening, studied the guidebook I bought in Paris. In the past, it says, Jerusalem looked quite different. Nine tenths of the splendours of the world were to be found in this magnificent city. Desert caravans brought spices, precious stones, silk and gold. From the sea ports of Jaffa and Askalon, merchandise came up in abundance. The arts and commerce were in full flower. Before the walls, carefully tended gardens lay outspread, the valley of Jehoshaphat was canopied with cedars, there were streams, springs, fish pools, deep channels, and everywhere cool shade. And then came the age of destruction. Every settlement up to a four-hour journey away in every direction was destroyed, the irrigation systems were wrecked, and the trees and bushes were cut down, burnt and blasted, down to the very last stump. For years the Caesars deliberately made it impossible to live there, and in later times too Jerusalem was repeatedly attacked, liberated and pacified, until at last the desolation was complete and nothing remained of the matchless wealth of the Promised Land but dry stone and a remote idea in the heads of its people, now dispersed throughout the world.

4th December: Last night dreamt that Cosmo and I crossed the glaring emptiness of the Jordan valley. A blind guide walks ahead of us. He points his staff to a dark spot on the horizon and cries out, several times, *er-Riha, er-Riha*. As we approach, er-Riha proves to be a dirty village with sand and dust swirling about it. The entire population has gathered on the edge of the village in the shade of a tumbledown sugar mill. One has the impression that they are nothing but beggars and footpads. A noticeable number are gouty, hunchbacked or disfigured. Others are lepers or have immense goitres. Now I see that all these people are from Gopprechts. Our Arab escorts fire their long rifles into the air. We ride past, and the people cast malevolent looks after us. At the foot of a low hill we pitch the black tents. The Arabs light a small fire and cook a dark green broth of Jew's mallow and mint leaves, and bring some of it over to us in tin bowls, with slices of lemon and crushed grain. Night falls rapidly. Cosmo lights the lamp and spreads out his map on the colourful carpet. He points to one of the many white spaces and says: We are now in Jericho. The oasis is a four-hour walk in length and a one-hour walk in breadth, and of a rare beauty perhaps matched only by the paradisal orchard of Damascus – *le merveilleux verger de Damas.* The people here have all they want. Whatever they sow grows immediately in this soft, fertile soil. The glorious gardens flower forever. The greening corn sways in the bright palm groves. The fiery heat of summer is made bearable by the many watercourses and pastures, the crowns of the trees and the vine leaves over the pathways. The winters are so mild that the people of this blessèd land wear no more than a linen shirt, even when the mountains of Judaea, not far off, are white with snow. – Several blank pages follow the account of the dream of er-Riha. During this time, Ambros must have been chiefly occupied with recruiting a small troop of Arabs and acquiring the equipment and provisions needed for an expedition to the Dead Sea, for on the 16th of December he writes: Left over-crowded Jerusalem with its hordes of pilgrims three days ago and rode down the Kidron Valley into the lowest region on earth. Then, at the foot of the Yeshimon Mountains, along the Sea as far as Ain Jidy. One wrongly imagines these shores as destroyed by fire and brimstone, a thing of salt and ashes for thousands of years. I myself have heard the Dead Sea, which is about the size of Lac Leman, described as being as motionless as molten lead, though the surface is ruffled at times into a phosphorescent foam. Birds cannot fly across it, they say, without suffocating in the air, and others report that on moonlit nights an aura of the grave, the colour of absinthe, rises from its depths. None of all this have we found to be true. In fact, the Sea's waters are wonderfully clear, and break on the shore with scarcely a sound. On the high ground to the right there are green clefts from which streams come forth.

There is also to be seen a mysterious white line that is visible early in the morning. It runs the length of the Sea, and vanishes an hour or so later. No one, thus Ibrahim Hishmeh, our Arab guide, can explain it or give a reason. Ain Jidy itself is a blessèd spot with pure spring water and rich vegetation. We made our camp by some bushes on the shore where snipe stalk and the bulbul bird, brown and blue of plumage and red of beak, sings. Yesterday I thought I saw a large dark hare, and a butterfly with gold-speckled wings. In the evening, when we were sitting on the shore, Cosmo said that once the whole of the land of Zoar on the south bank was like this. Where now mere traces remained of the five overthrown cities of Gomorrha, Ruma, Sodom, Seadeh and Seboah, the oleanders once grew thirty feet high beside rivers that never ran dry, and there were acacia forests and oshac trees as in Florida. There were irrigated orchards and melon fields far and wide, and he had read a passage where Lynch, the explorer, claimed that down from the gorge of Wadi Kerek a forest torrent fell with a fearful roar that could only be compared with the Niagara Falls. – In the third night of our stay at Ain Jidy a stiff wind rose out on the Sea and stirred the heavy waters. On land it was calmer. The Arabs had long been asleep beside the horses. I was still sitting up in our bed, which was open to the heavens, in the light of the swaying lantern. Cosmo, curled up slightly, was sleeping at my side. Suddenly a quail, perhaps frightened by the storm on the Sea, took refuge in his lap and remained there, calm now, as if it were its rightful place. But at daybreak, when Cosmo stirred, it ran away quickly across the level ground, as quail do, lifted off into the air, beat its wings tremendously fast for a moment, then extended them rigid and motionless and glided by a little thicket in an utterly beautiful curve, and was gone. It was shortly before sunrise. Across the water, about twelve miles away, the blue-black ridge-line of the Moab Mountains of Araby ran level along the horizon, merely rising or dipping slightly at points, so that one might have thought the watercolourist's hand had trembled a little.

The last entry in my Great-Uncle Adelwarth's little agenda book was written on the Feast of Stephen. Cosmo, it reads, had had a bad fever after their return to Jerusalem but was already on the way to recovery again. My great-uncle also noted that late the previous afternoon it had begun to snow and that, looking out of the hotel window at the city, white in the falling dusk, it made him think of times long gone. Memory, he added in a postscript, often strikes me as a kind of dumbness. It makes one's head heavy and giddy, as if one were not looking back down the receding perspectives of time but rather down on the earth from a great height, from one of those towers whose tops are lost to view in the clouds.

MAX FERBER

*They come when night falls
to search for life*

Until my twenty-second year I had never been further away from home than a five- or six-hour train journey, and it was because of this that in the autumn of 1966, when I decided, for various reasons, to move to England, I had a barely adequate notion of what the country was like or how, thrown back entirely on my own resources, I would fare abroad. It may have been partly due to my inexperience that I managed to weather the two-hour night flight from Kloten airport to Manchester without too many misgivings. There were only a very few passengers on board, and, as I recall, they sat wrapped up in their coats, far apart in the half-darkness of the cold body of the aircraft. Nowadays, when usually one is quite dreadfully crammed in together with one's fellow passengers, and aggravated by the unwanted attentions of the cabin crew, I am frequently beset with a scarcely containable fear of flying; but at that time, our even passage through the night skies filled me with a sense (false, as I now know) of security. Once we had crossed France and the Channel, sunk in darkness below, I gazed down lost in wonder at the network of lights that stretched from the southerly outskirts of London to the Midlands, their orange sodium glare the first sign that from now on I would be living in a different world. Not until we were approaching the Peak District south of Manchester did the strings of street lights gradually peter out into the dark. At the same time, from behind a bank of cloud that covered the entire horizon to the east, the disc of the moon rose, and by its pale glow the hills, peaks and ridges which had previously been invisible could be seen below us, like a vast, ice-grey sea moved by a great swell. With a grinding roar, its wings trembling, the aircraft toiled downwards until we passed by the strangely ribbed flank of a long, bare mountain ridge seemingly close enough to touch, and appearing to me to be rising and sinking like a giant recumbent body, heaving as it breathed. Looping round in one more curve, the roar of the engines steadily increasing, the plane set a course across open country. By now, we should have been able to make out the sprawling mass of Manchester, yet one could see nothing but a faint glimmer, as if from a fire almost suffocated in ash. A blanket of fog that had risen out of the marshy plains that reached as far as the Irish Sea had covered the city, a city spread across a thousand square kilometres, built of countless bricks and inhabited by millions of souls, dead and alive.

Although only a scant dozen passengers had disembarked at Ringway airport from the Zurich flight, it took almost an hour until our luggage emerged from the depths, and another hour until I had cleared customs: the officers, understandably bored at that time of the night, suddenly mustered an alarming degree of exactitude as they dealt with me, a rare case, in those days, of a student who planned to settle in Manchester to pursue research, bringing with him a variety of letters and papers of identification and recommendation. It was thus already five o'clock by the time I climbed into a taxi and headed for the city centre. In contrast to today, when a continental zeal for business has infected the British, in the Sixties no one was out and about in English cities so early in the morning. So, with only an occasional traffic light to delay us, we drove swiftly through the not unhandsome suburbs of Gatley, Northenden and Didsbury to Manchester itself. Day was just breaking, and I looked out in amazement at the rows of uniform houses, which seemed the more run-down the closer we got to the city centre. In Moss Side and Hulme there were whole blocks where the doors and windows were boarded up, and whole districts where everything had been demolished. Views opened up across the wasteland towards the still immensely impressive agglomeration of gigantic Victorian office blocks and warehouses, about a kilometre distant, that had once been the hub of one of the nineteenth century's miracle cities but, as I was soon to find out, was now almost hollow to the core. As we drove in among the dark ravines between the brick buildings, most of which were six or eight storeys high and sometimes adorned with glazed ceramic tiles, it turned out that even there, in the heart of the city, not a soul was to be seen, though by now it was almost a quarter to six. One might have supposed that the city had long since been deserted, and was left now as a necropolis or mausoleum. The taxi driver, whom I had asked to take me to a hotel that was (as I put it) not too expensive, gave me to understand that hotels of the kind I wanted were rare in the city centre, but after driving around a little he turned off Great Bridgewater Street into a narrow alleyway and pulled up at a house scarcely the width of two windows, on the soot-blackened front of which was the name AROSA in sweeping neon letters.

Just keep ringing, said the driver as he left. And I really

did have to push the bell long and repeatedly before there was a sign of movement within. After some rattling and shooting of bolts, the door was opened by a lady with curly blonde hair, perhaps not quite forty, with a generally wavy, Lorelei-like air about her. For a while we stood there in wordless confrontation, both of us with an expression of disbelief, myself beside my luggage and she in a pink dressing gown that was made of a material found only in the bedrooms of the English lower classes and is unaccountably called candlewick. Mrs Irlam – Yes, Irlam like Irlam in Manchester, I would later hear her saying down the phone time and again – Mrs Irlam broke the silence with a question that summed up both her jolted state, roused from her sleep, and her amusement at the sight of me: And where have you sprung from? – a question which she promptly answered herself, observing that only *an alien* would show up on her doorstep at such an hour on a blessed Friday morning with a case like that. But then, smiling enigmatically, Mrs Irlam turned back in, which I took as a sign to follow her. We went into a windowless room off the tiny hall, where a roll-top desk crammed to bursting with letters and documents, a mahogany chest stuffed with an assortment of bedclothes and candlewick bedspreads, an ancient wall telephone, a keyrack, and a large photograph of a pretty Salvation Army girl, in a black varnished frame, all had, it seemed to me, a life entirely of their own. The girl was in uniform, standing in front of an ivy-covered wall and holding a glistening flugelhorn in the crook of her arm. Inscribed on the slightly foxed *passe-partout*, in a flowing hand that leant heavily to one side, were the words: *Gracie Irlam, Urmston nr Manchester, 17 May 1944.* Third floor, she said, and, nodding across the hall, her eyebrows raised, added: the

lift's over there. The lift was so tiny that I only just fitted in
with my case, and its floor was so thin that it sagged beneath
the weight of even a single passenger. Later I hardly used it,
although it took me quite some time before I could find my
way around the maze of dead-end corridors, emergency exits,
doors to rooms, toilets and fire escapes, landings and staircases. The room that I moved into that morning, and did not
move out of until the following spring, was carpeted in a large
floral pattern, wallpapered with violets, and furnished with
a wardrobe, a washstand, and an iron bedstead with a
candlewick bedspread. From the window there was a view
onto semi-derelict slate-roofed outbuildings below and a
back yard where rats thronged all that autumn until, a week
or so before Christmas, a little ratcatcher by the name of
Renfield turned up several times with a battered bucket
full of rat poison. He doled the poison out into various
corners, drains and pipes, using a soup spoon tied to a short
stick, and for a few months the number of rats was considerably reduced. If one looked out across the yard, rather than
down into it, one saw the many-windowed deserted depot
of the Great Northern Railway Company, a little way beyond
a black canal, where sometimes lights would flit about
erratically at night.

The day of my arrival at the Arosa, like most of the days,
weeks and months to come, was a time of remarkable silence
and emptiness. I spent the morning unpacking my suitcase
and bags, stowing away my clothing and linen, and arranging
my writing materials and other belongings; then, tired after
a night of travelling, I fell asleep on my iron bed, my face
buried in the candlewick bedspread, which smelled faintly of
violet-scented soap. I did not come to till almost half past

three, when Mrs Irlam knocked at my door. Apparently by way of a special welcome, she brought me, on a silver tray, an electric appliance of a kind I had never seen before. She explained that it was called a *teas-maid*, and was both an alarm clock and a tea-making machine. When I made tea and the

steam rose from it, the shiny stainless steel contraption on its ivory-coloured metal base looked like a miniature power plant, and the dial of the clock, as I soon found as dusk fell, glowed a phosphorescent lime green that I was familiar with from childhood and which I had always felt afforded me an unaccountable protection at night. That may be why it has often seemed, when I have thought back to those early days in Manchester, as if the tea maker brought to my room by Mrs Irlam, by Gracie – you must call me Gracie, she said – as if it was that weird and serviceable gadget, with its nocturnal glow, its muted morning bubbling, and its mere presence by day, that kept me holding on to life at a time when I felt a deep sense of isolation in which I might well have become completely submerged. Very useful, these are, said Gracie as she showed me how to operate the teas-maid that November afternoon; and she was right. After my initiation into the mysteries of what Gracie called an *electrical miracle*, we went on talking in a friendly fashion, and she repeatedly emphasized that her hotel was a quiet establishment, even if sometimes in the evenings there was (as she put it) a certain commotion. But that need not concern you. It's travelling gentlemen that come and go. And indeed, it was not until after office hours that the doors would open and the stairs creak at the Hotel Arosa, and one would encounter the gentlemen Gracie had referred to, bustling characters clad almost without exception in tattered gabardine coats or macs. Not until nearly eleven at night did the toings and froings cease and the garish women disappear – whom Gracie would refer to, without the slightest hint of irony, with a hold-all phrase she had evidently coined herself, as *the gentlemen's travelling companions*.

Every evening of the week, the Arosa was bustling with salesmen and clerks, but on Saturday evening, as in the entire rest of the city centre, there was no sign of life. Interrupted only occasionally by stray customers she called *irregulars*, Gracie would sit at the roll-top desk in her office doing the books. She did her best to smooth out the grey-green pound notes and brick-red ten-shilling notes, then laid them carefully in piles, and, whispering as if at some mystical rite, counted them until she had come up with the same total at least twice. She dealt with the coins no less meticulously; there was always a considerable quantity, and she stacked them in even columns of copper, brass and silver before she set about calculating the total, which she did partly by manual and partly by mathematical means, first converting the pennies, threepenny bits and sixpences to shillings and then the shillings, florins and half crowns into pounds. The final conversion that then followed, of the pound total thus arrived at into the guineas which were at that time still the customary unit in better business establishments, always proved the most difficult part of this financial operation, but without a doubt it was also its crowning glory. Gracie would enter the sum in guineas in her ledger, sign and date it, and stow the money in a Pickley & Patricroft safe that was built into the wall by the desk. On Sundays, she would invariably leave the house early in the morning, carrying a small patent leather case, only to return, just as unfailingly, at lunchtime on the Monday.

As for myself, on those Sundays in the utterly deserted hotel I would regularly be overcome by such a sense of aimlessness and futility that I would go out, purely in order to preserve an illusion of purpose, and walk about amidst the city's immense and time-blackened nineteenth-century buildings, with no particular destination in mind. On those wanderings, when winter light flooded the deserted streets and squares for the few rare hours of real daylight, I never ceased to be amazed by the completeness with which anthracite-coloured Manchester, the city from which industrialization had spread across the entire world, displayed the clearly chronic process of its impoverishment and degradation to anyone who cared to see. Even the grandest of the buildings, such as the Royal Exchange, the Refuge Assurance Company, the Grosvenor Picture Palace, and indeed the Piccadilly Plaza, which had been built only a few years before, seemed so empty and abandoned that one might have supposed oneself surrounded by mysterious façades or theatrical backdrops. Everything then would appear utterly unreal to me, on those sombre December days when dusk was already falling at three o'clock, when the starlings, which I had previously imagined to be migratory songbirds, descended upon the city in dark flocks that must have numbered hundreds of thousands, and, shrieking incessantly, settled close together on the ledges and copings of warehouses for the night.

Little by little my Sunday walks would take me beyond the city centre to districts in the immediate neighbourhood, such as the one-time Jewish quarter around the star-shaped complex of Strangeways prison, behind Victoria Station. This quarter had been a centre for Manchester's large Jewish community until the inter-war years, but those who lived there had moved into the suburbs and the district had meanwhile been demolished by order of the municipality. All I found still standing was one single row of empty houses, the wind blowing through the smashed windows and doors; and, by way of a sign that someone really had once been there, the barely decipherable brass plate of a one-time lawyers' office, bearing names that had a legendary ring to my ear: Glickmann, Grunwald and Gottgetreu. In Ardwick, Brunswick, All Saints, Hulme and Angel Fields too, districts adjoining the centre to the south, whole square kilometres of working-class homes had been pulled down by the authorities, so that, once the demolition rubble had been removed, all that was left to recall the lives of thousands of people was the grid-like layout of the streets. When night fell upon those vast spaces, which I came to think of as the Elysian Fields, fires would begin to flicker here and there and children would

stand around them or skip about, restless shadowy figures. On that bare terrain, which was like a glacis around the heart of the city, it was in fact always and only children that one encountered. They strayed in small groups, in gangs, or quite alone, as if they had nowhere that they could call home. I remember, for instance, late one November afternoon, when the white mist was already rising from the ground, coming across a little boy at a crossroads in the midst of the Angel Fields wasteland, with a Guy stuffed with old rags on a hand-cart: the only person out and about in the whole area, wanting a penny for his silent companion.

It was early the following year, if I remember correctly, that I ventured further out of the city, in a southwesterly direction, beyond St George and Ordsall, along the bank of the canal across which, from my window, I could see the Great Northern Railway Company depot. It was a bright, radiant day, and the water, a gleaming black in its embankment of massive masonry blocks, reflected the white clouds that scudded across the sky. It was so strangely silent that (as I now think I remember) I could hear sighs in the abandoned depots and warehouses, and was frightened to death when a number of seagulls, squawking stridently, all of a sudden flew

out of the shadow of one of the high buildings, into the light.
I passed a long-disused gasworks, a coal depot, a bonemill,
and what seemed the unending cast-iron palisade fence of the
Ordsall slaughterhouse, a Gothic castle in liver-coloured
brick, with parapets, battlements, and numerous turrets and
gateways, the sight of which absurdly brought to my mind the
name of Haeberlein & Metzger, the Nuremberg *Lebkuchen*

makers; whereupon that name promptly stuck in my head, a bad joke of sorts, and continued to knock about there for the rest of the day. Three quarters of an hour later I reached the port of Manchester, where docks kilometres in length branched off the Ship Canal as it entered the city in a broad arc, forming wide side-arms and surfaces on which one could see nothing had moved for years. The few barges and freighters that lay far apart at the docksides, making an oddly broken impression, put me in mind of some massive shipping disaster. Not far from the locks at the harbour mouth, on a road that ran from the docks to Trafford Park, I came across a sign on which TO THE STUDIOS had been painted in crude brush-strokes. It pointed in to a cobbled yard in the middle of which, on a patch of grass, an almond tree was in blossom. At one time the yard must have been part of a carriage business, since it was enclosed partly by stables and outbuildings and partly by one- or two-storey buildings that had formerly been living quarters and office premises. In one of these seemingly deserted buildings was a studio which, in the months to come, I visited as often as I thought acceptable, to talk to the painter who had been working there since the late Forties, ten hours a day, the seventh day not excepted.

When one entered the studio it was a good while before one's eyes adjusted to the curious light, and, as one began to see again, it seemed as if everything in that space, which measured perhaps twelve metres by twelve and was impenetrable to the gaze, was slowly but surely moving in upon the middle. The darkness that had gathered in the corners, the puffy tidemarked plaster and the paint that flaked off the walls, the shelves overloaded with books and piles of newspapers, the boxes, work benches and side tables, the wing armchair, the gas cooker, the mattresses, the crammed mountains of papers, crockery and various materials, the paint pots gleaming carmine red, leaf green and lead white in the gloom, the blue flames of the two paraffin heaters: the entire furniture was advancing, millimetre by millimetre, upon the central space where Ferber had set up his easel in the grey light that entered through a high north-facing window layered with the dust of decades. Since he applied the paint thickly, and then repeatedly scratched it off the canvas as his work proceeded, the floor was covered with a largely hardened and encrusted deposit of droppings, mixed with coal dust, several centimetres thick at the centre and thinning out towards the outer edges, in places resembling the flow of lava. This, said Ferber, was the true product of his continuing endeavours and the most palpable proof of his failure. It had always been of the greatest importance to him, Ferber once remarked casually, that nothing should change at his place of work, that everything should remain as it was, as he had arranged it, and that nothing further should be added but the debris generated by painting and the dust that continuously fell and which, as he was coming to realize, he loved more than anything else in the world. He felt closer to dust, he said, than to light, air or water. There was nothing he found so unbearable as a well-dusted house, and he never felt more at home than in places where things remained undisturbed, muted under the grey, velvety sinter left when matter dissolved, little by little, into nothingness. And indeed, when I watched Ferber working on one of his portrait studies over a number of weeks, I often thought that his prime concern was to increase the dust. He drew with vigorous abandon, frequently going through half a dozen of his willow-wood charcoal sticks in the shortest of time; and that process of drawing and shading on the thick, leathery paper, as well as the concomitant business of constantly erasing what he had drawn with a woollen rag already heavy with charcoal, really amounted to nothing but a steady production of dust, which never ceased except at night. Time and again, at the end of a working day, I marvelled to see that Ferber, with the few lines and shadows that had escaped annihilation, had created a portrait of great vividness. And all the more did I marvel when, the following morning, the moment the model had sat down and he had taken a look at him or her, he would erase the portrait yet again, and once more set about excavating the features of his model, who by now was distinctly wearied by this manner of working, from a surface already badly damaged by the continual destruction. The facial features and eyes, said Ferber, remained ultimately unknowable for him. He might reject as many as forty variants, or smudge them back into the paper and overdraw new attempts upon them; and if he then decided that the portrait was done, not so much because he was convinced that it was finished as through sheer exhaustion, an onlooker might well feel that it had evolved from a long lineage of grey, ancestral faces, rendered unto ash but still there, as ghostly presences, on the harried paper.

As a rule, Ferber spent the mornings before he began work, and the evenings after he left the studio, at a transport café near Trafford Park, which bore the vaguely familiar name Wadi Halfa. It probably had no licence of any kind, and was located in the basement of an otherwise unoccupied building that looked as if it might fall down at any moment. During the three years I spent in Manchester, I sought out Ferber at least once a week at that curious hostelry, and was soon as indifferent as he was to the appalling dishes, a hybrid of the English and the African, that were prepared by the Wadi Halfa's cook, with an incomparable stylish apathy, in a set-up behind the counter that resembled a field kitchen. With a single, sweeping, seemingly slow-motion movement of his left hand (his right was always in his trouser pocket) the cook could take two or three eggs from the box, break them into the pan, and dispose of the shells in the bin. Ferber told me that this cook, who was almost two metres tall, had once been a Maasai chieftain. Now close to eighty, he had travelled (said Ferber), by which highways and byways he could not say, from the south of Kenya to the north of England, in the postwar years. There he soon learnt the rudiments of local cooking, and, giving up the nomadic life, had settled in to his present trade. As for the waiters, noticeably more numerous than the customers, who stood or sat around at the Wadi Halfa wearing expressions of the utmost boredom, Ferber assured me that they were without exception the chieftain's sons, the eldest probably somewhat over sixty, the youngest twelve or thirteen. Since they were each as slim and tall as the other, and all displayed the same disdain in their fine, even features, they were scarcely distinguishable, especially as they would take over from each other at irregular intervals, so that the team of waiters currently on duty was continuously changing. Nonetheless, Ferber, who had observed them closely and used the differences in their ages as an aid to iden-tification, was of the opinion that there were neither more nor less than a dozen waiters, all told, whereas I for my part could never manage to picture those not present at any given moment. It is also worth mentioning that I never once saw any women at the Wadi Halfa, neither family or companions of the boss or his sons nor indeed customers, the clientèle being chiefly workmen from the demolition companies then busy throughout Trafford Park, lorry divers, refuse collectors and others who happened to be out and about.

At every hour of the day and night, the Wadi Halfa was lit by flickering, glaringly bright neon light that permitted not the slightest shadow. When I think back to our meetings in Trafford Park, it is invariably in that unremitting light that I see Ferber, always sitting in the same place in front of a fresco painted by an unknown hand that showed a caravan moving forward from the remotest depths of the picture, across a wavy ridge of dunes, straight towards the beholder. The painter lacked the necessary skill, and the perspective he had chosen was a difficult one, as a result of which both the human figures and the beasts of burden were slightly distorted, so that, if you half shut your eyes, the scene looked like a mirage, quivering in the heat and light. And especially on days when Ferber had been working in charcoal, and the fine powdery dust had given his skin a metallic sheen, he seemed to have just emerged from the desert scene, or to belong in it. He himself once remarked, studying the gleam of graphite on the back of his hands, that in his dreams, both waking and by night, he had already crossed all the earth's deserts of sand and stone. But anyway, he went on, avoiding any further explanation, the darkening of his skin reminded him of an article he had recently read in the paper about silver poisoning, the symptoms of which were not uncommon among professional photographers. According to the article, the British Medical Association's archives contained the description of an extreme case of silver poisoning: in the 1930s there was a photographic lab assistant in Manchester whose body had absorbed so much silver in the course of a lengthy professional life that he had become a kind of photographic plate, which was apparent in the fact (as Ferber solemnly informed me) that the man's face and hands turned blue in strong light, or, as one might say, developed.

One summer evening in 1966, nine or ten months after my arrival in Manchester, Ferber and I were walking along the Ship Canal embankment, past the suburbs of Eccles, Patricroft and Barton upon Irwell on the other side of the black water, towards the setting sun and the scattered outskirts where occasional views opened up, affording an intimation of the marshes that extended there as late as the mid nineteenth century. The Manchester Ship Canal, Ferber told me, was begun in 1887 and completed in 1894. The work was mainly done by a continuously reinforced army of Irish navvies, who shifted some sixty million cubic metres of earth in that period and built the gigantic locks that would make it possible to raise or lower ocean-going steamers up to 150 metres long by five or six metres. Manchester was then the industrial Jerusalem, said Ferber, its entrepreneurial spirit and progressive vigour the envy of the world, and the completion of the immense canal project had made it the largest inland port on earth. Ships of the Canada & Newfoundland Steamship Company, the China Mutual Line, the Manchester Bombay General Navigation Company, and many other shipping lines, plied the docks near the city centre. The loading and unloading never stopped: wheat, nitre, construction timber, cotton, rubber, jute, train oil, tobacco, tea, coffee, cane sugar, exotic fruits, copper and iron ore, steel, machinery, marble and mahogany – everything, in fact, that could possibly be needed, processed or made in a manufacturing metropolis of that order. Manchester's shipping traffic peaked around 1930 and then went into an irreversible decline, till it came to a complete standstill in the late Fifties. Given the motionlessness and deathly silence that lay upon the canal now, it was difficult to imagine, said Ferber, as we gazed back at the city sinking into the twilight, that he himself, in the postwar years, had seen the most enormous freighters on this water. They would slip slowly by, and as they approached the port they passed amidst houses, looming high above the black slate roofs. And in winter, said Ferber, if a ship suddenly appeared out of the mist when one least expected it, passed by soundlessly, and vanished once more in the white air, then for me, every time, it was an utterly incomprehensible spectacle which moved me deeply.

I no longer remember how Ferber came to tell me the extremely cursory version of his life that he gave me at that time, though I do remember that he was loath to answer the questions I put to him about his story and his early years. It was in the autumn of 1943, at the age of eighteen, that Ferber, then a student of art, first went to Manchester. Within months, in early 1944, he was called up. The only point of note concerning that first brief stay in Manchester, said Ferber, was the fact that he had lodged at 104, Palatine Road – the selfsame house where Ludwig Wittgenstein, then a twenty-year-old engineering student, had lived in 1908. Doubtless any retrospective connection with Wittgenstein was purely illusory, but it meant no less to him on that account, said Ferber. Indeed, he sometimes felt as if he were tightening his ties to those who had gone before; and for that reason, whenever he pictured the young Wittgenstein bent over the design of a variable combustion chamber, or test-flying a kite of his own construction on the Derbyshire moors, he was aware of a sense of brotherhood that reached far back beyond his own lifetime or even the years immediately before it. Continuing with his account, Ferber told me that after basic training at Catterick, in a God-forsaken part of north Yorkshire, he volunteered for a paratroop regiment, hoping that that way he would still see action before the end of the war, which was clearly not far off. Instead, he fell ill with jaundice, and was transferred to the convalescent home in the Palace Hotel at Buxton, and so his hopes were dashed. Ferber was compelled to spend more than six months at the idyllic Derbyshire spa town, recovering his health and consumed with rage, as he observed without explanation. It had been a terribly bad time for him, a time scarcely to be endured, a time he could not bear to say any more about. At all events, in early May 1945, with his discharge papers in

his pocket, he had walked the roughly forty kilometres to Manchester to resume his art studies there. He could still see, with absolute clarity, his descent from the fringes of the moorlands after his walk amidst the spring sunshine and showers. From a last bluff he had had a bird's eye view of the city spread out before him, the city where he was to live ever after. Contained by hills on three sides, it lay there as if in the heart of a natural amphitheatre. Over the flatland to the west, a curiously shaped cloud extended to the horizon, and the last rays of sunlight were blazing past its edges, and for a while lit up the entire panorama as if by firelight or Bengal flares. Not until this illumination died (said Ferber) did his eye roam, taking in the crammed and interlinked rows of houses, the textile mills and dying works, the gasometers, chemicals plants and factories of every kind, as far as what he took to be the centre of the city, where all seemed one solid mass of utter blackness, bereft of any further distinguishing features. The most impressive thing, of course, said Ferber, were all the chimneys that towered above the plain and the flat maze of

housing, as far as the eye could see. Almost every one of those chimneys, he said, has now been demolished or taken out of use. But at that time there were still thousands of them, side by side, belching out smoke by day and night. Those square and circular smokestacks, and the countless chimneys from which a yellowy-grey smoke rose, made a deeper impression on me when I arrived than anything else I had previously seen, said Ferber. I can no longer say exactly what thoughts the sight of Manchester prompted in me then, but I believe I felt I had found my destiny. And I also remember, he said, that when at last I was ready to go on I looked down once more over the pale green parklands deep down below, and, half an hour after sunset, saw a shadow, like the shadow of a cloud, flit across the fields – a herd of deer headed for the night.

As I expected, I have remained in Manchester to this day, Ferber continued. It is now twenty-two years since I arrived, he said, and with every year that passes a change of place seems less conceivable. Manchester has taken possession of me for good. I cannot leave, I do not want to leave, I must not. Even the visits I have to make to London once or twice a year oppress and upset me. Waiting at stations, the announcements on the public address, sitting in the train, the country passing by (which is still quite unknown to me), the looks of fellow passengers – all of it is torture to me. That is why I have rarely been anywhere in my life, except of course Manchester; and even here I often don't leave the house or workshop for weeks on end. Only once have I travelled abroad since my youth, two years ago, when I went to Colmar in the summer, and from Colmar via Basle to Lake Geneva. For a very long time I had wanted to see Grünewald's

Isenheim paintings, which were often in my mind as I worked, and especially the "Entombment of Christ", but I never managed to master my fear of travelling. So I was all the more amazed, once I had taken the plunge, to find how easily it went. Looking back from the ferry at the white cliffs of Dover, I even imagined I should be liberated from that moment; and the train ride across France, which I had been particularly afraid of, also went very well. It was a fine day, I had a whole compartment, indeed the entire carriage to myself, the air rushed in at the window, and I felt a kind of festive good spirits rising within me. About ten or eleven in the evening I arrived in Colmar, where I spent a good night at the Hotel Terminus Bristol on the Place de la Gare and the next morning, without delay, went to the museum to look at the Grünewald paintings. The extreme vision of that strange man, which was lodged in every detail, distorted every limb, and infected the colours like an illness, was one I had always felt in tune with, and now I found my feeling confirmed by the direct encounter. The monstrosity of that suffering, which, emanating from the figures depicted, spread to cover the whole of Nature, only to flood back from the lifeless landscape to the humans marked by death, rose and ebbed within me like a tide. Looking at those gashed bodies, and at the witnesses of the execution, doubled up by grief like snapped reeds, I gradually understood that, beyond a certain point, pain blots out the one thing that is essential to its being experienced – consciousness – and so perhaps extinguishes itself; we know very little about this. What is certain, though, is that mental suffering is effectively without end. One may think one has reached the very limit, but there are always more torments to come. One plunges from one abyss into the next. When I was in Colmar, said Ferber, I beheld all of this in precise detail, how one thing had led to another and how it had been afterwards. The flood of memory, little of which remains with me now, began with my recalling a Friday morning some years ago when I was suddenly struck by the paroxysm of pain that a slipped disc can occasion, pain of a kind I had never experienced before. I had simply bent down to the cat, and as I straightened up the tissue tore and the *nucleus pulposus* jammed into the nerves. At least, that is how the doctor later described it. At that moment, all I knew was that I mustn't move even a fraction of an inch, that my whole life had shrunk to that one tiny point of absolute pain, and that even breathing in made everything go black. Until the evening I was rooted in one place in a semi-erect position. How I managed the few steps to the wall, after darkness had fallen, and how I pulled the tartan blanket that was hanging

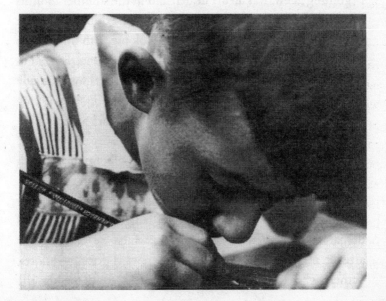

on the back of the chair over my shoulders, I no longer remember. All I now recall is that I stood at that wall all night long with my forehead against the damp, musty plaster, that it grew colder and colder, that the tears ran down my face, that I began to mutter nonsense, and that through it all I felt that being utterly crippled by pain in this way was related, in the most precise manner conceivable, to the inner constitution I had acquired over the years. I also remember that the crooked position I was forced to stand in reminded me, even in my pain, of a photograph my father had taken of me in the second form at school, bent over my writing. In Colmar, at any rate, said Ferber after a lengthy pause, I began to remember, and it was probably those recollections that prompted me to go on to Lake Geneva after eight days, to retrace another old memory that had long been buried and which I had never dared disturb. My father, said Ferber, beginning anew, was an art dealer, and in the summer months he regularly put on what he called special exhibitions in the lobbies of famous hotels. In 1936 he took me with him to one of these exhibitions at the Victoria Jungfrau in Interlaken and then to the Palace at Montreux. Father's shows usually consisted of about five dozen salon pieces in the Dutch manner, in gold frames, or Mediterranean genre scenes in the style of Murillo, and deserted German landscapes – of these, I remember a composition that showed a gloomy heath with two juniper trees, at a distance from each other, in the blood-red glow of the setting sun. As well as I could, at the age of twelve, I helped Father with the hanging, labelling and despatch of these exhibition pieces, which he described as artistic merchandise. By way of a reward for my efforts, Father, who loved the Alps passionately, took me up the

Jungfraujoch in the mountain railway, and from there he showed me the largest glacier in Europe, gleaming snow-white in the midst of summer. The day after the exhibition at the Palace closed, we drove out of Montreux in a hired car, some way along the Rhône valley, and presently turned off to the right, up a narrow and twisting road to a village with a name that struck me as distinctly odd, Miex. From Miex it was a three-hour walk, past the Lac de Tanay, to the summit of Grammont. All the noontide of that blue-skied day in August I lay beside Father on the mountaintop, gazing down into the even deeper blue of the lake, at the country across the lake, over to the faint silhouette of the Jura range, at the bright towns on the far bank, and at St Gingolph, immediately below us but barely visible in a shaft of shadow perhaps fifteen hundred metres deep. On my train journey through Switzerland, which truly is amazingly beautiful, I was already remembering these scenes and images of thirty years before, said Ferber; but they were also strangely threatening, as I saw with increasing clarity during my stay at the Palace, so that in the end I locked the door of my room, pulled down the blinds, and lay in bed for hours at a stretch, which only worsened my incipient anxiety. After about a week it somehow occurred to me that only the reality outside could save me. But instead of strolling around Montreux, or going over to Lausanne, I set off to climb Grammont a second time, regardless of my condition, which by now was quite frail. The day was as bright as it had been the first time, and when I had reached the top, utterly exhausted, there below me was the country around Lake Geneva once again, seemingly completely unchanged, and with no trace of movement but for the one or two tiny boats that left their white wakes on the deep blue water as they proceeded, unbelievably slowly, and the trains that went to and fro at intervals on the far bank. That world, at once near and unattainably far, said Ferber, exerted so powerful an attraction on him that he was afraid he might leap down into it, and might really have done so had not a man of about sixty suddenly appeared before him – like someone who's popped out of the bloody ground. He was carrying a large white gauze butterfly net and said, in an English voice that was refined but quite unplaceable, that it was time to be thinking of going down if one were to be in Montreux for dinner. He had no recollection of having made the descent with the butterfly man, though, said Ferber; in fact the descent had disappeared entirely from his memory, as had his final days at the Palace and the return journey to England. Why exactly this lagoon of oblivion had spread in him, and how far it extended, had remained a mystery to him however hard he thought about it. If he tried to think back to the time in question, he could not see himself again till he was back in the studio, working at a painting which took him almost a full year, with minor interruptions – the faceless portrait "Man with a Butterfly Net". This he considered one of his most unsatisfactory works, because in his view it conveyed not even the remotest impression of the strangeness of the apparition it referred to. Work on the picture of the butterfly man had taken more out of him than any previous painting, for when he started on it, after countless preliminary studies, he not only overlaid it time and again but also, whenever the canvas could no longer withstand the continual scratching-off and re-application of paint, he destroyed it and burnt it several times. The despair at his lack of ability which already tormented him quite enough during the day now invaded his increasingly sleepless nights, so that soon he wept with exhaustion as he worked. In the end he had no alternative but powerful sedatives, which in turn gave him the most horrific hallucinations, not unlike those suffered by St Anthony on the temptation panel of the Isenheim altarpiece. Thus, for instance, he once saw his cat leap vertically into the air and do a backward somersault, whereupon it lay where it fell, rigid. He clearly remembered placing the dead cat in a shoebox and burying it under the almond tree in the yard. Just as clearly, though, there was the cat at its bowl the next morning, looking up at him as if nothing had happened. And once, said Ferber in conclusion, he dreamt (he could not say whether by day or by night) that in 1887 he had opened the great art exhibition in the purpose-built Trafford Park, together with Queen Victoria. Thousands of people were present as, hand in hand with the fat Queen, who gave off an unsavoury odour, he walked through the endless halls

containing 16,000 gold-framed works of art. Almost without exception, said Ferber, the works were items from his father's holdings. In amongst them, however, there were one or two of my own paintings, though to my dismay they differed not at all, or only insignificantly, from the salon pieces. At length, continued Ferber, we passed through a painted *trompe-l'oeil* door (done with astounding skill, as the Queen remarked to me) into a gallery covered in layers of dust, in the greatest possible contrast to the glittering crystal palace, where clearly no one had set foot for years and which, after some hesitation, I recognized as my parents' drawing room. Somewhat to one side, a stranger was sitting on the ottoman. In his lap he was holding a model of the Temple of Solomon, made of pinewood, papier-mâché and gold paint. Frohmann, from Drohobycz, he said, bowing slightly, going on to explain that it had taken him seven years to build the temple, from the biblical description, and that he was now travelling from ghetto to ghetto exhibiting the model. Just look, said Frohmann: you can see every crenellation on the towers, every curtain, every threshold, every sacred vessel. And I, said Ferber, bent down over the diminutive temple and realized, for the first time in my life, what a true work of art looks like.

I had been in Manchester for the best part of three years when, having completed my research, I left the city in the summer of 1969 to follow a plan I had long had of becoming a schoolteacher in Switzerland. On my return from a soot-blackened city that was drifting steadily towards ruin, I was deeply moved by the beauty and variety of the Swiss country-side, which by then had almost slipped my memory, and the sight of the snowy mountains in the distance, the high-lying forests, the autumn light, the frozen watercourses and fields, and the fruit trees in blossom in the meadows, touched my heart more powerfully than I could have anticipated; but nevertheless, for various reasons partly to do with the Swiss attitude to life and partly to do with my position as a teacher, I did not care to stay in Switzerland for long. A bare year had passed when I decided to return to England and to take up the offer of a post I found attractive from several points of view, in Norfolk, which was then considered off the beaten track. If I had still occasionally thought of Ferber and Manchester during my months in Switzerland, my memories faded steadily in the period in England which followed and which, as I sometimes note with amazement, has continued up to the present. Of course Ferber did come to my mind at various times over the long years, but I never succeeded in picturing him properly. His face had become a mere shadow. I assumed that Ferber had been drowned in his labours, but avoided making any closer enquiries. It was not until late November 1989, when by sheer chance I came across a painting bearing his signature in the Tate Gallery (I had gone to see Delvaux's "Sleeping Venus"), that Ferber came alive again in my mind. The painting, about one and a half by two metres, bore a title which struck me as both significant and improbable: "G.I. on her Blue Candlewick Cover". Not long after, I came across Ferber in a Sunday colour supplement, again pretty much by chance, since I have long avoided reading the Sunday papers and especially the magazines that come with them. According to the article, his work now fetched the highest prices on the art market, but Ferber himself, ignoring this development, still lived as he had always done, and continued to work at the easel ten hours a day in his studio near the Manchester docks. For weeks I carried the magazine around with me, glancing time and again at the article, which, I sensed, had unlocked in me a sort of gaol or oubliette. I studied Ferber's dark eye, looking sideways out of a photograph that accompanied the text, and tried, at least with hindsight, to understand what inhibitions or wariness there had been on his part that had kept our conversations away from his origins, despite the fact that such a talk, as I now realized, would have been the obvious thing. In May 1939, at the age of fifteen, Friedrich Maximilian Ferber (so the rather meagre magazine account informed me) left Munich, where his father was an art dealer, for England. The article went on to say that Ferber's parents, who delayed their own departure from Germany for a number of reasons, were taken from Munich to Riga in November 1941, in one of the first deportation trains, and were subsequently murdered there. As I now thought back, it seemed unforgivable that I should have omitted, or failed, in those Manchester times, to ask Ferber the questions he must surely have expected from me; and so, for the first time in a very long while, I went to Manchester once again, a six-hour train journey that criss-crossed the country, through the pine forests and heathlands near Thetford, across the broad lowlands around the Isle of Ely, black at wintertime, past towns and cities each as ugly as the next – March, Peterborough, Loughborough, Nottingham, Alfreton, Sheffield – and past disused industrial plants, slag heaps, belching cooling towers, hills with never a soul about, sheep pastures, stone walls, and on through snow showers, rain, and the ever-changing colours of the sky. By early afternoon I was in Manchester, and immediately set off westwards, through the city, in the direction of the docks. To my surprise,

I had no difficulty in finding my way, since everything in Manchester had essentially remained the same as it had been almost a quarter of a century before. The buildings that had been put up to stave off the general decline were now themselves in the grip of decay, and even the so-called development zones, created in recent years on the fringes of the city centre and along the Ship Canal, to revive the entrepreneurial spirit that so much was being made of, already looked semi-abandoned. The wasteland and the white clouds drifting in from the Irish Sea were reflected in the glinting glass fronts of office blocks, some of which were only half occupied, and some of which were still under construction. Once I was out at the docks it did not take me long to find Ferber's studio. The cobbled yard was unaltered. The almond tree was about to blossom, and when I crossed the threshold it was as if I had been there only yesterday. The same dull light was entering by the window, and the easel still stood in the middle of the room on the black encrusted floor, a black piece of card on it, overworked to the point of being unrecognizable. To judge by the picture clipped to a second easel, the model that had served Ferber for this exercise in destruction was a Courbet

that I had always been especially fond of, "The Oak of Vercingetorix". But Ferber himself, whom I had not noticed at first as I came in from outside, was sitting towards the rear in his red velvet armchair, a cup of tea in his hand, watching his visitor out of the corner of his eye. I was now getting on for fifty, as he had been then, while Ferber himself was almost seventy. By way of welcome he said: Aren't we all getting on! He said it with a throwaway smile, and then, not seeming to me to have aged in the slightest, gestured towards a copy of Rembrandt's portrait of a man with a magnifying glass, which still hung in the same place on the wall as it had twenty-five years before, and added: Only he doesn't seem to get any older.

Following this late reunion, which neither of us had expected, we talked for three whole days far into the night,

and a great many more things were said than I shall be able to
write down here: concerning our exile in England, the immigrant city of Manchester and its irreversible decline, the Wadi
Halfa (which had long ceased to exist), the flugelhorn player
Gracie Irlam, my year as a schoolteacher in Switzerland, and
my subsequent attempt, also aborted, to settle in Munich, in
a German cultural institute. Ferber commented that, purely
in terms of time, I was now as far removed from Germany
as he had been in 1966; but time, he went on, is an unreliable way of gauging these things, indeed it is nothing but
a disquiet of the soul. There is neither a past nor a future.
At least, not for me. The fragmentary scenes that haunt
my memories are obsessive in character. When I think of
Germany, it feels as if there were some kind of insanity lodged
in my head. Probably the reason why I have never been to
Germany again is that I am afraid to find that this insanity
really exists. To me, you see, Germany is a country frozen in
the past, destroyed, a curiously extraterritorial place, inhabited by people whose faces are both lovely and dreadful. All of
them are dressed in the style of the Thirties, or even earlier
fashions, and wearing headgear that does not go with their
clothing at all – pilots' helmets, peaked caps, top hats, ear
muffs, crossover headbands, and hand-knitted woollen caps.
Almost every day a beautiful woman wearing a ball gown
made of grey parachute silk and a broad-brimmed hat
trimmed with grey roses visits me. Hardly have I sat down in
my armchair, tired from work, but I hear her steps outside on
the pavement. She sweeps in at the gate, past the almond tree,
and there she is, on the threshold of my workshop. Hastily she
comes over to me, like a doctor afraid that she may be too late
to save a sinking patient. She takes off her hat and her hair

tumbles about her shoulders, she strips off her fencing gloves and tosses them onto this little table, and she bends down towards me. I close my eyes in a swoon – and how it goes on after that point, I do not know. One thing is certain: we never say a word. The scene is always a silent one. I think the grey lady understands only her mother tongue, German, which I have not once spoken since I parted from my parents at Oberwiesenfeld airport in Munich in 1939, and which survives in me as no more than an echo, a muted and incomprehensible murmur. It may possibly have something to do with this loss of language, this oblivion, Ferber went on, that my memories reach no further back than my ninth or eighth year, and that I recall little of the Munich years after 1933 other than processions, marches and parades. There seems always to have been a reason for them: May Day or Corpus Christi, carnival or the tenth anniversary of the Putsch, Reichsbauerntag or the inauguration of the Haus der Kunst. They were forever bearing either the Sacred Heart through the city centre or what they called the *Blutfahne*, the banner of blood. On one occasion, said Ferber, they put up trapeziform pedestals draped in chestnut-coloured cloth on either side of the Ludwigstrasse, all the way from the Feldherrnhalle into the heart of Schwabing, and on every one of the pedestals a flame was burning in a shallow iron bowl. At these constant assemblies and parades, the number of different uniforms and insignia noticeably increased. It was as if a new species of humanity, one after another, was evolving before our very eyes. I was filled with wonderment, anger, yearning and revulsion in equal measure; as a child, and then as a teenager, I would stand silently amidst the cheering or awe-struck crowds, ashamed that I did not belong. At home, my parents never talked about the new order in my presence, or only did so obliquely. We all tried desperately to maintain an appearance of normality, even after Father had to hand over the management of his gallery across from the Haus der Kunst, which had opened only the year before, to an Aryan partner. I still did my homework under Mother's supervision; we still went to Schliersee for the skiing in winter, and to Oberstdorf or the Walsertal for our summer holidays; and of those things we could not speak of we simply said nothing. Thus, for instance, all my family and relatives remained largely silent about the reasons why my grandmother Lily Lanzberg took her own life; somehow they seem to have agreed that towards the end she was no longer quite in her right mind. Uncle Leo, Mother's twin brother, with whom we drove from Bad Kissingen to Würzburg after the funeral, at the end of July 1936, was the only one I occasionally heard talk outspokenly about the situation; but this was generally met with disapproval. I now remember (said Ferber) that Uncle Leo, who taught Latin and Greek at a grammar school in Würzburg until he was dismissed, once showed Father a newspaper clipping dating from 1933, with a photograph of the book burning on the Residenzplatz in Würzburg. That photograph, said Uncle, was a forgery. The burning of the books took place on the evening of the 10th of May, he said – he repeated it several times – the books were burnt on the evening of the 10th of May, but since it was already dark, and they couldn't take any decent photographs, they simply took a picture of some other gathering outside the palace, Uncle claimed, and added a swathe of smoke and a dark night sky. In other words, the photographic document published in the paper was a fake. And just as that document was a fake, said Uncle, as if

his discovery were the one vital proof, so too everything else
has been a fake, from the very start. But Father shook his head
without saying a word, either because he was appalled or
because he could not assent to Uncle Leo's sweeping verdict.
At first I too found the Würzburg story, which Ferber said he
was only then remembering for the first time, somewhat on
the improbable side; but in the meantime I have tracked
down the photograph in question in a Würzburg archive, and
as one can easily see there is indeed no doubt that Ferber's

uncle's suspicions were justified. Continuing his account of
his visit to Würzburg in summer 1936, Ferber said that one
day when they were strolling in the palace gardens Uncle Leo
told him that he had been compulsorily retired on the 31st of
December the year before and that, in consequence, he was
preparing to emigrate from Germany, and was planning to go
to England or America shortly. Afterwards we were in the
great hall of the palace, and I stood beside Uncle, craning up

at Tiepolo's glorious ceiling fresco above the stairwell, which at that time meant nothing to me; beneath the loftiest of skies, the creatures and people of the four realms of the world are assembled on it in fantastic array. Strangely enough, said Ferber, I only thought of that afternoon in Würzburg with Uncle Leo a few months ago, when I was looking through a new book on Tiepolo. For a long time I couldn't tear myself away from the reproductions of the great Würzburg fresco, its light-skinned and dark-skinned beauties, the kneeling Moor with the sunshade and the magnificent Amazon with the feathered headdress. For a whole evening, said Ferber, I sat looking at those pictures with a magnifying glass, trying to see further and further into them. And little by little that summer day in Würzburg came back to me, and the return to Munich, where the general situation and the atmosphere at home were steadily becoming more unbearable, and the silence was thickening. Father, said Ferber, was something of a born comedian or play-actor. He enjoyed life, or rather, he would have enjoyed it; he would have liked to go to the Theater am Gärtnerplatz still, to the revues and wine bars; but, because of the circumstances, the depressive traits that were also in his character overlaid his essentially cheerful nature towards the end of the Thirties. He began to display an absent-mindedness and irritability which I had not seen in him before; both he and Mother put it down to a passing nervousness, which for days at a time would dictate his behaviour. He went to the cinema more and more often, to see cowboy films and the mountaineering films of Luis Trenker. Not once was there any talk of leaving Germany, at least not in my presence, not even after the Nazis had confiscated pictures, furniture and valuables from our home, on the grounds that we had no right to the German heritage. All I remember is that my parents were particularly affronted by the uncouth manner in which the lower ranks stuffed their pockets full of cigarettes and cigarillos. After the Kristallnacht, Father was interned in Dachau. Six weeks later he came home, distinctly thinner and with his hair cropped

short. To me he said not a word about what he had seen and experienced. How much he told Mother, I do not know. Once more, in early 1939, we went to Lenggries for the skiing. It was my last time and I think it was Father's, too. I took a photo of him up on the Brauneck. It is one of the few that have survived from those years, said Ferber. Not long after our trip to Lenggries, Father managed to get a visa for me by bribing the English consul. Mother was counting on their both following me soon. Father was finally determined to leave the country, she said. They only had to make the necessary arrangements. So my things were packed, and on the 17th of May, Mother's fiftieth birthday, my parents took me to the airport. It was a fine, bright morning, and we drove from our house in Sternwartstrasse in Bogenhausen across the Isar, through the Englischer Garten along Tivolistrasse, across the Eisbach, which I still see as clearly as I did then, to Schwabing and then out of the city along Leopoldstrasse towards Oberwiesenfeld. The drive seemed endless to me, said Ferber, probably because none of us said a word. When I asked if he remembered saying goodbye to his parents at the airport, Ferber replied, after a long hesitation, that when he thought back to that May morning at Oberwiesenfeld he could not see his parents. He no longer knew what the last thing his mother or father had said to him was, or he to them, or whether he and his parents had embraced or not. He could still see his parents sitting in the back of the hired car on the drive out to Oberwiesenfeld, but he could not see them at the airport itself. And yet he could picture Oberwiesenfeld down to the last detail, and all these years had been able to envisualize it with that fearful precision, time and time again. The bright concrete strip in front of the open hangar and the deep dark inside it, the swastikas on the rudders of the aircraft, the fenced-off area where he had to wait with the other passengers, the privet hedge around the fence, the groundsman with his wheelbarrow, shovel and brush, the weather station boxes, which reminded him of bee-hives, the cannon at the airfield perimeter – he could see it all with painful clarity, and he could see himself walking across the short grass towards the white Lufthansa Junkers 52, which bore the name Kurt Wüsthoff and the number D–3051. I see myself mounting the wheeled wooden steps, said Ferber, and sitting down in the plane beside a woman in a blue Tyrolean hat, and I see myself looking out of the little square window as we raced across the big, green, deserted airfield, at a distant flock of sheep and the tiny figure of a shepherd. And then I see Munich slowly tilting away below me.

The flight in the Ju52 took me only as far as Frankfurt, said Ferber, where I had to wait for several hours and clear customs. There, at Frankfurt am Main airport, my opened suitcase sat on an ink-stained table while a customs official, without touching a thing, stared into it for a very long time, as if the clothes which my mother had folded and packed in her distinctive, highly orderly way, the neatly ironed shirts or my Norwegian skiing jersey, might possess some mysterious significance. What I myself thought as I looked at my open suitcase, I no longer know; but now, when I think back, it feels as if I ought never to have unpacked it, said Ferber, covering his face with his hands. The BEA plane in which I flew on to London at about three that afternoon, he continued, was a Lockheed Electra. It was a fine flight. I saw Belgium from the air, the Ardennes, Brussels, the straight roads of Flanders, the sand dunes of Ostende, the coast, the white cliffs of Dover, the green hedgerows and hills south of London, and then, appearing on the horizon like a low grey range of hills, the island capital itself. We landed at half past five at Hendon airfield. Uncle Leo met me. We drove into the city, past endless rows of suburban houses so indistinguishable from one another that I found them depressing yet at the same time vaguely ridiculous. Uncle was living in a little émigré hotel in Bloomsbury, near the British Museum. My first night in England was spent in that hotel, on a peculiar, high-framed bed, and was sleepless not so much because of my distress as because of the way that one is pinned down, in English beds of that kind, by bedding which has been tucked under the mattress all the way round. So the next morning, the 18th of May, I was bleary-eyed and weary when I tried on my new school uniform at Baker's in Kensington, with my uncle – a pair of short black trousers, royal blue knee-length socks, a blazer of the same colour, an orange shirt, a striped tie, and a tiny cap that would not stay put on my full shock of hair no matter how I tried. Uncle, given the funds at his disposal, had found me a third-rate public school at Margate, and I believe that when he saw me kitted out like that he was as close to tears as I was when I saw myself in the mirror. And if the uniform felt like a fool's motley, expressly designed to heap scorn upon me, then the school itself, when we arrived there that afternoon, seemed like a prison or mental asylum. The circular bed of dwarf conifers in the curve of the drive, the grim façade capped by battlements of sorts, the rusty bell-pull beside the open door, the school janitor who came limping out of the darkness of the hall, the colossal oak stairwell, the coldness of all the rooms, the smell of coal, the incessant cooing of the decrepit pigeons that perched everywhere on the roof, and numerous other sinister details I no longer remember, conspired to make me think that I would go mad in next to no time in that establishment. It presently emerged, however, that the regime of the school – where I was to spend the next few years – was in fact fairly lax, sometimes to the point of anarchy. The headmaster and founder of the school, a man by the name of Lionel Lynch-Lewis, was a bachelor of almost seventy, invariably dressed in the most eccentric manner and scented with a discreet hint of lilac; and his staff, no less eccentric, more or less left the pupils, who were mainly the sons of minor diplomats from unimportant countries, or the offspring of other itinerants, to their own devices. Lynch-Lewis took the view that nothing was more damaging to the development of young adolescents than a regular school timetable. He maintained that one learnt best and most easily in one's free time. This attractive concept did in fact bear fruit for some of us, but others ran quite disturbingly wild as a result. As for the parrot-like uniform which we had to wear and which, it turned out, had been designed by Lynch-Lewis himself, it formed the greatest possible contrast to the rest of his pedagogical approach. At best, the outré riot of colour we were obliged to wear fitted in with the excessive emphasis placed by Lynch-Lewis on the cultivation of correct English, which in his view could mean only turn-of-the-century stage English. Not for nothing was it rumoured in Margate that our teachers were all, without exception, recruited from the ranks of actors who had failed, for whatever reason, in their chosen profession. Oddly enough, said Ferber, when I look back at my time in Margate I cannot say whether I was happy or unhappy, or indeed what I was. At any rate, the amoral code that governed life at school gave me a certain sense of freedom, such as I had not had till then – and, that being so, it grew steadily harder for me to write my letters home or to read the letters that arrived from home every fortnight. The correspondence became more of a chore, and when the letters stopped coming, in November 1941, I was relieved at first, in a way that now strikes me as quite terrible. Only gradually did it dawn on me that I would never again be able to write home; in fact, to tell the truth, I do not know if I have really grasped it to this day. But it now seems to me that the course of my life, down to the tiniest detail, was ordained not only by the deportation of my parents but also by the delay with which the news of their death reached me, news I could not believe at first and the meaning of which only sank in by degrees. Naturally, I took steps, consciously or unconsciously, to keep at bay thoughts of my parents' sufferings and of my own misfortune, and no doubt I succeeded sometimes in maintaining a certain equability by my self-imposed seclusion; but the fact is that that tragedy in my youth struck such deep roots within me that it later shot up again, put forth evil flowers, and spread the poisonous canopy over me which has kept me so much in the shade and dark in recent years.

In early 1942 (Ferber concluded, the evening before I left Manchester), Uncle Leo embarked at Southampton for New York. Before he left he visited Margate one last time, and we agreed that I would follow him in the summer, when I had completed my last year at school. But when the time came I did not want to be reminded of my origins by anything or anyone, so instead of going to New York, into the care of my uncle, I decided to move to Manchester on my own. Inexperienced as I was, I imagined I could begin a new life in Manchester, from scratch; but instead, Manchester reminded me of everything I was trying to forget. Manchester is an immigrant city, and for a hundred and fifty years, leaving aside the poor Irish, the immigrants were chiefly Germans and Jews, manual workers, tradesmen, freelancers, retailers and wholesalers, watchmakers, hatters, cabinet-makers, umbrella makers, tailors, bookbinders, typesetters, silversmiths, photographers, furriers and glovers, scrap merchants, hawkers, pawnbrokers, auctioneers, jewellers, estate agents, stockbrokers, chemists and doctors. The Sephardic Jews, who had been settled in Manchester for a long time and had names like Besso, Raphael, Cattun, Calderon, Farache, Negriu, Messulam or di Moro, made little distinction between the Germans and other Jews with names like Leibrand, Wohlgemuth, Herzmann, Gottschalk, Adler, Engels, Landeshut, Frank, Zirndorf, Wallerstein, Aronsberg, Haarbleicher, Crailsheimer, Danziger, Lipmann or Lazarus. Throughout the nineteenth century, the German and Jewish influence was stronger in Manchester than in any other European city; and so, although I had intended to move in the opposite direction, when I arrived in Manchester I had come home, in a sense, and with every year I have spent since then in this birthplace of industrialization, amidst the black façades, I have realized more clearly than ever that I am here, as they used to say, to serve under the chimney. Ferber said nothing more. For a long time he stared into space, before sending me on my way with a barely perceptible wave of his left hand. When I returned to the studio the following morning to take my leave of him he handed me a brown paper package tied with string, containing a number of photographs and almost a hundred pages of handwritten memoirs penned by his mother in the Sternwartstrasse house between 1939 and 1941, which showed (said Ferber) that obtaining a visa had become increasingly difficult and that the plans his father had made for their emigration had necessarily grown more complex with every week that passed – and, as his mother had clearly understood, impossible to carry out. Mother wrote not a word about the events of the moment, said Ferber, apart from the odd oblique glance at the hopeless situation she and Father were in; instead, with a passion that was beyond his understanding, she wrote of her childhood in the village of Steinach, in lower Franconia, and her youth in Bad Kissingen. In the time that had passed since they were written, said Ferber, he had read the memories his mother had committed to paper, presumably not least with himself in mind, only twice. The first time, after he received the package, he had skimmed over them. The second time he had read them meticulously, many years later. On that second occasion, the memoirs, which at points were truly wonderful, had seemed to him like one of those evil German fairy tales in which, once you are under the spell, you have to carry on to the finish, till your heart breaks, with whatever work you have begun – in this case, the remembering, writing and reading. That is why I would rather you took this package, Ferber said, and saw me out to the yard, where he walked with me as far as the almond tree.

The manuscript which Ferber gave me on that morning in Manchester is before me now. I shall try to convey in excerpts what the author, whose maiden name was Luisa Lanzberg, recounts of her early life. At the very beginning she writes that not only she and her brother Leo were born at Steinach, near Bad Kissingen, but also her father Lazarus, and her grandfather Löb before him. The family was recorded as living in the village, which had formerly been under the jurisdiction of the prince-bishops of Würzburg and a third of whose inhabitants were Jews long resident there, at least as far back as the late seventeenth century. It almost goes without saying that there are no Jews in Steinach now, and that those

who live there have difficulty remembering those who were
once their neighbours and whose homes and property they
appropriated, if indeed they remember them at all. From Bad
Kissingen the road to Steinach goes by way of Grossenbrach,
Kleinbrach, and Aschach with its castle and Graf Luxburg's
brewery. From there it climbs the steep Aschacher Leite,
where Lazarus (Luisa writes) always got down from his
calèche so that the horses would not have so hard a job of it.
From the top, the road runs down, along the edge of the
wood, to Höhn, where the fields open out and the hills of the
Rhön can be seen in the distance. The Saale meadows spread
before you, the Windheim woods nestle in a gentle curve, and
there are the tip of the church tower and the old castle –
Steinach! Now the road crosses the stream and enters the
village, up to the square by the inn, then down to the right to
the lower part of the village, which Luisa calls her real home.
That is where the Lions live, she writes, where we get oil for
the lamps. There lives Meier Frei, the merchant, whose return
from the annual Leipzig trade fair is always a big event. There
lives Gessner the baker, to whom we took our Sabbath meal
on Friday evenings, Liebmann the slaughterer, and Salomon
Stern, the flour merchant. The poorhouse, which usually had
no occupants, and the fire station with the slatted shutters on
the tower, were in the lower part of the village, and so was the
old castle with its cobbled forecourt and the Luxburg arms
over the gateway. By way of Federgasse, which (Luisa writes)
was always full of geese and which she was afraid to walk
down as a child, past Simon Feldhahn's haberdashery and
Fröhlich the plumber's house with its green tin shingle
cladding, you come to a square shaded by a gigantic chestnut tree. In the house on the other side – before which the

square divides into two roads like waves at the bow of a ship, and behind which the Windheim woods rise – I was born and grew up (so the memoir in front of me reads), and there I lived until my sixteenth year, when, in January 1905, we moved to Kissingen.

Now I am standing in the living room once again, writes Luisa. I have walked through the gloomy, stone-flagged hall, have placed my hand cautiously on the handle, as I do almost every morning at that time, I have pushed it down and opened the door, and inside, standing barefoot on the white scrubbed floorboards, I look around in amazement at all the nice things in the room. There are two green velvet armchairs with knotted fringes all round, and between the windows that face onto the square is a sofa in the same style. The table is of light-coloured cherrywood. On it are a fan-like frame with five photographs of our relatives in Mainstockheim and Leutershausen and, in a frame of its own, a picture of Papa's sister, who people say was the most beautiful girl for miles around, a real Germania. Also on the table is a china swan with its wings spread, and in it, in a white lace frill, our dear Mama's evergreen bridal bouquet, beside the silver menora which is required on Friday evenings and for which Papa cuts paper cuffs especially every time, to prevent the wax dripping from the candles. On the tallboy by the wall, opened at a page, lies a folio-sized volume ornately bound in red with golden tendrils of vine. This, says Mama, is the works of her favourite poet, Heine, who is also the favourite poet of Empress Elisabeth. Next to it is the little basket where the newspaper, the *Münchner Neueste Nachrichten*, is kept, which Mama is immersed in every evening despite the fact that Papa, who goes to bed far earlier, always tells her that is is not

healthy to read so late at night. The hoya plant is on the cane
table in the bay of the east window. Its leaves are firm and
dark, and it has a lot of pink-hearted umbels consisting of
white, furry stars. When I come down early in the mornings,
the sun is already shining into the room and gleaming on the
drops of honey that cling to every little star. I can see through
the leaves and flowers into the grassy garden where the hens
are out pecking. Franz, our stable boy, a very taciturn albino,
will have hitched the horses to the calèche by the time Papa is
ready to leave, and over there, across the fence, is a tiny house
under an elder, where you can usually see Kathinka Strauss at
this time. Kathinka is a spinster of perhaps forty, and people
say she is not quite right in the head. When the weather
permits, she spends her day walking around the chestnut
tree in the square, clockwise or anti-clockwise according to
whim, knitting something that she plainly never finishes.
Though there is little else that she can call her own, she always
wears the most outrageous bonnets on these walks; one,
which featured a seagull's wing, I remember particularly well
because Herr Bein the teacher referred to it in school, telling
us we should never kill any creature merely in order to adorn
ourselves with its feathers.

Though Mother is long reluctant to let us out of the
home, Leo and I are sent to the day nursery when we are four
or five. We do not need to go till after morning prayers. It
is all very straightforward. The Sister is already in the yard.
You go up to her and say: Frau Adelinde, may I have a ball,
please? Then you take the ball across the yard and down the
steps to the playground. The playground is at the bottom of
the broad moat that circles the old castle, where there are now
colourful flower beds and vegetable patches. Right above the

playground, in a long suite of rooms in the almost completely deserted castle, lives Regina Zufrass. As everyone knows, she is a terribly busy woman and is always hard at work, even on Sundays. Either she is looking after her poultry or you see her in amongst the beanpoles or she is mending the fence or rummaging in one of the rooms, which are far too big for her and her husband. We even saw Regina Zufrass up on the roof once, fixing the weather vane, and we watched with bated breath, expecting her to fall off at any moment and land on the balcony with every bone in her body broken. Her husband, Jofferle, jobs as a waggoner in the village. Regina is none too pleased with him, and he for his part, so they say, is frightened to go home to her. Often people have to be sent to look for him. They tend to find him drunk, sprawled out beside the overturned hay-cart. The horses have long been used to all this and stay patiently by the up-ended waggon. At length the hay is loaded back on and Jofferle is fetched home by Regina. The next day, the green shutters at their windows remain shut, and when we children are eating our sandwiches down in the playground we wonder what can be going on in there. And then, every Thursday morning Mama draws a fish on the waxed paper she wraps the sandwiches in, so that we won't forget to buy half a dozen barbels from the fish man on our way home from the kindergarten. In the afternoon, Leo and I walk hand in hand along the Saale, on the bank where there is a dense copse of willows and alders, and rushes grow, past the sawmill and across the little bridge, where we stop to look down at the golden ringlets round the pebbles on the riverbed before we go on to the fish man's cottage, which is surrounded by bushes. First we have to wait in the parlour while the fish man's wife fetches the fish man. A fat-bellied white coffeepot with a cobalt blue knob is always on the table, and sometimes it seems as if it fills the whole room. The fish man appears in the doorway and takes us straight out through the slightly sloping garden, past his radiant dahlias, down to the Saale, where he takes out the barbels one by one from a big wooden crate in the water. When we eat them for supper we are not allowed to speak because of the bones, and have to keep as quiet as fish ourselves. I never felt particularly comfortable about those meals, and the skewed fish-eyes often went on watching me even in my sleep.

In summer, on the Sabbath, we often take a long walk to Bad Bocklet, where we can stroll around the colonnaded hall and watch the fashionably dressed people taking coffee; or, if it is too hot for a walk, we sit in the late afternoon with the Liebermanns and the Feldhahns in the shade of the chestnut trees by the bowling alley in Reuss's beer garden. The men have beer and the children have lemonade; the women can never decide what they want, and only take a sip of everything, while they cut up the Sabbath loaves and salted beef. After supper, some of the men play billiards, which is thought very daring and progressive. Ferdinand Lion even smokes a cigar! Afterwards they all go to the synagogue together. The women pack the things up and as dusk falls they make their way home with the children. Once, on his way home, Leo is wretched because of his new sailor's outfit, made of starched bright blue and white cotton – mainly because of the fat tie and the bibbed collar that hangs over his shoulders, sporting crossed anchors which Mother sat up very late embroidering the night before. Not until we are sitting on the front steps, by which time it is already dark, watching the storm clouds shift in the sky, does he gradually forget his misery. Once

Father is home, the candle made of many interwoven strands of wax is lit to mark the end of the Sabbath. We smell the little spice-box and go upstairs to bed. Soon dazzling white lightning is flashing across the sky, and the crashes of thunder set the whole house shaking. We stand at the window. There are moments when it is brighter than daylight outside. Clumps of hay are afloat on the swirling waters in the gutters. Then the storm passes over, but presently returns once more. Papa says it cannot make it over Windheim woods.

On Sunday afternoon Papa does his accounts. He takes a small key out of a leather pouch, unlocks the gleaming walnut bureau, opens the centre section, puts the key back into the pouch, sits down with a certain ceremony, and, settling himself, takes out the hefty account book. For an hour or so he makes entries and notes in this book and a number of smaller ones, and on pieces of paper cut to various sizes; softly moving his lips, he adds up long columns of figures and makes calculations, and, depending on what the results are like, his face will brighten up or cloud over for a time. A great many special things are kept in the numerous drawers of the bureau – deeds, certificates, correspondence, Mama's jewellery, and a broad ribbon to which large and small pieces of silver are attached by narrow braids of silk, as if they were medals or decorations: the *hollegrasch* coins that Leo is given by his godfather Selmar in Leutershausen every year, which I covetously marvel at. Mama sits in the living room with Papa, reading the *Münchner Neueste Nachrichten* – all the things she did not get round to reading during the week, for preference the spa columns and a miscellany feature. Whenever she comes across something incredible or remark-able she reads it out to Papa, who has to stop his adding up for a while. Perhaps because I couldn't get the story of Paulinchen, the girl who went up in flames, out of my head at that time, I can hear Mama even now telling Papa in her very own theatrical way (in her youth she had dreamt of being an actress) that ladies' dresses could now be fireproofed, for an exceedingly low cost, by immersing the material they were to be made from in a solution of zinc chloride. Even the finest of materials, I still hear Mama informing Papa, can be held to a naked flame after it has been thus treated, and it will char to ash without catching fire. If I am not with my parents in the living room on those eternally long Sundays, I am upstairs in the green room. In summer, when it is hot, the windows are open but the shutters are closed, and the light that enters makes a slanted Jacob's ladder pattern in the twilight around me. It is very quiet in the house, and throughout the neighbourhood. In the afternoon, the carriages out on excursions from the spa at Kissingen pass through the village. You can hear the horses' hooves from a long way off. I open one of the shutters a little and look down the road. The coaches drive via Steinach to Neustadt and Neuhaus and on to Salzburg castle, and in them the summer spa clientèle sit facing each other, grand ladies and gentlemen and, not infrequently, real Russian celebrities. The ladies are very finely turned out in feather bonnets and veils and with parasols of lace or brightly coloured silk. The village boys turn cartwheels right in front of the carriages, and the elegant passengers toss them copper coins by way of reward.

Autumn arrives, and the autumn holidays are approaching. First comes Rosh Hashanah, bringing in the New Year. The day before, all the rooms are swept, and on the eve Mama and Papa go to the synagogue, wearing their festive best: Papa in his frock coat and top hat, Mama in her deep blue velvet dress and the bonnet made entirely of white lilac blossom. Meanwhile, at home, Leo and I spread a starched linen cloth on the table and place the wine glasses on it, and under our parents' plates we put our New Year letters, written in our finest hand. A week and a half later is Yom Kippur. Father, in his death robes, moves about the house like a ghost. A mood of rue and penitence prevails. None of us will eat until the stars rise. Then we wish each other *ein gutes Anbeißen.* And four days later it is already the Feast of Tabernacles. Franz has put up the trellis for the sukkah under the elder, and we have decorated it with colourful garlands of glossy paper and long chains of threaded rosehips. From the ceiling hang ruddy-cheeked apples, yellow pears and golden-green grapes which Aunt Elise sends us every year from Mainstockheim in a little box lined with wood-shavings. On the two main and four half feast days we shall take our meals in the sukkah, unless the weather is exceptionally bad and cold. Then we stay in the kitchen, and only Papa will sit out in the bower, eating all by himself – a sign that winter is gradually coming. It is also at this time of the year that a wild boar the Prince Regent has shot in the Rhön is brought to Steinach, where its bristles are singed off outside the smithy on a wood fire. At home we study the May & Edlich catalogue from Leipzig, a thick compendious volume that reveals the entire wondrous world of merchandise, page after page, classified and described. Out of doors the colours gradually fade away. Our winter clothes are fetched out. They smell of naphthalene. Towards the end of November the Young Progressives' Club holds a masked ball at Reuss's. Frau Müntzer from Neustadt has made Mama a dress of raspberry-coloured silk for the occasion. The gown is long and flounced very elegantly at the hem. The children are allowed to watch the opening of the ball from the doorway to the next room. The hall is abuzz with festive murmuring. To set the mood, the band plays tunes from operettas, softly, till Herr Hainbuch, who works for the forestry commission, climbs onto the dais and, by way of an official start to the occasion, delivers a speech in praise of the fatherland. Glasses are raised, a flourish from the band, the masks gaze seriously into each other's eyes, another flourish, and the landlord, Herr Reuss, carries in a black box with a tulip-shaped metal funnel – the new gramophone, which pours forth real music without one's needing to do a thing. We are speechless with wonder. The ladies and gentlemen take their positions for a polonaise. Silberberg, the cobbler, quite unrecognizable in his tails, black tie, tie pin and patent leather shoes, walks ahead, conducting with a baton. Behind him come the couples, wheeling and twirling about the hall in every conceivable kind of way. The loveliest of them all, by far, is Aline Feldhahn as the Queen of the Night, in a dark dress bestrewn with stars. She is partnered by Siegfried Frey, wearing his hussar's uniform. Aline and Siegfried later married and had two children, but Siegfried, who was said to have a taste for dissipation, suddenly disappeared, and neither Aline nor old Löb Frey nor anyone else ever found out what became of him. Kathinka Strauss, though, claimed that Siegfried emigrated, to Argentina or Panama.

We have been going to school for a few years now. It is a school where we are all taught together in one form, exclusively for Jewish children. Our teacher, Salomon Bein, whose excellence the parents miss no opportunity to praise, imposes strict discipline, and sees himself first and foremost as a loyal servant of the state. Together with his lady wife and his unmarried sister Regine, he lives in the schoolhouse. In the mornings, when we cross the yard, he is already there in the doorway, spurring latecomers along by shouting *hopp! hopp!* and clapping his hands. In the classroom, after the blessing – *Thou who hast made the day, O Lord* – and after we have sharpened our slate pencils and cleaned our quill pens, jobs I dislike and which Herr Bein supervises closely, we are delegated to various tasks in rotation. Some are assigned to practise their handwriting; others have to do sums; yet others have to write an essay, or draw in their local history books. One group has visual instruction. A scroll is fetched out from the back of the cupboard and hung in front of the blackboard. The whole picture is of nothing but snow, with one coal-black raven in the middle. During the first one or two periods, especially in winter when the daylight never really brightens, I am always very slow about my work. I look out through the blue panes and see the deaf and dumb daughter of Stern, the flour merchant, on the other side of the yard, sitting at her work bench in her little room. She makes artificial flowers out of wire, crêpe and tissue paper, dozens of them, day in, day out, year in, year out. In nature study we learn about real flowers: larkspur, Turk's cap lily, loosestrife and lady's smock. We also learn about red ants and whales, from the animal kingdom. And once, when the village street is being newly surfaced, the teacher draws a picture on the blackboard, in coloured chalks, of the Vogelsberg as an erupting volcano, and explains where the blocks of basalt come from. He also has a collection of colourful stones in his minerals cabinet – rose quartz, rock crystal, amethyst, topaz and tourmaline. We draw a long line to mark how much time it has taken for them to form. Our entire lives would not even show as the tiniest dot on that line. Even so, the hours at school stretch as vast as the Pacific Ocean, and it takes an eternity till Moses Lion, who is sent to fetch wood almost every day by way of punishment, comes back up from the wood store with a basketful. Then, before we know it, Hanukkah is upon us, and it is Herr Bein's birthday. The day before, we decorate the walls of the classroom with branches of fir and little blue and yellow flags. We place the present on the teacher's desk. I remember that on one occasion it was a red velvet blanket, and once a copper hot-water bottle. On the morning of the birthday we all gather early in the classroom, in our best clothes. Then the teacher arrives, followed by his wife and the slightly dwarfish Fräulein Regine. We all stand up and say: Good morning, Herr Bein! Good morning, Frau Bein! Good morning, Fräulein Regine! Our teacher, who has of course long since known what was being prepared, affects to be completely surprised by his present and the decorations. He raises a hand to his forehead, several times, shaking his head, as if he does not know what to say, and, deeply touched, walks up and down the class, thanking each one of us effusively. There are no lessons today; instead, stories and German legends of old are read aloud. We also have a guessing game. For instance, we have to guess the three things that give and take in infinite plenty. Of course no one knows the answer, which Herr Bein then tells us in tones of great significance: the earth, the sea, and the Reich. Perhaps the best thing about that day is that, before we go home, we are allowed to jump over the Hanukkah candles, which have been fixed to the threshold with drops of wax. It is a long winter. At home, Papa does exercises with us in the evening. The geese are gone from their hutch. Soon after, parts of them are preserved in boiling hot fat. Some village women come to slice the quills from the feathers. They sit in the spare room, each with a heap of down in front of her, slicing almost the whole night long. It looks as if snow has fallen. But the next morning, when we get up, the room is so clean, so devoid of feathers, that you'd think nothing had ever happened. Early in the year, spring cleaning has to be done in preparation for Passover. It is worse at school. Frau Bein and Fräulein Regine are at it for at least a week. The mattresses are taken out to the yard, the bedding is hung over the balcony, the floors are newly waxed, and all the cooking utensils are immersed in boiling water. We children have to sweep the classroom and wash the shutters with soapsuds. At home, too, all the rooms and chests are cleared out. The bustle is dreadful. The evening before Passover, Mama sits down for a while for the first time in days. Meanwhile, Father's job is to go around the house with a goose feather checking to see that not a single crumb of bread is still to be found.

It is autumn again, and Leo is now at grammar school in Münnerstadt, a two-hour walk from Steinach, where he is living at Lindwurm the hatter's. His meals are sent to him twice a week – half a dozen little pots, stacked in a carrier. Lindwurm's daughter only has to warm them up. Inconsolable at having to go to school alone from now on, I fall ill. At least every other day I run a temperature and sometimes I am quite delirious. Dr Homburger prescribes elder juice and cold compresses. My bed has been made up on the sofa in the yellow room. For almost three weeks I lie there. Time and again I count the pieces of soap in the pyramid stacked on the marble top of the washstand, but I never arrive at the same total twice. The little yellow dragons on the wall-paper haunt me even in my dreams. I am often in great turmoil. When I wake up, I see the jars of preserves ranged on the chest and in the cold compartments of the tiled stove. I try in vain to work out what they mean. They don't mean anything, says Mama, they're just cherries, plums and pears. Outside, she tells me, the swallows are already gathering. At night, in my sleep, I can hear the swishing flight of great flocks of migrating birds as they pass over the house. When at last my condition improves somewhat, the windows are opened wide one bright Friday afternoon. From my position on the sofa I can see the whole Saale valley and the road to Höhn, and I can see Papa returning from Kissingen by that road, in the calèche. Just a little later, still wearing his hat on his head, he comes into my room. He has brought me a wooden box of sweets with a peacock butterfly painted on it. That evening, a hundredweight of apples, goldings and red calvilles, are laid down for winter on the floor of the next room. Their scent puts me to a more peaceful sleep than I have known for a long time, and when Dr Homburger examines me the next morning he pronounces me perfectly healthy again. But then, when the summer holidays are starting nine months later, it is Leo's turn. He has a lung complaint, and Mama insists that it comes from his airless lodgings at Lindwurm's, and the lead vapours from the hatter's workshop. Dr Homburger agrees. He prescribes a mixture of milk and Selters water, and orders Leo to spend a lot of time in the healthy air of the Windheim pine forests. Now a basket of sandwiches, curd cheese and boiled eggs is made up every morning. I pour Leo's health drink through a funnel into green bottles. Frieda, our cousin from Jochsberg, goes to the woods with us, as supervisor, as it were. She is already sixteen, very beautiful, and has a very long, thick, blonde plait. In the afternoon, Carl Hainbuch, the chief forester's son, invariably just happens to make an appearance, and walks for hours beneath the trees with Frieda. Leo, who reveres his cousin more than anyone, sits on the very top of one of the erratic boulders, watching the romantic scene with displeasure. What interests me most are the countless glossy black stag beetles in the Windheim woods. I track their crooked wanderings with a patient eye. At times it looks as if something has shocked them, physically, and it seems as if they have fainted. They lie there motionless, and it feels as if the world's heart had stopped. Only when you hold your own breath do they return from death to life, only then does time begin to pass again. Time. What time was all that? How slowly the days passed then! And who was that strange child, walking home, tired, with a tiny blue and white jay's feather in her hand?

If I think back nowadays to our childhood in Steinach (Luisa's memoirs continue at another point), it often seems as if it had been open-ended in time, in every direction – indeed, as if it were still going on, right into these lines I am now writing. But in reality, as I know only too well, childhood ended in January 1905 when the house and fields at Steinach were auctioned off and we moved into a new three-storey house in Kissingen, on the corner of Bibrastrasse and Ehrhardstrasse. Father had bought it one day, without hesitation, from Kiesel the builder, for a price of 66,000 gold marks, a sum which struck us all as the stuff of myth, and most of which he had raised on a mortgage with a Frankfurt bank, a fact which it took Mama a long time to accept. The

Lazarus Lanzberg stables had been doing better and better in recent years, supplying as far afield as the Rhineland, Brandenburg and Holstein, buying everywhere, and leaving all their customers well pleased and satisfied. The contract Papa had won as supplier and provisioner to the army, which he proudly mentioned whenever he had the chance, had doubtless been the decisive factor in giving up farming, moving from backwater Steinach, and finally establishing a position in middle-class life. At that time I was almost sixteen, and believed that a completely new world, even lovelier than that of childhood, would be revealed to me in Kissingen. In some respects that was really how it was, but in others the Kissingen years up until my marriage in 1921 seem in retrospect to have marked the first step on a path that grew narrower day by day and led inevitably to the point I have now arrived at. I find it difficult to think back to my youth in Kissingen. It is as if the gradual dawn of what was called the serious side of life, the minor and major disappointments that soon began to mount up, had affected my ability to take things in. And so there is a good deal I can no longer picture. Even of our arrival in Kissingen I have only fragmentary memories. I know it was bitterly cold, there was endless work to be done, my fingers were frozen, for days the house refused to warm up despite the fact that I poked the coals in the Irish stoves in all the rooms; the hoya plant had not survived the move; and the cats had run away, back to the old home, and, though Papa went back especially to Steinach, they were nowhere to be found. To me the house, which the people of Kissingen soon took to calling the Lanzberg Villa, always remained essentially a strange place. The vast, echoing stairwell; the linoleum flooring in the hall; the corridor at the

back where the telephone hung over the laundry basket and
you had to hold the heavy receivers to your ears with both
hands; the pale, hissing gaslight; the sombre Flemish furniture

with its carved columns – there was something distinctly creepy about all of it, and at times I feel quite definitely that it did steady and irreparable harm to me. Only once, if I remember rightly, did I ever sit on the window seat in the drawing room, which was painted with foliage and tendrils like a festive bower, and from the ceiling of which a brand new brass Sabbath-lamp hung down, also fuelled by gas; I leafed through a page or two of the blue velvet postcard album which had its place on the shelf of the smoking table, and felt like a visitor, passing through. Often in the mornings or evenings, when I looked out of my top floor window across the flower beds of the spa nursery gardens to the green, wooded hills all around, I felt like a maid. From the very first spring we rented out several rooms in the house. Mother, who ran the household, was an exacting teacher of domestic management. At six o'clock, right after I got up, my first task was to give the white chickens in the garden their measure of grain and fetch in the eggs. Then breakfast had to be made, the rooms tidied, the vegetables trimmed, and lunch cooked. In the afternoons, for a while, I did a course in shorthand and book-keeping that was taught by nuns. Frau Ignatia was very proud of me. At other times I took the children of visitors to the spa for walks in the public gardens – for instance, Herr Weintraub's fat little boy. Herr Weintraub was a timber merchant and came every year from Perm in Siberia, because Jews (so he said) were not allowed at watering places in Russia. From about four o'clock I would sit out in the chalet darning or crocheting, and in the evening there was the vegetable patch to be watered, with water from the well – the tap water cost too much, claimed Papa. I could go to evening concerts only if Leo was home from the grammar school.

Usually his friend Armand Wittelsbach, who later became an antiques dealer in Paris, would collect us after dinner. I would wear a white dress and stroll through the park between Armand and Leo. On occasions the spa gardens were illuminated: there would be Chinese lanterns strung across the avenues, shedding colourful, magical light. The fountains in front of the Regent's building would jet silver and gold alternately. But at ten o'clock the spell broke and we had to be home. Part of the way, Armand would walk on his hands beside me. I also remember a birthday outing with Armand and Leo. We set out at five in the morning, first towards Klausenhof and from there through the beech woods, where we picked big bunches of lily of the valley, back to Kissingen. We had been invited to breakfast with the Wittelsbachs. It was about that time, too, that we looked out for Halley's comet at night, and once there was a total eclipse of the sun in the early afternoon. It was dreadful to see the shadow of the moon slowly blotting out the sun, the leaves of the rambling rose on the balcony (where we stood with our soot-darkened pieces of glass) seeming to wither, and the birds flapping about in a frightened panic. And I recall that it was on the day after that Laura Mandel and her father first visited us from Trieste. Herr Mandel was nearly eighty but Laura was just our own age, and both of them made the greatest imaginable impression on me, Herr Mandel on account of his elegant appearance – he wore the most stylish linen suits and broad-brimmed straw hats – and Laura (who only ever called her father Giorgio), because of her firm, freckled forehead and her wonderful eyes, which were often rather misty. During the day, Herr Mandel would usually sit somewhere that was partly in the shade – by the silver poplar in our garden, on a

bench in Luitpold Park, or on the terrace of the Wittelsbacher
Hof hotel – reading the papers, making occasional notes, and
often simply lost in thought. Laura said he had long been
busy projecting an empire in which nothing ever happened,
for he detested nothing more than enterprises, developments,
great events, changes, or incidents of any kind. For her part,
Laura was all for revolution. I once went to the theatre in
Kissingen with her when some Viennese operetta – I no
longer know if it was the *Zigeunerbaron* or *Rastlbinder* – was
being performed to mark the Austrian Emperor Franz Josef's
birthday. First the orchestra played the Austrian national
anthem. Everyone stood up except Laura, who remained
demonstratively seated because – coming from Trieste – she
could not stand Austrians. What she said concerning this was
the first political thought I ever came across in my life, and
how often have I not wished, of late, that Laura were here
again to discuss things with me. For several years she stayed
with us during the summer months, the last time being that
especially lovely season when both of us turned twenty-one,
myself on the 17th of May and she on the 7th of July. I
remember her birthday particularly. We had taken the little
steamer upriver to the salt-vapour frames, and were strolling
about in the cool salty air near the timber scaffold down
which the mineral water continuously flows. I was wearing
my new black straw hat with the green ribbon which I had
bought at Tauber's in Würzburg, where Leo was now reading
classics. It was a beautiful day, and as we were walking along
the paths a huge shadow suddenly fell upon us. We looked up
at the sky, at the same time as all the other summer guests out
walking by the frames, and there was a gigantic zeppelin
gliding soundlessly through the blue air, apparently only just

clearing the tops of the trees. Everyone was amazed, and a young man standing nearby took that as an excuse to talk to us – taking his courage in both hands, as he later admitted to me. His name, he told us right away, was Fritz Waldhof, and he played the French horn in the spa orchestra, which consisted chiefly of members of the Wiener Konzertverein who took jobs at Kissingen during the summer break every year. Fritz, for whom I had an instant liking, saw us home that afternoon, and the following week we went on our first outing together. Again it was a glorious summer day. I walked ahead with Fritz, and Laura, who had distinct doubts about him, followed with a Hamburg cellist named Hansen. Needless to say, I no longer remember what we talked about. But I do remember that the fields on either side of the path were full of flowers and that I was happy, and oddly enough I also recall that, not far out of town, just where the sign to Bodenlaube is, we overtook two very refined Russian gentlemen, one of whom (who looked particularly majestic) was speaking seriously to a boy of about ten who had been chasing butter-flies and had lagged so far behind that they had had to wait for him. This warning can't have had much effect, though, because whenever we happened to look back we saw the boy running about the meadows with upraised net, exactly as before. Hansen later claimed that he had recognized the elder of the two distinguished Russian gentlemen as Muromzev, the president of the first Russian parliament, who was then staying in Kissingen.

I spent the years which followed that summer in the usual way, doing my household duties, handling the accounts and correspondence in the stables and provisioning business, and waiting for the Viennese horn player to return to

Kissingen, which he did regularly, together with the swallows. Over the nine months of separation each year we always grew apart somewhat, despite the many letters we wrote, and so it took Fritz, who like myself was essentially an undemonstrative person, a long time before he proposed to me. It was just before the end of the 1913 season, on a September afternoon that trembled with limpid loveliness. We were sitting by the salt-frames and I was eating bilberries with sour cream from a china bowl, when suddenly Fritz, in the middle of a carefully worked out reminiscence of our first outing to Bodenlaube, broke off and asked me, without further ado, if I should like to marry him. I did not know what to reply, but I nodded, and, though everything else around me blurred, I saw that long-forgotten Russian boy as clearly as anything, leaping about the meadows with his butterfly net; I saw him as a messenger of joy, returning from that distant summer day to open his specimen box and release the most beautiful red admirals, peacock butterflies, brimstones and tortoiseshells to signal my final liberation. Father, however, was reluctant to agree to a speedy engagement. He was not only troubled by the rather uncertain prospects of a French horn player, but also claimed that the proposed attachment was bound to cut me off from the Jewish faith. In the end it was not so much my own petitioning as the unceasing diplomatic efforts of Mother, who was not so concerned about upholding our traditional life, that won the day; and the following May, on my and Leo's twenty-fifth birthday, we celebrated our engagement at a small family gathering. A few months later, however, my dearest Fritz, who had been called up into the Austrian Musicians' Corps and transferred to Lemberg, suffered a stroke in the midst of playing the *Freischütz* over-

ture for the garrison's officers, and fell lifeless from his chair.
His death was described to me a few days later in a telegram
of condolence from Vienna, and for weeks the words and
letters danced before my eyes in all sorts of new combinations.
I really cannot say how I went on living, or how I got over
the terrible pain of parting that tormented me day and night
after Fritz's death, or indeed whether I have ever got over
it. At all events, throughout the war I worked as a nurse
with Dr Kosilowski. All the spa buildings and sanatoria in
Kissingen were full of the wounded and the convalescent.
Whenever a new arrival reminded me of Fritz, in appearance
or manner, I would be overwhelmed afresh by my tragedy,
and that may be why I looked after those young men so well,
some of whom were very seriously injured – as if by doing
so I might still save the life of my horn player. In May 1917
a contingent of badly wounded artillerymen was brought in,
among them a lieutenant whose eyes were bandaged up. His
name was Friedrich Frohmann, and I would sit at his bedside
long after my duties were over, expecting some kind of a
miracle. It was several months before he could open his seared
eyes again. As I had guessed, they were Fritz's greyish-green
eyes; but extinguished and blind. At Friedrich's request we
soon began to play chess, describing the moves we had made
or wanted to make in words – bishop to d6, rook to f4, and
so on. By an extraordinary feat of memory, Friedrich was soon
able to retain the most complex games; and if his memory did
fail him, he resorted to his sense of touch. Whenever his
fingers moved across the pieces, with a delicate care that I
found devastating, I was always reminded of the fingers of
my horn player moving upon the keys of his instrument. As
the year neared its end, Friedrich came down with some

unidentifiable infection and died of it within a fortnight. It was almost the death of me, too, as they later told me. I lost all my beautiful hair and over a quarter of my body weight, and for a long time I lay in a profound, ebbing and flowing delirium in which all I saw was Fritz and Friedrich, and myself, alone, separate from the two of them. To what it was that I owed thanks for my utterly unexpected recovery late that winter, or whether "thanks" is at all the right word, I know as little as I know how one gets through this life. Before the war's end I was awarded the Ludwig Cross in recognition of what they called my self-sacrificing devotion to duty. And then one day the war really was over. The troops came home. The revolution broke out in Munich. The Freikorps soldiers gathered their forces in Bamberg. Eisner was assassinated by Anton Arco Valley. Munich was re-taken and martial law was imposed. Landauer was killed, young Egelhofer and Leviné were shot, and Toller was locked up in a fortress. When everything was finally back to normal and it was business more or less as usual, my parents decided that now was the time to find me a husband, to take my mind off things. Before long, a Jewish marriage broker from Würzburg by the name of Brisacher introduced my present husband, Fritz Ferber, to our home. He came from a Munich family of livestock traders, but was himself just in the process of setting himself up in middle-class life as a dealer in fine art. Initially I consented to become engaged to Fritz Ferber solely because of his name, though later I did come to esteem and love him more with every day. Like the horn player before him, Fritz Ferber liked to take long walks out of town, and, again like him, he was by nature shy but essentially cheerful. In the summer of 1921, soon after our marriage, we went to the

Allgäu, and Fritz took me up the Ifen, the Himmelsschrofen and the Hohes Licht. We looked down into the valleys – the Ostrachtal, the Illertal and the Walsertal – where the scattered villages were so peaceful it was as if nothing evil had ever happened anywhere on earth. Once, from the summit of the Kanzelwand, we watched a bad storm far below us, and when it had passed the green meadows gleamed in the sunshine and the forests steamed like an immense laundry. From that moment I knew for certain that I was now Fritz Ferber's and that I would be glad to work at his side in the newly established Munich picture gallery. When we returned from the Allgäu we moved into the house in Sternwartstrasse where we still live. It was a radiant autumn, and a hard winter to follow. True, it did not snow much, but for weeks on end the Englischer Garten was a miracle of hoar frost such as I had never seen, and on the Theresienwiese they opened up an ice-rink for the first time since the outbreak of war, where Fritz and I would skate in wonderful, sweeping curves, he in his green jacket and I in my fur-trimmed coat. When I think

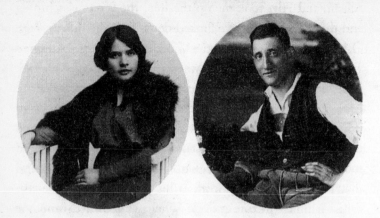

back to those days, I see shades of blue everywhere – a single empty space, stretching out into the twilight of late afternoon, crisscrossed by the tracks of ice-skaters long vanished.

The memoirs of Luisa Lanzberg have been very much on my mind since Ferber handed them over to me, so much so that in late June 1991 I felt I should make the journey to Kissingen and Steinach. I travelled via Amsterdam, Cologne and Frankfurt, and had to change a number of times, and sit out lengthy waits in the Aschaffenburg and Gemünden station buffets, before I reached my destination. With every change the trains were slower and shorter, till at last, on the stretch from Gemünden to Kissingen, I found myself in a train (if that is the right word) that consisted only of an engine and a single carriage – something I had not thought possible. Directly across from me, even though there were plenty of seats free, a fat, square-headed man of perhaps fifty had plumped himself down. His face was flushed and blotched with red, and his eyes were very close-set and slightly squint. Puffing noisily, he dug his unshapely tongue, still caked with bits of food, around his half-open mouth. There he sat, legs apart, his stomach and gut stuffed horribly into summer shorts. I could not say whether the physical and mental deformity of my fellow-passenger was the result of long psychiatric confinement, some innate debility, or simply beer-drinking and eating between meals. To my considerable relief the monster got out at the first stop after Gemünden, leaving me quite alone in the carriage but for an old woman on the other side of the aisle who was eating an apple so big that the full hour it took till we reached Kissingen was barely enough for her to finish it. The train followed the bends of the river, through the grassy valley. Hills and woods passed slowly, the shadows of evening settled upon the countryside, and the old woman went on dividing up the apple, slice by slice, with the penknife she held open in her hand, nibbling the pieces, and spitting out the peel onto a paper napkin in her lap. At Kissingen there was only one single taxi in the deserted street outside the station. In answer to my question, the driver told me that at that hour the spa clientèle were already tucked up in bed. The hotel he drove me to had just been completely renovated in the neo-imperial style which is now inexorably taking hold throughout Germany and which discreetly covers up with light shades of green and gold leaf the lapses of taste committed in the postwar years. The lobby was as deserted as the station forecourt. The woman at reception, who had something of the mother superior about her, sized me up as if she were expecting me to disturb the peace, and when I got into the lift I found myself facing a weird old couple who stared at me with undisguised hostility, if not horror. The woman was holding a small plate in her claw-like hands, with a few slices of *wurst* on it. I naturally assumed that they had a dog in their room, but the next morning, when I saw them take up two tubs of raspberry yoghurt and something from the breakfast bar that they had wrapped in a napkin, I realized that their supplies were intended not for some putative dog but for themselves.

I began my first day in Kissingen with a stroll in the grounds of the spa. The ducks were still asleep on the lawn, the white down of the poplars was drifting in the air, and a few early bathers were wandering along the sandy paths like lost souls. Without exception, these people out taking their painfully slow morning constitutionals were of pensioner age, and I began to fear that I would be condemned to spend the rest of my life amongst the patrons of Kissingen, who were in all likelihood preoccupied first and foremost with the state of their bowels. Later I sat in a café, again surrounded by elderly people, reading the Kissingen newspaper, the *Saale-Zeitung*. The quote of the day, in the so-called Calendar column, was from Johann Wolfgang von Goethe, and read: *Our world is a cracked bell that no longer sounds*. It was the 25th of June. According to the paper, there was a crescent moon and the anniversary of the birth of Ingeborg Bachmann, the Austrian poet, and of the English writer George Orwell. Other dead birthday boys whom the newspaper remembered were the aircraft builder Willy Messerschmidt (1898–1978), the rocket pioneer Hermann Oberath (1894–1990), and the East German author Hans Marchwitza (1890–1965). The death announcements, headed *Totentafel*, included that of retired master butcher Michael Schultheis of Steinach (80). He was extremely popular. He was a staunch member of the Blue Cloud Smokers' Club and the Reservists' Association. He spent most of his leisure time with his loyal alsatian, Prinz. –

Pondering the peculiar sense of history apparent in such notices, I went to the town hall. There, after being referred elsewhere several times and getting an insight into the perpetual peace that pervades the corridors of small-town council chambers, I finally ended up with a panic-stricken bureaucrat in a particularly remote office, who listened with incredulity to what I had to say and then explained where the synagogue had been and where I would find the Jewish cemetery. The earlier temple had been replaced by what was known as the new synagogue, a ponderous turn-of-the-century building in a curiously orientalized, neo-romanesque style, which was vandalized during the Kristallnacht and then completely demolished over the following weeks. In its place in Maxstrasse, directly opposite the back entrance of the town hall, is now the labour exchange. As for the Jewish cemetery, the official, after some rummaging in a key deposit on the wall, handed me two keys with orderly labels, and offered me

the following somewhat idiosyncratic directions: you will find
the Israelite cemetery if you proceed southwards in a straight
line from the town hall for a thousand paces till you get to the
end of Bergmannstrasse. When I reached the gate it turned
out that neither of the keys fitted the lock, so I climbed the

Dieser Friedhof wird dem Schutz
der Allgemeinheit empfohlen. Beschädigungen,
Zerstörungen und jeglicher beschimpfende Unfug
werden strafrechtlich verfolgt / §§168, 304 StGB\

Stadt Bad Kissingen

wall. What I saw had little to do with cemeteries as one thinks of them; instead, before me lay a wilderness of graves, neglected for years, crumbling and gradually sinking into the ground amidst tall grass and wild flowers under the shade of trees, which trembled in the slight movement of the air. Here

and there a stone placed on the top of a grave witnessed that
someone must have visited one of the dead – who could say
how long ago. It was not possible to decipher all of the
chiselled inscriptions, but the names I could still read –
Hamburger, Kissinger, Wertheimer, Friedländer, Arnsberg,
Auerbach, Grunwald, Leuthold, Seeligmann, Frank, Hertz,
Goldstaub, Baumblatt and Blumenthal – made me think that
perhaps there was nothing the Germans begrudged the Jews
so much as their beautiful names, so intimately bound up
with the country they lived in and with its language. A shock
of recognition shot through me at the grave of Maier Stern,

who died on the 18th of May, my own birthday; and I was
touched, in a way I knew I could never quite fathom, by the
symbol of the writer's quill on the stone of Friederike
Halbleib, who departed this life on the 28th of March 1912.
I imagined her pen in hand, all by herself, bent with bated
breath over her work; and now, as I write these lines, it feels
as if *I* had lost her, and as if *I* could not get over the loss

despite the many years that have passed since her departure. I stayed in the Jewish cemetery till the afternoon, walking up and down the rows of graves, reading the names of the dead, but it was only when I was about to leave that I discovered a more recent gravestone, not far from the locked gate, on which were the names of Lily and Lazarus Lanzberg, and of Fritz and Luisa Ferber. I assume Ferber's Uncle Leo had had it erected there. The inscription says that Lazarus Lanzberg died in Theresienstadt in 1942, and that Fritz and Luisa were deported, their fate unknown, in November 1941. Only Lily, who took her own life, lies in that grave. I stood before it for some time, not knowing what I should think; but before I left I placed a stone on the grave, according to custom.

Although I was amply occupied, during my several days in Kissingen and in Steinach (which retained not the slightest trace of its former character), with my research and with

the writing itself, which, as always, was going laboriously, I felt increasingly that the mental impoverishment and lack of memory that marked the Germans, and the efficiency with which they had cleaned everything up, were beginning to affect my head and my nerves. I therefore decided to leave sooner than I had planned, a decision which was the easier to take since

my enquiries, though they had produced much on the general history of Kissingen's Jewry, had brought very little to light concerning the Lanzberg family. But I must still say something about the trip I took up to the salt-frames in a motor launch that was moored at the edge of the spa grounds. It was about one o'clock on the day before I left, at an hour when the spa visitors were eating their diet-controlled lunches, or

indulging in unsupervised gluttony in gloomy restaurants, that I went down to the riverbank and boarded the launch. The woman who piloted the launch had been waiting in vain, till that moment, for even a single passenger. This lady, who generously allowed me to take her picture, was from Turkey, and had already been working for the Kissingen river authority for a number of years. In addition to the captain's cap that sat jauntily on her head, she was wearing a blue and white jersey dress which was reminiscent (at least from a distance) of a sailor's uniform, by way of a further concession to her office. It soon turned out that the mistress of the launch was not only expert at manoeuvring her craft on the narrow river but also had views on the way of the world that were worth considering. As we headed up the Saale she gave me a few highly impressive samples of her critical philosophy, in her somewhat Turkish but nonetheless very flexible German, all of which culminated in her oft-repeated point that there was no end to stupidity, and nothing as dangerous. And people in Germany, she said, were just as stupid as the Turks, perhaps even stupider. She was visibly pleased to find a sympathetic ear for her views, which she shouted above the pounding of the diesel engine and underlined with an imaginative repertoire of gestures and facial expressions; she rarely had the opportunity to talk to a passenger, she said, let alone one with a bit of sense. The boat ride lasted some twenty minutes. When it was over, we parted with a shake of hands and, I believe, a certain mutual respect. The salt-frames, which I had only seen in an old photograph before, were a short distance upriver, a little way off in the fields. Even at first glance, the timber building was an overwhelming construction, about two hundred metres long and surely twenty metres high, and yet, as I learnt from information displayed in a glass-fronted case, it was merely part of a complex that had once been far more extensive. There was currently no access – notices by the steps explained that the previous year's hurricane had made structural examinations necessary – but, since there was no one around who might have denied me permission, I climbed up to the gallery that ran along the entire complex at a height of about five metres.

From there one could take a close look at the blackthorn twigs that were bunched in layers as high as the roof. Mineral water raised by a cast-iron pumping station was running down them, and collecting in a trough under the frame.

Completely taken aback both by the scale of the complex
and by the steady mineral transformation wrought upon the
twigs by the ceaseless flow of the water, I walked up and down
the gallery for a long time, inhaling the salty air, which the

slightest breath of air loaded with myriad tiny droplets. At length I sat down on a bench in one of the balcony-like landings off the gallery, and all that afternoon immersed myself in the sight and sound of that theatre of water, and in ruminations about the long-term and (I believe) impenetrable process which, as the concentration of salts increases in the water, produces the very strangest of petrified or crystallized forms, imitating the growth patterns of Nature even as it is being dissolved.

During the winter of 1990/91, in the little free time I had (in other words, mostly at the so-called weekend and at night), I was working on the account of Max Ferber given above. It was an arduous task. Often I could not get on for hours or days at a time, and not infrequently I unravelled what I had done, continuously tormented by scruples that were taking tighter hold and steadily paralysing me. These scruples concerned not only the subject of my narrative, which I felt I could not do justice to, no matter what approach I tried, but also the entire questionable business of writing. I had covered hundreds of pages with my scribble, in pencil and ballpoint. By far the greater part had been crossed out, discarded, or obliterated by additions. Even what I ultimately salvaged as a "final" version seemed to me a thing of shreds and patches, utterly botched. So I hesitated to send Ferber my cut-down rendering of his life; and, as I hesitated, I heard from Manchester that Ferber had been taken to Withington Hospital with pulmonary emphysema. Withington Hospital was a one-time Victorian workhouse, where the homeless and unemployed had been subjected to a strict regime. Ferber was in a men's ward with well over twenty beds, where much muttering and groaning went on, and doubtless a good deal of dying. He clearly found it next to impossible to use his voice, and so responded to what I said only at lengthy intervals, in an attempt at speech that sounded like the rustle of dry leaves in the wind. Still, it was plain enough that he felt his condition was something to be ashamed of and had resolved to put it behind him as soon as possible, one way or another. He was ashen, and the weariness kept getting the better of him. I stayed with him for

perhaps three quarters of an hour before taking my leave and walking the long way back through the south of the city, along the endless streets – Burton Road, Yew Tree Road, Claremont Road, Upper Lloyd Street, Lloyd Street North – and through the deserted Hulme estates, which had been rebuilt in the early Seventies and had now been left to fall down

again. In Higher Cambridge Street I passed warehouses where the ventilators were still revolving in the broken windows.

I had to cross beneath urban motorways, over canal bridges and wasteland, till at last, in the already fading daylight, the façade of the Midland Hotel appeared before me, looking like some fantastic fortress. In recent years, ever since his income had permitted, Ferber had rented a suite there, and I too had taken a room for this one night. The Midland was built in the late nineteenth century, of chestnut-coloured bricks and chocolate-coloured glazed ceramic tiles which neither soot nor acid rain have been able to touch. The building runs to three basement levels, six floors above ground, and a total of no fewer than six hundred rooms, and was once famous throughout the land for its luxurious plumbing. Taking a shower there was was like standing out in a monsoon. The brass and copper pipes, which were always highly polished, were so capacious that one of the bathtubs (three metres long and one metre wide) could be filled in just twelve seconds. Moreover, the Midland was renowned for its palm courtyard and, as various sources tell, for its hothouse atmosphere, which brought out both the guests and the staff in a sweat and generally conveyed the impression that here, in the heart of this northern city with its perpetual cold wet gusts, one was in fact on some tropical isle of the blessed, reserved for mill owners, where even the clouds in the sky were made of cotton, as it were. Today the Midland is on the brink of ruin. In the glass-roofed lobby, the reception rooms, the stairwells, the lifts and the corridors one rarely encounters either a hotel guest or one of the chambermaids or waiters who prowl about like sleepwalkers. The legendary steam heating, if it works at all, is erratic; fur flakes from out of the taps; the window panes are coated in thick grime marbled by rain; whole tracts of the building are closed off; and it is presumably only a matter of time before the Midland closes its doors and is sold off and transformed into a Holiday Inn.

When I entered my room on the fifth floor I suddenly felt as if I were in a hotel somewhere in Poland. The old-

fashioned interior put me curiously in mind of a faded wine-red velvet lining, the inside of a jewellery box or violin case. I kept my coat on and sat down on one of the plush armchairs in the corner bay window, watching darkness fall outside. The rain that had set in at dusk was pouring down into the gorges of the streets, lashed by the wind, and down below the black taxis and double-decker buses were moving across the shining tarmac, close behind or beside each other, like a herd of elephants. A constant roar rose from below to my place by the window, but there were also moments of complete silence from time to time. In one such interval (though it was utterly impossible) I thought I heard the orchestra tuning their instruments, amidst the usual scraping of chairs and clearing of throats, in the Free Trade Hall next door; and far off, far, far off in the distance, I also heard the little opera singer who used to perform at Liston's Music Hall in the Sixties, singing long extracts from *Parsifal* in German. Liston's Music Hall was in the city centre, not far from Piccadilly Gardens, above a so-called Wine Lodge where the prostitutes would take a rest and where they had Australian sherry on tap, in big barrels. Anyone who felt the urge could get up on the stage at that music hall and, with the swathes of smoke drifting, perform the piece of his choice to a very mixed and often heavily intoxicated audience, accompanied on the Wurlitzer by a lady who invariably wore pink tulle. As a rule the choice fell upon folk ballads and the sentimental hits that were currently in vogue. *The old home town looks the same as I step down from the train*, began the favourite of the winter season of 1966 to 1967. *And there to greet me are my Mama and Papa.* Twice a week, at a late hour when the heaving mass of people and voices verged on the infernal, the heroic tenor known as Siegfried, who cannot have been more than one metre fifty tall, would take the stage. He was in his late forties, wore a herringbone coat that reached almost to the floor and on his head a Homburg tilted back. He would sing *O weh, des Höchsten Schmerzenstag* or *Wie dünkt mich doch die Aue heut so schön* or some other impressive arioso, not hesitating to act out stage directions such as "Parsifal is on the point of fainting" with the required theatricality. And now, sitting in the Midland's turret room above the abyss on the fifth floor, I heard him again for the first time since those days. The sound came from so far away that it was as if he were walking about behind the wing flats of an infinitely deep stage. On those flats, which in truth did not exist, I saw, one by one, pictures from an exhibition that I had seen in Frankfurt the year before. They were colour photographs, tinted with a greenish-blue or reddish-brown, of the Litzmannstadt ghetto that was established in 1940 in the Polish industrial centre of Lodz, once known as *polski*

Manczester. The photographs, which had been discovered in 1987 in a small suitcase, carefully sorted and inscribed, in an antique dealer's shop in Vienna, had been taken as personal souvenirs by a book-keeper and financial expert named Genewein, who came from near Salzburg and who was himself in one of the pictures, counting money at his bureau. The pictures also showed the lord mayor of Litzmannstadt, one Hans Biebow, on his birthday, well scrubbed and with a neat parting, at a table adorned with asparagus ferns and groaning beneath potted plants, bouquets, cakes and cold cuts. There were German men too with their girlfriends and wives, all – without exception – in high spirits. And there were pictures of the ghetto – street cobbles, tram tracks, housefronts, hoardings, demolition sites, fire protection walls, beneath a sky that was grey, watery green, or white and blue – strangely deserted pictures, scarcely one of which showed a living soul, despite the fact that at times there were as many as a hundred and seventy thousand people in Litzmannstadt, in an area of no more than five square kilometres. The photographer had also recorded the exemplary organization within the ghetto: the postal system, the police, the courtroom, the fire brigade, soil disposal, the hairdresser's, the medical services, the laying out of the dead, and the burial ground. More important to him than anything else, apparently, was to show "our industry", the ghetto works that were essential to the wartime economy. In these production sites, most of which were designed for basic manufacture, women were sitting making baskets, child apprentices were busy in the metalwork shop, men were making bullets or working in the nail factory or the rag depot, and everywhere there were faces, countless faces, who looked up from their

work (and were permitted to do so) purposely and solely for
the fraction of a second that it took to take the photograph.
Work is our only course, they said. – Behind the perpendicular frame of a loom sit three young women, perhaps aged
twenty. The irregular geometrical patterns of the carpet they
are knotting, and even its colours, remind me of the settee in
our living room at home. Who the young women are I do not
know. The light falls on them from the window in the background, so I cannot make out their eyes clearly, but I sense
that all three of them are looking across at me, since I am
standing on the very spot where Genewein the accountant
stood with his camera. The young woman in the middle is
blonde and has the air of a bride about her. The weaver to her
left has inclined her head a little to one side, whilst the
woman on the right is looking at me with so steady and
relentless a gaze that I cannot meet it for long. I wonder what
the three women's names were – Roza, Luisa and Lea, or
Nona, Decuma and Morta, the daughters of night, with
spindle, scissors and thread.

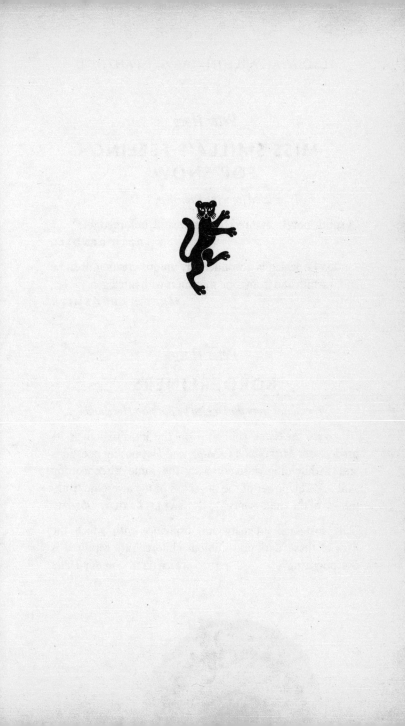

Peter Høeg

MISS SMILLA'S FEELING
FOR SNOW

Translated from the Danish by F. David

"A subtle novel, yet direct, clever, wistful, unforgettable"
RUTH RENDELL

"Smilla Jaspersen is a wonderfully unique creation of snow
and warmth and irony. She shimmers with intelligence"
MARTIN CRUZ SMITH

Peter Høeg

BORDERLINERS

Translated from the Danish by Barbara Haveland

"It exerts the same chill grip on the imagination as its
predecessor *Miss Smilla's Feeling for Snow*, posing questions
and withholding answers with the same disconcerting
skill . . . The power of the novel lies in the awesome truth-
fulness of the child's voice"   **SALLY LAIRD**, *Observer*

"The sustained intensity and brilliance with which the
lives of these 'dark and dubious children' are captured is
overpowering"   **JOHN MELMOTH**, *Sunday Times*

Cees Nooteboom

THE FOLLOWING STORY

Translated from the Dutch by Ina Rilke

Winner of the 1993 Aristeion European Literature Prize

"He is a fabulist who tells profound, elegant and disturbing stories, and meditates on the way stories are essential parts of our lives and thoughts. He is a major European writer, and *The Following Story* is a slender masterpiece"

A. S. BYATT, *Daily Telegraph*

"Sharp elegant prose . . . It recalls, in tone, Vladimir Nabokov. The language is, by turns, delicately allusive and rich, even ripely comic"

D. J. ENRIGHT, *Times Literary Supplement*

"Nothing is what it seems in this deceptively light and enchantingly amusing novella . . . one puts the novel down, only to start again, immediately, at page one"

MICHAEL IGNATIEFF, *Sunday Times*

Richard Ford

INDEPENDENCE DAY

Winner of the 1995 Pulitzer Prize and
the PEN/Faulkner Award

"It is nothing less than the story of the twentieth century
itself . . . Ford has created an extraordinary epic"

PENNY PERRICK, *The Times*

"Confirmation of a talent as strong and varied as American
fiction has to offer"

ELIZABETH HARDWICK, *New York Review of Books*

"A book that leaves you feeling more uplifted, more consoled,
than you did before reading it"

MICK BROWN, *Daily Telegraph*

"Frank Bascombe has earned himself a place beside Willy
Loman and Harry Angstrom in our literary landscape"

CHARLES JOHNSON, *New York Times*

Dermot Healy

A GOAT'S SONG

Winner of the 1994 Encore Award

"*A Goat's Song*, the story of two savage break-ups, is a rare and powerful book . . . At the end, intellectually aroused, emotionally wrenched, stunned with the imagery of place and drink and crumpled hopes, I was literally shaking"

E. ANNIE PROULX

"Intensity, passion, vivid characterization and a bold way with big themes" JAN DALLEY, *Independent on Sunday*

"It is a beautiful piece of work; no doubt about it, the real stuff" JAMES KELMAN

"I have read *A Goat's Song* three times now and I am going back to read it again . . . It haunts my dreams"

PATRICK MCCABE, *Sunday Tribune*

Giuseppe Tomasi di Lampedusa

THE LEOPARD

Translated from the Italian by Archibald Colquhoun

"The poetry of Lampedusa's novel flows into the Sicilian countryside . . . a work of great artistry" **PETER ACKROYD**

"Every once in a while, like certain golden moments of happiness, infinitely memorable, one stumbles on a book or writer, and the impact is like an indelible mark. Lampedusa's *The Leopard*, his only novel, and a masterpiece, is such a work" **BRUCE ARNOLD**, *Independent*

Boris Pasternak

DOCTOR ZHIVAGO

Translated from the Russian by
Manya Harari and Max Hayward

"The first work of genius to come out of Russia since the Revolution" **V. S. PRITCHETT**

"A book that made a most profound impression upon me and the memory of which still does . . . not since Shakespeare has love been so fully, vividly, scrupulously and directly communicated . . . The novel is a total experience, not parts or aspects: of what other twentieth-century work of the imagination could this be said?"

ISAIAH BERLIN, *Sunday Times*

Eduardo Mendoza

THE YEAR OF THE FLOOD

Translated from the Spanish by Nick Caistor

"A magnificent short novel . . . a rural elegy and political fable and an adventure story all in one"
MICHAEL EAUDE, *Times Literary Supplement*

"All the characters and relationships are sharply and subtly drawn"
JOHN SPURLING, *Sunday Times*

Jan Wiese

THE NAKED MADONNA

Translated from the Norwegian by Tom Geddes

"Certainly one of the finest pieces of fiction to have emerged from Norway in the last decade. Beautifully translated . . . it carves a curious niche somewhere between Umberto Eco and Hans Christian Andersen, crossing complex historical mystery with moral fable"
PAUL SUSSMAN, *Spectator*

Georges Perec

LIFE, A USER'S MANUAL

Translated from the French by David Bellos

"A dazzling, crazy-quilt monument to the imagination"

PAUL AUSTER, *New York Times*

"One of the great novels of the century"

GABRIEL JOSIPOVICI, *Times Literary Supplement*

Robert Hughes

THE FATAL SHORE

"An extraordinary, vivid, yet authentic account of the birthpangs of a nation. A work of real distinction"

PHILIP ZIEGLER

"An enthralling account of the convict settlement of Australia, thoroughly researched and excellently written, brimming over with rare and pungent characters, and tales of pathos, bravery, and horror" **PETER MATTHIESSEN**

To join the mailing list and for a full list of titles please write to

THE HARVILL PRESS
84 THORNHILL ROAD
LONDON N1 1RD, UK

enclosing a stamped-addressed envelope

The Good Enough Mother

by

Anoushka Beazley

First published in Great Britain in 2016 by Larchwood Press.

Copyright © 2016 by Anoushka Beazley.

The right of Anoushka Beazley to be identified as the Author of the Work has been asserted by her in accordance with the Copyright, Designs and Patents Act of 1988.

British Library Cataloguing in Publication Data: a catalogue record for this title is available from the British Library.

Library of Congress Catalog Card Number: on file.

ISBN: 978-0-9934368-0-2

Cover design: I Do Book Covers: www.idobookcovers.com

Printed and bound in Great Britain.

For Max

Part One

If you're happy and you know it, go fuck yourself

Drea Peiris, age 9

September 6th – Monday

Today was the day I was planning to kill myself but then I read Alex's note and, from there, I became unreservedly and altogether distracted. Alex was a school teacher. A linguaphile. A lover of young minds still malleable and awaiting instruction. The fact that he couldn't keep it in his trousers long enough to leave the classroom was but a casual digression. Despite this penile lapse, Alex was a staunch patriot of the learned institutional experience so leaving me and his fourteen-year-old daughter on the first day of the new term was more organised than pointed. You had to know Alex. He wasn't trying to hurt us, he just adored school – he used to tell me, 'Drea, all manner of good things begin on that first day.'

It was auspicious, apparently.

School was also a big thing for Ava. Alex's daughter from his first marriage, Ava had come to live with us when she was four years old. It might have been nice to think that some of me had rubbed off on her. However, the things that bond us to our children are not always obvious and her need to achieve was more than a little disappointing.

School was a similarly big thing for me. It filled me with a dreaded sense of foreboding anticipation. A nervous apprehension about I don't know what. There was still, after all these years, an indescribable but escalating anxiety that chilled me to my bones, made me shudder in the playground and quiver at the gates.

'Aren't you taking me in today? I can't be late.' I couldn't bear her dedication. Was that meant to mean something to me – this unspoken threat of an isosceles triangle? She was so eager to learn and completely oblivious to my scholastic emotional landmines. Ava belonged to a species insensitive to any activity not occurring within a millimetre of their physical body. Teenagers.

She callously ripped open the curtains, steering the sunlight in my direction and searing my face. I felt like a vampire touched by the hand of an irreverent hellion hunter. The heavy brown velvet had resisted yellowing, these aged and depressing curtains epitomising the mausoleum that was our house. We lived in the type of place that developers offer a lot of money for so they can gut it and start again. Knock down walls, raise ceilings, install bi-fold doors as the focal point of large, open-plan spaces, rip out carpets and shine up floor boards to capture that modern period feel. We, instead, shimmied dust from one small pokey room to another, a rotten wooden door opening out to a shapeless garden full of weeds and rubbish. Nicotine-stained, embossed wallpaper matched worn fabric lampshades. The most modern thing about our house was our neighbours.

The thing about being left by someone was the time it took to start again. He'd left the letter – that was Alex, ever the cliché – under my pillow, which he knew I turned over incessantly in efforts to recover its first fluffiness, so I was bound to find it. After a time, people just know things about one another. Reams of data never efficiently utilised but acquired all the same. It had sat suspiciously amidst loose, curly black strands of hair that lay rough like knotted bed weed. I crumpled it into the palm of my hand and, sliding it along the bed sheet, shoved it back where it had come from. It wasn't fit reading for a child/teenager – even I knew that. It had come dressed in a small cream envelope.

Innocuous. Like it was dressed for a wedding or a birthday
or even a fucking bar mitzvah. Not that Alex was religious,
more atheist than anything. In fact, what did Alex believe
in? Himself. And that in having a younger woman on his
arm he'd at least be offered the promise of eternal youth.
It was irritating that my anger might have been mistaken,
under the circumstances, for jealousy. I was not jealous of
Poppy. I knew I wasn't because I honestly wished her no
harm. Even when I thought of the two of them together,
being usurped provoked no reaction. But the more I thought
about it, the more I realised that it wasn't the other woman
who was the issue here. For me, although obviously not for
Alex, my thoughts kept returning to Ava. As her parents, were
we not responsible for ensuring she'd receive the best start
in life? Today didn't seem like the definition of a good start.
Why hadn't I slept? The newlyweds next door had kept me
awake. The girl had got all excited when she discovered
I was from Sri Lanka, as if that made us the same. Like this
connected us. Like our parents coming from the same country
could magically make our life experiences interchangeable.
She was a baking soda milkshake, all frothy and bland. It was
coming back to me now: her incessant panting through the
wall, sounding like an asthmatic puppy; no doubt his over-
exuberant cock causing the clamour. I could hear them going
at it in the kitchen. I hoped she'd slide off the counter and
do herself a spinal injury, but that probably wouldn't solve
anything. He seemed to be the kind of guy that would get off
on screwing a paraplegic – although I'm sure the paraplegic
would prove a far more interesting fuck than the wife. She
was one of those save-the-world types. The ones who, no
matter how busy they are, will always stop for the unemployed
university graduate swinging a clipboard, collecting credit-card
details for emaciated children in Africa. With a half-smile and
a deep sigh, these dearly accosted martyrs always trot off the

long number on the front as if they are coerced somehow, like they didn't have a choice and they couldn't have kept on walking past the debt-ridden smiling monkey. Choices. They were a marvellous invention. What was the point of limiting them when life took care of that all on its own?

The morning spilt brightly into the room like a peppy girlfriend. September was unashamedly still in bed with summer. Another wonderful day to be alive. Maybe I could make a noose for myself out of the curtains. Roll up, roll up, and welcome everyone to the greatest show on earth. Life? Bollocks. I had limited interest in life and even less interest in the school run. Or more accurately, I fucking HATED the school run.

'Where's Dad?' asked Ava.

'How should I know?' Oh God. My breath smelled foul. Was this why he left me? Left us?

'Are you okay?'

'Head… thing. Ache,' I muttered.

'Do you want some tablets?'

'No thanks. I've got.'

My mind went straight to the container at the bottom of my bag. Years ago I'd counted out fifty paracetamol and placed them in an empty plastic medicine bottle for this very day. As time went by, the only thing that changed was which bag they travelled in. They were my blankie. My crystal. My talisman. They were there so that when life got rough I knew there was a panic button I could press. I carried them everywhere.

I had always thought I'd make a day of it. Go and see a movie, maybe visit the National Gallery, have a nice steak and a couple of good single malt whiskies, and then take the lot. Probably in a park. Not because I liked parks. I couldn't actually bear parks. In my whole life, I had never been to as many parks as I had since Ava came along. Were children born loving parks? Pasta I could understand, but parks? Hideous places, which only goes to confirm how stupid children are. My main issue with them was the grass. Nasty stuff hiding a veritable multitude of creepy crawlies, not to mention canine excrement that lay in wait. How in God's name was this faecal cesspit supposed to induce calming meditative strolls in the peaceful solitude of one's thoughts? I personally did not know as, without warning, there could be a squelch, telling you that the sole of your shoe is now covered in dog poo. You are then left with the delightful task of finding something wet enough, large enough and strong enough to remove the offending substance. No, the park was not to be mistaken as an essential place to visit before I killed myself. The park was chosen specifically because of its respect for oblivion. People often closed their eyes on a park bench and no one thought twice about it. They were left alone in the soliloquy of their thoughts, unfettered by life. No one would notice me until it was too late and I liked the idea of being *in* the outside. A refreshing change from being on the outside. Sadly, the park would have to wait. Damn you, Alex.

Ava started brushing her teeth in the bedroom. Alex must have written only to me as Ava's casual demeanour suggested she knew nothing. He hadn't meant to be so deliberately aggravating; I was sure of that. It actually wasn't his style. Alex was far less obtuse than he appeared, which always meant that people only liked him once they'd heard about his likeable qualities from someone else. And despite the fact that leaving his partner and child after ten years wasn't the most congenial thing he'd ever done, he would not have intended to encumber me as well as leave me. Alex was old English: an upper-middle-class socialist, a repressed an awkward communicator – they all were in his family. And yet oddly, they'd all chosen to go into teaching. Maybe it was their way of connecting. However, despite Alex's general good character, nothing changed the fact that his leaving was a huge inconvenience. The bastard had stolen my idea. The professor was a plagiarist. I was the one who should be leaving. I was all ready to leave and I was going forever. It was my denouement, not his. How dare he sabotage my solo, which I had been preparing for no less than my whole life, for his paltry attempt at a dramatic exit? And not only was I still alive, I was alone. With a kid. In private school.

'I wondered if Amelia could come over for a sleepover soon. Maybe you could call, Mum,' said Ava through a mouthful of toothpaste. 'I'm sure her mother would appreciate you calling as they always need help for the bake sale.'

Dear Lord. This morning was turning into a fucking onslaught. A military attack. Were recent events – and by recent, I do mean in the last hour – not traumatic enough that I must be injected with this fatal cocktail of mundane and obligation? A sleepover with Amelia Salter *and* a bake sale? Seriously? Ava and I had unspoken agreements. I wasn't interested in any of her friends or her school life and she, in turn, would not force me into situations where I needed to behave as if I was. Plus, a sleepover was by no means as innocent as it sounded. Amelia's mother was a colossal bitch with a pole of some considerable thickness admirably, and firmly, wedged within her anal passage and, if Amelia stayed over at ours, I would have to engage in a conversation with said anal wedger. What's the big deal right – it's just conversation. I should point out here that I had never had a conversation with the woman, but I suspected even a banal and fleeting encounter with Regina Salter required effort. No doubt she thought I was weird, unemployed and slightly overweight; neither middle-class enough nor the right sort of Asian to be living in the affluent suburb of Gatlin (and that's if she thinks of me at all). The truth being accurate is hardly the point. Not to mention the fact that it could summon a barrage of childhood traumas rushing out of the rotting woodwork. Memories of chases down school corridors. Gangs of girls racing to see which one could slam me into a wall first. Taunts such as 'Wipe that dirt off your face?' and 'Go home, Paki' come flooding back like a montage sequence for club med sponsored by the Ku Klux Klan. Not that Regina Salter was racist. Well, she could be – wasn't everyone? But it wasn't even about Regina Salter. It was more to do with the fact that I hated school with every inch of my being and wanted nothing to do with anyone that might remind me of it. But because I will be the one unable to hide my buoyant tedium, it is me who will appear the one with the problem. Regina Salter will talk about her concerns regarding a teacher I don't know – and don't care to – or an over-subscribed-with-a-waiting-list extra-curricular class in intensive Mandarin for eight-year-olds, and I will find it impossible to keep the 'are you fucking having a laugh?' expression off my face. Boredom standing by, ready to inflate around my body like an emergency life vest. And I will need to smoke some weed to even contemplate the fucking bake sale.

'I know it's not really your thing, but—'

A bake sale? Not my thing? How about I make a dozen red velvet cupcakes with a heavy dusting of ricin sprinkles, PTA consumption only?

'All the mums bring something and last year some people were saying that...' Ava trailed off.

Some people, hmmm?

'Saying what?'

'Just that you don't really participate much,' Ava replied coyly, knowing full well that she was treading on dangerous ground. Her lamentable obsession with Amelia Salter was making her do things she shouldn't, asking me to do things I normally wouldn't. Given that her father had just left her, I chose to overlook her impudence. 'I'll bring something, Ava.' I kicked my legs around under the covers to get the blood moving. And just to kick.

'You're great, Mum. Oh, and Grandpa has left his porn on again.' Ava bounced out of my room, thankfully taking that awful stench of youth and optimism with her.

When I looked at Ava, I couldn't remember ever being that happy at her age – maybe at any age – being that together with myself. Sure, she had her fourteen-year-old moments of childish indecision, but they were few and far between and, for the most part, it was she who stabilised me rather than the other way around. How would she feel about her dad leaving? Were they close? No, not particularly. Alex was a difficult man to get close to. He craved adulation but wasn't in a position to offer much insight the other way. Outwardly, Ava didn't appear to need him, but doesn't every girl need her father? Didn't 'absent father' syndrome unite the whores and the virgins? I personally wouldn't have settled down with an older man, or indeed taken my panties off for so many cab drivers, if I'd felt closer to my father. Someone told me once that children choose their parents before they're even born. Ramblings of a new age psychopath, definitely. It's as well thought out a plan as racial profiling at airport security or the pro-life movement. Even so, Ava didn't choose this.

The sun twinkled like a girlish courtesan, hopping from cupboard to dresser, unsure where to lay her balmy touch. A yellow bath of colour tinged the bedroom from the large bay windows, all the way to the faded flowery wallpaper behind the bedstead. The seat beneath the window was the only part of the house not silently trapped in the seventies and screaming out for modernisation. It wound around the entire width of the bay, the leaves of the oak on the street reaching out to touch the glass. We'd picked the house up at auction in a probate sale. This seemed to bother other people, but not us. I felt comforted knowing that someone had made memories in the house, and now they were dead. Actually, it would have freaked me out, knowing the people who had lived in the house before us were still alive but somewhere else. As if their memories were alive too, but cast aside – not good enough anymore, resentful and suspicious of new residents. I slipped my hand back underneath the pillow to retrieve the letter. Alex was leaving. Fine. But what about the money? Isn't that the reason most couples stay together – it's too expensive not to?

What a difference twenty-four hours can make. It could have been Alex sat here reading my suicide note. Instead, it was I who was the proud owner of fifty redundant, killer paracetamol, imminent contributor to a PTA bake sale and mother. 'Mother' was the label that caused the most confusion. What made me a mother? My complete lack of maternal instinct? My overwhelming feeling of hatred for any and all activities associated with mothering, motherhood and, especially, the thought of other mothers? Or was it simply that I had a child? That seemed too easy.

My pyjamas went past my ankles, which I liked because it allowed me to dispense with slippers. I grabbed a cigarette from the drawer in the bedside table and foraged hard through a bunch of uninteresting correspondence, loose blister packs of out-of-date medicines and empty biscuit wrappers, searching for a lighter. I eventually closed my fingers around one. Eureka! Something needed to go right today and this would do for now. The flame crackled around the circular edge as the tobacco burned. Finally, a comforting sound.

Dear Drea,

Maybe this letter won't surprise you. I think it may have surprised me more. Poppy and I have decided to give France a try. I don't mean it to sound as trite as it might. She's got some research work at the university here and, well, I have to give it a shot. I know it was never your idea of heaven but it has always been mine, and she laughs at my jokes – like you used to.

The downside to my new life is that Poppy doesn't want Ava. I've tried to reason with her but she's young. I cannot even pretend that Poppy wants me all to herself, she just doesn't want someone else's kid. I know it's not very fair. After all, Ava is my daughter, but she likes you. We'll have to put her in a state school as I just won't have enough for fees and maintenance on the chateau (it's a very small chateau). Ava will be fine, it'll build character.

I am truly sorry about all this,
                    Alexander

Oh, Alex, you prick. It wasn't the younger woman I begrudged him for. Wasn't the French country mid-life crisis or even the shame and embarrassment he'd put on special order for me to last the duration of the entire school year. No, it was the way he'd just pronounced me a mother. A single mother no less. Go be with your younger, perkier whore, Alex. It's not like I don't know how it works – that was how we had met. I was Alex's student; he was twice my age and unhappily married to Ava's mother. Clearly some men had a type. Alex had a pattern. But leaving Ava? She did not deserve that. Ava deserved to have a dad who gave a shit. How was pulling her from her school that she loved going to do anything other than make her hate school? Hate her life. And he expected me to stand by and watch this car crash just happen? The dissolution of a perfectly good girl via badly managed secondary education. Fuck you, Alex.

I thought I knew what my life looked like. I knew that when I opened my eyes in the morning, I'd be in my house where I lived with my twisted-up, geriatric father, my cheating boyfriend and his philanthropic daughter. I knew that this was my life because it's what I saw every day. But now Alex had left and had removed his whole self out of the house to live somewhere else, leaving only a chalk marking of where a person used to be. I thought of Ava and suddenly felt a flash of panic. It could have been Ava who was gone and that would have felt completely different. It's only when something unexpectedly changes that you truly get to see what your life looks like by what's left behind. And in my life, I had a fucking daughter. She might have come from Alex and that narcissistic ex-wife of his, but for ten years she had lived with us and now I was kind of glad that Poppy hadn't wanted her.

Ava stormed back into the bedroom and started opening drawers and cupboard doors in a minor frenzy. I folded the letter and stretched over the bed to slip it into my handbag.

'Why are all Dad's papers gone from the study?' she demanded. 'And his clothes aren't in the drawers.'

'Yes, we should talk about that,' I needed an ashtray, coffee, some uninterrupted time to kill myself and some advice on how to drop a bomb. 'Your father has decided to live with Poppy.'

'His research assistant?' she asked incredulously. Ava had a square jaw, a lot like a cat. And like a cat, her features oscillated from scared to wise very quickly. Perplexity left her face at the mention of Poppy's name; her brain subliminally processing past information – what harm could come from a herbaceous red flower? She folded her arms in front of her chest. She had questions. This was the kind of discussion that could get frustrating without answers.

'I mean "Poppy",' I said, 'really? There's about as much substance in a name like Poppy as there is in a—'

'Why would Dad live with Poppy?' she interrupted, arching her eyebrows. Ava was tall and gangly, and I was always surprised when she appeared remotely vulnerable – as if tall people should be immune from such sensitivities, sort of like giraffes, the way they walked around the zoo thinking it a charity luncheon of their choosing rather than a caged enclosure.

'Good question Ava. I'm pretty sure it's because…'

'Oh my God, he's having an affair!'

'That would be the right answer.'

'Again?' Ava started to pace, waving her hands around like a bipolar lollipop lady. 'Did you know?' That last question was accusatory. I felt it. As if it was my ignorance alone that had lit Alex's flame of desire underneath Poppy's stamen.

'"Again" is unfair. There has been no proper proof of others. Your father may have had a fondle here and there, a careless caress of the buttocks by the photocopier at a Christmas party, but I really don't think there's been anything like Poppy since, well, since me.'

'I don't believe this.'

'I think your father is in love, again.'

'And you didn't stop it?' demanded Ava.

'Stop it? Because I should have known that "research" is what the kids are calling fucking your assistant? No, I did not stop it because I did not know.'

'You didn't know?' she repeated.

'This is fun,' I said, lighting another cigarette.

'Well maybe if you made dinner once in a while, you'd have noticed he was eating somewhere else,' she spat priggishly.

'I didn't know he was eating out so often – fish.'

'Ugh. I'll be in the car. My first day at my new school and you've both turned me into another statistic. Just another product of a failed marriage. You haven't done any better than my real mum.' She slammed the door so hard it bounced opened again.

'I never actually married your father and I'm the only mother you've got coz the real one doesn't give a shit,' I screamed.

There is an outside possibility I could have handled that better. I pulled some jeans on and threw a baggy jumper over my pyjama top. And that's when I felt it: a pain, shooting and sudden in my abdomen. It took me by such surprise that I needed to hold onto the bedpost to steady myself. I grabbed my car keys and tried to walk it off. As I moved through the hallway, one hand on my stomach, I could see flashing images coming from Papa's room. I peered in. Ava was right; he had fallen asleep with the television on again, his headphones still in place. The framed picture of my mother on their wedding day made me gaze a moment longer. She wore a knee-length white dress with three-quarter length sleeves and a gold brooch in the shape of a flower pinned to her chest. On the screen, there was another woman, bent over the kitchen table; her sari hitched up past her buttocks. A man was behind her, thrusting clumsily as she gyrated with the force of his hands on her shoulders, waiting for him to ejaculate – presumably so she could finish cutting the onions for his chicken curry.

At seventy-five, Papa had acquired a fervid taste for Tamil porn. We discovered his new pastime when he came to live with us. Would it have been less disconcerting if the films had higher production values? The fact was we didn't get involved in each other's business; it wasn't who we were. The headphones were a compromise saving the whole house from climaxing together.

Stab. There it was again, but this time in my chest. I tried to breathe, but the air felt shallow and hard to find. I looked at my father asleep on the bed. This was a man I'd never known. I saw blurry images of me as a child, about three years old; someone was crying. Colours, Papa smoking a cigarette. He had not raised me, had never been around to know who I was or who I was trying to be. Anger rose up in me like flames; the true realisation of Alex leaving me – what his absence really meant – sucker-punched me.

I was a mother now. In being abandoned I had suddenly been charged with protecting my young, and it was this feeling, this untenable responsibility that had dug into my flesh and caused me to wince in pain. This hideous urge to give another human being what I had never had. To afford her a better life. From some unknown source, there ran an unconditional river of magnanimity. It was all on me now. Alex had forced me to grow up, without asking if that was something I even wanted to do. By having a child of my own, the fact that once I'd been someone's child automatically became less important, a watered-down version of the truth. I was not the main story anymore. Alex had taken my innocence when he left me with Ava. Plunging me into motherhood severed all nostalgic ties with my own childlike identity. I read the letter again. Yadda, yadda, yadda. Ha! State school. You dick. I don't think so. Thanks for the heads up on the affair, but there would be no state school for Ava. My daughter would be staying at Gatlin Private School for Girls.

I put Alex's letter in my bag. It would serve as a reminder that I was on my own and –though I didn't know how – somehow I would find the money for Ava's school fees.

30 Minutes Later

The car was quiet. We travelled in silence. I smoked a joint out of the window whilst Ava, glowering, had turned most of her body sideways as if she'd rather be strapped to the roof rack than inside with me. I was enjoying the peace. I'd let the little bitch stew. She thought she'd wounded me with that 'real mum' dig. She'd have to do better than that. I wasn't her real mum, fact. Another fact was my boiling abhorrence for reverse parking and people who forced me to reverse park.

'What are you eating?' I growled.

'Nothing,' said Ava, her mouth chewing and her hand covering what suspiciously resembled a piece of toast.

'Are you eating toast in my car?' I asked, my voice candied, interspersed with interested overtones.

'Yes,' she admitted. Foolishly.

'With jam?' I enquired lightly.

'Yes,' she answered.

'Are you fucking having a laugh?' I screamed. 'Jam? In my car. I fucking hate jam! There will be no jam in my house *or* in my car, do you fucking understand me?'

I grabbed the toast from her trembling fingers and threw it out of the window. The toast flew further than I'd expected, which diverted my attention and caused me to brake suddenly. A gigantic black Land Rover, which had stopped ten feet in front of us, was unable to pass as an even bigger Range Rover was blocking it. We were behind the car that was behind the Range Rover and there were two more cars behind us.

My stomach began to fold into knots at the thought of turning the steering wheel into various positions, all guaranteed to cause offence. It was exactly this kind of shit that was impossible to avoid on the school run, no matter how careful one might be, because there were just so many idiots behind the wheel. I burned with rage that no one had yet declared the road a one-way street, which would have prevented this daily debacle. There were no more than ten inches between my car and those parked on either side of me. At the top of the thin, tree-lined road sat Gatlin School for Girls. A gargantuan mansion house that extended much further back than its modest double doors implied. At the same time every day, as if under a spell, mothers all over the town would leave what they were doing, get in their cars, and drive towards Gatlin. Handmaids of their own volition.

A black door swung out and a slim woman with perfectly blow-dried chestnut hair descended from the Range Rover. As she did, a khaki green door opened and a tall, slender, dip-dyed-blonde exited the Land Rover.

'There's Amelia's mum, Regina,' said Ava, who had found the strength and necessity to interrupt her staged silence with this breaking news bulletin. It seemed to light something up in Ava. It was unclear at this point who she wanted to be friends with more, Regina or her daughter. 'Ooh, she's highlighted her hair. Can I go?'

'No, I think these people want me to reverse,' I said with hesitation.

'You don't know how to reverse,' said Ava.

'I'm aware of that.' My driving skills were completely acceptable and totally functional, except in situations where I needed to reverse in a straight line.

'So what are you going to do?'

'I'll just have to do my best,' I answered.

'Shouldn't your best and your worst be easier to tell apart?'

'Who is the other woman?' I asked. 'The one with the brown hair.'

'That's Catherine's mum, Ann Donnington.'

Yes, I'm sure it was. I mean, did it get any more lacklustre than 'Ann'? Maybe, in fact, I knew who it was, but had forgotten. Maybe that was the truth about the Boleyn woman – it wasn't uxoricide, it was suicide. She just couldn't bear the tedium of her forgettable moniker one minute longer – 'off with my head,' she cried gaily! 'Henry, you can say it was all your idea!' I grinned at the thought.

'What's so funny?' Ava demanded.

'Nothing.'

'They're both on the PTA,' she chirped. It appeared all was forgotten between Ava and me. Simply being in the general vicinity of these women, I had redeemed myself through osmosis.

The owners of the houses on Gatlin Road began to emerge. I looked in the mirror behind me. There was a five-car tailback at least. This was the height of excitement for the residents of Gatlin. The only time life had been so scintillating was when the dustmen had arrived on a Friday instead of a Monday. It was that kind of town. All the front doors were painted in different shades of matt: breakfast-room green and mole's breath grey. There were stained-glass, luminous coloured window panels in original Edwardian designs, ornate door handles and restored tiled paths.

Regina and Ann air-kissed, exchanging brief pleasantries, and I found myself momentarily drawn to these women. Ann, Regina and two other mothers, Henrietta and Penelope, were all very close and had a lot in common. They were all moneyed, all owners of environmentally unsound motor vehicles and all mothers of monstrosities. But that was not

what interested me. Regina's coat had the letters P-R-A-D-A
written on the back in white plastic lettering. As she pointed
and gesticulated, explaining her grand plan to reverse into
a space on the left, a leather tote with the gold lettering of
Mulberry swung gently off her arm like a metal rod from
a wind chime. Ann's coat had the letters C-H-A-N-E-L on
the side panels, as if it was a badly kept secret, and her black
leather bag bulged grotesquely around the letters D-K-N-Y. I
watched these women, their fashion alphabets dancing in the
air. They broke away, heading back to their respective off-
road army vehicles. As they did, Regina's gigantic rock-sized
diamond ring hit a sunray. It sat fat on her yoga-stretched
fingers, like the missing aid for a third world country.

'Mum, you need to go.' Ava's strained, high-pitched plea
brought me back to a cacophony of honking. Okay then. The
car behind had already reversed to give me more space to do
the same. How kind. I turned the wheel to the left and pressed
the accelerator. I regretted the manoeuvre as soon as my foot
touched the pedal, but it was too late. Unintentionally, I had
forced the vehicle into an impossible dichotomy where we
either scraped the body of the car on my left or knocked out
the wing mirror of the car on my right. A physics equation
floated across the windscreen. Force equals mass times
velocity. I decided that the extent to which I would damage
either the body or the mirror all depended on how fast we
went. I put my hand on the gear stick whilst pushing my foot
down hard on the accelerator.

'Mum!'

The car screeched and shuddered as I tried to gain control
of the steering wheel. 'Wheee!'

Everyone was honking. Regina, Ann, passing cars, parked
cars. I heard a crack. That's ok; it wasn't my mirror. I careered
all the way around the corner where I parked and tried to
get my breath back. I figured if anyone to whom those cars

belonged had actually seen me, they'd find me soon enough. Now I was out of the way, I was less bothered. And even less interested in the opinions of house owners shouting out their disapproval, feeling the need to inform me that they thought I should drive better. Get in line.

'I can't believe you just did that,' said Ava, aghast.

'I think you're probably better off on your own from here,' I replied. Ava slammed the door as she got out and the car gave a desultory shake.

A silver BMW estate space wagon pulled up alongside me.

'Excuse me,' I shouted. 'What are you doing?'

'I'm parking,' said Penelope Coultard.

'Then I can't get out,' I said.

'There's plenty of room,' she replied. I stared at her, fascinated. Her mouth was moving, although her recently lifted face, unfortunately, could not do the same.

'Have you seen the size of your car?'

'Sorry?' She did not seem sorry.

'I said, have you seen the size of your car?'

'I don't believe the size of my car is any of your concern,' she said, hissing slightly.

'Look, you need to understand that if you choose to drive a tank to school, you need to park in a way that allows other people to move their normal-sized cars.'

'Drea Peiris isn't it? It's your husband that has that nice young research assistant helping him with his work.'

'Boyfriend.'

'You're not married? I see. Wake up on the wrong side of the bed? Well, as there's no call for rudeness I'll say good morning.' So she knew. She was always at the school involving herself in one thing or another and had probably seen them together. I could bet Alex wasn't discreet – not enough for Penelope's beady eyes, anyway.

'Next time you go to bed, I hope you die in it, bitch. Then

we'll see who wakes up on what side.' Her mouth dropped
open. I left her standing on the pavement.

Gatlin village green had one of every kind of shop that a
middle-class family needed to survive. As I walked down the
street, I pondered on where I should go. A butcher whose
meat and sausages were farmed in the spacious green fields
of Kent, where cattle listened to Bach whilst grazing. A
fishmonger – purveyors of fish caught leaping in and out of
clear freshwater streams. A dressmaker with an elite handful
of appropriately sized designer brands and some essential yet
seasonal accessories. A ceramic store proud to house clay-fired
art in an 'experimentation with form and time.' An apothecary
where, at short notice, you could pick up a fennel and birch
hand cream for the completely natural price of £19. A tea
room producing such creations as loin of venison with a red
wine jus served with prosecco. And last, but by no means least,
a milliner.

This morning I did not need the milliner. I had not, in
fact, ever needed a milliner, but I wasn't ruling it out. A good
funeral was always just around the corner. Today I needed
the apothecary as the eczema on Papa's hands had flared up
again from all his wanking. The doctor had said as much the
last time it had happened and had recommended a mild steroid
cream for dermatitis. It was evident his latest batch of Tamil
porn possessed a more emotionally charged storyline. As I was
about to cross the road, I saw Tabatha Crosly-Burke running
out of the apothecary. She had a hoodie over her head and was
so intent on looking down that she didn't see the car until it
screeched to a halt inches from her feet.

'What the hell are you doing?' screamed the cabbie. That
was when I saw her wet-streaked face with her small and puffy
eyes. Hunched and crying, she was trying desperately to go
unnoticed in the world. How radical a transformation this was

from the girl who ruled Gatlin; mini breasts projected in a push-up bra, blonde hair swishing in a high ponytail and her body taking up space, needlessly imposing, like her father. She had obviously left the house without her usual 'my name is Tabatha Crosly-Burke, daughter of Henry Crosly-Burke, largest financial donor to Gatlin School, Managing Director of Stellar Sportswear (and massive twat)' face. It was this face that enabled her to walk the halls of Gatlin as if they were hers. Her father's money was literally woven into the rugs that covered the Gatlin floors, and the girl acted as if it were at her behest that the teachers and students walked upon them. I wondered what could possibly cause such upset in the life of Tabatha Crosly-Burke.

The classic quiz show Family Fortunes came to mind where a family of five attention-starved individuals appeared on television hoping to win a car, a holiday or a cash sum in a valiant attempt to transform their dull existences. They were asked to guess which answers to questions were to be found amongst the top five answers collated from a general survey. The question: why was Tabatha upset? The most obvious five answers, in ascending order, would be: the Crosly-Burke heated pool was being drained for cleaning; Henry has refused to pay for all thirty of her best friends to ski in Aspen; a venereal disease; parents are divorcing. But most likely – and what I'd put my money on – a chipped nail. Thinking about it, Alex's recent actions had a good chance of turning me into one of those idiots who fantasised about going on one of those awful game shows myself. The cash they paid you for the humiliation could serve as Ava's tuition. Don't knock populism 'til you need it.

Tabatha made eye contact with the cabbie momentarily. He honked his horn as she ran in front of his car and disappeared down a side road. The cabbie screeched off muttering expletives. Maybe I could ask Henry Crosly-Burke to make a few donations to me. I could become the 'Drea Foundation' – that's what you needed to announce a charity case: a worthy foundation. However, I suspected that helping my daughter to remain in private school after her father had absconded with an opiate would not be high on Henry's to-do list. This was a great shame as they had more than enough money and probably wouldn't even notice. An insidious throbbing crept up on my left temple, reappearing whenever I thought about Ava's school fees.

I opened the white wooden door to the apothecary and a loud bell reverberated unsubtly. Not that I cared, but it crossed my mind that, for those customers who might be less inclined to share with the entire shop that they were about to purchase dermatitis cream to soothe their father's out-of-control masturbating, a more muted method of customer announcement might be more appropriate. But this was the brainchild of Dick Spencer. A transparent invention to repeatedly declare his symbolic arrival into his own shop. I thought it admirable that Dick embodied his name with such passion. For women called 'Joy' or 'Hope', it might be wearing having to display such eternal joviality and optimism, yet for Dick to continually be nothing but a dick, it seemed effortless. The apothecary had been in the Spencer family forever, but Dick was the only Spencer who had not trained as a doctor. It was a true feat of organisation that he managed to accommodate that many products as well as the extremely large chip on his shoulder.

Dick was anal. The white wooden shelves were neatly stacked and he immediately replaced every empty space with another item so the shop always looked as if it had just opened for business. Row upon row of potions of promise, lotions and creams, herbal concoctions for everything from collagen to coughs sat in square and rectangular boxes with simple gold lettering, although there was nothing simple about them. The ladies of Gatlin cleansed with the nectar of Hawaiian hibiscus flowers and moisturised with fine particles of Japanese sea urchins. I handed Dick the prescription for Papa's wanking ointment and noticed a flush of red pass his cheeks. A bead of sweat sat just underneath his nose and his face was stretched tight with irritation.

'We're closed,' he snapped, looking straight at me. He wore a yellow bow tie, black braces and a white shirt. Glasses would have softened his face, but instead, his sharp eyes stared angrily out onto the world. He stood more than a foot taller than me, but his inherent rigidity and stiffness shortened him slightly on his left side.

'That's not what the sign says.'

In reaction to my inflammatory comment, he stormed out past the counter, flung the roped plastic sign round so it faced the other way and stomped back. 'Closed.'

Hurricane Dick knocked me sideways as he brushed roughly past, but his leaving had revealed a gaping hole in the display behind him. A packet of anti-depressants was missing from the top shelf and I remembered that his last customer had been Tabatha Crosly-Burke.

'That's fine. I just need my cream.' Clearly something had rattled Dick's cage. 'Maude told me last time I came in that she'd put some on order.'

Dick was silent. He looked straight into my eyes with a steely glare and only then did he robotically move one arm, and, without averting his gaze, retrieve a notepad from underneath the counter.

'My wife ordered you some ointment last week. It's in the back.' My wife. Dear Lord. Who does that? Maude was the secretary at Gatlin. I saw her every day at school and she was actually one of the normal ones. Dick knew we were friends but always insisted on referring to her as 'my wife' as if I didn't know, as if I were an outsider, not worthy of being included in his world. Given her appearance of normality, I concluded that it must have been an unfortunate absence of sanity that had caused Maude to take an oath to spend the rest of her life with this man. What a dick. I really hated it when he spoke to me like that. He thought nothing of me or of the consequences of such dickishness. Few people do. For instance, leaving the ledger on the counter so provocatively… so open.

I looked up and could see his profile in the back of the shop searching through drawers. My hand stealthily moved forwards, my eyes on Dick. Twisting the ledger around, I brought it inches closer. The name Tabatha Crosly-Burke appeared every few weeks, and the order was always the same: Prozac. A popular anti-depressant for teenagers. I should know. What could a fourteen-year-old girl possibly be that depressed about? Then again, what wouldn't a fourteen-year-old girl be depressed about?

Dick had found Papa's cream. I tried to flick the ledger back to its original place but it spun across the counter with more force than I'd intended. Oh no. This situation was about to become an incident. In moments, it would be on the floor. If I reached out to grab it, he'd know for sure I'd read it. Dick strode back to me, his only objective being to get me out of his shop, and as his body became flush with the counter, it froze the runaway ledger.

'Thank you for your custom. Now, as I said, we are closed.' Dick had an annoying habit of believing that if he was overly polite, then he wasn't being rude. He had managed to be factual and factious. And Maude had thought it sensible to have a child with this man. I hoped it was their last.

It was a grey day. Unapologetic. Grey because it could be. It was pathetic the way people constantly worshipped the sun as if, without its blessing, their happiness was in jeopardy. Plenty of happy things could happen on a grey day. A prime example was Tabatha Crosly-Burke – moments away from a positively delirious bout of happiness that had all been made possible by collecting her Prozac. In fact, Tabatha was an inspiration. She was turning her life around. At the tender age of fourteen, Tabatha had come to the practical realisation that being the product of Henry and Henrietta Crosly-Burke and burdened by such pompous DNA precluded any predisposition to normality. I couldn't wait to tell Ava. Not that Ava would ever use such information to take Tabatha down, Ava was far too morally afflicted to be that genius. However, it would just be good for her to know, just to keep in the back of her mind for the next time Tabatha patronised her, which she had done before and would no doubt do again. The audacity of the little bitch. To stand there and get Ava to run errands when she was running around town with her little pills. It appeared she was a completely different girl out of school. Unrecognisable, like the mimic octopus – a magician of the sea who could literally change colour and texture to impersonate other creatures and avoid or intimidate predators. It was the work of a true survivor. Someone who found themselves in a predicament they were determined to overcome.

I walked to the tea room. Maude's younger sister Felicity was the manager. The Whitefields, Maude and Felicity's parents, were Christian missionaries, descendants of the Methodist Whitefields. Whilst Maude had married Dick Spencer, believing in her heart that his dictatorial demeanour would keep her on the straight and narrow, young Felicity had absconded to India with her Indian boyfriend and a backpack where she saw fit to donate stolen missionary funds to the boy's village. After the two survived a serious motorcycle accident in the Himalayas and, in an effort to curtail all future fraternising with girls on motorbikes, the boyfriend's family forced him into an arranged marriage with an armless local girl. Felicity's family brought her back to Gatlin with nothing but a book on Hinduism and a broken heart. He was the love of her life, but Christian missionaries save little Indian boys in order for them to grow up and become good Christians, not to grow up and marry their good Christian daughters. There wasn't enough Christian charity in the kitty for that kind of a scandal. The Whitefields needed to explain her mood, her tears and her desperate sadness, so the family re-named her broken heart 'a breakdown'. Much less shame in that.

I sat outside and lit a cigarette. The tar hit the back of my throat and the nicotine filled my lungs. It felt good. I became aware of a presence and looked up. Felicity's thinning gold hair was swept to the side and pinned with a fake blue flower. She wore a red silk dress with lavish gold embroidery, tights, flip-flops and a woolly hat. She scrubbed the table down.

'Hot chocolate please.'

'Nice hot drink to warm you up? Above 4,880 metres, the Himalayas are below freezing and permanently covered in snow,' said Felicity, with an incredulous air. I got the flask out of my bag and set it on the table. 'Whereas in the southern foothills, it can rise to about 30 degrees, which is not at all like the climate in Gatlin. Today we have some lovely scones with raspberry jam,' she went on.

I tried not to leave the house without my flask of whisky. Really, I just needed to take the edge off. In truth, the whole day had been so unbearably stressful, and I had this niggling feeling that Alex leaving me had been the least stressful part.

The parking had unnerved me considerably, as reversing manoeuvres on the school run always did. And my encounter with Dick was the last thing I needed today of all days. Though an encounter with Dick was the last thing I needed on any day.

'I don't eat jam. Just the hot chocolate.'

When Felicity returned, she had red powder marks on her forehead. I poured a whisky shot into my cup and looked up.

'After prayer we apply the holy ash,' she said, noticing me staring. 'I have just offered flowers to Goddess Kali, the all-worldly and all-masterful.'

Two grey lines were drawn across her forehead. Hadn't Dorothy and her merry band of misfits mentioned something similar about the Wizard of Oz?

'What are you praying for?' I asked. The whisky started to relax me around the edges. I felt the alcohol hitting my nerve receptors, slowing them down, telling them softly that 'everyting gon' be aiiight'.

'Success in my endeavours. I am embarking on a new vocation,' beamed Felicity, proudly.

The hot chocolate was helping to blanch the traumas of the morning, incidental though they were. Ava was the real problem. Or rather how to pay Ava's school fees. That was the weight on my mind – the unease that settled tightly around my chest like a Victorian bodice.

There was no ashtray so I flicked my cigarette onto the street. Unholy ash landed on Felicity's foot.

'I will accompany the students of Gatlin and introduce them to my homeland,' she said, shaking it off.

'England?'

'India. For the exchange programme. I am the co-ordinator. India is for me...' She went silent and I wondered at first whether she'd forgotten what it was she was trying to say, but then I saw her misting up. 'India, for me, is the place of my true birth. It is where my soul is the happiest. Where my essence and purpose unite. You understand?'

'You like it there,' I surmised.

'Goddess Kali teaches all of us that our dreams are who we are and that they are achievable by becoming strong and fierce women of our destinies. Tonight I'm taking a self-defence class,' said Felicity, her clear blue eyes smiling. 'Crime is big in India.' And that was when I had my epiphany. It was simple. Easy. Just follow the signs. The entire morning had been constructed on my behalf. Hand-stitched together like an intricate tapestry just for me. And everyone had played a part. I knew what I had to do. They were completely right: the mystics, the fate chasers and the destiny believers. Everything did happen for a reason. I looked up at Felicity and felt my mouth widen into a long, broad, satisfied smile.

That Evening

The houses of Gatlin clung to each other as the ferocious wind beat down upon their doors. I was home hours before the dark settled. I always smelled the weather before it came. Ever since I was young, I could tell if a storm was coming by the way my skin started to feel damp from the inside. Papa said it ran in the family. I'd instinctively turn the radiators up or put on an extra layer and then it would rain. Tonight I could feel an echo in my ears. Occasionally, a hollow flutter: the winds were on their way. The autumn nights heralded the end of the hedonistic summer. They could come suddenly, whispering secrets and following in long shadows as you walked home. However, tonight's wind was merely a warning, autumn simply a blind messenger – winter will see you soon.

Monday night. Exercise night. The mothers from the school would do an after-the-kids-had-gone-to-bed hour of pilates or yoga, or even yogalates if they were feeling frisky. An hour's workout aimed at tightening the unfortunate and unfairly designed inches of flab that replaced stomach muscle after childbirth. Exercising on a Monday got it out of the way, assuring no guilty interference with that 'small glass of wine' from Tuesday to Sunday.

There was no word from Alex. He had left his poetic offering under my pillow and ceased all contact. Alex was doing a Tabatha – being that octopus, re-inventing his life.

Could we really chastise the man for that? If anything, the opportunity to take the high road already existed as it was simply a matter of time before Poppy left him. She was letting him tag along on her adventure – which he thought was his own. However, it was one he would never have done if not for her.

I looked at the clock in the hall. It was a peculiar piece from a flea market – a wooden mermaid holding a glass face in her hands. Nearly time.

'Where are you going?' Ava sloped into my room and lay herself flat on the bed. Staring at the ceiling, she stretched out her arms wide by her side.

'I'm… taking a class,' I answered.

'What class?' Ava turned over, raising her head off the bed a few inches.

'Self-defence.'

'Why?'

'Because, Ava… listen to the weather out there. Anything can happen.'

'You're going to kick your way out of the wind?'

'My point being… be prepared. Have you had dinner?' I asked, trying to change the subject. I wore tracksuit bottoms and a sweatshirt with trainers. On the way home, I had driven out of town for some essentials, items not sold in Gatlin – such wares would have significantly affected house prices.

'No I haven't, but maybe you could drop me at Amelia's house?' Ava said coyly. She began twisting a ring of her curly brown hair around her fingers. Everybody had a tell.

'Has she invited you?' I knew the answer but I wanted to see if she'd lie; to see if she had a plan.

'No. Not yet, but I'm hoping, thinking, maybe she'll call soon as some of the girls are going over there and—'

'Ava, she doesn't even know who you are. You wait for this girl to notice you when you're right in front of her face and you think you're going to her house? And when you say girls, do you mean friends of yours? People I know?'

'No. Not exactly. I mean, I say hello to Tabatha sometimes.'

'Tabatha Crosly-Burke. These are the friends you think she's going to invite you to hang out with? Ava, seriously, have some pride. Get a life.' Ava rolled her eyes. She shifted over onto her side and curled into a ball. Of course she didn't have a plan. She wasn't my biological daughter. Ava's philosophy was hope for the best and then hope some more. She must get that from her father.

'Tabatha Crosly-Burke is average. If average is what you're aiming for to improve your social cachet, then fine. But maybe if you stopped trying to be so nice to these people, you'd have a chance to be interesting.' Ava winced. Somebody had to educate the girl. 'And next time Tabatha pisses you off, just so you know, she's clinically depressed and popping pills. So find a nice quiet time and whisper softly in her ear "Had any suicidal thoughts lately?"'

Ava's lips fell apart. Over-active receptors buzzed in a frenzy of empathy, you could tell by her face. She was processing. She had better not be trying to formulate some 'Save Tabatha' plan of hers. I couldn't let the martyrdom distract me. As a young child, Ava's only identifiable hobby had been altruism. As she got older, it became clearer that her lack of confidence was what fuelled such a drive. Personally, I would have preferred she take up taxidermy. Her fondness for Amelia Salter was unnerving and I wondered whether my revelation about Tabatha had unwittingly unleashed the brain-damaged monster of Florence Nightingstein.

I smuggled my small plastic sack of supplies under the crook of my arm.

'Well, do you want to do something? We could watch a movie after your class,' she asked.

'Not tonight.' I'm busy earning some money so I can pay those extortionate fees at that prissy school of yours so that maybe you won't end up becoming an out-of-work physics tutor like me.

'Ok. Do you want me to make some dinner and keep it for you?' Ava offered. The panting was getting louder as we approached Papa's room.

'No. I don't want dinner. But you don't have to cook, I bought you a pie.'

'Oh that's nice. What kind of pie?' She lit up.

'Steak and kidney.'

'I'm vegetarian.' Her voice sank.

'Still?' I asked. We both slowed down seeing the door ajar. In a familiar scene, a female policewoman was bent over a desk and a Tamil police officer stood behind her smacking her bottom with his truncheon. In a slightly more unfamiliar scene, Papa was leaning forward trying to recreate his own version using the tube of cream I'd bought him to smack the air. His sarong fell and, as he moved forwards to smack his imaginary policewoman, he tripped and landed face first on the floor. Ava and I shared a laugh caught in a gasp as he dusted himself off and got back up like a professional.

My breath was cold. I stood at the edge of the park at the point where the rose bushes ended and the thick blackish brambles and wild berries began. The early night-time air was invigorating. People were still awake, but had begun to retreat. Disappearing inside cars or houses, restaurants or gyms. Their sounds were muffled behind walls and windows and the world appeared distinctly emptier. Annoyingly, Alex flashed into my mind. I wondered what he and Poppy were doing right at that moment, the same moment I stood in my exercise trousers and trainers on the brink of my own personal reinvention. They were probably sharing a foul-tasting Gauloise and finding

Poppy's love of arbitrary metaphors in French avant-garde poetry just oh-so-amusing. Ok Alex, maybe you do deserve your new life. We were never about happiness after all, we were about functionality. The fact that I am here and you are there just proves that.

I heard a crackle in the leaves. It was loud, but I couldn't see anyone. There was a reason they advised people to use the park in the daytime. Instantly, my stomach lurched and I hung back quietly in the shadows. My heart started to beat a little faster. I tried to breathe more quietly but my breath just got shallower and louder. The bracken had grown long over the trellis and arch, affording me a hidden alcove in which to turn my body sideways and remain unseen. I tried to still my quivering legs. The crackling became more regular. Someone was coming.

Heavy footsteps crunched the gravelly floor. A full, fat moon lit up the silhouette and, as she passed by me, my foot fell out of my hiding place. Slamming into her back I pushed her sideways into the undergrowth and, pulling from my pocket my recently purchased hunting knife, hooked my arm under her chin, blade to her throat. I'd asked specifically for a serrated edge to try and prevent any accidental slicing. The element of surprise made her body easy to re-position. She stayed still and upright. We were the same height. I smelled her hair; sweet orange lacquer. I moved the knife to the side of her neck so she could feel the metal ridges against her skin. Then I swallowed, took a deep in-breath and prepared to talk, hoping to sound like a man.

'Give me your bag, your coat, your rings and I'm gone. If you don't, I'll gut you right here, right now.' I tried to rein in my anatomy so she wouldn't feel my breasts, which I'd bound with bandages. My heart was racing so fast. I was scared it would give me away and she'd know I'd never done this before. The voice was good, though – I was very pleased with that.

Any hope of sounding like a husky phone sex operator had been put to bed – I sounded like I pissed standing up and liked my bitches fat. Maybe my new balaclava helped. I gave her collar a yank and pulled her coat off her shoulders to give her a head start. She took off the rest like a scared prostitute, dropping it on the ground. The bag fell and, stretching her arm out to the side but without turning her face around, she offered me three shiny diamond rings in the palm of her hand.

'Now you're going to run and you're not going to stop 'til you get to the other end of the park. And if you tell anyone about this… I'll be coming for your daughter too, Regina Salter.'

She inhaled a small, scared breath. I re-positioned her away from me, gave her the tiniest push between the shoulder blades and she took off like an Olympian. I watched her run. She was fast. I guess exercise night paid off. She fell, recovering like a true athlete – pulling herself up and darting through the night. Watching her was addictive. I felt like I was a hunter allowing my prey to live, but only if it pushed itself to the limit. Anything less and they were mine again. Soon the darkness ate her up and she was gone. I ran like hell the other way with considerably more effort, but then I had things to carry. I ripped off my balaclava and saw the car exactly where I'd left it. I was covering every role on this job, doubling up as my own get-away driver. I guess that's how all small business ventures start out.

I threw Regina's stuff onto the passenger seat and put the keys in the ignition. The engine started first time. This night could not have been any more perfect. I started laughing. I couldn't help it, it just bubbled out. I hadn't considered what might have gone wrong, but I never imagined it would be so easy. I'd only worried tentatively about my voice and whether I could disguise it well enough. Though I had never spoken to

Regina, our paths did cross on a daily basis and my head was full of her trill speech. Yet tonight, she was so silent, so different than at the school gates where she looked through me as though I was somebody's nanny, not even worthy of a smile, knowing full well that Ava was my daughter. I had never imagined Regina had it in her to be so obliging – if only she showed this side of her more often. The adrenalin had kicked in and I could almost feel the blood as it surged around my body. My face stung a little from the cold, so I whacked up the heating. Even the movement of my fingers felt reckless. I could feel the rush and the power pulsing through my body. The lights flipped up and I saw a man with a dog up ahead. Maybe he walked his dog every night – let him sniff the hedge, piss under a tree, wander round the park in the hope he'd see another dog. Their night would go on unchanged. Regina Salter, however, might think of using another route home from now on. I turned on the radio. One of those slow, drive-time songs they played at this hour would do the trick. Something slushy and infested with lyrics about love to calm the frenetic pace of my mind. I lit a cigarette, leaned my head against the headrest and drove.

Everyone had gone to bed; I could tell from the street: all dark windows and motionless curtains. I turned the key with one hand and carried my loot inside with the other. I thought it suited Gatlin, trying desperately with its million-pound townhouses re-designed and re-restored to recreate a past era, that someone should revive the sixteenth-century idea of the 'footpad.' A footpad was a common criminal; different to a highway robber only by virtue of the fact that he robbed without a horse. Often found lurking behind a hedge, footpads were seen as being more brutal than highway robbers due to their get-away being that much slower. I suppose in that sense I was cheating by jumping into my car at the other end of the park, though it was only a Ford Estate.

In my kitchen, I opened the laptop. The computer started whirring as it came to life, I took the opportunity to multi-task and rolled myself a well-deserved joint. Weed had never tasted so good. For the first time, I saw a link between marijuana and the criminally active. It was a bit like ice-cream after a hot curry. It just made sense. I inhaled the smoke and the last hour of my life seemed to evanesce.

The label of Regina's coat said PRADA. I touched the fabric. Soft, luscious and inviting. I went to the website and searched for the very same one that I held in my hands. There were so many. If not for the fact that my one had a hood, I could have sworn they were all the same. Pages and pages went by and I finally got to the very last one. Prada Wind Hawk, it was called. OK, and how much do you cost Mrs Wind Hawk?

What the fuck! £2,750. That couldn't be right. I shook my head and blinked a few times to disperse the weed over my eyeballs. £2,750. Jesus, Regina.

Next up was Regina's brown leather Mulberry bag, which I was fully expecting to prove as fun an experience as Mary Poppins' bag. Could Mary P have had a Mulberry too? It was the latest one. First page, no waiting around. £1,600. The model in the photos seemed to love it so much she took it everywhere. There was a photo of her with it at the beach, one of her wearing just an oversized man's shirt and some socks whilst the bag sat relaxed on the bed and then one where it rode with her in the passenger seat of an open-topped Porsche like an old friend.

I put the bag on eBay for £800. It was positively thrilling, watching the photo I had taken instantly appear on the internet for all the world to see with just one click. I put the coat up for £1,000. I couldn't bring myself to put in on for higher – it seemed pure insanity to pay even that. Then there were the three shiny diamond rings. The jewellery was decidedly more complex. I didn't know where to look for its initial value as I couldn't tell where it was from. There was a much higher probability of seeing bacteria with my naked eye than identifying the name of the shop where Mr Salter had chosen to give away his latest bank bonus. All three rings were similar in their sparkly wonder, but also different. I looked at them cradled in the palm of my hand. Were they lonely? Lost without their mistress? Was she lost without them? Which one of her stolen accoutrements did she miss the most? Was she cold without her coat? Beside herself without her bag? Or suffering from a severe identity crisis – 'Who am I if I don't have my diamond rings announcing my marital status to the world, securing all future concerns regarding my inner peace and happiness?'

I put them on. Or tried to, at least. My ring finger was too fat. I pulled them all over my little finger instead. First the engagement ring – a thin band with one humungous diamond on the top. Then the wedding ring – a more expansive width of platinum with two diamonds lodged together within it. The third, an eternity ring, customarily given after the birth of a child, and littered with diamonds.

I waved my fingers in the air. It wasn't the same as when Regina did it. She didn't wear them on her pinky, for starters. And secondly, these were rings that I had taken from her perfect life. What did Regina's perfect life look like? What would Regina do in her rings? She'd make delectable dinners for her family, sophisticated recipes like sea bass lasagne. Yes, that's what she'd do. That couldn't be so hard. I could make dinner. I could make dinner for my family. Sod it if one member had publicly derailed us by leaving. And sod it if I didn't have sea bass, I could use pollock.

The internet said I needed a béchamel sauce. Lasagne is more inflexible than it lets on. It gives the impression with its pasta heritage that it's easy, quick. What the fuck was a béchamel sauce? A béchamel sauce is essential, said the recipe.

I was unflustered – as I imagined Regina would be. The ring was changing me. Or was it the weed?

I didn't have any butter so I used margarine. The recipe also said plain flour, which I didn't have either, but I did have some almond flour that Alex had bought months ago to make cupcakes for a student called Poppy who was showing promise. That would do. And milk. The recipe wanted full-fat milk. I had goat's milk, which was presumably from a full-fat goat.

It was the early hours of the morning before I was able to look down and admire my efforts. I stared at the first lasagne I had ever made. I hoped Ava would like it. She could have it for dinner that evening. The light was different in the kitchen – I think because it was so close to morning – a kind of stark, thin grey. The table was strewn with every saucepan I had in the cupboard; somehow I had used them all. I was tired, but not too tired to feel an immense sense of pride in my work. And I wasn't one for sidelining another creative. Regina and I made this pollock and almond lasagne together. It wouldn't have happened without Regina and I wasn't too proud to admit it. She was my muse. Her rings – my rings – sparkled. It was time for a nap.

Tuesday

Despite my tirelessly cooking dinner for her in the early hours of the morning when most people were in bed, not to mention severely stretching the limits of my cordon bleu expertise, Ava woke up in a strop. How her intuitive ingratitude knew to strike at the very moment I had given all of myself was a feat of mastery. If I had to hazard a guess, I'd say that she was smarting from Amelia not having invited her to anything the previous evening. If she were lucky, she may have been in the midst of the realisation, as was obvious, that she was never going to be invited to anything by Amelia Salter. However, I didn't have to guess for long. Ava was unable to be emotionally complex and create an environment where anyone needed to assume anything at all.

'Plus, I feel very sad today,' she continued.

The 'plus' was a clue. It meant I should have started listening earlier than I had. 'I am sad that Amelia doesn't want to be my friend. I felt very alone last night when you went out. I was left feeling vulnerable,' she said, perched on the side of my bed. Through half of one eye, I squeezed the time into my vision: I had been asleep for three hours. I tried to focus on Ava. Who spoke like that? How did she even know what she was feeling, let alone find a way to label it? Was that a class at school? 'Austen's Feelings and Sensibilities for the Modern World.' Is this the shit she's learning that I'm robbing this bitch to pay for?

Robbing? Shit! Fuck! What had I done? Had I really put Regina's stuff on eBay last night? Was that wise? Stolen goods straight onto eBay, it didn't sound clever. But they were only stolen goods if someone reported them. As long as Regina actually believed that her family might be in danger and kept her mouth shut, then eBay was the best place for them. Ava's soft melodic droning soothed the sharp peak in my cortisol.

I turned my face away from her, but knew I had to get up for the fucking school run. Oh, how I hated the school run. It was like a living thing. Every day, just at the point I thought I had no more hate left in me, I found a way to hate it more. It was like a mutated lizard's tail that, if cut off, would not only grow back but grow back even bigger, with festering pustules, making it even more loathsome. I was also beginning to recall that, not so long ago, I had had a very important engagement with a park bench and fifty paracetamol, which happened not to be a whimsical flight of fancy but a hugely important event in my life. The type of event I had been rehearsing and preparing for, similar to a Christian child preparing for holy communion. I was feeling more than a little put out about everything, as if my thoughts and desires had been hijacked during the past twenty-four hours of my life. The plan to execute may have been abstract – the location of the park, what restaurant, which steak? – but the intention had been absolute. My one, true ambition, that I would not see forty-one. Of this I was sure, and over the course of my life it had always been in the comfort of my bed that I had spent the most time fantasising about how this would play out. Only under the safety of my blankets could I have the time to bring my heart and mind to work together in unison. For a project of this magnitude, there could be no differences of opinion. The heart and mind both needed to be on board or it wouldn't work. Living under the shadow of a failed suicide attempt would have been the most malicious self-destruction. But it seemed as if, since Alex's departure, now even my bed was under attack.

'You may think what I'm feeling has been born out of some kind of transference,' said Ava, lifting the covers off my head and exposing me.

'I think babies are born. I think wolf cubs in the wild are born.'

'Don't be pedantic, Mum. What I'm saying is this isn't about Dad because I've fully examined his leaving.'

'Gynaecologists examine, Ava.'

'I've unravelled it as far as it can go,' she continued undeterred.

'String unravels,' I said.

'For fuck's sake, Mum,' she shouted.

'Aha!' I said, springing up to sitting. 'You see. Unconscious boiling venom. UBV. Similar to CBT, but angrier. Anger that is probably for your father. Do they talk about that in those fucking self-help books you're constantly reading?'

'Mum,' she said, rolling her eyes to the heavens where the wallpaper was desperately trying to peel itself off the ceiling. 'I'm not saying I'm not hurt and it's not pathetic, but he'll be back. My self-help books do help with honouring my emotions, so how I say I feel is exactly how I feel.'

The hubbub at the school gates was the same as usual. Mothers reliving the horror of their chronically traumatic childhoods, the memories of which were alive and well and laughing behind the thin veil of half-smiles and cursory nods. They speedily bundled their children through the school gates so they could get out to where the air was easier to breathe. Where it was less polluted by the competitive mouth farting.

Then there were the mothers finding popularity at school for the first time in later life and, having had a view of the school from the winner's circle, determined never to let it go.

This was often characterised by the overzealous organisation of play dates and a sycophantic need to network; to solidify relationships between other parents with an eventual view to sharing holiday homes and indeed holidaying together.

Lastly, there were the renaissance mothers. These women ruled the school as they always had. Now back after a brief hiatus, during which time they sought the appropriate mate with whom to reproduce, they returned to the playground to piss with their steel vaginas on all those less important – which would be everyone. Savages. The baboons of the monkey kingdom – violent and superior – their revival was nature at its best. It was natural selection of the upper echelons with their biological and moral traits filtering down to become the genetic basis of the middle classes. Darwin himself had talked about the domination of the expanding middle-class family in his nascent allegorical comic *On the Origin of Species*. Individuals who are better equipped with money, social connections and education will survive for longer. And the families in Gatlin – with their direct substitution of childhood innocence for extra tuition in three languages, two instruments and a specialist sports subject – assured that same legacy for the Amelia Salters and Tabatha Crosly-Burkes of this world. In fact, if Alex were here he would say that by doing what I was doing, I was trying to ingratiate myself into the natural order of selection, which was in direct opposition to the young socialist philosophies we had once bonded over. But if Alex had been here, I wouldn't be doing this at all. Couldn't I be a secret socialist? This wasn't about Karl Marx; this was about Ava.

The tea room was busy. Extreme fatigue was beginning to encroach on my ability to do anything that did not involve a bed. I needed one of my special hot chocolates to perk me up. There were a few odd bods I didn't know and had never seen, but at this kind of time it was mostly mothers from the school. A particularly gruesome table in the corner caught my attention. Ann Donnington, with a deceptively normal side profile, opposite a woman who I recognised as being Henrietta Crosly-Burke. I walked up to the counter trying to avoid looking in their general direction. Maude was second in line, carrying two polystyrene trays with inbuilt cup holders.

'Coffee bean crisis at the school?' I asked, standing by her.

'Oh! Hello, Drea. Busy in here today,' she said, obviously startled. 'Actually the admin staff prefer the coffee here, Felicity imports it from India, you know. I like to come once a week and treat them all to a decent cup. It's the little things in life that make people happy.'

'Is it, Maude? Well, judging by what a big dick your husband is I beg to differ.'

'Oh, Drea! You are naughty,' she said blushing a little.

'How's Molly?' Maude's daughter was still on the fence. She had a fifty per cent chance of inheriting her father's genes and being a hundred per cent mongoloid. Until I knew for certain, I asked after her.

'Oh well, you know. She's four now, so we're applying for primary schools at the moment,' she answered, smiling strangely, multiple worry lines instantly appearing on her forehead.

'That's bollocks,' I said.

'Yes, it's a stressful time,' said Maude.

'No, I mean, don't you get into Gatlin automatically?' I asked, slightly confused.

'Because we live nearby?'

'Because you're the school secretary,' I said, with conviction.

'Oh yes. Well, not exactly. It's not in the new contract.' She was trying not to look crestfallen, but her eyes looked down before she'd finished speaking and gave it away.

'And what about the £30,000 in donations made by certain banker parents to ensure their place at the school?'

'Drea,' she said sternly but in a thin voice whilst looking around to see whether anyone had heard me. 'Please. That's just a rumour. A silly rumour.'

She was next up, but as she waited for her drinks, she chose to make idle chit-chat with Felicity about the weather in India instead of continuing her conversation with me. This was a flimsy diversion as anyone who had been to the tea room at least once knew all there was to know about the weather in India. Meanwhile, the two mothers behind me were engrossed in a most amusing tittle-tattle.

'So we had Mary and Ben Stern over for dinner last Saturday because their daughter Mabel and our Ella are inseparable,' said the first. Really? Are they? Are they conjoined twins? I'm sure that the upstanding parents of Gatlin would have found that a huge violation of the school's non-existent disability policy.

'Oh that's nice. What did you make?' asked the second.

'Well, nothing fancy. It was the nanny's night off, and between Hugo's rugby and Ella's swimming… it's Monday, Wednesday, Saturday and Sunday now because you know she's competing nationally, don't you?'

'No, I didn't know that. I'm still trying to get my two to brush their teeth on Monday and Wednesday!' The first one looked horrified. 'They're very young. That was a complete joke, ha!' said the second, delirious with regret.

'Yes, well, I made a simple coq au vin followed by île flottante for dessert, and we broke open the Merlot we brought back from France last summer.'

'Did you?' squealed the second, like a stuck pig.

'So again, we've done the double,' said the first, looking mightily pleased with herself.

'You absolutely have. I've yet to do the double, but I really want to. We were close last week, but then Charlie said he found Mrs Rajesh just a little too ethnic – although if it weren't for her colour you couldn't even tell their daughter is from Bangladesh. She's so integrated and doesn't proselytise at all,' said the second.

'How ethnic is ethnic?' asked the first in a slight whisper.

'Charlie said the day she picked up Poonam from our house, he thinks he saw a plastic Ganesh on the dashboard with a wobbly head. Quite garish.'

'I suppose it's better than fluffy dice,' said the first.

'Is it?' queried the second, earnestly.

'I'm not sure. Try not to be too despondent. As soon as you do it once you'll be doing the double all the time, you'll see. Best friends with the parents of our children's best friends – double fun.

'That is so great.'

'It really is.'

Why couldn't Mrs Rajesh just stick a Christmas tree air freshener on the dashboard like everybody else? Oh well, I'm sure her daughter Poonam's facial hair was a much bigger priority, although I think Asian parents intentionally encouraged facial growth as a form of contraception. That was definitely the motivation for my teenage fuzz, although it didn't work. Asian men'll shag anything. The more facial hair, the better because it's like two in one; the perfect homo-hetero fantasy. I'm not sure what all the repression is all about. The Hindus, authors of the Kama Sutra, have got bare-breasted women and heavily endowed men in weird tantric positions all over the shop, but for God's sake don't mention sex or let your children see you kissing. And then there are the Muslims with their women in black burkini suits at the local public pool looking like a school of killer whales have found their way into the water whilst their husbands ogle every other woman in a regular bikini. Either way, it's a hypocritical mess.

'Hot chocolate.' I was at the front of the queue.

I had no choice about where to sit – there was only one table left. It was a foot away from Ann Donnington and her cronies. I put my bag on the chair as a deterrent, hoping the tea room clientele would have the same healthy and shared respect for misanthropy as I did. But just as the leather touched the chair Felicity arrived out of nowhere. She lifted my bag up and set it down on the one empty seat next to Ann and Henrietta.

'Sorry Drea, table's rickety. Safety hazard. You might think in India that driving is the main cause of death but it's actually circulatory disease.' The ladies at the table seemed just as perturbed by this intrusion as me. I turned, poised to object, vehemently.

'Felicity, I don't care about—' But before I could finish there was a bang. The wooden door to the toilet flew open, smashing against the wall, and Regina rushed out like a bull at a rodeo.

Her eyes were swollen and red, and she had a scarf tied around her blonde hair. This in itself was evidence of a tragedy, as most mornings she had her Brazilian blow-dry on such show that I wondered how she didn't give herself whiplash. Unsurprisingly, she was carrying a coat and bag I had not seen before. Both items appeared to be far inferior to the previous night's acquisitions but, as I had seen from perusing the internet for prices, what did I know about the luxury female outerwear and accessories market? She strode straight over to the table where her friends, saving her seat from me and waiting for her to return, were just about to announce to both Felicity and myself that Regina's chair was decidedly taken.

'I'm sorry,' she said, flustered. She hadn't seemed to even notice me standing there. Her speech was staccato and wavering a little. She spoke directly to her friends, 'I'm not feeling too well all of a sudden. I just need to lie down.' And with that she ran out of the shop.

'Well, looks like it's all yours,' said Felicity, clearing away Regina's half-drunk cup of coffee and wiping down the area where she had been.

'Umm…well,' said Ann, looking wistfully at the door from which Regina had just exited letting in a chilly breeze. I was about to make my excuses to leave when Crosly-Burke spoke to me.

'I'm Henrietta. Henrietta Crosly-Burke.' She extended her hand.

'Your husband is called Henry,' I blurted.

'Yes. I should be tired of it by now but I still think it's quite sweet, don't you? Henry had wanted to name the baby Harriett so we'd all have the same initials but once I had a Persian show cat called Tabatha and so I insisted.'

'Poor, poor Regina,' said Ann, shaking her head before I could reply regarding the idiocy of their shared-couple moniker.

'Is she alright?' I asked. To this, both women looked subtly around the room and then back to each other. It seemed as though they were telepathically agreeing on how best to answer.

'Sit down,' said Ann, quietly but firmly patting the seat of the chair. 'I think all the women of Gatlin have a right to know what's happened, don't you?' she declared officiously, looking at Henrietta. My bag became heavier with the weight of my flask's seclusion.

'Cancel that hot chocolate, Felicity, I'll just have some water,' I said. Hot chocolate without whisky made no sense.

'Last night, Regina was robbed at knifepoint in the park on the way back from pilates,' announced Ann abruptly. I was horrified. How dare that little bitch break our confidence. Ann choked a little at the end and it was as if her voice broke, but I couldn't be sure. Could she have been moved by what Regina had been through? I suppose it was possible, I just hadn't entertained the thought that these women could feel interchanging emotions in this way. I felt a rush. A flicker of power surged through my skin. I had done this. I was the master who had made Barbie's head move; made one plastic friend feel empathy for another.

'She won't go to the police,' Ann continued. 'He threatened her. Threatened her family. He even knew her name!'

'Can you believe it?' Henrietta asked me.

'No, I cannot.' But I do like that we think it's a man.

'It could happen to any of us,' said Henrietta.

Well, I'm glad you think that because it's true – although it couldn't happen to me.

'Do you think so?' I asked.

'Of course,' screeched Ann emphatically, waving her manicured hands in the air. All I could notice were her diamond rings. 'We were all in that pilates class,' she said, her mouth stressing the 'p'. I imagined she gave a perfunctory blow job. Comprehensive. Going everywhere she needed to go: up, down, left, right, slow to fast with as much sex appeal as a car wash.

'I wasn't,' said Henrietta ruefully.

'Well, be grateful. It could have been you,' Ann reprimanded flatly.

'I don't think so. I never walk across the park. I've always thought it strange that Regina did. I've always worried that something could happen. What if one of those out-of-work layabouts from Brigham accosted her one night, then what?' She paused as a thought struck her. 'Oh my God. And now they have. Have I done this? Have my thoughts caused this tragedy?' she exclaimed, hand flying to her mouth. Was she trying to stop more prophetic lunacy from coming out?

'Don't be ridiculous Henny, but you're right. It's stupid how she always walked home through the park. Why wouldn't you take the car?' confirmed the oracle that was Ann Donnington.

'Exactly!' agreed Henny. 'I'm not saying she deserved it but people do talk and, when they do, this might be what other people say.'

'Like dressing inappropriately invites unwanted male attention,' said Ann, her eyebrows coming together slightly, nodding her agreement at her own transparent judgements. 'From this moment on, no woman walks home alone. Everybody in twos.'

'Ann, you're so clever the way you make these connections,' marvelled Henrietta. 'I just wouldn't have thought.' Why doesn't that surprise me? Any idea your daughter's on her way to a successful career in popping prescription drugs?

'Well, I was formerly an industrial psychologist. Before we decided to concentrate on Oswald's career.'

'And the training never leaves you,' nodded Henrietta. 'I think the most important event in my life has been my wedding to Henry, and all I can think about is how devastated I would be if someone stole all my rings,' Henrietta looked at her glittering hand and then down at my bare and less-than-slender fingers.

'It's shocking. Chopard you know. Andrew always buys everything from Chopard. It's her favourite. She says wearing Chopard makes her float the same way as the jewels, suspended in their settings.' Chopard? Chopard! Hallelujah! What a joyous morning. The fortuitousness of my day was so suddenly overwhelming that I was hit with an unexpected surge of generosity towards these women.

'Ladies, shall I get us something to eat. Some cake?'

'They've got some lovely jam scones here,' said Henrietta.

'The jam is off,' I said. 'Let's have some *carat* cake instead.'

Back at home, the noise of the laptop firing up had become my favourite sound. Akin, I'm sure, to those who find birdsong soothing or children laughing to be anything other than nauseating. I entered 'Chopard' into the search field. Oh, I was so excited. An innocent childlike excitement and I realised how long it had been since I'd felt it – this liberated freedom of true happiness and contentment. No guilt or limits.

I moved the cursor across the rings. There were lots of photos and lengthy descriptions detailing the qualities of small, metal circles – which in itself seemed absurd – but none of these were the rings I needed. No pictures of Regina's rings. Similar models perhaps, but not the same. I paused and lit a cigarette. Defeated slightly, I blew smoke at the kitchen window. I had thought that this would be it. Simple. I got up from the laptop and went to put some water in a pan to boil for a hot toddy. Whilst I was waiting, I looked out at the wild forest of abandon that was our garden. The weeds had claimed Ava's old bike for themselves. Bushes had turned into trees, thorny bare-rooted roses climbed around the ramshackle fences, and the old apple tree – which we all thought had died last winter – knocked on the kitchen window with its large rotten red fruit, waiting to be let in.

I put a teaspoon of minced ginger into the pan along with a couple of cloves, a cinnamon stick, a piece of lemon rind and a dash of nutmeg. I let the spices get acquainted, turning it down to simmer. The shop website dazzled on the screen. I tapped their number into my phone. It rang twice.

'Good afternoon, Chopard head office, may I help you?'

'Oh, good afternoon. My name is Lucinda Lace and I am personal secretary to one of the largest Saudi families currently visiting the UK. My employer would like to purchase engagement, wedding and eternity rings for some of his wives. Is it possible you have some rings he might be interested in that would not be on your website?'

'Yes Madam, our more expensive rings with larger carats are not listed online.'

'Would it be possible for you to send me pictures of the rings you do not advertise, along with some costings?'

'Umm… yes, yes of course. Could I get your email, please?' Shit. Email. Uggh. I saw a letter on the table addressed to Papa from the hospital.

'A-N-A-N-D-P-E-R-E-R-A@hotmail.com'

'And your phone number?'

'The email is sufficient. If we need any more information, we will be in touch. Thank you.' I poured some whisky into a glass, added in a bit of water, honey and lemon juice and waited. Whilst it seemed certain that Regina, despite running her mouth off, was too traumatised to go to the police, there was something about Ann's demeanour that worried me. It felt like she could be easily tipped to play the annoying activist and take it all up as some sort of bloody cause. 'Scared to be rich? Stand up and unite, women of the spa!! We want you!' I'd be keeping an eye on her.

I logged into Papa's account. Ping. My email had arrived. I opened it. What the…? No, it couldn't be. £1 million? I mean it wasn't £1 million to be exact, it was £1,204,320.00. That was the engagement ring. The wedding ring was £1,926,640.00 and the eternity ring was £3 million!! Fuck! £3 million?

We were set. Ava would never have to worry about her education ever again – or rather, I would never have to worry. Ava wasn't thinking beyond the next twenty-four hours at the moment, but one day she'd get to my age where it became routinely possible to regret entire stretches of one's life. She could even go to university if she wanted. I smiled. Ava at university. She'd be brilliant. Not spoiled or wasteful, drinking and sexing her three years down the drain the way most people did. She'd study something important, meaningful, and probably go on to win a Nobel Prize. And then, without warning and out of nowhere, an unbidden tear sat at the edge of my bottom left eyelid. I caught the pesky intruder before it could plop. What the hell was that about? Pull it together, Drea. Ava is the mushy one in the family. Mush turns to slush. You can't walk the path of glory in a blur of slush. The bell rang. I downed my toddy before I went to open the door. Ava must have forgotten her key again.

I was entirely unprepared for the sight that was to greet me. It rendered me quite speechless.

Tuesday Evening

Whatever drugs I took, however much I drank, I never threw up.

I have just thrown up, and the wretching was agony. It wasn't prolific. I'm not talking gutter rivers of sick that flow on a Friday night next to the bar with the all-day happy-hour sign. In fact, a small stream of water from the tap washed the putrid juices away. But it was involuntary, not my style, and it had all been brought on by opening the door to see Ava flanked by one Amelia Salter and one Tabatha Crosly-Burke.

Neither of these two degenerate whores had given Ava a second glance in their spoiled, clueless lives, despite Ava a-wishing and a-hoping. At junior school, these self-pronounced cool girls would take her money, demand she hand over her lunch and repeatedly pull down her knickers in the playground to see if she had started her period. Now Satan's sisters were here standing outside my house. Seriously? This was insane enough, but after last night in the park with Regina Salter? I didn't believe in God – but if I did, I'd say he was fucking with me.

'We'll be in the living room, Mum,' said Ava casually. Just to be clear, we do not have a living room – at least not a place we referred to as one. It was called the 'front room' if it ever needed a name. Mostly it was called 'here,' 'there' or maybe 'downstairs' if we were upstairs, but never the 'living room.' Didn't that imply that people lived there? Was this her point?

'Amelia,' I acknowledged. I just needed to play it cool. Hopefully I'd wiped the sick from my mouth. With any other friend of Ava's, I'd never chat that much anyway, or ask too many questions, get involved. I wasn't one of those mothers. Some mothers needed to feel like all their children's friends really liked them. They wanted to be thought of as funky, approachable, pretty. I personally didn't give a shit. I had enough on my hands dealing with Ava, I wasn't running a fucking orphanage. Just say hello and move on.

'Mrs Thorn,' said Amelia and Tabatha in stereo, curled up on the sofa like large cats. All of a sudden I had become hyper-aware of my house. This was an odd, unfamiliar sensation, as out of all the things the world brought to my awareness from time to time, my house was rarely one of them. But people who should not be in my house were in my house. People who, according to the laws of gravity and social class, should not have wanted to sit inside my house, on my sofa, resembling fat cats. I blinked. The cats got bigger. Tabatha swished her spiralling black tail and Amelia snarled, causing her long whiskers to twitch.

'It's Miss Peiris. Mrs Thorn is Ava's biological mother.'

'Mum, the most awful thing happened to Amelia's mother last night. She was robbed! You can't say anything to anyone,' Ava broke eye contact with me and put a reassuring hand on Amelia's arm. She turned to her, 'Don't worry, she won't.' She looked back at me. 'But I told her – Amelia, not her mum – about your self-defence classes and thought maybe you could talk to her, Amelia's mum not Amelia, about coming with you?'

I am very capable of keeping a secret, but when I told Regina not to say anything to anyone or I would hurt her daughter, it is apparent that she did not keep my confidence the way I would have listened if someone had assaulted me with such a comminatory order. I know this because if she had, I would not be hearing about it now from my fucking daughter in my living room. Did we live in it? I wouldn't have said our living room was either big or small, but I doubted anyone's – apart from maybe a sniper's – would have had the necessary items I'd require to actually live. Ah, that was the problem. The definition of living was not unilateral. Most people's idea of a living room was somewhere they could breeze in and out of, watch a bit of television, read a book. For me to exist in a room named the 'living room', it would have to have everything in it to prevent me from dying. And as I had been planning my death for more than thirty years and hadn't come across anything to change that plan yet, I sincerely doubted such a room could exist.

Our 'living room' comprised a faded velvet three-seated sofa from a car boot sale that still held sporadic flourishes of the original turquoise despite the patches I'd stuck on over the years to hide the rips, a television, although not one of these oversized domestic use cinema screens – twenty-three inches was plenty; a tall lamp, leaning slightly to the left, with a yellow barrel shade, threw suspicion onto a few paintings and their innocuous Neptunium etchings; and a chess table. The latter was a quirky piece consisting of two chairs with an adjoining plank of wood. The pieces were just how Alex and I had left them in our last game. I could see now how I'd left myself open. My pawns had gone too far and I couldn't go back. Instead of being my secret weapon, my fianchettoed bishop rendered my king side utterly vulnerable.

'Mum?'

'What?'

'Self-defence classes for Amelia's mum. And maybe you should tell your mum too, Tabatha. The more women can stick together, the better, don't you think?'

For fuck's sake, Ava. Why don't you just run down to the cemetery and dig up the fucking suffragettes? 'Sounds good. You girls want something to drink?' I headed straight for the kitchen and out of the room in which we 'lived', where it seemed completely obvious – although only to me – that the walls were inching closer and closer towards each other.

Daylight upon the kitchen wooden worktops gave them a homely sheen. I didn't wait for the water to boil, and poured myself a shot of whisky. Where was I? Oh yes, that's right – three million pounds! Those kids out there were fucking with my brain, but there were three million reasons why none of it mattered. Half a joint sat in an ashtray next to the spices. I lit it up, inhaled hard and took a deep lug. None of this was a problem. Ava and I had a game plan. We were sorted. And the fact that Regina's daughter was now in my living room was circumstantial flea shit. Ava had somehow proclaimed herself prom queen and had been allowed, for an afternoon at least, into the Freemasons. Her annoying, do-gooder attitude had finally proved useful, and now here she was with Amelia and Tabatha in her house as her girl crush turned into a real ménage-a-trois. And that's all that was happening here. Great. Happy for her. Nothing to do with me. My work would continue. However, did it mean I needed to advance timescales? Do the next one tonight, instead of waiting. There were now five people who shouldn't know who already knew. Between Ava and Ann, I dreaded to think what further damage could be done.

There was a light rapping on the kitchen door and it swung open. 'You didn't wait,' said Tabatha, standing in the doorway.

'Excuse me?'

'You asked us what we wanted to drink, but you didn't wait to hear,' she said with her perfectly pouty lips and irritating self-confidence.

'If you're going to knock, you should *wait* for someone to say "come in",' I said.

'What?'

'Go on.'

'Sorry?' said Tabatha confused.

'Go back out, knock and wait,' I said. I don't think I'd ever spoken to this girl before. Of course I knew all about her, through Ava's fantasies and the prominent position her family held in the Gatlin community, but I'd never encountered her like this. It was funny how well you can intimately know the idea of someone and, if you've known that idea long enough, you can say anything to them. Tabatha turned around and went back into the hallway leaving the door slightly ajar. Then she knocked again. I said nothing. She said nothing. Both of us on either side of the door, waiting. I wondered how depressed she must have been feeling to warrant hanging out with Ava. The tablets can't have been working that effectively. In her right mind, she would never have set foot in our house. Or was this all about Amelia? Where Amelia went, Tabatha followed? Except she didn't seem the follower type.

I wondered how long she'd wait; I hoped she wouldn't knock again. Surely that would be demeaning. Go on, knock again.

The door burst open. I'd make her regret her insolence.

'Mum!' Ava looked cross.

'What?' I answered faking ignorance.

'Tabatha said you wouldn't let her into the kitchen.'

'Rubbish. I didn't hear her knock.'

'Mum!'

'Oh, ok. But why are they here?'

'I found Amelia in the toilets crying. She said her mum is a mess since it happened. That she's been drinking—'

'Didn't I say those girls were a bad influence?'

'Not Amelia, Regina.'

'Oh. I'd be drinking if I got robbed—'

'She's been sober for five years. She's a recovering alcoholic.'

'Well, it sounds like she really needed a drink then,' I said, pouring another shot.

'Amelia really needed a friend and I think Tabatha is the only one out of her group that she trusts, so she came too. Please can you come and talk to her?' she pleaded.

'What! Why me? You're the one shopping for new friends.'

'Because I think she really needs to hear from a mother that her mum is going to be okay, which means that Amelia's going to be okay too.' Oh, Ava. Why can't you smoke pot and shoplift like normal teenagers?

'Now?' I made no attempt to hide my reluctance.

'Yes. Now,' insisted Ava, also making no attempt to hide her newly acquired diva persona.

I exhaled deeply and followed her into the living room. Tabatha leaned against the wall, her bored tongue pressing out the inside of her cheek as if in time with a metronome. She looked up, her face without scorn. I smiled inwardly, wondering if her throat was parched. Ava stood next to Amelia, who held her head in her hands, and gestured for me to sit next to her friend on the sofa. Gingerly, I lowered myself down to the girl. As soon as she felt me next to her, she swung her whole body sideways and lunged her face into my chest. My hand was trapped under her torso and I was caught. If I moved it, I'd have no choice but to drape it around her. I chose to leave it where it was. I didn't like the way that Tabatha was looking at me. I sensed a low level of scrutiny beginning to pervade. Ava moved behind the sofa. She leaned over and pulled my arm out, laying it gently around Amelia's shoulders. After Ava had arranged me I realised that, without too much effort, I could probably make myself throw up again all over Amelia's head.

'Don't cry,' I said. 'Your mum'll be alright. One in three people will be mugged, assaulted or murdered in their lifetime. It's the best one out of the three.'

Ava smiled down at us proudly. I imagined she must have confused today with Christmas. Amelia seemed less anxious – maybe it was the secondary weed smoke. Tabatha had left the room, quite possibly to get herself a drink.

Hours later, I emerged from my bedroom and headed straight to Ava's.

'Ava, have you seen Papa today?' Papa's room had been quiet when I had peered round the corner earlier to see whether he'd fallen into a self-induced coma. I'd had a horrible image of what every child fears will be the end for their elderly parent – extreme geriatric sexual exertion. I was more than a little thrown to see the bed had been made and the pillows fluffed. Amongst Papa's many eccentricities was his love of fine bed linen. He dressed like a tramp, considered the cost of travelling anywhere to be extortionate, but took his thread count very seriously. I washed his sheets separately because he feared the cheap colours from ours – 'if you can call that trash bed linen' – would run. I looked at his ivory Egyptian cotton sheets, his vintage-style embossed hand-stitched duvet and the delicately matching pillows, and wondered where he could go for the whole day and why he still wasn't home. Ava breezed out of her room still wearing her school uniform.

'Why aren't you in your pyjamas,' I asked.

'Because I'm not sleepy and Amelia's still here,' Ava replied, as if bedtime was something to be negotiated.

'In there?' I shrieked. 'Bedtime is not a debate Ava. You don't get to decide if you feel it suits you.' I grabbed her, marching her back into my bedroom doorway. 'And what do you mean she's still here? It's nine o'clock at night.'

'I never go to bed before nine.'

'It's a school night. You probably haven't even done your homework. But more to the point, what can you possibly have to say to that girl for so long, Ava? Aren't you bored?'

'Mum! She's in the other room,' sushed Ava.

'But why?' I asked, pulling her inside.

'Look I know why you're behaving like this,' said Ava.

'Why I'm behaving like this? I am not the one who feels the need to go on some sort of charity expedition, befriending the school's over-privileged fuckwits,' I said in the most strenuous whisper I could manage from across the room. I was looking for my tracksuit bottoms and sweatshirt that seemed to be missing from the armchair that masqueraded as a clothes horse.

'You think she's going to be a bad influence on me, but really it's the other way around. Oh, not me being a bad influence on her, that came out wrong,' she laughed, 'we've already done our homework and we also went over some extra physics. Motion matter and energy,' she said proudly.

'Extra physics?' My voice was calm.

'Yes,' she smiled.

'Topics you haven't covered in class yet?'

'Yup.' The smile got wider, although how she managed it I don't know as it already took up most of her face.

'And what do you get out of this, Ava? I can see why it works for her but how do you benefit? Not to mention that for years – way before you were born, in fact – the government of this country has had a system in place for just this very thing. They call it education, from the Latin word *educatus*. Did you know that was the school's job, Ava? And that it is still the school's job. Did you know that is why you go to school? That by law I need to educate you, me educate you, not her,' I said gesticulating wildly to Ava's bedroom where I guessed Amelia lay waiting. 'You see, her parents pay for the school to do that job, and they pay very comfortably. And if their kid needs extra tuition, they'll just pay for that too and they do all of this by using just an iota, a mere atom of the money that is perpetually in an ever constant flow out of their a-hole. Did you know that, Ava? Did you know that these people don't actually need you to tutor their imbecile progeny for free due to the steady stream of fucking money continuously flooding out of their arseholes Ava, which I don't have, you see,' I stamped off my jeans and yanked my knickers down presenting her my naked bottom. 'You see, arsehole, but no fucking money!'

I couldn't be sure if I had raised my voice. It seemed likely. Ava was quiet. She glanced sideways for a moment. I used the opportunity to pull my knickers up.

'I don't think you always need to get something out of it, but as benefit is so important to you, I have benefitted. I've made a friend.'

I had nothing to say. Not because I thought what she said was so profound, but because this fantasy that had her believing Amelia Salter had the ability to form friendships was the precursor to Ava having her heart stamped on, and for this I did not need to see a preview. Soon she'd have the choice of three million new friends and she wouldn't need these losers.

'Where are you going?' she asked.

'Out, and I can't find my clothes.' I picked up piles of things and moved them onto mounds of other things.

'Your self-defence class?'

'No.'

'I put your clothes in the wash.'

'Ava! Don't touch my stuff.'

'Okaayyy. Maybe Amelia and I should go with you. Then she can show her mum the moves.'

'That is not where I'm going but if it was I wouldn't take you because it's not a fucking dance class!!' Heading towards the bathroom to dig my jogging bottoms out of the dirty linen basket, I bumped straight into Amelia. She stared at me. Wondering perhaps why I was standing in my knickers? What's it to her? It's my house. Who does she think she is? Fucking knicker police?

Ava came running down the corridor throwing her arms around my waist from behind and nuzzling her head on my back like she used to do when she was little and she'd make me guess who I thought it was.

'I think we both know what happened in there,' she whispered turning me around to face her. 'Transference. Don't be sad. He'll be back. I just know he will.' She kissed me on the cheek and, taking Amelia by the hand, skipped downstairs.

Technically the moon was waning but it didn't show. Fat and heavy, she hung in the sky looking like she was about to drop. Give birth. Push a huge, painful second moon from a tiny air pocket in her atmosphere that she'd spend the rest of her lunar life worrying about. I could feel the energy had shifted since the full moon. My body felt less porous, my mind less brittle, my thinking felt more concise, which it needed to be as Ann Donnington had rammed her spanner right up my works with her 'everybody in twos' plan. There was no way I could rob two people at once. Maybe if Alex was here we could have done it together – like a hobby. There was something sexy about robbing as a couple. The camaraderie, the shared instinct and the risk. But maybe the sexiest part was just in being together. Alex and I had done nothing together. I sighed. I guess it had been just a matter of time before he left. What is the point of staying together if you never do anything together? Robbing as a single mother was far less sexy. Necessary and functional and just another parenting job that single mothers find themselves having to do alone, like cleaning out the litter tray. If we'd had a cat.

The last time I had travelled to Brigham was to purchase my balaclava and untraceable hunting knife from a camping store owned by a man called Charlie. In an impressive demonstration of upselling, Charlie told me about his brother-in-law Lenny, just out of prison for fencing, who I'd arranged to meet tonight in the old supermarket car park on the edge of town between Gatlin and the extremely long road that led into deep, dark Brigham. I had never ventured this far north of the border. As I drove, the road turned gravelly, less even under the tyres. The rose baskets of Gatlin hung underneath street lamps next to painted wooden benches were gone, replaced by coil-sprung mattresses, broken prams and bins with overflowing rubbish. This is where the immigrants with no obvious skills had been shuttled. This is where councils didn't clean the streets or repair dilapidated houses. This is where people survived when they would rather have lived.

As I thought of that three million, my stomach started to flutter. Images floated through my head of going back home and telling Ava we were moving house to one of the wide double-fronted ones on East Hill with the outstretched front lawns and corridors leading to hidden attics and secret studies. The houses in Brigham were noticeably smaller. The cars on the road seemed to have more of a purpose than those in Gatlin, which gave off a 'we're just cruising' vibe. My car felt more at home in Brigham. I considered it; I think I'd change that too. Get Ava a small banger for herself and get me a bicycle with a basket for my flask. No reversing with a bicycle.

This was the address Charlie had given me. It was a deserted, hidden place with the disused car park I'd arrived at boarded up. I got out of the car and a feisty cold chill smacked my face. It was agreeably warmer in Gatlin. Tall sheets of dirty corrugated cardboard blocked up spaces where the old brick walls had been half-demolished. But despite the 'danger' and 'no entry' signs, I could hear something happening inside. I pushed on a large rectangular piece that seemed more unstable than the others and it fell back. Unidentifiable grease slid onto my fingers.

Once in, I let my eyes grow accustomed to the torches and old, battered glow-in-the-dark toys turned into makeshift fairy lights. Clusters of industry offered various services. Twin towers of electrical goods proffered in the distance. A trio of painted ladies in tight faux leather skirts and high heels drank coffee from plastic cups on sacks of sand. A white woman wearing a nightdress under a fur coat with trainers pushed a dinner trolley. This was a night market of salubrious goods and matching proprietors.

'What can I do you for, darlin'?' Her breath stank of rum and halitosis, and she had sores on her face. 'Welcome to Alphabet Street. A–Z of all you need. I gotcha A-bombs, Base, Chicken Fever, Donkey Dust, Eggs—'

'I'm looking for Lenny.' I thought it best to get in quick, but I appreciated she'd created a brand.

'Oh, I got rocks. I gotcha Rolex—'

'Let me stop you there. I don't think you're talking about jewellery so this isn't the stall for me.'

She looked at me straight in the eye, looking scarily how you'd imagine the devil would if he caught you out late at night and was deciding how best to devour you.

'Back right,' she nodded over into the corner. It was too dark to see what lurked there. Guess I'd find out. She put her face so close to mine I could see one of her facial craters seeping.

'You tell Lenny he owes me.'

'Owes you what?' As soon as I'd asked, I realised I didn't really need to know.

'He knows what he owes,' she hissed.

'I will tell him that. Thanking you.'

The interesting part about this specialised night market was the family feel. Children were running around playing tag or on skateboards whilst the older ones were being introduced to the family business. Heading into the lion's den, or at least in the direction that the kindly drugs rep had sent me, I stared at two Mexican kids, twins, holding torches over a chess board. The girl hovered dubiously over her bishop.

'Don't do that,' I warned.

She glared up at me, needing to hear a good reason in ten seconds or less.

'He's still got his on the board, see,' I explained, pointing to her brother's bishop. If you do this and then he exchanges his, you'll expose all these squares.' I was still wincing from my own game with Alex. I felt embarrassed that this amateur move had been my last chess play. No good for anyone else to suffer. She had seen the light and her eyes widened as she moved her fingers over to her last remaining rook.

'You want something love?' The twins took after their father. No bad thing: he was a good-looking man but from the aged gash on his neck and sheer size and definition of his body, I'd say he'd endured some in prison. He clipped the boy lovingly round the ear.

'Lenny?' I checked.

'Who are you?' the man squinted.

'Charlie said you could help me. I've got some jewellery to sell.' Lenny had long hair in two plaits and tattoos poking out from everywhere. His body was a walking battleship. Large with scars, impenetrable. But despite the brawn and the lines around his eyes his discriminating feminine hands belied brains.

'Whatcha got?'

I pulled out my purse and took out my lottery winnings, also known as Regina's rings. 'These are all from Chopard. This one is £1,204,320.00,' I said showing him the engagement ring. I thought it best to be exact with the figures. 'This one is £1,926,640.00 and this one is three million. It's actually £3,000,525.00 but I'm happy to round down. Funny numbers aren't they? Something to do with the prices of the carats, so I'm told…' I trailed off. I had expected Lenny's reaction to be a little bigger. In fact, I had expected Lenny to have a reaction. 'I'm thinking I'd like to round up the wedding ring to two mil, just because it seems rude not to, and the engagement ring well maybe we'll say two hundred grand round down for depreciation. So that's six million pounds. Now I understand that straight into my bank account is going to alert some managerial heads, so I'm happy with cash and if you don't have that much to hand, I can take what you have now and come back for the rest – taking the jewellery with me, of course. I know the way things work.'

Lenny stared at the rings in my hand. He didn't try to reach for them or look at me but just focussed on the diamonds. I moved my hand closer to his face, but he didn't flinch. Lenny's stoicism was creating unnecessary tension. Perhaps such tension was paramount in six-million-pound stolen jewellery negotiations. I felt I should recap.

'So like I said, all the rings are Chopard—'

'I'll give you four grand for the lot,' he said, straightening his body up. I must have misheard. Four million pounds was two million short of my asking price. That was a tall order and a deal I had no intention of making. This was our nest egg. Ava was about to have everything she deserved and I wasn't giving this man an extra two million no matter how hard his children were working to beat the odds of their social standing.

'Four million pounds—'

'Four grand,' he interrupted.

Maybe he was dyslexic. I should tread lightly. He could be harbouring feelings of resentment because of a condition he felt had held him back from a more legitimate career in jewellery retail.

'I'm not sure you heard me properly—'

'Lady, I heard you. I'm giving you four grand cash total for the lot, take it or leave it.'

'These rings total a recommended retail price of six million pounds!' I exclaimed, somewhat hysterically.

'It don't work like that. Jewellery depreciates Mama, don't matter what it is and if these are Chopard and worth whachu say they worth, then they're tagged baby. Completely traceable. It's too hot at that price, so even I can't get rid of them. I'm sorry but that's how it is. Now, you wanna talk drugs – that's a different story. I can move meth to Mumbai before the police can say meconophagist. You see, that's a family business. That woman who sent you here, that's my ex-wife, and I'm still tight with her old man coz he knew she was trouble.'

I sat in the car and ate biscuits. I systematically demolished the packet and then began another, my mouth unable to chew as fast as my hands were putting them in. I felt the refined sugar act as a barrier to my emotions, blocking tears of disappointment from entering the world. I ate until the disillusionment had turned to fat. Manically, I searched for fallen crumbs that had dropped from my mouth onto my trousers and into the car seat. The money he'd given me smelled like arse. Four thousand pounds in crumpled dirty fifties. The coat and the bag had gone for what I'd asked for on eBay so now I had a grand total of £5,800. Ava's school fees for the year were £17,310. I needed £11,510 more. I hoped Alex was enjoying himself in Normandy. I'd hate for him to choke on a snail and die, leaving what little he had to Ava.

Yogalates was tonight's offering in the church hall. I had been once. Never again. It was more strenuous than I'd imagined and I'd pulled a muscle in my back which I'd not even known I possessed. Remarkably, it wasn't a strained back ligament that put me off but something much worse; the stench of desperation. Entrenched in the unwashed rubber mats that the yummy mummies of Gatlin sweated upon, a virus of lost youth virulently permeated the air. Overweight women held together in swatches of lycra tried with leaden

thighs to scissor kick their way to thinner bodies, only to
return home after the class and reward themselves with a tub
of salted caramel ice-cream. There were the women who had
just given birth with a deadline to return to work in six weeks
or less. Was it meant to amuse women how, written in the
poisonous pen of inequality, hidden in the maternity package
amongst the 'Get Well Soon' cards, it also read 'or lose your
job for "poor performance"'? Despite having just popped out
a person from a hole so small it had been given the task of
excreting liquids, they found themselves in yogalates, trying to
shrink their uterus to the beat of heinous dance tracks so they
are able to fit into just one old work dress and save their jobs,
maybe even tiring their co-workers of the 'What's going on in
there, I thought you'd already had your baby!' office banter.

Then there were the dieters – purporters of the slow-
carb-release diet, the weight-watchers diet and the eat-nothing-
but-kale-for-two-weeks-and-then-nothing-but-kale-whilst-
skipping diet – hoping to entice their lost husbands back into
the marital forest, where weeds grew rampant and beautiful
flowers of spontaneity had once bloomed. Desperation city.
Couldn't do it. I preferred my all-butter biscuits.

I parked far enough down the road and turned the lights
off. A full joint was still in the ashtray. That would do nicely.
I'd wondered momentarily after the decision to put the stolen
goods on eBay whether the distinction between weed clouding
or clearing my judgment was becoming less certain. I sparked
the joint up and leaned my head onto the headrest. It was
skunk – stronger than my normal stuff. Grey clouds billowed
up around my face and hung in the air, promising to be the
only good news I'd had all day. As the smoke hit the back of
my throat, I felt my mind care a bit less, but I couldn't say
about what.

Between 10 and 11pm

I felt as though there was an uninvited presence in the car. A vague and self-conscious wariness sat in judgement on my shoulders. I tried to block it out by taking a deeper drag. Who needs critics? Let people be who they want to be. That was our family motto. No obligations to anyone. Papa did whatever he wanted and Mother certainly had. So what the fuck was this voice in my head? Put down the joint. Be sharp. Be quick. Be aware. Robbery means get in fast, get out faster. 'Fuck you,' I said to no one. 'I'll do what I want.'

The large wooden doors of the church hall opened, casting a small pool of light into which heads bobbed back and forth, quickly morphing into shadows in the dark again. Doors on the driver and passenger sides opened simultaneously as people got into their cars to travel home in pairs. Some set off on foot, striding defiantly down the street. Animals scared to enter the ark alone. Ann was a fucking liability. This was all her doing. She had cast doom over the town like a tortured soothsayer and been the ringleader of this meddling community watch.

The loss of our millions was slowly becoming a distant memory. That's what weed did – it made life bearable, and skunk made it bearable just that bit faster. It took all the prickly bits and smoothed them out. What was that Chinese shit? Feng Shui? The ancient art of living in balance. Even they said it. Don't keep cacti in the house, too pointy – replace with plants with rounded edges. Weed made you rounded. More than medicinal, it was essential. Mother taught me that. It was the only thing she did teach me: to rely on something other than her. Okay, maybe weed wasn't necessary or essential for everyone. Maybe there were those out there with charmed lives who didn't need to sand down the rough edges because there were none. Those like Henrietta Crosly-Burke.

She was the last one to exit the church and get into her Lexus, alone. I grinned. Game on. I sat up straight in my seat and felt the steering wheel tilt to the left a little. Did it really tilt? Was that my eyes or the joint? Could it be what the joint had done to my eyes? Fuck, weed was so much more complex than people understood. I needed to focus. It was strong skunk, I could admit that, but it was fine. Totally fine. It would level out soon, I mean that was the point of it. It was a leveller.

My throat was dry. I swigged a lug of whisky from my flask. The lights from the church went out and a figure emerged from inside and stood fiddling at the door. The silhouette got into the Lexus on the passenger side. Shit, she wasn't alone after all, but now the seed had already been planted in my mind, germinating as she turned on her bright red brake lights. I started up the engine and began to follow.

Gatlin was quiet. It was the beginning of the week; people were just getting back into life again after the weekend. That's how the Western world lived. Their salvation consisted of two days. Even the Jews, with their special Friday and Saturday, were doing it. Everybody living for the weekend. This meant five out of every seven days were bullshit. A means to an end. And for most people, Sunday started bleeding into Monday by the afternoon anyway, so it was really just one and a half. What kind of life was that? The days of the week needed a resurgence. Their own special meaning and purpose again. I'd start with Tuesday. I was renaming Tuesday as national robbery day. After national robbery Monday.

I wondered about this other person who had got into Henrietta's car. Could I handle them both? I could with a gun. Guns killed people. You chopped onions with a knife, spread butter with a knife. Yes, it could cause damage, but there were lots of other uses. There was only one use for a gun. Two people felt ambitious. Clearly this person was someone responsible as they had been tasked with locking up the church. This was also worth pondering as these righteous types often became overly courageous when accessing the strength of the divine. This wasn't just anybody's house – this was God's house. I'd have to wait for Henrietta to be alone.

She drove slowly, slowing down even more as she approached red lights and always waiting for green before she started up again. It was practically dangerous. I was tempted to make a citizen's arrest for reckless driving. People thought they were doing something better than everyone else when they approached traffic lights in this idiotic way but it just made amber totally redundant and no one likes to feel as though they're not important, not even colours. Amber was there for a reason.

She seemed to be driving towards the school when she suddenly made a left onto Elm Street and then a right to the Gatlin village shops. Why were they going to the shops at this time of night? Henrietta parked outside the apothecary. I thought about what I was going to do. How was this supposed to work? Assuming she was going straight home, could I do it right outside her house? Fuck. That sounded dangerous. Was that dangerous? Was that such a bad idea? I needed £11,510. Would there ever be any good ideas? That was the beauty of the park. That was what parks were for. Strolls in the day, crime at night.

She turned to wave. It was Maude. Instinctively I put my hood up. Of course. That made complete sense. I should have realised that. There was no one more responsible than Maude.

She let herself into the apothecary and went upstairs where she would take up her position in the bed next to her large man-shaped penis.

So now what? What a pointless excursion. I might as well just go home. There was no way I was going to have the elements of surprise and privacy in the driveway outside her house. I might as well ring the doorbell and ask her for her bag and coat. But I was curious to see where she lived. Whether she slept in a double-fronted house with an outstretched front lawn. And I was wired.

Henrietta drove faster now. A lot faster in fact. Maybe she was in a hurry. Maybe at midnight all her diamonds turned into flesh-eating pumpkins. To be fair, I had nothing against her personally. She was as soporific as they come. In fact, there was a slim chance her pill-popping teenage daughter was more enigmatic. The road began to climb, and pretty soon we had turned onto East Hill, where the truly affluent of Gatlin resided. Even the Salters and the Donningtons were out of their league on East Hill.

For a time, there were only trees for either of us to look at. I kept a three-car distance between us until the branches started shaping into the arched contours of the Gatlin golf course. The road felt smoother and the car wanted to go faster. Just over the top of the hill, houses began to reappear again, but not like before. These were mansions, separated from each other by out-buildings and garages, parked cars and land. Every property appeared to be its own estate. It was pretty outstanding that this was how some people lived, but in the night it was kind of eerie. All that space freaked me out.

I slowed down as the road had no street lamps. If there was any light at all, it seemed to come only from the windows, of which there were many. She had dropped her speed and was doing around twenty now. I assumed that she was approaching her own palace, yet when she stopped, it was by a barren emptiness. The door opened on the driver's side and she got out and walked to the back of the car. The boot lifted up. I wasn't sure what happened next, or rather how it all happened. I knew I needed gloves, although I didn't have any. I also knew as badly planned as it all was, it was still an opportunity, one I couldn't miss. I rifled around the car and found a fluffy pink pair of Ava's. I put them on, and the next thing I knew I was pushing both my hands down on Henrietta's back, forcing her face into the boot of her own car. Her legs flipping frantically up and down, like a fish out of water, as she straddled the edge of the boot. I was flattening her body with the palm of my hand when I realised that I'd bolted out of the car without my balaclava or my hunting knife. I could also now see that she must have taken her coat off whilst she was driving and left it in the front of the car, along with her bag.

'Give me your rings,' I said gruffly, suddenly aware of how fast I had run from my car to hers. My throat lurched for air as I spoke.

'Mmha Iccha rmmeme ha,' she mumbled.

'What?' Enunciate for God's sake woman. Did you not attend a private school?

'Mmha Iccha rmmeme ha,' she repeated. I moved my hands off the top of her back and neck and she immediately flipped her head to the side, freeing her mouth from the rough felt of the base of the boot and the weight of my hand.

'My hands. I can't reach my hands,' she said. 'Take whatever you want just please don't hurt me. Please God, don't hurt me.'

Either she believed that it was God who was car-jacking her or that God was about to help her stop me from car-jacking her, now that she had announced that she was being car-jacked. It was fairly evident that she could use some assistance – why did people always over-complicate the God thing, inadvertently proving his non-existence?

Now that she was free to speak, I pressed down hard on the side of her head, concerned about how quickly she might raise herself up and realise it was me. I leaned my body into her side, mainly so she could feel my weight and not do anything stupid.

'Stick your fingers in your mouth and take off your rings,' I growled.

'What?'

'Do it!' I pushed her head down harder. Strands of thick, conditioned hair felt silky on my fingers.

'Ok, Ok.' She opened her legs. I don't know why. Maybe it released some panic-calming endorphins or made for an easier repose. She stuck her index finger in her mouth as far as it would go, searching for metal so her teeth knew from where to pull. She moved her finger ever so slightly in and out like a bulimic whore in an effort to remove all three rings.

To be clear, there was nothing remotely attractive about Henrietta. At least not to me. If I was going to do it with a woman, this is not the ice-cream I'd be licking. However, right now – spread-eagled face down in the boot of her car sucking on her long slender fingers – she was kind of sexy. Her mouth started to move in succinct but elongated spasms. She spat out the rings, more as a precaution against choking than a defiant final act.

I scooped up the wet rings in my hand and stuffed them in my pocket. Now for the coat and the bag. Yes, she was obsequious, but how long would she remain that way? And if I took my hand off her back, who wouldn't get up and run if they had the opportunity? That was a chance I simply could not take. I grabbed what looked like the end of a sort of string sticking out from underneath her thigh. As I pulled, the coloured spotty triangles of bunting just kept on coming as though from a magician's hat. Who the fuck has bunting in their boot? I tied it around her ankles, folded up her legs and pushed both them and her deeper into the boot. She toppled over like a broken doll.

'No, please don't do this,' she begged. 'Please. I implore you.'

Shut up will you? I was trying to talk as little as possible, feeling completely exposed having forgotten my balaclava. I banged the boot down hard. Once it was firmly shut, I ran round to the front of the car to grab the coat and the bag. There was no way to know whether she'd be able to climb through from the boot to the front and I was too scared to turn around and look.

I flung open the driver's door and stretched my body over into the passenger seat when I felt something move. The inside lights of the car had turned off and it was so dark I couldn't see a thing. My hand patted around the seat searching for the bag and the... ah, got the coat.

'Ow!' What the fuck? The coat bit me. Hang on a minute, that wasn't a coat, it was a fucking dog. Shit. It was one of those rat dogs, small and pointless, that were bred to look like furry handbags, as well as live in one. This one was clearly trained to kill.

'Ow!' The fucking thing was snapping at me now, jumping up and down on the seat, trying to sink its teeth into me.

'Bite him, Miss Congeniality, go on poppet, do it for Mummy. Bite him hard.' Henrietta was barking muffled orders at her rat bitch from the boot. I pulled my hood around, hoping to cover the left side of my face. I found the bag. I think I was bleeding. It hurt like hell, and felt like teeth were still in my flesh. I grabbed the bag with my other hand whilst trying to follow the trajectory of the incessant yelping. I saw the pale devil-yellow glow of its eyes and whacked the bag solid against its body. It flew hard, straight, thudding against the windscreen. There was a descending thump onto the dashboard, a short whimper, then nothing.

'Miss Congeniality? Miss Congeniality?' Henrietta called hysterically. 'Are you okay, poppet?' I was moved. Moved to wonder if, after I was finished robbing the bitch, I should have her sectioned.

'Are you seriously more concerned for the life of this rat than your own?' I asked in the deepest man-rasp I could muster.

'Miss Congeniality is a Shih Tzu! Is she hurt? She's hungry. Her food is in the back.' So that's why she was looking in the boot. I had wondered what she could possibly be searching for if her car had broken down. Henrietta Crosly-Burke change a tyre? Food or no food, this was clearly a trap. No one could care more about the nutritional needs of their canine at this point in their life and I was no idiot. I grabbed the coat and the bag and slammed the door. Some people deserved to be robbed.

I ran back to my car and threw the loot inside. I tried to reverse, but my hand hurt like hell from the bite and I lost control of the wheel. The car skidded backwards into a muddy patch of grass. Pressing hard on the accelerator to get back on the road I could feel my body sweating. I turned the engine off, and counted to twenty, my eyes fixed on Henrietta's car in front of me. Any minute now, I expected a demonic-looking banshee to break out.

Thank God the car started first time. I pushed hard on the pedal, spun the wheel round as I reversed the car and drove back down the road towards Gatlin. As I sped away, I looked in my rear-view mirror to see a dark mass slump out onto the pavement. Fuck! I drained what was left of the whisky in the flask and breathed out, winding down both windows. I needed air. Shit.

What was I thinking? I slowed down a touch as I saw a street light and tried to raise my hand to examine the damage. Blood. Great. The missing ingredient in every perfect crime.

'Jesus fucking Christ!'

In a remarkable twist of fate, I arrived home without encountering a tsunami, running over a child or indeed receiving a speeding ticket, all of which were entirely plausible possibilities considering a dog the size of a fucking hamster and pretending to be a coat had bitten me during my incredibly badly planned robbery and I would now need to go to the doctor and get a tetanus.

I needed my bed. I put my handbag on the table and heard the soft rattle of my bottle of paracetamol. I suddenly felt a real sense that I had been neglecting myself. I'd been so overwhelmed with Ava, the school fees, what to make for dinner and motherhood in general, that I had no time for myself, for the things I wanted to do, a little me time. Oh to have just five minutes of uninterrupted peace so I could kill myself.

I heard voices. Taking the stairs two at a time, I went to check. They were coming from Papa's room. A woman's voice. I leaned into the door. Ugh! Dirty talk. Dirty and panting. Geriatric intercourse. I hoped he was still wearing his pacemaker. Unbelievable. Was I the only one in this house acting responsibly?

Wednesday

I could not believe I was here of all places. Pink rose bushes bordered the front garden. A grey wooden fence opened onto a winding path and led to a thick oak-panelled yellow front door. Lace curtains were hanging in the bay window. From the outside, it looked like any other house; however, from the inside it was a hot box of staphylococcus that was also known as Gatlin Medical Practice.

The practice straddled two boroughs so half the patients actually lived in Brigham. Posters covered most of the walls at eye level. 'Prostate cancer – don't wait until it's too late.' 'Alzheimer's – don't forget we're here to help you.' 'Cystitis – The Gatlin Apothecary now sells over-the-counter medication.' Yet I would bet money that none of these people had an enlarged prostate, that if there was an Alzheimer's question they would need reminding to ask it, and that the majority would want to talk about a burning sensation experienced whilst urinating. It was unlikely that any of these people were dying or even close to dying, or that their illnesses would not pass on their own in their own time without the aid or interference of a doctor's supposedly expert opinion. I was already suspicious of how efficiently this tetanus would be administered.

'I need to see the doctor,' I said to the woman behind the glass.

'Name?' Her accent was heavy and the Jamaican lilt made

me feel sleepy. Her fake nails were so long that I had no idea how she managed to input any name into the system.

'Drea Peiris,' I said.

She yawned, pressing down on the keys with an upside down pencil. 'Don't have an appointment,' she said, making no attempt to hide her disdain.

'I know, but it's an emergency,' I saw my breath steam as I whispered into the glass.

'Can't do nothin',' she said, shaking her head from side to side.

'You can't do anything?'

'That's what I said. Can't do nothin'.' She looked right at me, one side of her lips slung down.

'Well I have to see a doctor this morning,' I said.

'I got nothin' to give you,' she said.

'I'd like to speak to your manager,' I said.

'She ain't 'ere.'

'Who is in charge?'

'Priti! Next.'

I moved along the counter. No one asked me to but I thought that if I was courteous, it might play to my advantage. A woman in a niqab appeared. All I could see were her brown eyes. It reminded me of the Steve Martin film 'The Man with Two Brains' where he had an intimate relationship with a cerebrum in a glass jar.

'I'm Priti,' she said. But are you? How can I tell?

'I need an emergency appointment.'

'What's it for?' she said, eyes soft.

'A tetanus shot.'

'Why do you think you might need one?' she said, eyes curious.

'I got bitten by a rat.'

'A rat! Oh no,' she exclaimed, eyes wide. 'Where?' she said, eyes sensitive.

'What difference does it make? I got bitten by a rat and I need a tetanus now.'

She looked at me with eyes hurt and pointed to a poster behind her head. I looked up. Big black letters on a yellow background. 'ABUSE – Any patient who is verbally or physically abusive to our staff will be told to leave the premises.'

'You think that was abusive?' I asked.

I was seething with rage at this fucking jobsworth, but I needed to get this tetanus before Henrietta and her rat had the last laugh.

'I think we were getting there,' she said, eyes calm.

I took a deep breath. 'Could you give me an emergency appointment for a tetanus shot please?' Why people appreciated politeness even when they knew it was completely fake, I had yet to fathom.

She bent over the head of the receptionist and, scanning the computer screen, said, 'the doctor can see you at 11.20,' eyes cold.

'Thanks. I'll go and come back.' I was already half a shoulder turn away before I caught myself on the end of her dulcet tones.

'Then you'll miss your appointment,' she said, eyes flat.

'No I won't. I'll definitely be back on time.'

'You'll miss your appointment because it will be given to someone else if you're not here,' she said, eyes determined.

'Why?' Was it me or was she being really fucking facetious? 'Because that's the way it works,' she answered, eyes defiant.

'That doesn't make any sense. If you give me an appointment that I intend to keep, what's it got to do with what I do with my time in the interim?'

'If it's an emergency, you stay in the surgery,' she said, eyes smug. I looked up at the clock. Ten past nine. I walked backwards keeping constant eye contact with her. She looked at me suspiciously. When the back of my thighs hit the plastic chair, I sat down. Once I was seated, she pointed behind her again to the poster.

It was my lucky day: baby clinic. The clinic was supposedly confined to the back room but toys, babies, and no doubt diseases still to be discovered from these potent infant carriers, spilled out all over the surgery. It attracted a certain crowd, namely hormonally challenged women finding their lives unrecognisable. They arrived with a clipped and forced gaiety, essential in their need to befriend other women of the same ilk experiencing the same hostile takeover of mind and body. These women wandered around in a timeless fug, content to waste time – time, I assumed, that must now be a precious commodity as it cannot fail to be once motherhood begins to drain the life blood out of you. Convincing each other and themselves that merely having squeezed a human out of their vagina is basis enough to both begin and sustain a friendship. To say nothing of the pond green, snotty-nosed children they arrived with – the precocious older siblings of pond green snotty-nosed babies. I listened with tedious fascination.

'Hello. It's so nice to see you.'

'Oh and you too.'

'Wow! She's really enjoying her food isn't she?'

'I thought you usually go to the other baby clinic?' I'd seen hyenas with more sincerity. Why not just say 'your baby is so fat' and 'I was hoping not to see you here'? A cacophony of banal high-pitched incomprehensible chatter, and that was just from the mothers. I picked up the magazine on top of the pile. French interior design. They had a special supplement on country houses in Normandy. I was intrigued and started reading about Alex and Poppy's new life. From over the top of my pages I could see Priti gliding officiously back and forth behind the reception like Darth Vader's secret mistress.

'How old is she?'

'Three months.'

'And how old is she?'

'Just turned four.'

Seriously, do any of us really give a shit?

'She's got so much hair.'

'Oh I know; I don't know where she gets it.'

Really. You don't think it might be from either you, your husband, a sperm donor.

'It's an unusual colour.'

'Yes, it's kind of a red tinge with some copper undertones.' She's a ging-a. Dear God, can this get any more fucking boring?

'Is she eating yet?'

'I gave her some vanilla fromage frais yesterday for the first time, but I don't think she was too impressed.'

Yes, looks like it can get more boring and it's happening right here right now. Ye of little faith.

'That's a shame. I read they need calcium from as many dairy sources as possible.'

'We don't do dairy at all. Cow's milk has been found to cause all sorts of health problems. Especially allergies,' she whispered. 'We do soy,' she said returning to normal volume, as if soy was something to shout about, 'it's so much better for you.'

'Really? They've said the isoflavones that mimic estrogen in the soy could be linked to early puberty. Gosh, it's all so confusing isn't it! Soy, cow, which one is it?'

It's less confusing if you stop talking. If I tried to kill myself here, would they notice in time to resuscitate me? The surgery door opened and a mother in a velour tracksuit with her hair pulled tight into a high ponytail entered. She pushed a double buggy with an older child in tow. The mother was white, the kids in the pram were mixed race and looked nothing like either each other or the teenage boy sloping in alongside them, who was black. Soy and Cow exchanged glances and raised eyebrows.

'You've just shat yourself again haven't you?' the young mother demanded from the babies. Nobody owned up although probably down to lack of speech than insolence. 'Uhh, I forgot to bring the wipes,' she said to herself. She looked around. She had come to the right place. You could not swing a dead cat without hitting a baby or a pack of moistened tissues.

'Got any wipes?' she asked.

Soy and Cow locked eyes and then answered in stereo. 'Sure!'

'Here you go,' smiled Soy. 'They're infused with chamomile,' Soy said off-handedly.

'Or you can try these ones,' said Cow. 'These have lavender,' she said in a most deprecating manner, as if she wasn't sure why, as if it didn't matter, and like she would be just as happy to purchase baby wipes without herbal infusions. This was where the mothers of Gatlin met the mothers of Brigham and not even a packet of baby wipes could establish common ground.

'Anyone sittin' there?' asked Brigham.

'No. No,' they answered in perfect unison. Where they divided over the benefits of differing baby milk, they united over the benefits of non-differing baby fathers. The babies in the double pram started to cry as if someone had stabbed them.

The door opened and a Chinese-looking man in a suit and briefcase coughed his way towards reception. It was a chesty cough with bass tones that echoed in deep pockets where you'd expect bacterial organisms to lay nesting. He got in line.

'Did you see the papers this morning?' asked Soy.

'I certainly did,' answered Cow with a displeased face. 'My husband is beyond furious. That property has been promised to Gatlin for a year. We need a new badminton court.'

'Completely. It is outrageous,' agreed Soy. 'Totally unacceptable. We don't actually need another school.'

'Especially not a faith school,' said Cow, leaning in over their wonderfully beautiful babies playing together on the mat.

'Where do your kids go, then?' asked Brigham, taking Soy and Cow by surprise as they had intended for their conversation, which they were having out loud in a doctors' waiting area, to remain members only.

'Gatlin,' said Soy and Cow through forced, straight smiles. It was quite something to be able to smile in a straight line. I tried to do it behind my magazine, but failed. The supplement advised using trees instead of fencing to add to the rustic charm of your French country house. Had Alex been able to tear himself away from the cunnilingus, his newest hobby, long enough for him and Poppy to discuss the merits of trees versus fence?

'That's a private school innit?' asked Brigham whilst shovelling out wipes full of shit from her child's bottom. I wondered how much food this child ate that this amount of waste could be extracted. Ava was four when I'd met Alex. I'd missed this part and now found regret to be absent.

'Yes,' confirmed Soy and Cow.

'We can't all afford to send our kids to fancy schools,' said Brigham matter-of-factly.

'While I do sympathise, that land had been in development for Gatlin for over a year,' said Soy and then, turning exclusively to Cow, 'my eldest boy has been selected to play for County juniors. Where is he supposed to practise?' Cow showed suitable disappointment regarding Soy's first world tragedy. China had alerted reception to his arrival and was seated, hunched forward, coughing up bits of lung.

'We've been on a waiting list for three months. My eldest hasn't been to school all that time, so I'm really happy about it,' said Brigham.

'It's a faith school,' answered Cow quickly, 'so I doubt you'll even be able to get in.' She pursed her lips to show that she was simply the bearer of bad news, the fact that this bad news might make her happy was merely a coincidence.

'I'm Cafolic,' replied Brigham, wrapping up an enormous nappy which she dropped in the bin.

'Excuse me,' called out a thin and pretty Eastern European accented woman in smart trousers and a tailored blouse, a Croatian newspaper in her hand. 'You're can't leave that nappy there?'

'Why?' asked Brigham, adjusting the baby back into the pram and returning the wipes to Soy and Cow.

'That's not a nappy bin,' said Croatia.

'It's just shit. It's no big deal,' answered Brigham.

'If you're going to have children, then you should know how to look after them,' said Croatia, her accent thickening the more riled she became.

'It's none of your business how I look after my children,' Brigham said, her chest expanding. However, her path was blocked by prams and other children, so she resigned herself to protruding her neck like an aggressive pigeon. I tried to look away. The supplement advised making the extra effort to get to know one's neighbours as this was often how land was acquired in France. Croatia walked over to reception, tutting loudly as she passed the bin – which was, in truth, emitting a less than fresh odour.

'My appointment was for nine o' clock,' she said.

Priti was alone at the helm. 'Sorry about the delay,' her eyes smiled. 'The doctor was running late, but he's here now. You're next.'

'Why didn't anyone make an announcement? If you know

the doctor is running late, you should say something, not keep us all waiting.' Croatia made valid points.

'I'm very sorry about that. You should have been told,' apologised Priti, eyes contrite. One of the consulting room doors opened and a black woman emerged in a smart suit with a shiny stethoscope around her neck like medical jewellery.

'Good luck with everything,' said the doctor to an exiting patient before closing the door quickly, maybe in case we all ran in demanding consultation, which was possible. Croatia sat back down. China had started to hack bits of phlegm into a tissue that I wished was man-size.

Soy was still explaining religion to Brigham. 'Well, as a practising Catholic, I suppose you're lucky to have a free source of education,' she said.

'Free ain't the only thing. The girl's' school, opened a year back, is already number three in the league tables,' said Brigham.

'Really?' chimed Soy and Cow with a double splash of angry and envy.

'But we're not proper cafolics. I mean, seriously, if there was a God, you'd think He would have made one of their fathers stick around,' she nodded in the direction of her kids. 'But I've started going recently coz you have to play the game to make sure you get in. Nuffin's for certain.' Being a good Catholic school, I was sure that one of the priests would be willing to let one slip in for a little extra holy communion.

'I'm going to find out what's going on. Nancy's going to start getting antsy, aren't you, poppet?' Nancy looked as if she was born antsy. Soy approached reception. 'Excuse me, our appointment was for ten past nine.'

'I know. I'm very sorry about that,' said Priti, eyes humble. 'The doctor was running late so the nurse has been covering for him, but she's just started seeing the babies now so you'll be in next.'

'There is a poster right there detailing the patients' charter. This lack of communication is poor form,' said Soy.

'I'm really very sorry. We will endeavour to do better,' said Priti, eyes ashamed.

China dropped his tissue on the floor. One of the babies made a beeline believing it to be food.

'I'm not really sure how I feel about pretending to be religious,' pondered Cow to Brigham.

'You don't have to feel anything about it,' stated Brigham.

'I mean, what sort of a message is it sending our children?' Cow continued. 'What do we have left to call sacred if even our faith becomes fraudulent.'

'My Dad paid his taxes his whole life and now his grandchildren don't even have a school to go to. That's fraud in my book,' answered Brigham angrily. At this, Croatia stood up and walked to reception.

'How much longer?' she said.

'We've got a TB clinic this morning so we're busier than normal. Sorry.'

Croatia strutted back to her seat, puffing out hot air. She looked straight at China and then shouted loudly at reception. 'We wouldn't even need a clinic for a disease that was wiped out of England years ago if they didn't keep letting in every Tom, Dick and Harry. What's this afternoon, the Bird Flu Clinic?'

I approached reception. 'Excuse me, my hand is really hurting. Have there been any cancellations?'

'The doctor won't be able to see you after all. There are too many people. You'll have to come back this afternoon,' snapped Priti.

'What! That's ridiculous! You gave me an appointment. I'm not here because my nose is running, I need a tetanus.' Priti pointed to the poster behind her head.

'Now look here,' I said swivelling round to the side where

there was a gap in the glass and no one could hear me. 'How come you're only pointing to that poster for me?' I asked.

'Because you should know better,' Priti answered, eyes burning.

'Why?'

'Because you're Asian,' she said, eyes dead.

'So?'

'So. I see the way you look at me.' she said.

'I doubt you see as much as you think.'

'You disgust me,' said Priti.

'You're... racist,' I said, knowing it was tenuous.

'I'm the manager.'

I turned to leave the surgery and, as I did, I heard the doctor call China in. 'Peter Lu, room two.' On his way, he stopped in front of Croatia and said, 'Lady, if you have bird flu, this place not for you. You need animal doctor. And wear a mask for goodness sake.'

I lay still in my bed. The twilight tried to force its way past the curtains. It wasn't hard as they didn't hang properly. They never had, falling down at the centre, the very place they should have been able to support themselves. I hoped the dark would find me.

The leaflet I'd picked up from the surgery after my afternoon injection listed side effects of the tetanus jab: redness, swelling, hives, fever, nausea. No mention of sadness, which seemed to be the only side effect I was experiencing. I guess that came from somewhere else. Though it was also true that happiness didn't interest me. It had nothing to do with my life. What had always been of greater fascination was the line. The thin line between looking in the mirror and seeing the day ahead or looking in the mirror and seeing nothing. Nothing at all. A complete absence of essence. When I was younger, the absence was disconcerting and I allowed it to disturb me. But as I got older, there came a numbing. An acceptance. I've heard people refer to it as wisdom, and I wondered if my need to end it all was the same pill by a different name.

I opened the bottle. Still fifty left. Fifty faithful friends. I'd put an end to this business with Ava, this motherhood thing. It was a huge responsibility. It was a fucking insane amount of expectation on one person and not just a little claustrophobic; there was simply no room to breathe. To be able to kill yourself without the guilt of having to be alive for another person. It was a selfish set-up. I felt as if for the last few days I had joined an activist group to protest against giving up on life, but that wasn't me. It wasn't who I was. It wasn't where I came from, and a person's roots are important. Do whatever you want to do – that was me. I swallowed the first two. I thought twos would be manageable. This wasn't the exit I'd planned. There was no steak or glass of red wine; no people watching or idle pre-death self-reflection. And doing it whilst being this sad, when for so long I had viewed it as an act of liberation, felt like cheating. But I didn't care anymore. I had looked after Ava since she was four. Having a mother for ten years was good innings. Two more down. The tablets stuck; I'd have to get some water. Better to do that now in case it got difficult to walk later on. I filled the plastic glass to the top and glanced in the mirror. I don't know why or what I thought I might find. There was nothing there.

Two more. Two or four. Four was better. Why hadn't I ever changed these truly awful curtains? Poppy wouldn't have stood for old curtains like these. She'd have had new ones up by now. Or no curtains so it would be as if they were making love in the wild. Their French neighbours could come by with some rank smelling cheese and red wine and sit on fold-up metal chairs watching through the windows.

Two more. Or four more? Four more. What was love really about? Had I ever really been in love? I'd said it, more than once, and I meant it at the time. But looking back, it had never felt completely true. I think that was because I didn't see how it could be true if these men were saying that they loved me back. Lovable, me? Two more. No four more. So how many was that? The pills hadn't remotely begun to take effect, yet the screaming seemed to be coming from somewhere. It had to be coming from somewhere other than my house and from someone other than Ava. As it continued, I began to identify my present state of denial. How I didn't want the noise to be coming from my house. How I didn't want it to be Ava's voice because if it was Ava hysterically screaming in such a manner, I was, unfortunately, still alive enough to have to go downstairs and see what the problem was. Which begged the question of why. Why was it so hard to kill oneself in the privacy of one's own fucking bedroom?

'MUM!! MUM!!' Begrudgingly I climbed out of bed wearing a just a torn T-shirt and full-size briefs. I downed a load more tablets before I left the room. Mother had been superstitious. She said you should never make someone turn around once they'd decided to go. I put the bottle of pills on the bedside table. Ava better have a good reason for calling me back.

Wednesday Evening

'Ava!' I snapped, running down the stairs two at a time, chips of hastily applied, cheap yellow paint from the wooden bannister coming off in my hands. 'What's the matter?'

I call to her without any idea of where she is or what has happened. Part of me, a scientific and statistical part, thinks if I am the mother and I am about to kill myself then whatever is happening to Ava will always be less dramatic, which is a good thing. But the irrational and emotional part compiles lists of all the random acts of tragedy that constantly befall people every day.

I fling myself off the penultimate step into the living room shot-put style where I find my daughter. On the sofa is a familiar sight, arousing in turn familiar feelings. Amelia Salter was in my house, again, crying. Well, sniffing loudly – as if she might have been crying before and could start again at any moment. Ava had her arms around her and a pained expression on her face.

'Ava?' I was no longer worried. No longer concerned that I had fallen into the minus 0.1 percent of people whose child has been ravaged by a bear in their home. The situation was much worse.

'Mum. It's so awful. You'll never believe what's happened?'

'Probably not.'

'Tabatha's mum was robbed last night. In her car! And they killed her dog!'

'What? No I didn't!' I exclaimed.

'They did, Mum. The robbers, they killed her dog,' stated Ava.

'How… why… how do you know this?'

'That's what Tabatha's mum said.'

The puzzle still didn't look right. So why is Amelia here crying? I felt like I should go back to the doctor's surgery and talk about my Alzheimer's. I was very confused.

'It's brought it all back for Amelia. What happened to her mum.' I looked at Ava like I still needed more information and, like a jack-in-the-box, Ava sprang up from her seat, grabbing me by the arm and turning me sideways. 'Mum. You need to be understanding. She needs our support.'

'Does she, Ava? Maybe we are "enabling" her with our support. Remember how your self-help books speak about taking responsibility for your own actions.' Ava gave a reproachful look. I was scraping the barrel and apparently not in secret. She sat back down on the sofa.

'Amelia is going to stay for dinner, and so is Tabatha,' said Ava definitively.

'Tabatha?'

'Yes,' she lowered her voice. 'She's gone to buy cigarettes. I said you wouldn't mind this once.'

I wouldn't have minded on any occasion, and much less so on this one because I had just run out of cigarettes, having bought no more, assuming it would be difficult to smoke when I was dead. It had barely been forty-eight hours since I'd robbed both these girls' mothers and had been bitten by Henrietta's fucking rat dog, for which I was still suffering. Now the bitch was lying saying I killed the damn thing. Shit. And her stuff was still all over my room.

'I need to put some clothes on,' I announced, hiking back up the stairs. Henrietta's coat and bag were lying on the floor by my bed like hostages, waiting to expose me, ready to run.

Panicking, I stuffed them at the back of the top cupboard, where they promptly fell back out. I pushed them in again more forcefully. Her rings were still in my pocket. I put them in my jewellery box. It was odd to finally have some jewellery to fill it instead of weed and rizlas. Back down the stairs again, I panted into the living room.

'Mum.'

'Yes Ava?'

'You're not dressed.' I looked down. How right you are. There I stood, still in my full-size briefs. The doorbell rang. Tabatha. I did not want to see her. And especially not whilst still in my knickers. I did, however, urgently need a cigarette. I was also feeling a little tired. I'd had a heavy day and a tetanus. It was probably one of the side effects. Everything had side effects these days. Even paracetamol.

Paracetamol? Ohhh, okay! So that was what was happening. This might be a problem. Not a big one – I wasn't dying. You couldn't die on eight paracetamol. I stopped in my tracks. Had it been eight? I couldn't swear on it. Though I could say that my body was receiving a message of some sort. This situation might need to be contained. Maybe a little lie-down.

'Amelia and I would like some chicken curry and rice please, Mum. And can you get the door? I blew my lips out and made a funny noise like those babies had been doing at the surgery. I walked, slowly. Tabatha wore skinny jeans and a Gatlin sweatshirt, her blonde hair tied up back and high. I was relieved to see something in her prettiness looking less than perfect.

'Come into the kitchen,' I said. Let's call it ten. It must be ten. What would ten paracetamol do? Hardly touch the sides, I'm sure. It was the number one choice for most women – probably because you could buy it at the same time you bought a bar of chocolate or a packet of cigarettes. It was as if the supermarkets wanted you to do it. Had enough? Doesn't seem worth it anymore? We agree. We won't make you walk down all these different aisles looking for a way out – we'll give you one right here at the till point. Won't break the bank either. Pop it in your handbag, mum's the word.

'Give me a cigarette,' I said. Tabatha unwrapped the packet and offered it to me.

'Do you mind if I smoke?' she asked.

I shrugged and fell into a chair. As long as she gave me one, I was indifferent to what she did with the rest. She held out the orange flame of her lighter and I blew out a long, lopsided ring of smoke. I pulled my knees up to my chest to hug them because I thought it might make the weird falling sensation in my chest go away, but it didn't so I lowered them down again. Tabatha pinched a floret of over-boiled, two-day-old broccoli from the saucepan, and popped it her mouth. I pushed the pan her way. The smell made me nauseous. Tabatha took another. She must have been starving. I wondered if the emptiness in my chest was hunger. I could smell myself a little. I wondered if Tabatha could smell me. I found teenagers customarily full of noise and angst and questions, but this girl was oddly appreciative of the silence. There were definitely two sides to her – as there are to most people – but these were two very extreme sides. There are people whose clothes and homes look like yours and you socialise with – people who only have one car, a mortgage on their one property, little thought to holidays, let alone a holiday home, and a slightly ropey, though well-intentioned plan to rob other people and pay for school fees. And on the opposite side of the coin, there are people who don't look anything like you who, from a precocious early age of wealth and access, begin a rapid metamorphosis into arrogance and entitlement. Yet here, in my kitchen, next to me in my knickers with the combined scent of my womanliness and that broccoli, Tabatha seemed oddly peaceful. I was witnessing her straddle two different worlds and I felt myself wanting to applaud her for fitting so well into mine.

Our reverie was slashed by none other than the lovely Ava, who seemed caught in the midst of some bizarre Victorian lesbian romance.

'Mum! I told you that Amelia was famished and languishing with hunger!' she exclaimed, bursting into the kitchen full of shock and outrage.

'Uh, no, you didn't Ava. I would have remembered.'

'Tab! Oh my God, how are you?'

'Ok,' said Tabatha.

'How's your mum?' asked Ava.

'Ok.'

'It's a terrible thing that happened to her. She didn't deserve it. No one deserves that,' said Ava confidently.

Actually, Ava, she did deserve it. Maybe not before but she definitely does now that she's lying about me killing her fucking dog.

'And her poor poor dog,' Ava continued.

'Violently gutted and his insides strewn over the street like party banners,' said Tabatha.

'What! Who said that?' I demanded, slowly.

'Mum,' answered Tabatha.

'Does she have people at home to look after her?' Ava always asked reasonable questions; questions I would never have asked because I failed to give a shit. However, I did have a more interesting line of enquiry.

'Did she report it to the police?'

'No.'

'Why not?' demanded Ava.

'I don't know,' replied Tabatha. There was a noticeable apathy to her mother's robbery that I could not help but find endearing.

'It must simply be because she is weak and needs to get her strength back. I'm sure she will once she's rested. Don't you think, Mum?'

'A woman must be rested before she trifles with the law,' I said, semi-laughing, but I didn't know why. I was feeling a trifle tired myself. The door opened and Amelia entered.

'Is my dinner ready?' she asked, in all seriousness.

Dinner. How did I get here? To this strange and twisted fairground of domesticity? What could I make for dinner? The three girls loomed large as the room became smaller. I don't think anything had been defrosted. I hadn't done a proper shop for weeks and although baked beans were an option, there was a tiny possibility that I might be dying. Having never spent too much time with Ava's actual friends, it was odd that the blurred, elongated faces of Amelia and Tabatha in my kitchen were the last thing I remembered before blacking out and waking up in paper knickers.

My eyes appeared to open independently from my brain. Like my mind and body had agreed to disagree and actions were now being completed without consultation. I had a sneaking suspicion that my body thought my mind could not be trusted. Bright lights flickered. Strip lighting? Never a good sign. I was either in a hospital or a prison. The last thirty-six hours tumbled into my head in jigsaw pieces. I hoped it wasn't a prison. I was on a bed. Pale baby-blue walls and white ceilings. And what was that beeping? Pip. Pip. Pip. I looked around without moving my head. In order of ascending shock, I saw one jug of water, one painting of a field of flowers, one drip, one heart monitor...one Tabatha Crosly-Burke? She leaned closer. I tried to speak but she couldn't hear me. 'It's ok,' she said jumping up from the chair. 'I'll get Ava.' She moved to go but I grabbed her wrist.

'Why are you... what happened?' I whispered.

'You don't remember? You took some pills. Not enough. I'll get Ava.' She ran outside and the door didn't have time to close before Ava burst in, her beautiful face looking like a football. She'd been crying.

'You woke up? What happened? They won't tell me anything. Oh, I was so scared I'd lost you.' She threw herself upon me. 'I don't know what I'd do if something happened to you.' She was upset, rambling as she tended to do when she was anxious.

My chest hurt. No, not my chest, my stomach. It was coming back to me. The pills. I'd taken some but then the doorbell had rung and I'd been interrupted. Story of my fucking life these days. And now Ava was crying.

'Have the doctors spoken to you yet?' she asked, sniffing, salty water from her eyes merging in the middle of her face, snot streaming from her nose. Hang on a minute. How does Tabatha know about the pills if Ava doesn't? There's no way Ava wouldn't have mentioned me swallowing a truckload of headache tablets.

'Not yet. Listen I'm fine. Run down, that's all.' This was exactly the kind of shit I wanted to make sure didn't happen. This is why it was so essential that suicide was successful. If not, then attempted suicide – the category I had been down-graded into – was a nightmare. An open cavity into which all manner of pestiferous incidentals found their way. Regret, recrimination, social services to name but a few. Oh why hadn't I got it right the first time? I should have planned it better and done it on a night where there was no one in the house. I didn't want to see Ava cry; I couldn't bear it. And I was angry that now the decision to kill myself was suddenly infected with Ava's tears. If Ava was in the dark about the pills, I needed to make sure it stayed that way. However, the fact that I was here in a hospital bed meant that Ava wouldn't be the only one with questions.

'Ms Peiris?' A young man in a white coat entered followed by two cherubs. The doctor looked too young to have read, digested and remembered any of the information about my situation whilst the medical students looked too young to be learning about the biology of flowers, let alone people. The doctor was also overly handsome. Not my kind of good looking, but chiselled and defined in a way that for the average woman would present a symmetrical attractiveness. However, I personally found it distrustful, as if he had slipped into medicine to be closer to gynaecology without looking like a pervert. Medicine was a respectable discipline and should be offering flawed but intelligent thinkers, God-complex sufferers, not catalogue models. And now he came to my bed to talk to me about death and how mine had been unsuccessful. But luckily, I was going to be fine. What did this boy know about death? He'd barely been alive long enough.

'Doctor, I think my daughter and her friend were just leaving.'

'I don't think so, Mum,' Ava flashed her eyes at Tabatha, who looked at me, and then the floor.

'Ava, I'll explain everything afterwards. These things can get pretty technical.'

'Mum, I'm not five. I'm staying.'

'I'm afraid you're going to have to wait in reception, please. Patient confidentiality.'

So the doctor wasn't just a pretty face. Ava and Tabatha left the room.

We all watched for the door to shut, me especially. 'Ms Peiris. How are you feeling?'

All three faces stared down at me with bated breath. It was obvious that these medical students had been dragged by the collar into my room with the promise of learning something; that their time here with me was intended to further medical science and develop their keen young minds.

'Like I tried to kill myself and did a spectacularly lousy job.'

'Was that your intention? Were you trying to kill yourself?' asked the doctor.

'Listen, Doctor, I was joking. I took too many headache pills because I wasn't concentrating on what I was doing,' I said smiling and trying to lighten the mood.

'You had over ten times the acceptable amount in your blood stream,' said the doctor, kindly but seriously.

'I know and I'm sorry about that,' I said.

'This is a serious situation. I see you have a child with you at home.'

'Yes, and I appreciate you not saying anything in front of her.' My stomach hurt and my ears were ringing. The medical students looked uncomfortable. Attempted suicide was aggravating for everyone.

'We need to know that you're in a position to look after yourself.'

'I am.'

'We're going to have the mental health team take a look at you...' Here we go... He kept talking, but I stopped listening. Now it was all about protocol. They were trying to get me into the system. No one really had the time to find out why I carried fifty paracetamol around with me all day, had done for years, and why I thought taking them all in one go would be such a great fucking idea. They just wanted to make sure they'd ticked all the right administrative boxes.

'There's really no need,' I said, trying to move my arms and feeling them heavy as though they had been pinned down with lead weights.

'Ms Peiris, you're not going anywhere,' he pushed my shoulders back onto the pillow firmly. I just needed to say what this man wanted to hear to get him out of my room so I could get out of this hospital.

'Doctor, you're right. I think it must have been a cry for help. Everyone feels better after a good cry.' The medical students seemed unconvinced.

'I'll check in on you tomorrow.' Tomorrow? Are these people crazy? I took a few pills; it wasn't cancer. In fact, even people with cancer lived at home.

'Doctor, I really need to go home tonight. I'm feeling a lot better. I think I got a lot of stuff out and now I just need to go home and live my life. Alive. You know.'

'Ms Peiris, I'm not discharging you today. You're still receiving treatment,' he pointed to the IV. 'You've been through an ordeal and you need to rest. I'm going to ask the mental health team to report to me and have a conversation with your daughter so everyone is on the same page.'

'No one is talking to Ava.'

'In situations like this, it's best if the whole family knows what's happening.'

'No one talks to Ava.'

'I'm not sure you're hearing me Ms Peiris. I don't think you're in the best place to be making decisions about your health right now.'

Oh, I heard you, doctor. I heard you so well that I'm now angry. Don't fucking tell me what to do. Truth be known, I am a little embarrassed, not that you'd understand. You see I had a plan: one that I made a very long time ago, and would have executed perfectly had I not been so rudely interrupted.

'Doctor. Thanks for saving my life. I'm going to give you that, even though there's no way of knowing whether I had even taken enough pills for my organs to fail, one by one, ensuring that I die the long and painfully drawn out death that paracetamol assures, or – because I was so rudely interrupted, and not for the first time may I add, and unable to swallow the entire bottle as planned – I would not have merely felt a little queasy and spent a couple of crampy days in bed watching

One Flew Over the Cuckoo's Nest. We don't know that because those idiot teenagers out there panicked and brought me here. But it's over now; your work here is done, so you can move on to someone more deserving, someone with pancreatic ulcers or a pulsating brain tumour, someone who wants and needs your help and is desperate for you to spend your time talking to their devastated family. I am not that person, and in regards to what I need I am discharging myself right now because I am fine. I no longer require your assistance, and mostly because as far as what's best for my family, I don't want to hear that you, these two simpletons you travel with or anyone else in this hospital has opened their mouth and said one thing to my fucking daughter. NO ONE TALKS TO AVA. Do you hear me, doctor?'

A loud bleeping filled the room. I seemed to have detached myself from my drip.

Thursday Morning

Life was testing me. I wasn't sure why, as it had been testing me for years and I thought we had an agreement. I was under the distinct impression that a truce had been negotiated. That if I showed willing and played my part in good faith then that would be it. That if I accepted the cards dealt to me without complaint, without comparison to the lives of others and, dare I say it, with charisma – a charismatic misanthrope – then there would be no more surprises. Nothing would be sent to try me that I couldn't handle, nothing to floor me because I had already been floored, and life and I had agreed that it was to be the last time. But over the last couple of days, I felt like the contract life and I had entered into was not worth the macrocosmic toilet paper it was written on. A car accident on the main road coming into Gatlin from Brigham had resulted in a three-car pile-up. What this meant for me is that Doctor Everyoung and his foetal cohorts could save people who wanted to be saved. I got dressed quick smart when I heard the commotion, pausing for a moment to marvel at my knickers, which actually were made of paper, and then took a taxi home.

My stomach hurt, and I was probably too weak for a triathlon, but aside from that I was fine. Had Ava not felt the need to come to the hospital with Amelia and Tabatha, and have them travel home with us in the taxi just in case I required any further assistance, and then have them stay the night so that they were there to help me when I woke up the next morning, it would have been the most perfect ride home from a failed suicide I'd ever had.

'Mum?'

'Yup.' I turned over in bed to face the door.

'I heard you moving. How did you sleep?' Ava was already dressed for school.

'Not sure.'

'I think you should have really simple food today. Nothing fancy.' That's right, I had told Ava last night that the doctors had confirmed it was food poisoning. What a pity, as I was starving and could really have done with a good curry right now.

'Yes, good idea,' I said, getting up. I was suddenly pining for my torn, worn, full-size briefs. There was something about paper knickers that made a woman feel desperate.

'You don't have to drive us,' said Ava. I looked at her. She looked nothing like Alex, thankfully for her, but had the same kindness in her eyes. Serious pupils in orbs washed of soft fennel green. The kind of people who, no matter how stupidly they behaved, were nice to have around.

'It's fine. I'm fine.'

'I've never heard you use the word "fine" as much you have in the last twelve hours – the same twelve hours in which you were rushed to hospital.'

'Okay. Good point. Perhaps it's times like this when asinine descriptions of feeling come into their own. Like a placebo, but the point is, I would still like to drive you to school because I need to get back to normal – an important part of a speedy recovery.'

'But you hate the school run.'

'Which is why it will help me get back to normal. Right before I got food poisoning, I was hating my week.'

The phone rang. The phone never rang this early.

'I'll get it,' said Ava, running downstairs. I wondered what went on in the lives of others that would bring us together this early in the day. Mornings were protected. Sacred time before forced interactions and soiling oneself with the rest of the world.

It was Alex. Typical. I opened the door to listen. Poor Alex, it made me laugh. Any other time, he would have found himself speaking to his logical, even-tempered, way-more-mature-than-any-of-us daughter. But off the back of my hospital visit, Ava was on shaky ground and Alex was first in the firing line.

'What do you want?' she asked gruffly. There was a pause.

'I'm fine—'

'I just don't know what you're calling for. You left—'

'I'm not really interested in what you and Poppy have been planting. Mum was rushed to hospital with food poisoning—'

'She's fine—'

'What do you care, you only think about yourself—'

'Oh Dad. Do whatever you want. I'm not in the mood.'

I could intervene. I bet Alex was sitting in Normandy gagging for someone to take the phone from her hands, but it was rare that the lividity of Alex's deceased vows and promises were examined and I was enjoying Ava uncensored.

'I am well. I am growing up without a father—'

Oh Alex. Poor Alex. This must be killing you. Such a bad time to call. Never mind. Life goes on and I have a number of stolen items that I need to exchange for cash today, so you will have to fend for yourself.

There was a hesitant knock at the door.

'Come in.' I was destined to keep meeting Ava's friends in my underwear.

'Ava told me to bring you this,' Tabatha said with more than a little awkwardness. She sat a tray down on my bed with

black coffee and plain toast. No butter or milk. Ava would
have made a great nurse during the war. I moved the tray to the
table, a flat wooden surface less inclined to cause hot coffee to
spill all over the bed. Teenagers had no peripheral vision.

'How did you know about the pills?' I asked.

'What pills?' Straight into coy. Bet the boys lapped that
shit up.

'You told me I'd taken pills when I asked you what
had happened?' This was precarious terrain. This girl had
been born and groomed to be a bitch from a long line of
thoroughbred bitches and there was no insouciance when
it came to one's lineage. And, though not as superstitious as
my mother – the proprietor of such gems as 'don't whistle in
the night or snakes will come,' and 'don't use chalk or you'll
lose your money' – I did believe in serendipity or, to be more
accurate, its nemesis. A nemesis I was much more familiar
with, and I was therefore unable to escape the increasing
suspicion that Tabatha Crosly-Burke just kept popping up into
my life to fuck with me.

'The same thing happened to me last year,' she admitted.

I remained impatiently silent.

'I took an overdose of pills. Was in hospital for three
days.' She looked scared. Maybe because I looked angry.

'That's what you think happened to me is it?'

'I—'

'And have you told Ava this preposterous theory you've
conjured up, being the medical graduate that you are?'

'No.'

'And are you planning to? Sorry, let me rephrase,' I moved
closer to her face. Her skin smelled of lily-of-the-valley. 'If you
open your fucking mouth and tell Ava any of this shit, I'll sew
those pretty lips of yours shut.'

She handled my threats as I suspected any self-respecting
pill-popping teenage whore would, with a passivity that neither

riled nor comforted me. That would do for today's confrontations, although the days seemed to be getting longer and longer and I suspected it had nothing to do with the solstice.

'I've got some Prozac if you want?' she added.

'Get out.'

She got up to leave, and then sat down again as if in mid-thought.

'But can you take Prozac if you've just had a tetanus,' she said. Note to self: how quaint and what the fuck?

'What did you say?'

'I heard the doctors talking last night. They were wondering about prescribing Prozac, and a nurse said you'd had a tetanus booster that morning. According to your records.'

I saw now how plainly they were related. Henrietta had proved herself to be as bothersome as a papercut on the labia and it appeared that the apple did not fall too far from the tree. In fact, it was still hanging, never to fall or ever be plucked off – being that it was maggot-ridden; fat, legless larvae crawling out of its rotten core.

'And why do you think I had a tetanus, Columbo?' I got up and began pacing, aware that this room was not conducive to pacing of any kind. It was cluttered without any empty stretches where striding could be practised and perfected and I had to turn around and come back before I'd been anywhere at all.

'Because you got bitten by a dog? Who's Columbo?' she asked, seeming genuinely confused on both counts.

'Firstly, you are too young to remember any television of real value. Secondly, it was NOT a dog, it was a rat, actually.'

'Oh no,' she sympathised.

'Why does everyone say that?'

'Where?'

'Why does everyone say *that*?'

'Everyone says what?' asked Tabatha.

'In the street. It's none of your business. Come on let's go,' I snapped.

Did she know? Was this a veiled threat? How could she know? Had Henrietta sent her here to spy? But then I remembered that she'd turned up even before the robbery. She was quite reticent, which allowed me to tolerate her. However, had I mistaken maleficence for aloofness? Had she been sent to look for evidence? Wasn't that entrapment? Truly, she seemed as if she knew nothing. Scrap that, she seemed as if she cared about nothing. That was different. She was apathetic and it was entirely possible that someone could care about nothing, but know everything. So assuming she was here with full disclosure of what I had done, it was only a matter of time before she would use what she had. The one piece of leverage I had, she had offered up herself – as if I couldn't get my own Prozac. A suicide attempt and these girls think they have the monopoly on prescription drugs. So that's what we were doing. Playing the friend. Well, I could put on a show too.

'Mum, that was Dad on the phone,' Ava announced, huffing at the trauma of her call with Alex. 'He asked to speak to you, but I said we were on our way to school.'

'Not before pancakes.'

'Excuse me?'

'I'm making pancakes. Come on Tabatha. You can't go to school without breakfast, darling. Where's Amelia?'

'Is breakfast ready yet?' called Amelia from Ava's bedroom.

How difficult could pancakes be? Flour, butter, milk? I'd throw an egg in – couldn't hurt. How much of each? Until it looked like pancake mixture.

The girls sat down at the table. Ava sandwiched herself between Tabatha and Amelia, her sweet face skidding with uncertainty.

'Your mum is so cool. My mum never makes pancakes for me,' whispered Amelia.

'My mum doesn't either,' murmured Tabatha.

'Neither does mine,' said Ava.

'I heard that,' I said, cracking an egg into a bowl.

The kitchen was a sun trap. Hitting straight to the face, sunlight forced the girls to sit together on one side, as it spread itself thickly along the counters and across the cupboard doors, demanding to be seen.

'Morning, Grandpa,' said Ava as Papa came into the room, squinting.

'Pull the curtains, somebody?'

'We've never had curtains in the kitchen, Grandpa.'

'What are you doing?' he asked.

'I'm making pancakes. Isn't a lovely day?'

'What's wrong with you?' he tried to probe.

'Grandpa, these are my friends. Tabatha and Amelia.' Ava was so proud to finally say those words.

Papa was dressed in tailored trousers, a shirt and a V-neck cashmere sweater. It was so obvious he had a girlfriend. The disruptive ligature that underpinned my parents' entire matrimonial existence was haunting and best forgotten. I was in no hurry to see which ill-suited elderly crackpot he had saddled himself with this time, so I didn't ask. Ava looked like she'd noticed his threads and was about to enquire. I glared at her from behind my bowl of batter.

'Is your hand better now?' Tabatha asked me. Oh, the little bitch. The hospital had redressed the wound and put a smaller plaster on it.

'Yes, thank you dear,' I crooned.

'What happened to your hand?' asked Papa lightly.

'Nothing.'

'Do you have any jam?' asked Amelia.

'We don't keep jam in the house,' whispered Ava.

'Why?' I could hear Amelia ask.

'Mum doesn't like it.'

'Who doesn't like jam?'

'I don't,' I stated, turning round from the cooker to lean in at the table, holding the whisk threateningly in my right hand.

'Gym today,' said Ava furtively, looking worried.

'I know,' Amelia hesitated.

'Just play it cool,' Tabatha purred.

'I just don't know if he likes me,' Ava said swiftly.

'Because he doesn't want you to know,' said Amelia. 'But if you like a boy,' she continued, 'there are ways to make him know what you want him to know, know what I mean?' I had no idea. Using a ladle, I lowered the batter into a hot buttered frying pan and the mixture morphed into the most perfect circle I'd ever seen. Almost self-sufficient in its development, it curled its edges up ready for me to flip it over. Papa sat at the table with a bottle of Sri Lankan chilli garlic pickle waiting for his pancake. I looked around at the customers in my cafe. Was it too soon to buy an apron?

'Like what?' asked Ava.

'I happen to know that he finds the world of maths a dark and scary place,' said Tabatha in a mock whisper. This was the Tabatha I knew. It was the Tabatha we all knew. The one on display, not the damaged sample on the shelf in the back that no one saw.

'And as I recall, didn't you get 93% on your last algebra test?' grinned Amelia in a questioning tone, though it was obvious she had all the answers.

'Yes. How do you know?' asked a stunned Ava.

'We know everything,' winked Amelia.

'But I bet it's a fraction of what Lex knows,' laughed Ava. Tabatha and Amelia exchanged glances, finding Ava endearing and wondering, as good friends do, how to make Lex feel the same way.

'A maths joke!' They chimed. 'Probably hold off on those in the beginning 'til he gets more confident. Boys can be surprisingly sensitive.' What was this Macbethian sorcery? Were they trying to initiate Ava to become the third witch? They were good. There was stuff for me to learn here too.

'Start a conversation,' said Amelia.

'Oh, I couldn't. I'd be way too nervous,' Ava said, practically shaking. 'Maybe if Bach were playing from the speakers in the hall.'

'Bach!' spat the witches.

'It calms her down,' I explained. 'Who's Lex and why haven't I heard about him before?'

'He's no one. I mean he's someone, but just not into me—'

'...yet,' they said, trying to bewitch her with their confidence in the intricate web of teenage intimacy. Ava was their latest project and they were proud of it. She alone had been deemed worthy to drink at the sows' trough and swallow the elixir of teenage seduction. The gonadotrophins had so much to answer for. This fucker Lex would be lucky to have her.

'So what's he like?' I asked, plopping a pancake on Ava's plate.

'He's… luminous.' Luminous? Seriously Ava? With everything going on at the moment, now I had to worry about this shit. If she only knew how ripe she was. I did not need Ava in love right now. Ava was responsible. Ava was disciplined. Ava was using words like 'luminous'.

'Well. That's just great,' I said.

'Ava, love is complicated,' mused Papa, chilli pieces on his lips and clear mucus running from one nostril. 'Love can lift you up, but it can be messy too… dirty,'

'Ok girls, let's go. Time for school.'

Nature versus nurture. Are you born into motherhood or do you learn it like any other learned behaviour? I certainly did not feel that driving Ava to school was a normal way to begin my day, but driving other people's children as well? Obviously I understood the convenience factor, but how did these women cope with the routine? The monotony of these actions at the same time every day was unbearable. The worst kind of claustrophobia: to suffocate within the confines of one's own life. How was adding someone else's offspring to the shit bucket meant to improve anything? This autistic excuse for adventure, this groundhog-day road trip, this driving to one's own death only to never drive off the cliff; some women found this a delight – I could see it in their eyes. They sprang out of their cars bubbling with joy to be reunited with their fellow inmates that they had seen just hours before doing the exact same thing. Metronomes were more spontaneous. No, I was not born to do this and neither had I learned to do this. What I had done was cultivated and grown a strong-rooted tree of hate whose leaves fell upon the road like autumnal foliage every time I did. As they crunched into fibrotic dust beneath my tyres, the sinuous roots twisted inward pulling me that inch further down into the belly of the earth, lowering me into the bowels of hell, which stank from the putrefied mummies of those whose had died insidiously, a little every day, on the school run.

'Did you like school, Ms Peiris? Can I call you Drea?' chirped Amelia.

'No, I did not and no, you cannot.'

'Ava says you're a physics teacher,' she bubbled.

'Those who can do, those who can't, teach. I was never going to become a physicist so I taught physics. Anyway, I don't do that anymore.'

'What do you do?'

'I kill rabbits, stuff them with formaldehyde and sell them at farmer's markets.'

'She doesn't,' said Ava hastily. The only nice thing about the drive to school was the way that East Hill brought the spectacular Gatlin oaks to meet you from the horizon one by one. Like debutantes from a forgotten time where nature ruled. So graceful how they barely rustled their large balls of leafy hair in the wind, intimidating and unique in their majestic size and dominance as they arrived, like beauty queens. It was quite breathtaking. Like a green baize backdrop of a puppet show, child's felt. I waited excitedly to see my trees, but what I saw were daffodils in bloom. Strange – I didn't know daffodils flowered in September. As we came closer, the yellow from my illusory daffodils thinned into an elongated linear strip. The roads of Gatlin were pristine. They couldn't possibly be laying down more tarmac. I saw a cluster of vehicles stationed outside the church. White ones. Vans and cars? No, not just white: blue and white. A police cordon.

'Why are the police here?' asked Ava, squinting up into the distance whilst lifting up off her seat to get a clearer view.

'Sit down,' I ordered.

'Maybe someone else has been robbed?' said Tabatha.

Maybe, Tabatha. It must be tough to carry such a burden of genius. But it would have been difficult for anyone to have been robbed whilst I had been asleep in my bed. We looked. Large German Shepherds yanked at their leashes, jumping into the air and barking with undiscerning clarity at every passer-by.

'There's Xavier Coultard,' pointed out Amelia. As we approached the road leading up to the school, we saw barriers and tape everywhere. It was as if a child had scribbled all over my nature scene with a fat marker pen leaking bright yellow police crime tape. I stopped the car. I couldn't go any further. There was a diversion sign for vehicles going anywhere else but the school. A few were reversing, but most just stopped at the top, creating a disciplined and well-behaved roadblock.

Over on the other side, I saw Ann Donnington in the middle of a group. I hadn't once seen a police cordon in Gatlin and, on any other day, Ann would never even notice me, but today was no ordinary day. I could see her weaving through the crowd in what seemed to be our direction.

'Tabatha? Amelia?' She stuck her head inside the car like a monkey on safari expecting to see humans inside, but finding other monkeys instead. We all registered the confusion as her eyebrow vaulting was not subtle.

'The girls stayed over,' I said, which actually explained nothing.

'Really?' she smiled a straight smile, her eyes inching closer together.

'What's going on?' asked Ava.

'Oh,' she said, returning to her focus, 'I can't quite say it out loud.'

'Try,' I said. She swallowed, looking at all of us in turn – long, lingering looks.

'Last night… Penelope Coultard was… murdered.'

Part Two

To be yourself in a world that is constantly trying to make you something else is the biggest accomplishment

Ralph Waldo Emerson

Two Days Later

I shouldn't even be here. Any minute now, the door will open and I will be entering a hostage situation, albeit voluntarily, but that's beside the point. Yes, I am here of my own choosing. I do not want to be and I most definitely do not want to talk about why. How has an entire profession – a burgeoning, over-subscribed and saturated profession to boot – managed to exist using completely opposite principles to every consumer-driven business model. You walk through the door of a high-street shop and it's because you want to be there. Everybody fawns on you, asking you repeatedly how you are or if they can help you with anything, and all of this is tolerated – the exception being the Disney store. The sales staff, the merchandising, the marketing are all tailored towards an individual who is confident enough to know that is where they want to be. Not here. Here is where they capitalise on the fact that this is the one place you don't want to be. And why wouldn't I want to talk to a perfect stranger about my intimate thoughts and feelings?

I look at the clock. Any minute now. I feel sick. It's all giving me a headache. The fear of what is behind that door is mounting like an ominous expanding mass and my throat is dry. However, when I look around the room for some water all I can see are boxes of tissues. Am I meant to drink my future tears? What kind of a world do we live in when our hearts and minds are not enough that we must pay a total stranger to listen to our problems – it seems a barbaric type of insanity, and yet here I am.

My therapist resided on the borders of Gatlin and Brigham. I knew the location would affect the price, but I was hoping not the quality. However, the room was situated above a law office. I stopped in my tracks, feeling much like the child of the devil before unsuspecting parents tried to take me inside a church. Was this a silly idea? Why had this happened? Why was the therapist not above a herbalist or a toy shop? Were the burning hot fires of ethics and justice right below us not enough of a sign that I should be somewhere, anywhere, else?

The building itself was shabby and in desperate need of re-plastering and a coat of paint. The door to the street moved uneasily when I pushed it. Scuffed, unopened letters addressed to various different people were wedged in stacks between the door and the wall, blocking my way. I pushed a bunch of pizza leaflets to the side and a woodlouse scurried away.

Upstairs. Room 4. I knocked.

'Miss Peiris? So sorry to have kept you waiting.' I wasn't waiting. I'd only just knocked. Why did people say things they didn't mean? She should be more sorry that there was nowhere to wait if I had tried.

'Not at all,' I said. 'I was early.'

She held the door for me to enter – like a lamb to the slaughter. Oh, how sweet of you to gut me open and rip away my secrets for your therapising. You'd like that, wouldn't you? To have created a new verb giving legitimacy to your cause. Inside the room, we entered a different country. A blue velvet sofa sat opposite a purple armchair. Art in gilded frames alongside sculptures and vases. A seduction in creative aesthetics. And books. Books and more books to confirm her intellect. Let's see, shall we?

'Did you find the place alright?'

'Oh yes. You gave excellent directions.' There you go. Tell you what: you can have that for free. Now sit down in your chair and pretend that my throwaway compliment didn't stroke your little ego, cowering away behind Freud and Jung lest you are spotted with a weakness in your armour. The soft speech, direct gaze, relaxed body language, comfy chairs; all weapons of entrapment. Pathetic, really. I can sit and play this game. Oh, and I can play it better than you. No, keep gently staring at me. I won't speak first, you will. We sat in front of one another, assessing each other's hormones.

'So why did you want to see a therapist, Drea? Can I call you Drea?' She broke first.

'Of course, please do. Ms Peiris is so formal. I've had some panic attacks.'

'And how long have these panic attacks been going on for?'

'This last week.'

'And have you ever experienced anything like this before?'

'No.'

She looked like she knew how to be happy. Like she'd worked at it the way some people train to be a lawyer or a doctor, and now she did it well. The frames on the wall enclosed documents to prove as much: a certified excellence in happiness. Maybe that's where I fell short. My limited training stemmed from Newton's law of motion. An object that is at rest will stay at rest unless an external object acts upon it. An object that is in motion will not change its velocity unless an external force acts upon it.

'And that's why you've come today?'

Newton's first law of motion was essentially why I was here. The law of inertia that governed my life, and to which I tried to give over all power, had been disturbed. Idly, I noticed that, apart from the paintings, everything she had on display was grouped in twos. Two glass vases, two tall black sculpted African women carrying babies on their back, two Chinese Buddhas. Two. Should I have come with a friend?

'Yes.' Further qualifications: she had a nice smile. Believable. Because let's be honest, if you look like an asexual trucker you're going to struggle in this profession. When I was selecting who would be the lucky recipient of my inner-most workings I noticed a lot of these therapists put their photo up on the websites. That's probably eighty percent of patients choosing a therapist on looks alone, no matter where they've trained. Why would the average person know the difference between psycho-dynamic or gestalt? Wasn't person-centred when they put the client in the middle of the room? No one really cared. I chose her because she had a nice smile and didn't look like she'd been abused. Recently.

'Drea, do you want to start from the beginning?'

No. For starters that was a closed question masquerading as an open question. And it was here, at the start, where it all broke down – the supposed trust we shared. It was here where she first demonstrated her lack of authenticity. Tell me what you really want, don't act as if it's up to me, my choice, as if once I'm here I even have a choice.

To tell the truth, the beginning was somewhat hazy for me to recall. Everyone was shocked. Penelope Coultard was dead. Murdered. Found outside the school slumped on the ground beside her car. Gatlin did not partake in criminal activity. If it did, no one knew about it, and what did exist consisted of littering, soft-sell marijuana on the borders of Gatlin and Brigham, and administrative fraud at the gym over badminton court bookings. As Ann spoke to us that day, the cogs started to turn in my head. Somehow crime had entered our town, which meant the police would be looking for things no one had ever looked for before. And if the police were here with their dogs and their vans and their noses for foul play, then I had to get Henrietta's stuff out of my cupboard. I'd already posted Regina's stuff the day I'd sold her rings.

'A woman was murdered at my daughter's school.'

'Oh my God.' Ha, gotcha. And I wasn't even trying.

'I'm pretty sure God has a good alibi.'

She smiled in spite of herself. 'And how did this make you feel?'

'Annoyed.' That after everything I went through to get the damn stuff, I'd now have to get rid of it as anything else was too risky and could attract unwanted attention. That coat and bag were money for Ava's school fees and it was selfish of whoever murdered Coultard not to boil away her body in a bath of acid as any self-respecting murderer would, so as to not drag innocent people into the fray.

'Why did you feel annoyed?'

'Because someone has left a poor little boy without a mother.'

'Did it make you feel anything else?'

'Sad.' Because I was that much further away from finding the money for Ava's school fees.

'Why sad?'

'Because someone has left a poor little boy without his mother,' I repeated.

Ann was pretty cut up about the whole affair. Large groups of the mothers just hung out at the tea room. It was as if they wanted to be close to her but her body was in the morgue, so this was the next best thing. They would drink coffee and cry, even if they'd never met her. One of them said to me, tears streaming: 'I wish I'd known her, spoken to her.' No, you don't. I spoke to her before she died and she was a bitch. That might not have been why she died, but it did mean you weren't missing out. I didn't say that, and it was a rare thing that I was able to detect a moment in life where the less said, the better.

'Did you know her?'

'No.'

'But it has affected you?'

'Apparently.'

'You are shocked by this?'

Shock doesn't begin to describe it. The girls got out of the car and went to school. I drove home. Straight home. Didn't even stop for cigarettes, although I wanted to, and I desperately needed a joint. I put the key in the door and raced up the stairs into my bedroom. I was thinking I'd burn it all in the back garden, but then I wondered if smoke at nine thirty in the morning would raise unwarranted suspicion – odd time for a barbecue. I could drive into Brigham and put the stuff in a bin. No one would know where to start looking in Brigham; the whole town was a crime scene. I opened the door to the cupboard I had shoved them in and reached into the back. My hand wiggled about in the air, finding nothing I wanted. I pushed my arm in further, vaguely remembering I had pushed them in quite far back, and wiggled again. Nothing. I stood on a chair to get a better reach. Henrietta's bag and coat were gone.

'Yes, you could say I was shocked.'

'Why shocked?'

'At the depth of feeling, I suppose.'

I had never had a panic attack, so at first the symptoms were unrecognisable. My breath became shallow and racy. I was breathing from my throat rather than my lungs but part of my throat was closing down, not letting in the air and stopping me breathing. Though I had been in Gatlin Hospital not so long ago for trying to take my own life, I felt now like my life was being taken away from me, but this time it wasn't my decision. Sepia-tinted images of Mother and Papa fighting raced before me, a little girl crying.

'You felt it strongly.'

'Very. I had a panic attack.'

'Drea, it's not uncommon. I don't know if that makes you feel any better, but you've experienced an unbelievably stressful event.'

'You're telling me.' I didn't understand where the stuff could have gone. I was sure I put it at the back of the cupboard. Ava? No, she wouldn't. The guilt would push her over the edge. Amelia? Maybe. Tabatha? Very possibly.

'One you could not have ever predicted or prepared for.'

'I know,' I agreed wholeheartedly.

'Death is our greatest certainty and our greatest challenge. Can you remember how the panic attack subsided?'

Thank fuck I'd had a joint that had rolled under the bed. Gasping for air, I leant under and grabbed it and, with my hands shaking, lit it up.

'It's hazy.'

'And am I right in thinking you've experienced more than one panic attack?

'Yes, but now they come randomly.'

'Without warning?'

'And for no reason.'

Were the paintings supposed to stimulate emotions? There was one with a lady lying on the bed in an orange robe. At first I thought she was just sleeping, but then I noticed what I thought was anguish on her face. I got the feeling that the contrast between the outside of the building and the inside of the room was just the beginning and that everything here had been deliberately placed to engineer some kind of reaction.

'It sounds as if you are suffering from what is known as a panic disorder. Because the attacks can come without warning and are often not connected to a specific event, it may feel that they are without reason. However, the reason can be a trauma no longer remembered or even registered as a trauma, and that has nevertheless sparked an overwhelming fear and anxiety.'

I can remember it and it is a trauma. Someone has stolen my stolen goods. They were in my bedroom cupboard and now they are gone. I can't report it because the police are obsessed with finding out who murdered Penelope Coultard, making them blind to the plight of others and unlikely to be sympathetic to the fact all the items I am reporting are stolen. And yes, it has sparked a fear. A fear that I will not be able to find the money to pay Ava's school fees and an anxiety about ripping her away from everything she loves and the opportunities she should have and – without stepping up the weed and the whisky this week – yes I agree, it could easily have slipped into overwhelming.

'Does that make sense to you?' she asked.

'Most definitely.'

'Panic disorders can take time to unravel. There are exercises I can show you to help you cope with them in the moment, and the work we do here will reduce their frequency until eventually they have no reason to exist anymore.'

She was calm. Calmer than me. Sure of herself. Surer than me. Did she steal my stuff? By her logic, the only way the attacks will stop is if the reason for the disorder goes away – I get my stuff back. Therefore, if she is saying that eventually they will stop because they'll have no reason to stay, she must know I have to get my stuff back; ipso facto she must have taken it.

'How does that sound?'

'Suspicious.'

'We're not afraid of scepticism here.'

Who's we? Who else was she working with? Who else was involved? Why would they steal my stuff? And how would they know it was there? Was this her legitimate business? Did she even know who I was? That I'm the one she's stolen from?

'What about paranoia?'

'What about it,' she asked.

'Could I have it? Is it part of the panic attacks?'

'Why do you think you're paranoid?'

'Or maybe anxiety? Anxiety and paranoia?'

'Anxiety and paranoia are two different conditions, but very closely related in that they both stem from fear. Anxiety is not purely psychological; it is biological too. When a person experiences anxiety, their brain chemistry changes. Emotions and moods are controlled by neurotransmitters, which then start to misfire and affect a person's thoughts. These can then become paranoid thoughts.'

Fuck. So she didn't steal my stuff. Then who had? No one knew it was there. Someone had got into the house without busting a lock or breaking a window. It had been nearly a week and no one had contacted me. I didn't know whether this was good or bad.

'Is there another way to get rid of the panic attacks?'

'What do you mean?'

'Like could you reason them away?'

'With logic?'

'Yes.'

'Actively changing one's thoughts would control paranoia.'

'Oh forget about that, I'm not paranoid,' I snapped.

'Sorry?'

'The paranoid thing was just a question. Go on.'

'Okay.' She took a moment to restart. She was frazzled. By me. So boring. 'Logic and reason can intellectualise and can soften the landscape for a while, but in my experience, only emotionally unravelling the trauma, doing the work here with me, can release it and set it free.'

Really. That's convenient. How could you not rely on logic? Logically, if no one had contacted me, my chances of avoiding a blackmail situation were increasing. If they were to find the stuff now, at least it was out of my house and I didn't have to trouble myself with disposing of it.

'Is that something you'd like to do?'

'What?'

'Work with me?' she asked. It was embarrassing how open she laid herself.

'Actually, no.'

'Okay.' She paused. 'Well, the first session is always a little staccato. I'm getting to know you and you're getting to know me. We're both seeing whether this is something we want to do.'

'How are you seeing if you want to work with me? This is your job.'

'Yes, it is. But it's still a partnership between two people, and our relationship becomes the site where most of the work happens, so I need to see how that works for me too.'

'I think that's bullshit.'

'You do? Why?'

'Because I thought therapy is meant to be this place that you come to and bare your soul, which you would never do unless it was a place where you could feel unconditionally accepted. But it sounds as if you have conditions.'

'I wouldn't call them conditions.'

'I would.'

'The work between therapist and client is intangible. It brings two people together on so many levels, spoken and unspoken. For both parties. There needs to be a chemistry. That said, I would very much like to work with you.'

'Changed your tune pretty quick. Too late.'

'Sorry?'

'You ruined it. With your judgement and your conditions. I don't want to work with you. I'm afraid I have no chemistry with you.'

'I must be honest, that makes me sad. I can't help feeling that although I had to be honest, somehow I've hurt you.'

'Listen, Dr Feelgood—'

'It's Armstrong.'

'Whatever. You guys, you therapists, you have your protocols. Your boundaries. Your conditions. And some people obviously have much lower standards than I do or you'd have cheaper art on the walls. But you are not the therapist for me. If I were you, I would be sad because you're just not good enough.'

The Crucible

I was on the school run. Ava had asked Amelia and Tabatha to stay over again. I hadn't protested. I had entered a phase of my life where I needed to choose my battles. Despite a desperate urge to win them all, I knew I wasn't as strong as I needed to be in order to wage such indiscriminating wars. I had withdrawn somewhat. Ava and her troll friends danced about my life like white noise on a television screen. I told Ava to sit in the back of the car in an attempt to separate myself from the madness. I drove them to school as if I were a taxi. And just like a taxi driver, I was uninterested in my job, unimpressed with the calibre of my passengers, yet incredibly knowledgeable. And this knowledge was weighing me down.

The man on the radio had called to make a point. It wasn't always the case. Many people have never spoken on the radio before and are too star struck by the fact that they are talking live to the nation to illustrate their point effectively, or even remember it, but Arthur Williams from Stoughton had definitely called to make a point.

'Arthur, this is a family show. I know you've called a few times so I want to give you a chance to be heard, but no more profanity Arthur, not this early in the morning.'

'I apologise, Abigail. I feel strongly about this issue.'

'That we can see, Arthur. Tell me, do you have children of your own who are being affected by the building of this new Catholic faith school? Listeners, if you've just tuned into

Abigail in the Morning, we are discussing the new school in Gatlin. I want to know your thoughts: do we need another faith school? Is this good for our children? Education and religion: oil and water, or chips and ketchup? Please no one call and say mayonnaise or I will hang up on you. All yours, Arthur.

'No, I don't have children at the school, but I have three grown-up children who went to state schools more than twenty years ago. At that time, our borders were not being used like cattle turnstiles and all the children knew how to speak English. But now my own children are having to find money for private schools they cannot afford for my grandchildren because there are playgrounds full of Romanian gypsy urchins swapping heather for marbles.'

'Even I know that's not a fair trade, Arthur, as I always lost my marbles. But do we not have a social responsibility here? Yes, things have changed and the world isn't what it was when your children were in school – it's not what it was when I was in school – but I've got to say, it also used to be easier to go on holiday, d'you know what I mean? Now you've got to check who's fighting where and it feels like people are fighting everywhere. So what I'm saying is, doesn't someone need to educate these children who are clearly collateral damage – as innocents always are – and who I'm sure would prefer to be in school in their various home countries.'

'Well, fuck off and go back then—'

'Oops, and we've lost Arthur. Who have we got on next? Betty Hale from Parris. Betty, how is this issue riling you up? Now, you saw what happened to Arthur. We had to pop him off the air because he wouldn't stop blowing the profanity bubble, so keep it clean.'

'Good morning Abigail. Thank you for having me. I've never been on the radio before—'

'You're on now, Betty. Let's make it count.'

'Well, I have an interesting job, Abigail. I work at the post office. It's part of my job to sort through the stamps and separate the first class and the second class and I also keep the jiffy bags stocked because it's remarkable how many people expect the items they're sending to be protected by a regular envelope until I suggest thicker protection and point them over to the bubble bag rack.'

'I know we're perilously close to a point here, Betty, don't let me down now—'

'Oh yes, sorry. Well, I watch the people who come to cash their government benefits for food and rent and it seems to me like the foreigners are in the minority.'

'What are you saying?'

'I'm saying, Abigail, that it's people who are living here and who have been born here who are claiming money off the government, not the so-called immigrants, so what difference does it make if children who can't speak English have a religious school to go to? If they grow up like their parents, then statistically there is more chance they will get a job and contribute to the economy, so that's a good thing, isn't it?'

'Well, I'd say so. Betty from Parris, thanks for your call. Who have we got next? Ann from Donnington. Ann, good morning to you. What's your stance here? Should we be worried that the blood of Christ and holy communion is coming to a cinema near us very soon?'

'I… I'm more concerned about the murder of Penelope Coultard.'

'That is a tragedy, no doubt about it, which we've actually got scheduled for discussion on our afternoon show with the silver-tongued Jon Proctor.'

'There were two muggings first and I think they're connected—' The line went dead. It took a minute for Abigail to speak again.

'Sorry about that, folks. Let's go to a quick ad break, but remember, tomorrow morning we've got Dr HRT herself, Hilary Rose Tremour, in the studio talking about her new book *From Suicide to Homicide* about women who have been plagued by hormone imbalances their whole life. Don't go anywhere.'

I turned the radio off. I had gone somewhere. Abigail had lost me as a listener despite her plea. Ann from Donnington! Well, didn't she have a lot to answer for? What did she think she was doing? Didn't Gatlin have enough going on without her injecting her bony body into an active investigation and complicating matters? I mean, for God's sake, there was a murderer at large. We were all unsafe. Not to mention I had been robbed myself. Although maybe the less said about that, the better. But it serves to illustrate my point. I am a person who knows when not to muddy the waters and stick in my tuppence. Ann 'from Donnington', on the other hand, knew nothing, not least how to keep her big fucking mouth shut.

'Mum, I've invited Catherine over tonight. She'll stay for dinner.'

'Catherine Donnington?'

'Yes.'

'That does seem the most likely thing to happen now.'

'Because I think she feels a bit left out with Tabs and Meels spending so much time at ours, and that's the last thing I want her to feel.'

'The very last thing,' I said. Despite such sickening nicknames sounding more like infections than real people, Ava's bonding with these nuisances was worryingly low down on my ever-increasing list of irritations.

The police tape had become stronger over the week instead of limp and flaccid as I'd visualised. I was hoping to see it broken from the stress and tension of being pulled between two trees and the responsibility of protecting the area. Two pieces of redundant, tattered tape hanging like party banners the day after, representing a dying or dead investigation. I was not so lucky. The road diversion was still being enforced with vigour, everyone still parking at the top of the road and, far from it being a hindrance, seemed to give the mothers even more time to bond. They discussed recent events and spread gossip like an eternal game of Chinese whispers – Mothers of Gatlin Unite. It was like a farmers' market without the farmers or the stalls, just groups of people who ate bio-dynamic eggs and discussed murder. The forensic team was still milling about, and I noticed more un-uniformed, unfamiliar faces. It appeared that they were talking to the children first.

'The police interviewed Catherine yesterday,' said Amelia. From the rear-view mirror, I could see her balance an open bottle of nail polish in the alcove of the door.

'Put the polish away,' I warned.

'Oh, sorry Drea, but it's just for one nail that's chipped.'

'I have no interest if you've chipped all ten of your nails. And it's Ms Peiris.'

'I wish our parents didn't insist on driving us to school. I want to go to school on my own,' sighed Amelia.

'And I too would love you to go to school on your own, Amelia, but I happen to think more parents should take their kids to school. You never know when something bad's gonna happen. Just look at Mrs Coultard.'

'This whole experience has upset Catherine really badly,' she continued, closing the bottle and putting it in her bag next to her compass and protractor and other actually essential items.

'You know she's got a bit of a thing going with Xavier,' Tabatha fizzed.

'Really?' exclaimed Ava. 'I didn't know.'

'Why would you, darling?' Catty but true.

'But there's no way he's going to ask her to go skiing with him and his family now as he'll have to spend some time grieving for his mum. It's understandable Catherine's upset. She had already bought her whole snow wardrobe,' explained Amelia.

'Although one quarter of his family is gone now,' pointed out Tabatha poignantly, 'so it's not like it would cost them any more.'

'See how your maths have improved,' smiled Ava. 'It's just so upsetting. They asked me lots of questions too that made me come away feeling awful,' she continued.

'Like what?' said Tabatha.

'Like had Penelope ever come to our house.'

'What? You didn't tell me that.' I interrupted them.

'I forgot.'

'They didn't ask me that,' said Amelia.

'Nor me,' echoed Tabatha.

'And did my mum and Penelope know each other,' Ava went on.

'What? You didn't tell me that!' I screeched.

'I didn't think it was important. It made me think that if you had known Xavier's mum then maybe she could have been at our house and then she wouldn't have been murdered so I completely understand what Catherine must be feeling. I'm sure she wonders if there was something she could have done, as we all do—'

'I don't think Catherine is thinking that,' assured Amelia.

'Neither do I,' agreed Tabatha.

'Although I don't know as I haven't just bought a brand new skiing wardrobe. In fact, I can't even ski,' continued Ava.

'You can't ski?' gasped Tabatha and Amelia, more horrified than when Ann told us Penelope had been murdered.

'Nope.'

'Not everyone skis,' I retorted.

'Then what do they do?' asked Tabatha.

'They bowl.'

I turned the radio back on. Anything had to be better than listening to this, but the music was dire. I turned the dial again. *This is Abigail in the Morning.* And we've got renowned psychic Cotton Mather coming into the studio tomorrow to talk about his new book, 'Those Familiar Spirits.' The time is eight-fifty on this grey and overcast Thursday morning. Ok I'm not a psychic but I'm predicting rain. No it looks like a storm's coming. Think of me as the crucible of current affairs – what matters to you at home – and there's a storm cooking up about this new Catholic faith school that's just been given the go ahead. We're taking your calls to find out what you have to say. Who do we have next? Sarah from Putnam, Hello Sarah—'

'Hi, Abigail—'

'And how's all this sitting with you, Sarah?'

'Abigail, I have three children. Conceived intentionally in December for Caesarean September births so they are the oldest in their years. Research shows that babies born in the autumn are more focussed, less likely to indulge in risky behaviour that might derail their education, and more likely to go on to Oxbridge. I engineered a precise three-month gap between pregnancies, partly to let my body recover but mainly to ensure that there are always at least two of them in the same age bracket for holiday camps. They have been tutored since the age of two and can all play two instruments and two sports, competitively. I am outraged that a property earmarked for a whole year for Gatlin's new sports court where Tarquin would have taken his already outstanding badminton to Olympic heights is now being turned into a faith school. Abigail? Are you there?'

'Sorry Sarah. Yes, I am here – very much here – and just taking it all in. I can definitely hear that you've put a lot of planning into this. Let's see if anyone wants to respond to Sarah in Putnam.'

'Hi, I'm Thomas. I just want to ask how do we know that the kids going to this school are even properly Catholic? You heard about that woman who dressed up as a guy to see a Saudi football match?'

'I'm not sure I follow, Thomas. You don't need to dress up to be Catholic?'

'Yes, but you see how people use religion to bend the rules.'

'Umm, noooo... The woman in question used gender to flout a rule that shouldn't have even been a rule in the first place, in my humble opinion.'

'Right, so if it's a mixed Catholic school, you agree we got problems?'

'And thank you, Thomas. Let's hear from Elizabeth in Tituba...

'...Aaaaaaahhhhhh!

'Elizabeth, turn your radio down. Elizabeth? Turn your radio off. Someone tell this girl she can't have her radio on whilst she's on the air! And we've lost Elizabeth in Tituba. Where is Tituba anyway?'

Afternoon school run, done. I was tired. The plants looked thirsty. I had bought a watering can. If I were going to be someone who watered plants, then I would have to use a proper metal can. Utensils had functions. The relationship between them should be respected. The plants were withered and their leaves were not the soft fennel green of Ava' eyes or even the childlike felt green of the Gatlin oaks, but a decrepit, dried-up algae green of plants that had seen better days, lived better lives. Of all the plants in the house, it was no surprise that the money plants were the ones begging loudest for burial. *Crassula Ovata.* They were all Alex's. It had felt as if whenever he left the house, he came back with a plant. I hated plants and told him the excess oxygen concerned me. Now he was gone and here I was, gently wiping the dust off the leaves, adding drops of plant food into the earth, watering the fuckers, silently willing them to live because I thought maybe Ava might like them around and even talking to them occasionally. My elderly father was more self-sufficient. I liked to think that they were suffering out of sympathy for me.

Ava, Amelia, Tabatha and Catherine were doing their homework at the table and, when they were not talking, the house felt a like the restricted section in a library. Catherine Donnington was proof that you didn't have to be pretty to be popular. Tabatha and Amelia had both angles covered. Ava had been trying for years to get 'pretty and unpopular' to catch on, but it never had. In this way, Catherine demonstrated, along with a slightly crooked nose, thin mousy brown hair and pursed lips, that she and Ann – one of the fiercest tiger mothers in the PTA – had more in common than merely looking undesirable.

However, I observed an insecurity in Catherine undetected by her peers. She had been invited last. The other three had already formed a bond. It wasn't impenetrable by any means – proven by the fact that she sat with them now – but its mere existence confused Catherine. Amelia had arrived at our house seeking comfort. Tabatha had arrived seeking refuge. It seemed as if Catherine didn't actually need anything from Ava, aside from perhaps an opportunity to reclaim her old friends and end this farce where tiger cub Ava showed her stripes.

'Cath, these sums,' Amelia pointed in Catherine's workbook, 'need doing as well.'

'How do you know?'

The girls exchanged glances. 'Because Miss Triloni said so, but it was when you were with the police.'

'Oh. Okay. These are really difficult,' she said, downcast.

'Actually, they're not that hard. I can show you,' offered Ava.

'I know I've been a bit upset, but I'm not so devastated that I'm going to take maths advice from you,' snarled Catherine.

'Meels got eighteen out of twenty on her last test,' said Tabatha, as if Catherine had made a fair point but she should know that there was new exculpatory evidence in play.

'You copied?' said Catherine glibly.

'Yes,' Amelia said with her head down. This was not a normal reaction for Amelia. Guilt. Girls like these ate guilt for breakfast and washed it down with a glass of fat-free shame. Amelia's reaction seemed especially weird because guilt in the face of plagiarism simply constituted a normal day in her world. There was something else going on here. I got the distinct smell of intimidation. It was not the done thing to be taking advice from Ava and especially not for something that Catherine found difficult and was clearly grappling with herself. It was good to see they could turn on each other, even if Ava was to get caught in the crossfire. Worse would have been if they spoke and thought from one body but with three separate heads. Cerberus in knee-high socks.

'Amelia! You didn't tell me that,' exclaimed Ava, hurt and astonishment flashed across her face as she dropped her pencil.

'Why does she have to tell you anything?' Catherine hissed back.

'She doesn't – I just thought… it doesn't matter,' mumbled Ava, clearly embarrassed.

'Ava, I saw Lex talking to you this morning on the field,' probed Tabatha, a glint in her eye.

'Yes,' smiled Ava. Bless my little girl and her ready-at-the-starting-line, raging teenage sex hormones. If I thought life was difficult now, I wasn't even ready to entertain the Ava and Lex scenarios. And why did that boy's name have to rhyme with 'sex'? It was more than a little disturbing. Why don't parents think about the names they give their babies for longer than the time it takes to make a baby?

'Well, what did he say?' nudged Amelia.

'He was asking if I knew who was running for class president.'

'What?' said Catherine, spitting out an oat cake I had made earlier. It was difficult to say whether she was shocked by what she had heard or sickened by what was in her mouth. I had run out of oats and used mung beans instead.

'I told him it was you.' Ava looked over at Catherine, 'It was a nice conversation.' Her head folded into her neck like a shy giraffe.

Amelia, Tabatha and Catherine held a moment of tension together across the table before Ava questioned the new elephant in the room.

'What's the matter?'

'I run for president every year,' stated Catherine. Any more unamused, she'd be dead.

'I know,' said Ava. 'Maybe Lex forgot—'

'He knows. I think he's suggesting you run,' stirred Tabatha, her brow creasing. She had clearly been thinking this whole time.

'It would seem so,' squealed Amelia. 'A conversation is easy enough to start, but why ask Ava what he already knows unless he's trying to sow a seed in her head? And I know where it would prove more fruitful to sow that seed,' she grinned.

Dirty slut. I restrained myself, trying to go unnoticed under my bamboo and let them have their private time.

'Me? Run? I wouldn't know what to do,' said Ava.

'Well, that is precisely why you shouldn't do it,' smiled Catherine tightly.

'Right,' agreed Ava.

'It's a stupid idea,' said Catherine.

'It is funny,' said Amelia.

'So funny,' added Tabatha.

That was enough restrained time. 'Why is it funny? I don't see any reason why Ava shouldn't run for president. The people need new blood. They want new blood. That's how the people work. Ava, you would make an excellent president and I think people would vote for you. There comes a time where the corrupt political crucible spits out change and that's you.'

Tabatha and Amelia laughed at the idea. Ava laughed with them and Catherine faked a tremor in her throat to join in with the joviality. I expected there was always an air of nervous hilarity on the eve of a presidential campaign idea. Presidents were made and broken during conversations as haphazard as this one. Things took time to sink in and propagate. And in every presidential campaign, there was always one person who thought that they should be president instead. As the laughter continued, Catherine smiled a wonderfully straight smile.

Groups

Even if I wanted to miss him, even if that possibility existed, I would not have had time. Since Alex's sudden departure face down into Poppy's fragrant bush, I had cooked more dinners than I could remember, spoken to Ava's friends more than necessary, botched a suicide attempt, experimented with therapy, robbed two women, been bitten by a rat dog and all this whilst still needing to find £11,510 for Ava's school fees as the formal yet threatening letter in today's post reminded me. Sometimes when people telephoned the house looking for Alex, I found myself replying, 'Alex who?' During our time together, I definitely had moments – moments, I would say, that turned into years – where I convinced myself that there was no way I could look after Ava without Alex. It was a shock when he said she was coming to live with us permanently. I didn't protest or try to prevent it, but I made sure Alex knew it was on him to cook the family dinner and involve himself in her schooling. These were two areas I needed to stay away from if Ava's presence in our house was not to upset me. But this week had proved a revelation. I didn't need Alex. Every utensil had a function and I was this family's watering can. I refused to dwell on the small bits of rust that had corroded around the spout.

Maybe I could sell the car. I wouldn't get much. It was old and battered, but it was something. I could put an advert up in the tea room. But was it a good idea to draw attention to the fiscal vice around my neck? The letter said the fees were due now. Probably wasn't good for people to know I was struggling with money. If the school contacted Alex, he would simply take her out of Gatlin. The last thing Alex would want would be a black mark for not paying the fees and keeping Ava enrolled under false pretences. Being so caught up in his last chance at happiness, he didn't have room to consider what Ava might want. The one thing that was working for me was everybody assuming that Alex was on sabbatical. Penelope Coultard knew about the affair – had known – but no one else had mentioned it and Penelope wasn't talking much anymore. If Alex wasn't rushing to tell anyone that he had left us, there was less chance that the school would be in touch with him. We were safe. For now.

I crumpled the letter in my palm, trying to crush the money I owed, and put it in my handbag. There was another letter lying at the bottom in an even sorrier state. It was the one from Alex. How much had happened in such a short space of time since that day? I'd carried that letter with me since then because I suppose I needed to, but I didn't need to anymore. Weird how that happens – the idea that, at one point, something is so essential, and then that point in life passes. The moment is gone and you can't even remember needing what you once thought you couldn't be without. Gone. Much like death.

All was quiet in the living room. The girls must have gone upstairs. I went to check that they'd finished dinner, see if they wanted dessert. I'd made a chocolate mousse. It was a lot of work. As soon as I had started making it, I'd regretted not buying a ready-made one from the shop and wished I'd just smoked a joint instead. The chocolate bubbled like a volcano in hot, molten pools of angry cocoa. The eggs followed suit, curdling organically as if this was the original recipe. Maybe it would still taste okay.

Papa's door was shut, but I knew he was out. I was never normally tempted to go inside. It smelled of old man: flatulence and semen. It would have made a horrific scented candle. I'd heard him talking to a woman. He was dressing smarter and spending time outside of the house instead of wanking off behind a closed door – although we were always grateful that he closed the door. He'd started to talk to the girls about love. That was a step too far, I couldn't listen. But I was curious to know what was going on. Had his life changed as much as mine? He seemed happier than me. But then he'd always been happier than me, even when he was sad. He said that was just how some people were. It wasn't their fault: it was just that whatever they'd come to this life needing, they just hadn't got. I had to try to see it less as a punishment and more of a reminder. A reminder of what? I'd asked as a child. An opportunity to remind yourself that despite the shitty cards you've been dealt, you are worth something. Not everybody was so lucky, apparently. According to the legend of Papa, God had a big needle. He sewed a badge on people's hearts with it that said 'You are special.' The pain they felt every day was God's needle reminding them to look at the badge. Not everybody got a badge. I remember hearing this story most days from the age of about seven. When I turned ten, I told Papa I didn't believe in God and he put God's special needle away. Stuck it in a pin cushion of harmless lies for children. But occasionally, as an adult, I'd tap the left side of my chest, like there was something missing.

The bed was made. Silk sheets with an embroidered valance and a purple duvet cover with stitching on the borders. Three plates with dried food waited patiently on the table to be collected, and a shirt that he had already ironed hung on the back of the chair. He loved to sprinkle talcum powder liberally over his whole body after a shower and puffs of white chalky dust had settled over the floor, leaving footprints where he had stood. He had a stack of about five books by his bed at all times and read them all at once. However, it was the Kamasutra by Vatsyayana jutting out of the middle of the tower that caught my attention. A piece of paper was dangling over the edge with handwriting I didn't recognise. Bending down, I tried to read it without pulling it out, but it made little sense – the contents were indecipherable. I removed the paper to inspect it more closely, keeping the pages that it sat between open with my fingers. I read it then wished I hadn't – a side effect of snooping. Someone had written Papa the filthiest of letters. I could not even describe it as a love letter because there was a sense of depravity that was absent from any love I had known. Was I a prude? How was my father more sexually adventurous than I was? Didn't he renounce all claims to his former identity when he became a parent? I wanted it off my hands. I felt as though I had opened Pandora's box and needed to get all the bad things back in between the pages quickly before they slipped out to infest the world. Who was this awful woman? Was Papa so lonely that he'd settle for any sort of debased individual? I'd have to talk to him. There came a time when the child became the parent.

The doorbell rang. A short hollow chime. I was grateful for the diversion. I had been meaning to change the bell and get something more pleasing to the ear. A couple of bars of a sonata. Something to give the impression that opening the door to the world would be a good idea. Ann Donnington stood on my steps. She had come to pick up Catherine. On second thoughts, that was a lot of pressure to put on a doorbell.

'Hello,' she said, looking around. The front garden hid its lawn well under sacks-of-cement-turned-rubbish-bins that had once belonged to discontinued building works. The bricks had come loose from the wall, some having been removed altogether to make handy space for crushed up empty beer cans, and weeds had forced their way through the cracks in the stone. It wasn't personal, but Ann seemed to take it that way.

'Weeds,' she announced. I wouldn't have known. She had been sent to guide me.

'Catherine's upstairs.' Following behind, I could hear her throwing her voice as she nosed around the house, peering into the living room, the downstairs toilet and the study on the way to the kitchen. The kitchen wasn't dirty; it wasn't even messy. The three wooden shelves above the counter with my mugs and spices looked very orderly, and the cooker and table had been wiped down as recently as this morning. However, as soon as Ann and I were both stood in it together and her eyes widened the way eyes do when getting accustomed to the dark, I got the distinct feeling it was missing an aga, an island, and some wall-to-wall, floor-to-ceiling glass doors.

'It's light,' said Ann, shocked by the revelation.

'It's the daytime,' I said.

'North-east facing houses are usually terribly dark.'

'We're south-west.'

'It's strange this new alliance,' Ann pondered as she pulled a chair and began dusting it off with her hand. With a look of disgust, she pulled her hand to her face to examine it more closely. A sticky red gloop attached to her fingers.

'Sorry about that,' I said tossing her a sponge, which she caught in a fluster. 'My Dad sometimes spreads jam on the chair and it really gets me because I fucking hate jam.'

'Your father spreads jam on the chair?'

'I think he wants me to like jam.'

'You live with your Dad?' she asked in disbelief.

'I'm Asian.'

'I've known Tabatha and Amelia since they were born,' she said changing the subject, handing me back the sponge with her thumb and index finger. 'Henrietta, Regina and I were all in the same NCT group. We've all been such a close group of friends that it just made sense that our children would form their own little group and become best friends too. I mean, of course we encouraged them, but we didn't have to – they all had so much in common it was inevitable. But Ava. I don't believe the group has ever been friends with Ava.'

'Nope. Don't understand it either. I think Ava's having a small psychotic break between you and me.' I stood on the other side of the wooden table. Her bag seemed welded under her arm and was far too small to carry the essential items that its size suggested should be its main priority. I lit a cigarette.

'You smoke in the house.' That wasn't a question. I just stared at her blankly. 'I hope you haven't been smoking around Catherine.'

'Do you want a drink? Coffee, tea. I've got wine. Do you want some wine?' Hosting made me nauseous. A commune would probably finish me off without the need of pills. Everybody checking in to see how the other person was doing or how they felt, needing to prove how worthy or good they were by being of some pointless service. When people came to the house, I preferred them to make themselves at home and get on with it – get their own drinks, make their own food – so I always forgot to ask. But most people weren't able to do that, especially not Ann.

'Well I'm driving, but I suppose one wouldn't hurt. Just one, mind. Will you be having some? I don't believe you and I had ever properly spoken before that day in the tea room,' she stated. Her fingers were long with French polish and prominent knuckles. Her rings sparkled. Look away, Drea. Step away from the shiny fingers.

'No, we had never spoken on any day,' I clarified. 'Wine doesn't agree with me.'

'How very odd.'

'I'll have a whisky,' I decided.

'A whisky. Now that's even odder. I'm not sure I know who your... I can't remember seeing you with... I'm sorry.' She shook herself to regain composure. 'Do you have a group? Is there a group of mothers you are friends with? Do you have friends at the school who form a group?' If I'd met her speed dating, I would not have lasted the full sixty seconds, which would have lead me to conclude that she was not for me. She tried the wine. Her lips recoiled slightly the way I thought she might look at point of entry if she was having sex. 'This wine is corked.'

'I know, I just opened it.'

'No, I mean—'

'I know what you mean, I'm just fuckin' witcha,' I drawled, exaggerating an accent. 'No, I hate groups.'

'I see.'

I wasn't sure she did. I threw her wine down the sink, a tiny piece of cork running behind it into the plug hole, and opened a new bottle. I puffed on my cigarette and she watched me smoke.

'Have you been interviewed yet?' she asked.

'I think they just finished the children. I'm tomorrow.'

'Mine is on Friday. I think the police are doing a wonderful job,' she said. I nodded. 'It's a terrible thing for Gatlin.'

'Yes, it is,' I agreed.

'I still can't quite believe it.'

'She's definitely dead,' I confirmed.

'It's affected Catherine deeply. She's a very sensitive girl and she's beside herself.'

My thoughts meandered. That sounded scary – two Catherines, side-by-side. 'She and Xavier, well let's just say I think they had a special bond. They'd known each other forever you see from our NCT baby group. I think Penelope imagined they might marry.'

'Child marriage is illegal.'

'Not now!' said Ann, open-mouthed.

'What happens at NCT?' I said.

'Well it's a fabulous group of parents that come together to learn about pregnancy, parenting—'

'No, I mean what really happens?'

'What do you mean?'

'Well, it's a cult right?' I asked.

'Sorry?'

'A load of parents who've never met each other manically desperate to make friends with other couples so they enter into some unspoken agreement that states by virtue of the fact that they've all had sex without protection at around the same time of year they will suddenly have everything in common, start having dinners together and bond in this weird, cultish – oh my God, it's a swingers' club!'

'No, it is certainly not!' Ann brayed loudly.

'Don't get mad. That's cool. You don't look that way inclined, but trust me, I think it's good for you. I just wanted to know from someone in the "group".'

'I'd like to get Catherine now,' Ann insisted.

'CATHERINE!' I screamed. The girls had the music on. I could feel the bass vibrating through the floorboards.

'Heard you on the radio.' I said.

'Did you?' she looked shocked.

'Ann from Donnington? Were you MI5 before PTA?'

'I… I didn't think about it in advance,' she mumbled.

'Really.'

'Someone needed to say something. It's obviously the same person. The same person who robbed Regina and Henny killed Penny,' she said, pouring herself another glass of wine. Wine gave me an awful headache, but seemed to be the staple drink of women with children. At events with mothers and children, it was usually the only alcoholic beverage on offer. Women breastfed and, once the milk dried up, their bodies distracted themselves from any potential sadness over the demise of the milk ducts through insatiable cravings for wine. White, mainly, and often in the afternoons, around 4pm.

'Maybe. Maybe not,' I contradicted.

'It has to be,' she practically snorted with authority.

'It's actually quite a large jump from robbery to murder,' I pointed out.

'I don't see how. They are both criminal acts!' Her little piggy snout stuck in the air as if she had never forged a signature, stolen a credit card, taken ecstasy, snorted coke, mugged anyone. Maybe she hadn't. Where was the life experience?

'Yes, but, I just think these things can be complicated,' I continued, 'and the last thing we want is to send the police in the wrong direction and away from the real killer. I bet you couldn't live with yourself if you did that.'

'Well that's not what I'm doing. I'm being a good, responsible friend. The girls would have reported these crimes already if they hadn't been so frightened. I mean, he killed Henny's dog, gutted Miss Congeniality right in front of her.'

Be calm. Henrietta was obviously a pathological liar. I smiled inwardly. In another lifetime maybe we could have been friends.

'The police need to have all the information at their disposal in order to conduct an informed investigation,' she proclaimed. I had to do something. Ann was out of control.

'I was robbed,' I blurted.

'What?'

'I haven't told anyone. I'm too frightened,' I lowered my head.

'You see! This is exactly what I mean. We have to unite and form a group. Mothers Of Gatlin Stand Strong.'

'No! No groups! He had a picture of Ava.' Ann slumped back into her chair. 'He said he would hurt her. You can't say anything to the police. Please. This is my daughter. Imagine if it was Catherine. Imagine if something bad was to happen to Catherine,' I paused to imagine. Ann thought for a minute. 'And you could have stopped a terrible tragedy by simply not opening your mouth,' I continued.

'Ann, promise me you won't say anything. We can't help them, anyway. None of us saw anything.'

'Okay,' she said reluctantly. 'Are you alright? I mean did he hurt you.'

'No. Yes. I mean, I'm shaken, but fine. I just need to put it behind me. Throw myself into something and forget about it.'

She looked up, excited. 'I've got just the thing,' she frothed. 'The school bake sale! Now that Penny's dropped out—'

'Died—'

'Now that she's dropped out, we're a man down, so to speak.'

'No. Sorry.'

'Why not? You said you needed something to take your mind off it. And it's for Gatlin. To be honest, Drea, I haven't really seen you do anything for the school before. You know the PTA encourages parents and teachers to get involved.'

For fuck's sake. The PTA. Another fucking cult. Like my life needed a bake sale right now.

'It's just so much work for us. Penelope was Treasurer and she did such a wonderful job, but we've raised so much money – about five thousand pounds this year alone – that we need time to really look at the finances. What is the best method of distribution and with all that work to do and being a man down for the bake sale—'

'Ok, you twisted my arm,' I jumped in.

'Really?'

'It's for Gatlin. And in memory of Henny,' I suggested.

'Henny's not dead.'

'No, she isn't. Thank God for that. Penny. Penelope. That's what I meant. This business is all so upsetting, isn't it?'

'It really is,' she said pouring another glass. 'With Penny gone the group is just… well, fragile.'

I had some ideas for re-distribution. In the quiet of my kitchen, I planned whilst Ann reminisced.

Interview

I could smell the rain that morning. The police had held the interviews for the children at the school to prevent any further disruption. Ironically, it was Penelope Coultard who had been disrupted the most. I wondered if she was bothered where the interviews were conducted or, indeed, if they were conducted at all. Did the dead need justice as badly as the living?

As so many of the parents had insisted they be present at their darlings' interviews – I had not, although, after Ava told me about her interview, I wished I had – the children had become used to seeing parents coming and going and generally milling about. It made sense, then, that the police announced that they would interview the parents at the school as well. The actual interviews were held in a portacabin at the edge of the premises, which normally served as a spill-over classroom or an exam room when needed. However, until it was your turn, or if you arrived early, you had to wait in the reception area by the principal's office.

My appointment was for ten o'clock, and it seemed that this was not one of those events at which to arrive fashionably late – or indeed any kind of late. I was there at quarter to ten.

An egg white-coloured dado rail separated the magnolia and cream painted walls that were adorned by multiple first-place awards for the school. Maude sat behind a green leather-topped desk looking up, her bifocals perched obediently on the bridge of her nose.

'Drea!' She quickly scanned a piece of paper next to her computer, 'I didn't even read my sheet this morning, I've had so much to do. It's been a bit manic to say the least,' she spluttered, flustered and pushing back hair that was not in her face. 'Oops, shouldn't really say that too loudly, should I?'

"You look tired,' I observed. She did, and this was unlike Maude. Maude did all the things you were supposed to do, including sleep at the right times. As a child of missionaries, it was that or burn in hell, I suppose.

'The truth is that without the PTA, God knows what we'd do… and well, Penny was treasurer. I can't do it all.'

'I'm helping out at the bake sale,' I admitted, as we were confessing to hideous responsibilities. It felt like the sort of thing that gets said in a room like this. The words reverberated around me and, when they came back to my ears, the sick, nauseous feeling I'd been left with after Ann had left the night before came rushing back.

'That's very school-spirited of you Drea. Don't take offence, but it's not something I'd have thought you'd be interested in.'

'No offence taken. It was a moment of weakness. I've been having a few of those lately.'

'Is Alex enjoying his sabbatical?'

'More than you know. More than any of us knew.'

'Some of our more creative types really need to take a break from the classroom and bury their heads in some good old-fashioned academia.'

'Maude, he's got his head so far up academia right now—'

'Oh Drea, you are terrible.'

I was regretting my eager arrival at the school and was suspecting I had come a little too early when Regina Salter walked in and promptly confirmed all my suspicions. I had not been this close to her since our fateful rendezvous in the park.

It wouldn't have been weird to avert my gaze and just not make eye contact, but then she looked right at me and smiled and it was too late. I was so shocked that I flashed her a convicted serial killer grin that should only be reserved for passport photo applications. She looked unperturbed and, with two chairs in front, chose to sit down in the one right beside me. I felt a slight tingling in my toes. Which was worse? The feel of her aerobically toned thighs next to my cupcake layered legs, or her sat opposite me, boring a hole into my face because she has a vague recollection that she's met me somewhere before? I could see the strain as she pushed her brain to start searching through its catalogue of memories and find a recognisable snapshot of the two of us together. Next to me was definitely the better seat. At least from there she could only see one side of my face and there was less chance of her saying something hideous like 'have I met you somewhere before?'

'Have I met you somewhere before?' she said sweetly. Oh it was getting so hot in here – why was it so hot in here?

'No.'

'Really?' she continued.

'No.'

'I know you come to the school. You have a...' she faltered, stumbling on the correct terminology for my relationship with a girl whose colour and features were nothing like mine.

'Step-daughter,' I offered.

'Right,' she drawled with confident uncertainty. 'But I feel like I know you from somewhere else too,' she confessed. I shrugged my shoulders apologetically. Please let that be the end of it. 'I can't remember the last time I was summoned to the principal's office,' Regina whispered. 'It's like I've done something naughty.' She was as interesting as cucumbers and dip – but without the dip.

'You haven't been summoned to the principal's office, you've been summoned to the portacabin,' I corrected, instantly wishing I'd suppressed my liminally disguised contempt.

Regina stared at me. 'I do know you. Is it NCT?'

'No.'

'PTA?'

'No.'

'WWF,' giggled Maude.

'I just feel... you know, when you just feel like you just know someone?'

'Well, you don't.'

'You sound so sure,' said Regina gaily, looking at Maude to draw her in.

'I am,' I said, standing up. 'Maude, should I go in now?'

'I'd wait here a couple more minutes, Drea. There's nowhere to sit at the cabin if you're early, so the police like everyone to be exactly on time.'

I sat down.

'Do you go to my exercise class?' asked Regina.

'Maude, I need the toilet,' I said standing up again.

'Ok,' smiled Maude nodding and when I looked back at her, she appeared to have turned into a sheep. A sheep sat on its hind legs behind the computer, bifocals on its face, typing with its animal hooves.

The hall started to spin. This was more than a slight dizzy spell. I knew my bearings were unreliable when I went to hold what I thought was a soft white wall and a student shouted, 'Get off me!' I tried to focus on the first door I could find with the picture of a stick figure in a dress. The third door on the left looked like the girls' toilet but three boys bundled out before I could enter. Someone had drawn a skirt on the stick boy. Everything was turning upside down. People were laughing with their heads the wrong way round so their mouths looked like their eyes.

I leaned up against the wall to steady myself. Breathe. If this was a panic attack, I just needed to tell it to go fuck itself. I could control this. I was waging a war, with my irrational thoughts going up against my anxious paranoia. I breathed deeply with my eyes closed, whilst simultaneously hoping that when I opened them, the whole corridor would not be gathered there, standing silently, to watch the weirdo. Deeply in. Hold it. And deeply out. Deep breath in. Hold it. And deep breath out. One more time. Okay. I opened my eyes. I saw girls and boys walking and talking and taking no notice of me and I saw them clearly, the right way up. Right. Off to the police.

The walk across the school playing field was brutal. Grass was scary enough on a good day, but the fear of what had just been and the fear of what was to come amalgamated into the most fearsome fucking walk through grass I'd ever had. And what was it all for? Penelope Coultard's death was starting to be the one thing that made sense around here that's how crazy everything had become. Death itself was certain and made so much more sense than life. People died; yes, sometimes people killed other people, but this was nature. Human nature. Crime itself was a social construct invented by humans needing to live in a world where they could judge others safely and stand apart from their own moral depravity. My life felt as though it wasn't mine anymore and I was detached from it, just playing a part. Was this weird? Don't we deliberately set ourselves apart from each other to construct our own identity? Maybe problems arose from trying to detach ourselves from what is inside us. If we could all look at the dark parts of ourselves, would it be better to bring them into the light? It started to rain. I felt the grass drink it up greedily and become flaccid under my feet. Penelope had got out. I bet if you asked her now, she'd say it wasn't such a bad thing. We are the only species cursed with the ability and need to know ourselves. If we gave up on this obsessive need and flushed it down the toilet what would be left? Nothing. Peace.

I knocked. A plump, rosy-cheeked woman in a uniform opened the door.

'Ooh, come in quickly from the rain.' I remembered what Maude had said about the police wanting people to arrive exactly on time and I wondered if this concern for my solubility would have existed at five to ten. Maybe the nicer they acted, the more likely it was that they were going to arrest you for murder. She gave me a big smile.

'It just started all of a sudden,' she stated. Could rain start any other way? For crime scene investigation purposes, maybe there was rain that washed evidence away and rain that could be tolerated depending on how suddenly it began. Or maybe this was another bullshit warm and fuzzy fill-in until the waterboarding started. I groaned inwardly. There was nothing like a conversation with the police to get the paranoia beans jumping.

'I'm Officer Frampton. But call me Jane. Have a seat, Drea.' And there it was. That thing they did when they used your name in conversation acting so casually, as if you had either just given it to them or the two of you had gone to Montessori together as infants and shared a history. She pulled a wooden chair out for me to sit at a large white melamine-topped desk. It didn't look in bad condition. Not too many scuffs and no readable graffiti, just faint marks where someone had tried rubbing the words away and left a light blue cloud in its place. She might have been cheery, but the room was not. Its sparseness screamed interrogation. She sat opposite me. A large pane of glass looked onto the miserable field I'd just walked across.

'Drea, I'm going to take some notes while we talk, are you okay with that?' she checked.

No, I'm not okay with that. And this is the part where I say no, we get physical, you claim I'm resisting arrest, and I sleep in a cell overnight – murder suspect number one. Loving these questions already.

'That's fine,' I lied. My first lie.

'Good.' She paused as if that was the first test and I had passed. As if she could conclude the interview here, if she wanted to. But she didn't.

'Let's start from the beginning shall we. You have a child at the school.'

'Yes.'

'Ava Thorn.'

'Yes.'

'But your name is Drea Peiris?

'She uses her father's name as we're not married.'

'And she's not your daughter?'

If you know the answers why ask the questions? 'Not my biological daughter, no.'

'And your husband's name is?'

'Boyfriend. Alex Thorn.'

'Alex Thorn. Why do I know that name?'

Because you saw it on the front cover of Philanderer's Weekly?

'Oh here it is.' She shuffled paper around as if she was going to perform some kind of magic trick: and now, ladies and gentlemen, out of this guilty-before-innocent-presumed interview, I produce from nothing a theory based on less than that. 'Here it is, yes I thought so. He's a teacher here at the school. Teaches English. He's at school today?' I couldn't yet work out if she knew more than she let on or if she was discovering these facts in real time.

'He's on sabbatical right now.' It was a hard line to walk, knowing how much information to give and look innocent and how much would be too much and lead to incrimination –

especially the way the police were known to intentionally obfuscate situations to further their own agenda.

'That's nice. Work or pleasure?' She seemed genuinely interested.

'Pleasure that will probably turn into work,' I replied grimly. I thought it best from now on to make sure that everything I said I could say again if I was strapped to a polygraph.

'I was never very good at school,' she said, reminiscing as though she was rocking in a home and chatting to her grandchildren. 'The deceased – Penelope Coultard – were you friends? Did you know her?'

'No, not really.'

'Not really? So you did or you didn't?'

'I knew who she was.'

'Ever talk to Mrs Coultard?'

'I think so.'

'You think? So you had spoken to her or you hadn't.' Fucking police.

'I think she might have sold me a cake at the bake sale last year,' I said. This was true. She might have sold me a cake, if I had gone.

'Bake sale. Mmm. I love cakes.' No need for you to take a polygraph there, Officer Fat Face.

'So that was last year. Anything more recent? In the last couple of weeks?'

'Umm. I think we had a conversation about a parking space.'

'Oh,' she laughed gaily. 'What about exactly?'

'The usual. Are you planning to park there? No, I'm just leaving, that sort of thing.'

'Mighty polite you lot round here. Do you think you might have said instead, "Next time you go to bed, I hope you die in it, bitch"?' she smiled, her happy-clappy demeanour not having changed in the slightest. That's when I knew the blue team had sent in one of their finest.

'Umm. I recall... something that might have sounded similar to that.'

'Well let's see.' She re-sorted her magic papers and created a slight fluttering, which I was very grateful for as I felt it getting warm again. 'Yes, it says here her son Xavier Coultard, heard you saying exactly those words to his mother on 6th September.'

What was the best course of action here? I felt we had come to a crossroads. Although there were two definitive roads for me to take, the writing on each sign was unclear and a flock of large black crows circled ominously in the distance. Think of the hubris it took to sit here all rosy cheeked, knowing everything, and still play it like she was Mother Teresa.

'Yes, I did say that.'

'Pretty strong words. Such strong words I'd go as far as to say you and Mrs Coultard weren't friends at all. Maybe even enemies?' She stopped, giving it time for the weight of this to sink in.

'Did you kill Mrs Coultard, Drea?' First-name basis again. Love it. She'd returned to intimacy to find the truth. And where else could truth reside?

'No, I did not.'

'Do you know who did?'

'No.'

'Did you have anything to do with Penelope Coultard's death?' Jesus, string it out why don't you?

'No.'

'Drea, you can understand my predicament.'

There was a small window here for a mini-closing argument, or if not that then at least for more evidence for the defence. Let's call our first witness: leading psychologist, Drea Peiris.

'Listen, I admit I was angry. But anger itself is not motive for murder. In fact, I have no motive as I don't know the woman from Adam. If you ask me, saying what I said is probably healthier. Maybe if the murderer had been able to express themselves better verbally Penelope would still be alive.'

She smiled, jotting a few things down.

'Where were you on the evening of Wednesday 8th?'

I hated when the simple act of trying to remember made you seem guilty, like you were having to make up some elaborate story entirely unrelated to not taking enough tablets to kill yourself but overdosing anyway and being taken to the hospital by your daughter and her two new BFFs. I was walking a tightrope. Wavering between falling down onto the cold hard truth – which would open up a whole foul-smelling can of worms about why I might want to end my life – or falling down onto a bouncy cushion of lies, slowly deflating as cushions of lies tend to do, especially in the presence of the police. Either way I was falling.

However, before I could pick a side, through the window I saw Regina walking across the field. She was wearing high black boots. She had known she'd be walking over wet grass and had chosen appropriate yet fashionable footwear, unlike me. There was a hole in my left trainer and my big toe felt moist. My throat tightened. It felt chalky and dry. Then right in the middle of the field, she stopped. She had forgotten something – no, she had heard something. She turned around, and walking briskly through the field towards Regina Salter was none other than my favourite pathological liar, Henrietta Crosly-Burke.

I went to breathe, but I couldn't. I opened my mouth and nothing. I began to sweat. Beads dropped down past my eyebrows and fell onto my lips. I had salt, but no oxygen. There was something blocking my throat. It was so tight I felt my hand fly up to try and loosen it. Officer Frampton flew off her chair and stood in front of me, but I couldn't hear what she was saying. I put my hand on the table to stand up but it wouldn't stop shaking and I couldn't raise myself. The thing in my throat felt like a ball, but a ball of what? It made me feel like I was choking, but choking on what? I knew her words made sense but I strained to hear them in the deafening quiet.

'Drea. Drea. Listen to me. Watch my lips. Can I touch you? Would it be okay if I bent down and put my hands on your knees?' She crouched so she was nearer me and I felt the pressure of her hands grounding my legs into the chair. She had tiny freckles above her lips and on the brow of her cheeks.

'Drea, you're having a panic attack. I know it feels like you can't breathe, but the body just needs to remember that it can. So we're going to distract it a moment.' A plan, yes at least one of us has a plan.

'I'm going to take your arms and lift them up and down a couple of times.' The slow, rhythmic beat of her voice felt good. I still couldn't breathe, but the ball in my throat was deflating. She moved my arms up and down, slowly at first but then faster and I started to feel my sweat-drenched blouse as the air moved around me. The ball deflated and suddenly all the oxygen in the room rushed into my throat.

'Okay. Good, Drea. Now we're going to breathe. Long, deep, relaxing breaths. In and out. Look at me.' I did what she said. I could feel the tidal waves of dread that had engulfed me, just moments before, subsiding, lolling against the rocks, almost as if I could trust them now; as if we were becoming friends. The trembling had stopped. Frampton set down a box of tissues and started wiping my forehead. No one said anything for a little while, just two strangers breathing. The peace I felt in that room was unexpected and not a feeling I could remember having had, ever. Was the possibility of non-existence the only thing that could make existing more than bearable? At the moment she brought me back to life, I caught a glimpse of a place – somewhere in the middle of nowhere, where I could put all my dark stuff and be a different person. It felt as though this body and this face were not mine, they did not belong to me and I could slither away from them and away from all the mess. The world was a deformed hallucination and we were prisoners of memories and consciousness.

'Drea. Are you feeling better?'

'Yes.'

'I'm sure that was quite an ordeal. I'd like to carry on if that's okay?' Wow. She giveth with one hand and with the other she taketh away.

'Okay.'

'Great. Panic attacks can seemingly arise for no reason at all, but there is always a reason. It is usually the body's way of coping with an overwhelming fear of something. Drea, the attack started when I asked you where you were the night of the murder, Wednesday September 8th. Are you ready to talk about that now?'

'I was in hospital.' The panic attack, as she called it, had gone and all that was left was the realisation that I was scared, really scared.

'In hospital?'

'I took an overdose. Tried to. My daughter and her two friends took me there in a taxi. My daughter has no idea and I want it to stay that way. She thinks I had food poisoning.'

'Can you tell me why you wanted to end your own life?' She wouldn't understand that killing myself was the least scary part of this whole twisted chess game. That I seemed to be caught up in a vortex of reacting, emotionally, and killing myself seemed the sanest thing to do.

'My boyfriend left me on Monday. He wrote me a note and ran off with his research assistant. The school have no idea and I want that too to stay that way. The school think he's on sabbatical.'

'Okay. There's certainly more to you than meets the eye, Drea, which is really one of the most wonderful aspects of my job. Finding out who people really are, you know, behind the mask,' she laughed. 'I'm assuming this was Gatlin Hospital?'

'Yes.'

'And are you receiving follow-up treatment? I understand you don't want your daughter to know, but are you talking to anyone? Maybe a support group the hospital has recommended?'

I nearly died and she was talking about joining a group. Did no one understand me? Why save me then ask me to join a group?

'I have a therapist.'

'Good.'

I hadn't seen the camera before and, looking at it now, I couldn't believe I hadn't noticed it as there was barely anything else in the room.

'You're filming this?' I asked.

'Yes. Rodman and I will film all the interviews. In a murder investigation like this one where there are so many susp— people, it's necessary. My colleague should have joined us by now,' she said brightly. The porter cabin door opened with a force.

'Speak of the devil.' And it really was. I saw his large hands first on the ends of long arms that were too long for his torso as he held the door open for himself and hurled his hefty and cumbersome body inside. His head lolled over hunched shoulders. His eyes looked unopened, slits, almost like he was in pain. Thick black hair fell over thick black eyebrows, casting shadows. His hard, carved cheekbones and wide mouth, took up most of his face.

'Drea, this is Detective Constable Rodman.' I nodded at him. His cheap suit smelled damp.

The cold blew through me as the door banged on its hinges, refusing to close. Frampton jumped up in front of him to pull it shut. He shuffled his brooding expression around the room.

'It's got so blustery all of a sudden,' she laughed, perkily. I wondered if she'd got her body stuck beside Rodman on purpose. Once we were all inside, the room was much too crowded. This man sucked up my air and, after my latest panic attack, I needed easy access. 'Rodman, we're done here for now with Drea,' she smiled, invitingly.

'Drea, I'm sure you understand we don't want anyone leaving Gatlin due to any sudden engagements. If you remember anything after you've left, here's my number. It's the little details that close the big cases like this.' I wanted to ask her why this constituted a big case. I saw Rodman flash her a look. Should she even have admitted that? Was it because Penelope Coultard was a celebrity Gatlin mother, drove a fancy car and had a seat on the school board? If I died would my social relevance demand the same furore?

'You're wondering why it's a big case?' Frampton was feeling chatty. 'When a case involves this level of brutality, it takes special priority.'

'Interview over.' Rodman had spoken with a sardonic smile and a frightening raucousness to his voice. No one was born with a voice like that. He looked as if he moved amongst the worst of human detritus trying not to let the shit he saw leak all over his soul. Immune to and muted in the face of everyday emotion. Could rosy-cheeked Frampton really see herself with a man like that? Maybe Frampton knew that a man like that was the only kind of man that could protect her from whatever was out there.

Chemistry

I couldn't go home. I needed to do something active but mundane so I drove around. No destination, just driving. I was too wired. The local paper had Penelope on the front page. Two photographs side-by-side to show the trajectory of her life: one from her graduation and one from her wedding. Woe betide you if were murdered and did not have the foresight to graduate and get married before this tragic event took you from the world, would you even get a byline? She wore pearls in both photos. She was probably stabbed in pearls. Maybe it was a professional hit. By an oyster. She'd been stabbed nine times in the back. Not that Penelope didn't have the ability to make people want to stab her, but nine times? There was someone running around Gatlin with even less cognitive control than me. Thoughts drove themselves in numbered sports cars around the race track of my mind. Bringing up the rear in number 7: a brutal murderer on the loose in Gatlin. Number 6 gaining speed: replays of the interview with Frampton. What did she think I was guilty of? How far would she go to prove my guilt? Burning rubber in number 5: Regina and Henrietta in the field. Had they spoken about their individual robberies? Had they compared notes and were they onto me? Taking no prisoners was number 4: Rodman's cold, angry eyes. This detective was different to Frampton, more disturbed. Something about him was frightening. More determined than 4 was number 3: my panic attack. Fucking uncontrollable feelings. I'd kept a lid on my emotions my whole life and now, just at the time I needed that lid to be sealed tight, everything was imploding around me. Steady at number 2: Ava's school fees. I had to find the money. It wasn't right that Ava suffer because of her parents' actions. It wasn't fair. But in the lead and showing the others how it's done was number 1: the motherfucking bake sale. If it hadn't been for such a heavy police presence in Gatlin, I could have substituted a bit of baking powder for cocaine, but now was not the time to get creative.

It was still raining, in fact it had got heavier, and the wind raged with a vendetta of its own. This made me drive faster. I don't know why. Stopping distances are supposed to lengthen in wet weather, but I thought maybe if I drove really fast, I could slow the thoughts down. Drive past them and leave them drenched and alone in my rear-view mirror by the side of the road. My windscreen wipers were shocked and unprepared for the strength of the downpour and they rattled against the glass trying to keep pace. The windows were all steamed up. I couldn't see out and no one could see in.

Before I knew it, I the car stopped. I'd been here before. I didn't think about why it had happened or how I felt about it, I just got out. Maybe there was a part of me that knew it had to look after the rest of me. A part that wasn't fucked up and hadn't robbed anyone or ever had a panic attack; a part of me that knew about Newton's second law of motion and knew that acceleration is produced when a force acts on a mass. That the greater the mass of the object, the greater the amount of force needed to accelerate the object. So here we were.

I went to knock on the door, but it pushed right open. The letters were all over the stairs, muddy from the rain. When I got to the top I knocked hard. I heard her footsteps.

'Hello.' I stared. She was now a he.

'I'm looking for Dr Feel… Dr Armstrong.'

'She's off today. We share this room. Can I help you?'

'I wanted to see her,' I said.

'Did you have an appointment?'

'No.'

'Oh.'

'I had another panic attack today. I didn't intend to come here. I got in the car and was driving around,' I blurted.

'Have you rung Dr Armstrong? Maybe she could arrange a special session.'

'She's not going to do that,' I confessed.

'I'm sure she would.' He was optimistic.

'I've had one meeting with her and at the end I told her she was crap.'

'Sounds like you regret that?' he said.

'No, but I don't know any other therapists.'

'You're very wet,' he observed astutely.

'It's raining.'

'Why don't you come inside. I'll give Dr Armstrong a call and we'll go from there.' With an elongated arm, he held the door open for me to enter, staying in the hallway to make his call. Tall, slender, a checked woollen tank top over a pale blue shirt, he looked normal. The other one had looked normal too. Maybe I'd try and hold off for as long as possible before calling this one crap. I felt like it was important for my therapist to be normal. If I was seeing a therapist because there was a part of me that was not normal, then my therapist needed all their parts to be completely normal. It's like girls on make-up counters with bad skin – why would you ever listen to anything they had to say on pore control?

I used the small towel he'd handed me to dry myself. It took a certain kind of rain to determine whether your coat was actually rain proof. This was that sort of rain and my coat was not. I walked over to the sculpture of the two black African women carrying their babies. How did they do it? How did they provide? Was the key to do it in twos? Find a friend and get a papoose for your back – after that it was plain sailing? These women did not look remotely bothered by the prospect of school fees. They were on a journey with their babies and their brethren through the Bayuda desert. The more they walked and talked, the taller and stronger they became, until their essence was captured in ebony and sat on a white man's shelf in a therapy room. Just so I could glean some understanding on how to provide for my non-biological child who had become so all-consuming I might as well have put my foot through my own pelvic floor.

'Hello,' he said, with a half-smile of commiseration. 'So I spoke with Dr Armstrong. Normally the way it works is we share a room, but we don't share patients. Continuity and confidentiality. But on this occasion, Dr Armstrong feels that, due to personalities, you guys weren't able to gel in the first session. As there's only been one so far, she's happy for you to see me.'

'One what?' I said.

'One session,' he replied.

'Oh.' So if there'd been two sessions she'd have carried on seeing me out of obligation without ever mentioning our ungellable personalities? None of this makes any sense. Why am I here?

'Why don't you have a seat?'

I sat down where I had sat before. He sat down where she had sat. Same shit, different therapist. 'Do you want to take your coat off?' he asked.

'I want to talk about my boyfriend leaving,' I announced.

'Has this been causing you a great deal of emotional distress?'

'No.'

'Why do you want to talk about it?'

'Because I'm having panic attacks and maybe it's… what's that thing you people say? The place where you think everything happens. Psychological parliament.'

'The unconscious.'

'That's it. Maybe it's my unconscious. Maybe I really miss him.'

'Do you really miss him?'

'No.'

He uncrossed his legs to stretch his body and brought over a pad from his desk. Pen poised. 'Do you mind?'

'No.'

'Okay, Drea, let's start from the beginning. Where are your parents?'

'Papa lives with me and Mother's in the cemetery.'

'When you say your mother's in the cemetery—'

'She lives there.'

'She lives there?'

'No, she isn't a sitting tenant, she's dead. Papa's usually at home watching porn, but he's got a new girlfriend now so maybe he's with her – with the girlfriend, not with Mother. Maybe they're both at home watching porn.'

'And your mother – how did she die?' He lowered his voice. I didn't lower mine in case he didn't hear me and then I'd have to repeat it. I would hate to have to repeat something I never talked about. But now it sounded like I was shouting to compensate.

'She killed herself.'

'How old were you?'

'Seven.'

'How old was she?'

'She was forty.'

'How old are you now, Drea?'

'I'm forty.'

'When are you forty-one?'

'Next week.'

'Have you ever thought about suicide?'

'Every day.'

'Is this of some concern to you?'

'I'm concerned I won't get a chance to do it, yes.'

'Have you ever attempted suicide?'

'Last week.'

'And what happened?'

'Worked like a charm.'

'Okay, Drea. So, I think there's quite a lot going on here. Is there anything going on in your life now that's causing you concern?'

'My ex-boyfriend is living in Normandy with a woman who is a lot better suited to him than I am but he can't pay my daughter's... his daughter's, my step-daughter's, school fees and Ava deserves to be at this school. She's bright, she's articulate, annoyingly moral and if I don't find £11,510 that will be the end of Ava's private school education.'

'You're anxious about finding this money?'

'Yes.'

'Have you tried to find this money from anywhere?'

'Yes. I robbed two of the mothers whose children have subsequently become Ava's best friends and are always in my house.'

'Robbed them?!'

'I bought a balaclava and a hunting knife for the first one and jumped her in the park taking her coat, bag and jewellery.'

'Why would you want her coat and her bag?'

'To sell.'

'To sell?' he queried.

'I got more than a grand on eBay.'

'More than a grand?' he exclaimed.

'Like you, I was unaware of the mark-up in the luxury-goods market.'

'On eBay?' he repeated.

'Yes. I'm not sure whether that part was completely thought through and, as it transpired, the next robbery was a little messier. I forgot my balaclava and my hunting knife so I had to push her into the boot of her car and then her dog bit me. Now there's a woman in need of therapy! She lied and told her friends and family I had killed her dog. The dog nearly fucking killed me. In fact, considering what a sociopath she is, she probably killed her own dog. I needed a tetanus shot! Anyway, I couldn't sell her shit because I thought it would arouse too much suspicion after the murder.'

'Murder?!'

'Yes. But I didn't do it. And therein lies the problem. You probably assumed that I killed Penelope because I robbed Henrietta and Regina. But I didn't. I have no idea who did. The police found out from her son Xavier that I'd said "Next time you go to bed, I hope you die in it, bitch," but I just said that because she passed a remark about my boyfriend leaving me and gave me no room to get out of my parking space, making me more nervous than I normally am on the school run because the roads just aren't wide enough to reverse park.'

'Okay. Well… this is certainly an inimitable state of affairs. Drea, now might be a good time to discuss confidentiality,' he said seriously.

'Now? You want to discuss that now?'

'I am obligated. If I think my client has killed another person or is planning to kill another person, to tell the police.'

'That's fine. I haven't and I'm not planning to, so if that's your line then you can stop worrying because no one's crossed it.'

'You mugged two women. I don't feel it's ethical for me to keep this information to myself.'

'Aha, but you said murder. That was the big one, so if it's not murder we're fine. We're okay. They haven't reported it to anyone, the robberies, nor are they going to, and I won't be doing it again because there is now a murderer on the loose. The fewer conversations I can have with Officer Frampton and DC Rodman, the better it is for my health – and that is really why I'm here, for my health. So it would be great if we could wrap up the moral and legal therapist dilemma debate and get back to my health.'

'Why would you possibly think that mugging these women was a good idea?' He'd stopped writing.

'It's not that I thought it would be a good idea, I just didn't have any other better ideas. These women have money. The worst thing that has happened to them this week is that they were forced to buy a brand new coat and bag from last season's Autumn collection. That is not a serious problem. I know it sounds like it is, but you need to relax. I understand your cut-off is murder, and it's a good one to have, but no one's been murdered. I mean someone has, but not by me, which is clearly the point. However, what is a serious problem is this business with Ava's school fees, and I hate to say it out loud, but I think it has got me really strung out.'

'Did you go to a private school, Drea?' He was younger than me. Not a lot, but enough to make his grilling me about my education feel like role-play.

'No.'

'So why is it so important for Ava to go to a private school?'

'Because Alex is gone and it's down to me.'

'I understand that, but why does that mean that Ava needs to go to private school? One which you clearly cannot afford?'

'I told you.'

'No you didn't.'

'Yes I did,' I insisted.

'Drea, lots of people would like to send their children to private school but can't because they don't have the money.

What they don't do is decide to mug people to find that money.'

'So I'm being penalised for my ingenuity?'

'Or if we take this back to the issue of your health, we could look at how you feel about boundaries?'

'Boundaries? You mean like where a sound wave encounters the end of one medium and another medium begins?' I mused.

'Umm. Yes, okay, let's try that. Newton's third law of motion, I believe. For every action there's an equal and opposite reaction.' He rapidly went up in my estimation. Check out the physics. 'Why do you think most people would choose to find the money another way?'

'Because they're scared of getting caught.' Obviously.

'So if we extend that rationale where the action is the mugging and the equal and opposite reactions are going to jail, why is the risk not enough for you to find your own boundaries?'

'Because she's my child.'

'So?'

'Because she deserves the best.'

'Because?'

'Because she has no one else?'

'And?'

'Because I can't kill myself now! Because that was my plan and it was a good one, but now it won't work because Ava will be all alone. I don't know how to do all this, it's just so hard and what about me? What about what I want, what I need? This is fucking bullshit! Are you gonna help me or what?!' I was shouting whilst the skin on his face finally relaxed into satisfaction. He'd started writing again. Seriously? I was paying for this shit?

'How are you feeling Drea?'

'Angry?'

'Why are you feeling angry?'

'Because I feel like you are missing the point here, as well as using my time to fixate on a tenuous, at best, issue of probity. If I had not demonstrated my desperate need to find the money by robbing those women, would we even be discussing the necessity of Ava going to private school?'

'What point am I missing?' he asked.

'That I'm having panic attacks without warning. That I'm here to give this therapy lark another go, despite your co-conspirator failing so abysmally, and that implying that I am morally bankrupt is… political.'

'Political?' He seemed genuinely taken aback.

'This is uncomfortable for you. Not for your profession. For you. You are uncomfortable in my company because I have behaved in ways that make you feel you need to judge me. Personally, I am irritated that you lack the finesse to conceal your motivations in a more sophisticated way instead of making your braying and baiting so obvious. However, it doesn't change the fact that you judge me and are pushing your feelings away, pushing away what you're scared you might like.'

Quiet. He put his pen down. We had a moment of self-reflection. I was thinking there was a possibility that maybe I wasn't completely angry and that I might also be a little sad. I was also thinking that he would call Dr Feelgood and agree with her that they had found a live one here. When he finally spoke, he took me by surprise.

'Would you like to go out with me?'

'Excuse me?'

'We've only had one session,' he continued. Was that therapy-speak for 'you've got nice eyes'?

'This one session caveat's pretty flexible,' I said.

'Would you?'

'Well… what about my panic attacks?'

'Let's discuss them over dinner.'

A Friend Indeed

'Chilean sea bass, sir?' The manager and the waiter were one and the same. His eyes were everywhere, hands gesturing to staff in the open kitchen as well as those working the floor of the restaurant.

'Thank you.'

'And your steak, Madam. Cooked rare.'

'Shouldn't I know your name?' I asked, touching the yellow gingham tablecloths.

'Giuseppe, Madam,' said the manager/waiter with a blank face that said that even if I had known his name, my food would not be delivered any faster.

'No, not yours,' I said. 'Yours,' staring at my dinner companion.

'Yes. Sorry. Michael. Flanders. Michael Flanders.' Giuseppe shrugged and left. Michael continued, 'Look, I know it's all been a little unorthodox,' he uttered nervously with a half-smile. He was an attractive guy. In the warmth of the restaurant, he'd taken off his tank top and his blue shirt reflected his eyes. Why was he single? Why was he a therapist? Did single people become therapists? Could I become a therapist? Did therapists become single? Maybe that was more likely.

'Why are we here?' I asked. I was wearing tracksuit bottoms and the hole in my trainer had opened up in the most defeatist way. Was my foot in danger of gangrene? Michael wouldn't know that. He was a mind doctor. I sighed. Why couldn't doctors just know everything?

'Could I get gangrene in my foot?' I asked.

'Sorry?'

'My foot is wet. It's been wet all day.'

'Isn't gangrene when there's a loss of blood to the limbs?' he smiled.

'Okay good.'

'You're probably more in danger of athlete's foot than gangrene.'

'I don't want either.'

'And you seem more concerned about gangrene than suicide.'

'That's a problem for you?'

'To have dinner.' he answered, cutting up his fish. The eyes in the fish's head stared at me knowingly. What did they know? How to get caught. Me and this fish had nothing in common.

'What?' I frowned. 'Your fish is staring at me,' I told him.

'Is it?' he asked, chuckling. 'You asked me before why we're here. To have dinner.' He looked up and saw me staring at the plate. 'Sorry,' he said, rotating the fish. 'I think he thinks you're pretty.'

'I want to talk about my panic attacks.'

'Okay,' he said slowly, looking around as though I'd chosen an unsuitable environment.

'Well, you're the one who wanted to have dinner,' I reminded him.

'Yes. Sorry. Go on.'

'I want them to stop.' The restaurant was busy. My steak was good. I was feeling… happy. The manager/waiter was at the next table now, asking a young couple if they'd like some wine. 'I'll have a whisky now,' I announced loudly, more to Giuseppe than to Michael.

'Fear. The root cause of all anxiety, but a slippery emotion to grasp because it hides,' Michael told me, chewing.

'Hides where?'

'Wherever it thinks we won't look. Behind anything that will lead us away from the true source of our fear.'

'So what I think I'm scared of, I'm not really scared of?'

'There'll be an element of truth to distract you so it's not entirely off base, but it won't be the real truth. Okay, for instance, let's say in chess – do you play?'

I nodded tentatively. Was this guy for real? Physics and now chess. If I was worth any money, I'd think this was a set-up. You know the guy who learns about a woman from a dossier then pretends to fall in love with her so he can steal her millions. We should be on a cruise ship. I should have millions.

'In chess, there's this great play called fianchetto.' Seriously? 'It's basically about getting the bishop to be more active so you move your knight pawns out and get the bishop on its long diagonal. It becomes a much more offensive piece, controlling the centre action from afar. That's what fear does. It controls the centre of your life from a safe and hidden distance. What are you scared of, Drea?'

'Is this a date?'

'Do you want it to be?' he asked, smiling.

'Answer the question.'

'Yes,' he said definitively, 'this is a date.'

'Why are you single?' I persisted.

'I work a lot and I suppose not everyone interests me.'

'So you're not a man whore?'

'No, I'm not a man whore.' He smiled a lot during dinner. He hadn't smiled at all during our session. Maybe it wasn't professional to smile. Obviously, it was far more professional to cut the session short and ask your client out. 'Why are you single?'

'I told you. My boyfriend left me. I'm recently out of a long-term relationship.'

'Which is causing you little, if any, emotional distress?'

'Correct.'

'Great,' he smiled.

'I'm not sure how functional I am in intimate relationships,' I admitted.

'I'm sure that's true, and it's probably what attracts me to you,' he said with the confidence of a man who had not yet explained his evening shenanigans to Dr Feelgood. 'What was your boyfriend like?'

'Fine. Nice. An English teacher. Into punctuation, but not very punctual. We were relaxed together. I guess too relaxed and you fall apart.'

'And Ava?'

'Wonderful. In spite of me.'

'Not because of you?'

I stiffened. 'This was a great idea. I was starving and that whisky hit the spot, but nothing else is going to happen here.'

'I see. I blew it with the compliment.'

I suddenly felt sad. 'I don't know. Maybe. Or maybe there was nothing to blow.' Giuseppe was heading in our direction in a flurry of napkins and hot plates.

'You've been very honest with me, I'd like to be honest with you now, if I may?' he said, edging closer. I moved in to meet him across my plate. 'I have... certain sexual preferences. I have a private room in my house, in the basement. It's sound proof.' He sat back.

'You're a musician?' I asked.

His face flashed with surprise and then horror as he realised I had no idea what he was talking about – until I suddenly did, and then my face looked as shocked and horrified as his.

'Oh!'

'Sorry. I thought that you might like… might be into… might… sorry,' he fumbled.

'No. Oh no. No, no, no – that's not me. Why would you? The balaclava? Anyway, no. The whole dominant submissive thing? No.'

'Is ok?' Giuseppe said over his back whilst en-route to another table.

'The bill please,' I said.

'I'll get it,' said Michael.

'I guess it's hard to be open about stuff like that?' I mopped some bread in olive oil. The thought of deviant sexual practices was making me hungry again.

'It's like any minority group that poses the threat of difference to others. You need to be secure in your environment before you can feel safe,' he said in a little voice.

The rain had stopped and I couldn't smell it anymore, but the wind still howled a lonely tune, searching desperately through the trees for something lost. The storm had lulled but was not finished. Michael walked me to my car, piles of leaves forming quick circles at the kerbside and then dispersing as though they had never known each other at all.

'I misjudged the situation. I feel stupid.' he said, hands in his pockets.

'I must give off that vibe.' My hair blew right into my face and he pushed it to the side. I might have flinched.

'Chemistry isn't an easy thing to figure out,' he said.

'Good thing you're into physics then.' I tried to keep it light but the wind was against me. Nothing light about this gale.

'Why does it feel futile to suggest we be friends?' he asked.

'I don't really do friends. It's nothing personal.'

'At least let me give you some numbers of other therapists. I owe you that.' He got his wallet out and started rifling through business cards.

'At the very least,' pleaded Michael, his face falling, for the panic attacks. You should speak to someone.' Tried that, twice. If I believed in signs, I'd have to try another way. Feelgood said they'd keep coming until they had no reason to exist. The only way out, the only way to stop the panic attacks, was to find the money. But how to find £11,510?

It fluttered down from the heavens. A sheet of paper, torn at the edges, heralded and abused by the wind. The poster bounced about on the bonnet of the car, uncertain if it should stay. Penelope's crumpled face staring at us – still wearing the pearls – and under her chin, the only words relevant to me, 'REWARD – £15,000.'

'What a beatific picture,' said Michael. 'That's a lot of money.'

'That's a fucking sign,' I said.

When I arrived back at home, the lights were blazing from every room like a lighthouse staring out across a dark sea. Furthermore, there were three ships parked outside that I'd never seen before. My house was my sanctuary. The unfamiliar had me decidedly wary.

The street was quiet, but the night air bristled with feverish secrets. People told stories behind closed doors. Stories to each other about why they were late home from work. How the bus was stuck in traffic and the train was delayed. About the seminar they had to attend suddenly, forcing them to lay their head on a different pillow. Stories to the children about which religion was the safest and the most true. About monogamy and the death of spontaneity, and about love and its malignant nemesis – duty. And in the safety of these warm yellow windows, they lived as normal a life as they could pretend to. The door opened before I could get my key out.

'Where have you been?' she howled.

'Ann?'

'You should have been here.' Reluctantly she turned to allow me to enter my own home. Mixed messages. She wore a loose camel roll neck and relaxed jersey trousers, but there was nothing weekend about Ann. Ann was a Monday morning for whom Tuesday never came.

'Is Catherine here, again? Have you come to collect her?' I asked, only slightly more interested in the answer to my second question and equally troubled by the fact I had to ask either.

'Yes she is, but that is very much beside the point.' I'll be the judge of that Little Miss Muffet. She craned her neck toward my ear and her breath was tinged with just the slightest trace of bad egg. 'The police are here.'

The police? Well, wasn't that just fucking great? The police were in my house. Ann Donnington was in my house. Ann had let me in to my house to see the police. If the world turned upside down right now, this scenario would probably stay exactly the same, that's how fucked up it was.

'Did you say anything about the robberies,' I whispered.

'No. But I feel ever so torn,' she answered with the angst of a woman who had been tasked with nothing more demanding than keeping her trap shut.

'Well it wasn't you who was torn, was it,' I whispered quickly back. 'It was me...' her eyes widened. 'My blouse torn,' I went on, 'my coat and bag torn from my shoulders, my rings torn from my fingers—'

'That's exactly what happened to Regina and Henny,' she said, astounded by the symmetry.

'Well there you go, Ann. We are the ones who were robbed, the lives of our children threatened, not yours. So zip it, okay? Not a word.' Her face slunk back into resigned agreement.

'Ladies.' Officer Frampton greeted us with the smile of a wide-mouthed frog.

'Officer.'

'Drea. We tried calling.' I'm sure you did. Lift your hand to your ear and dial your palm did you? She looked no less intimidating standing in my hallway than she had in the portacabin hours earlier. It was as though it was only seconds ago that I had seen Officer Frampton in the portacabin, and to see her again in my house was most disorientating. Like living the nightmare over again but worse because I already had the awareness of how fucking scary it was the first time.

'We've had a development in the case,' she said.

'Great.' This was great. Break the case, wrap this shit up and get the fuck out of Gatlin.

'We needed to talk to Ava.' Whoa there Tonto. Rewind.

'Ava?'

'Yes.' Ann gave me a reproachful flash of the eyes as if to say that if had I been home like I was supposed to be they wouldn't have spoken to Ava and would have decided to interview the cat instead. If we'd had a cat.

'I'll go and check on the girls,' said Ann, almost bowing out of the corridor.

'Why don't we go in here?' suggested Frampton, ushering everyone into the living room, closing the door on Ann. 'Come and sit down, Drea.' The presence of the law in one's own house was like a rank smell.

Looking at it through the eyes of strangers, our living room had the sense of being lived in – and was that pride I felt? Ava sat on the sofa looking as though she'd pissed her pants. Officer Frampton offered me the chair by the piano. Thanks. Rodman leaned up against the window behind Ava, ready to pounce, growling at me with his razor eyes and I felt myself tremble.

'One of the mothers has reported a mugging. It's a serious incident. Her dog was murdered.'

'Murdered,' I repeated.

'Yes. As I said, it's a serious incident.'

'How did you know... did she know the dog had been murdered?'

'How did she know? She saw the whole thing. Poor woman. Did it right in front of her. Gutted the animal.'

'That's... shocking,' I said. In shock.

'It is. We could be looking at a possible escalation. The same person who robbed this woman and gutted her dog having then murdered Penelope Coultard.'

'Surely not!' I said with over-elevated levels of disbelief and disregard for the trajectory of the criminal investigation.

'Yes.'

'Seems a stretch to go from robbery to murder? I'm sorry, I just can't believe what's happening in our town.'

'The robber wore gloves but we found a hair. It came up as Ava's.'

'What do you mean, it came up as Ava's?' As far as I knew, the state-controlled world we were heading towards did not yet have everyone's DNA on file, so how anything other than a repeat prescription for an inhaler she had used sporadically between the ages of four and five could have 'come up as Ava's' I was at a loss to understand.

'Ava was stopped a few months ago with marijuana on her person,' answered Frampton, gravely.

'Oh really?' This was news to me. Maybe that was the cardinal rule of being a teenager: don't ask, no fun in that, just steal. After all, it was more than likely she'd got it from my jewellery box and knew she didn't need to sneak around with it. If she'd asked, I would have given it to her and, if she'd told me she wanted to smoke, I would have smoked with her. But now, in front of officers of the law, I would have to be suitably appalled.

'I think there must be some mistake. I don't think that's something Ava would do.'

'I'm really sorry, Mum. I stole some from—' was she really planning to take us both down?

'Where you stole it from is irrelevant, Ava,' I interjected quickly, 'as that person should never have had it in the first place. Marijuana is illegal, punishable by law, and what I want to know is, why did you do such terrible thing?'

'Some girls at school wanted to try it. Dad knew.'

'Your father knew and didn't tell me?' I paced with mock outrage. 'Well, that's Alex all over isn't it? We'll just add it to all the other things he didn't tell me about before he ran off with that harlot,' I turned to Frampton, 'peer pressure at this age is staggering.' Rodman had his gaze firmly fixed on me and it was unsettling. I concentrated on Frampton.

'Well I think that's probably something best left explored after we've gone. Ava was let off with a caution,' said Frampton in a calming tone, trying to appease me. 'What we'd like to know, Ava, is how your hair found its way into Henrietta's Crosly-Burke's car?'

Fuck. I wore Ava's pink gloves. Oh God.

'I don't know,' Ava stammered, suitably traumatised. I could see her wondering how she might escalate from a caution on weed to a murder charge. This was the problem with DNA. Completely unreliable.

'She was with me.' The door burst open and even Rodman jumped when Tabatha walked in. I despised group events. People aren't themselves. It is impossible, as you have to dilute part of yourself to accommodate the others whilst, ironically, the pressure continues for you to try and remain yourself. A paradox of the worst kind. But Tabatha wasn't deterred by the complexities of group dynamics as tonight she was planning on perjuring herself instead of being herself.

'Tabatha?' said Officer Frampton with her eyebrow arched.

'We sat in my mum's car that night and had a cigarette.'

'What music did you listen to?' shot Rodman from the back of the room.

'Bach,' Tabatha replied instantly. Ha.

'Bach? You didn't mention that when we interviewed you, Tabatha.' said Frampton.

'You didn't ask.' Check. Your move.

'Ava, is this true?'

Please lie darling. For once in your honest, sainted fucking life, please lie.

'I love Bach.'

'Alright. Well uh, glad we cleared that up. Thank you guys. That's it, you can get on with your evening.' Ava jumped off the sofa, her head down when she passed me, and she and Tabatha ran upstairs.

'Teenagers,' mused Frampton, 'troublesome times. Well, I think we're done here for now. Thank you, Drea, we'll show ourselves out.' She smiled as Rodman heaved his unconvinced body off the windowsill and followed her, not moving his eyes away from me for a second. The front door banged shut.

I sat down at the piano and played some Bach for the first time in a long while. I didn't turn around but I knew he hadn't gone. Outside in the dark night, Rodman was watching.

Uninvited

'Wine?' asked Ann. 'Who was playing the piano?'

'I don't drink wine,' I reminded her. The kitchen was a mess. It was a small area and felt squalid very quickly if not regularly cleaned and tidied. Dried remnants of their contents sat clinging to used crockery. The bowls seemed larger than I remembered them to be and the plates looked like serving plates rather than side plates. Nothing looked right next to Ann.

'No, do you have any wine for me?' she snapped. I started aligning the cereal boxes so that they were flush with each other, no jagged edges and all facing the same way.

There had been some red on the counter from the other night but it was gone now. Maybe Papa and his lady friend had drunk it. I dreaded to think what they had done with the empty bottle. I pointed to the cupboard next to her but she already had her hand on the handle. Was Ann beginning to know where to find things in my kitchen? If so this was the beginning of the end.

'Glasses?' she barked. 'So what did they say?' She seemed very het up for a woman whose daughter had not been interviewed by the police and was also not a suspect. I turned a wine glass around in my hand and Ann grabbed it from my fingers.

'They know about Henrietta. About what happened to her,' I said.

'How?' she asked in astonishment. 'I didn't say anything,' she insisted, urgently filling her glass.

'She did.'

'Who?'

'Henrietta.'

'Why?'

'Good question,' I said.

'I always thought she should tell the police,' nodded Ann.

'What you think is irrelevant,' I reminded her.

'I wonder why she changed her mind.'

'Well that still leaves me and Regina who have not changed our minds, so there's no need for you to change your mind and say anything. Anything at all. Understand? The less people go about changing their minds, the better,' I said, pouring a large whisky. I started looking for the weed and then realised I had company. Bad company to boot. I lit a cigarette instead.

'I wish you wouldn't do that,' she said waving her arms around in the air as if she were burning alive. 'It's so bad for you.'

'Feels pretty good, thanks.'

'And what about Catherine?'

'You should take her home; it might collect in her lungs.' I blamed Ava for Catherine being here but Ann was definitely uninvited.

'Why did they want to talk to Ava?' she asked, perplexed.

'They're eliminating suspects. Tabatha and Ava had spent time in Henrietta's car.'

'It's amazing how they know that. How did they know that?'

'I don't know, Ann. I'm not a policeman, woman, officer... whatever. They just know.'

'Do you not find it peculiar how the girls are spending all this time together suddenly. Tabatha and Ava together – I mean, it's not right of course, but they did used to make fun of her.'

Yes, it was all very bizarre. And why would Tabatha lie to the police? Unless it were true – it could be true. But Ava didn't respond as if it was, plus Tabatha had used Bach. That was a clever move on Tabatha's part. But what was in it for Tabatha? Lying to the police. She must realise how serious that was, unless that was the point. I froze. She was stocking up. That was the second thing she had on me now. She was keeping my confidence by not telling Ava about my overdose and now this. She wanted something, but the question was what?

'Ava is bound to get bored of them soon. Yes, it is peculiar that she hasn't already, but when she does everything will return to normal,' I said.

'Do you think so?' asked Ann in a quieter voice.

'I fucking hope so.'

'I think in some ways maybe I don't.' Was she still talking about Ava and the girls? It was the fluctuation that alerted me – the surge from uptight Ann to wistful Ann. She seemed almost vulnerable. Now I wondered if it wasn't her who had finished that other bottle before I arrived.

'Don't what?'

'It sounds awful and I miss her terribly, I do. But Penny's murder – not specifically her murder, but her death – it's made me feel... alive. It's crazy isn't it?'

'No.'

'You don't think so?'

'Death is the closest thing to life,' I mused.

'I think we fell into this trap, you know, with the kids and work and Oswald and I, well, we... it changes doesn't it. Marriage. You think it's going to bring you closer, but it feels like, since the kids, we're just so far apart.' I wondered if she knew that she was talking to me. She was looking at me but I couldn't be sure.

'He stopped seeing me, and then I stopped seeing me, and now this whole thing happened with Penny, and I'm wondering who I am. I don't know anymore. I got lost.'

'Maybe we should cancel the bake sale,' I said. It seemed the kindest way to help her. If the poor woman didn't know who she was, she certainly wasn't going to find out at the bake sale.

'The bake sale!' This brought her back. She looked at me and she might not have known who she was, but she certainly remembered who I was. 'Oh my God. I've had too much to drink and don't know what I'm saying,' she laughed nervously. 'There's so much smoke in this room, I can barely breathe.' If only.

'The bake sale is this Saturday and there's so much to do,' she waffled.

Jesus! The fucking bake sale.

'Ava!' Usually, I had to call twice and then demand that whoever was not my daughter leave the house. The girls bowled down the stairs, sounding like charging elephants. Ann hurried out of the kitchen and I followed.

'Mum, Ann, you've got to see this!' Ava's cheeks were flushed and all three of them were out of breath. Catherine appeared, looking solemn, the face and body of a pall bearer. They headed straight past us and into the living room.

'Sit down,' Ava said, giggling. Ann and I followed them. 'Mum! Sit!' Ann and I sat down in reluctant continuance of our evening together. Catherine stood on the side with fiery eyes, whilst the three girls waited in a line at the front of the room.

Silence. Then Tabatha and Amelia started to clap a beat with Ava in the middle. Tabatha did a star jump – her legs practically horizontal – followed by a high front leg kick, whilst Amelia clapped. Then Amelia did a star jump as Tabatha clapped.

A-V-A! A-V-A!
IF YOU WANT CHANGE
THAT'S WHAT YOU SAY!
A-V-A!!'

Hi! My name is Ava and I'm the one to save ya
Let Ava get you in the mood
Want better canteen food?
Want a better library?
Just stand up and vote for me
Vote for Ava, vote for sport
Help save our badminton court
Vote for Ava one last chance
Want a kickin' school dance!

Ava and the girls ended with a side shoulder shimmy.

'And we'll also have pom-poms and be in little skirts,' said Tabatha, excited.

'And crop tops, obviously,' said Amelia.

'And music,' piped up Tabatha.

'So what do you think?' asked Ava.

'Some of the lines don't scan very well,' said Catherine. I didn't agree publicly, but she had a point.

'So you're running?' I said.

'Yes, I think so,' answered Ava smiling.

'Apparently,' stated Catherine, doing nothing that resembled smiling.

'You'll be a fucking brilliant president,' I said.

'Drea! Language,' said Ann.

'She will.'

'She needs to be elected first,' said Catherine. 'I am still the class president, despite Tabatha and Amelia having organised this bizarre social experiment.' The joy ran off Ava's face and Tabatha and Amelia crumpled from the spine, physically intimidated. 'Plus the badminton court is a matter for Gatlin council not the class president, or I'd be looking into it already,' she continued.

'Well, it's very late. Come on girls, I'll take you all home,' Ann huffed, angrily.

'I'll just get our stuff,' said Amelia.

'We'll be waiting in the car,' announced Ann, dragging Catherine. Ava ran upstairs and Tabatha was just about to follow when I pulled her back into the living room and closed the door.

'What do you think you're doing?' I demanded.

'What do you mean?' she asked, with bewildered eyes.

'Don't play innocent with me, you conniving little bitch. Why are you encouraging Ava to run for president and why did you lie to the police?'

'Catherine doesn't want Ava to run, but me and Meels do. And I wasn't lying,' she said. She was up against the wall and I only had a few inches with which to tower over her.

'So if I ask Ava right now if she was with you, she'll say yes?'

'No.'

'No, she won't say yes?'

'Yes.'

'Let's try this again. What's your fucking game?'

'I don't have a game.'

'Then tell me why you lied to the police.' I put my hand around her throat and tightened my fingers. 'Why did you say Ava was in the car with you?'

'Because she could have been,' she spluttered in an answer, which absurdly seemed to veer closer to the truth than her earlier lie. Ann tooted her horn from the street.

'What does that mean, "because she could have been"?'

'It means she could have been.'

'So she wasn't but you said she was?'

'Yes.'

'And you said she was because she could have been.'

'Yes.'

'But she wasn't?'

'No.'

The girl was as deranged as her fucking mother. These people made me look honest. I had no issue with lying. Lying was necessary, occasionally fun, but there was always a reason. Lying for the sake of lying?

'She seemed in trouble. I wanted to help'

Ann had started a continual pressing on the horn. The neighbours would be livid.

'You can go,' I said, pushing her out of the living room. She opened the door to leave but I slammed it shut.

'One more thing,' I said, 'stop taking those pills.' Tabatha looked scared. 'The happy pills. If you're taking them because you think you might top yourself, then either just top yourself or stop. If you're taking them because you think people don't know how great you are, fuck 'em. You don't need them to know. You know. Don't wait for people to educate themselves. People are stupid and will regularly let you down, understand?'

'Yes.'

'Now get out.' She ran out and I heard the door bang. People kept leaving the house yet I felt no more at peace. Ava emerged at the top of the stairs looking guilty.

'I'm so sorry I didn't tell you about the weed,' she said.

'Ava, I smoke weed. I'm not bothered about the weed.'

'And I'm sorry I lied about being with Tabatha in the car. I don't even know why I did that. She said that I was with her and it felt like she wanted me to agree and the police were acting all weird about finding my hair at the scene and I just thought—'

'Ava, it's fine, don't worry about it. It was the right thing to do. It was good you lied. We need to stop the police sniffing in the wrong direction. That's what they do, they just sniff everywhere for shit and when they can't find the right shit they go back to the last shit they smelled. But now Tabatha has done you a favour and we need to watch our backs.'

'Oh Mum. I suppose it does look weird that we're all friends considering I've wanted to be their friend for so long. Maybe they think it's weird – they probably think I'm weird.'

'I wonder what she wants.'

'I don't think she wants anything, Mum.'

'Sure. Ok. Watch yourself anyway. And if the police want to talk to you again, say nothing until I get there.'

'Ok Mum. I'm going to bed. Goodnight.' I watched her walk up the stairs, graceful, troubled, unsure, so sure.

'Mum,' she said, turning around half way up.

'Yup.'

'Do you think people will vote for me?'

'They should, but the world is full of idiots.' I was about to follow her up when I decided to put the chain on and double lock the door. Why did I do that? Maybe because the police had just been in my house. Maybe because there was a murderer on the loose in Gatlin – it dawned on me how easily people can feel unsafe. Maybe because my mind and my life were hurtling towards me like an out-of-control rollercoaster at a condemned carnival – every seat packed with loud, unbearable ghosts – and in locking the door I tried to lock them all out.

The stairs creaked underneath my feet. Houses held all our secrets. Every new day, new feelings, new lies, new secrets, same house. And when people got inside who were meant to stay outside, the house kept that quiet too. But it knew. It knew when something dark and unfamiliar had found its way in.

A joint balanced on the edge of the ashtray. I lit it up and sank back onto the bed blowing out rings of smoke, which suspended effortlessly in the air above me. I spread out my legs and my one free arm like a blow angel. What was the point of a double bed if someone else wasn't in it? It just became a large single bed. I was tired. I felt the mattress hold me. It reminded me of the way Officer Frampton had held me during the panic attack. That moment of such intense desperation where it's possible to let anyone in, even the police. As it happened, the truth provided an alibi I did not expect to need so urgently, but I did need to quickly become more organised. Despite its near-universally good reputation, the truth was usually complicated. Not everyone could handle it and there were plenty of 'truths' I'd rather didn't get out. Many said they wanted the truth but once in possession of it, it became a different story. These idiots who went about touting such idioms as 'the truth shall set you free,' were, like most people who claimed to have superior knowledge, ignorant. Freedom was in the mind – one's own mind. Owning your truth was better than sharing it.

I went to the window to draw the curtains. Time for bed. The street was already asleep. No lights shone from the houses and the engines in the cars were cold. I drew one across and was half way to drawing the other when something made me stop. One of the three cars that I'd seen on my way into the house but hadn't recognised was still parked in the same spot underneath the oak tree across the street. I peered so close to the window that my head hit the glass. It was hard to tell what was the dark and what was anything else until he moved his head and stared back at me. I saw for the first time that his eyes did open, intense and fixated. He wanted me to know he was watching me. He wanted me to know he'd been inside my house and now he could watch me anytime. And it was only after I'd pulled away from the window that I heard Rodman start up the car and drive away ever so slowly.

The day had brought a couple of strange comforts, a few unexpected dangers and one sign. A piece of paper floated through my mind. It floated past my mother's cemetery, past my old school, and through the deserted plains of adulthood where it was too arid for anything to grow for long. The reward poster finally came to rest right in front of my face. Penelope's face staring right back at mine. I knew then that I would need to solve this murder myself.

Wattalapan

I looked at my investigation notes.

Murderer - ?
Victim - Penelope Coultard
Suspects - Everyone
Motive - Bitch

Maybe they needed filling out. Not the murderer part, because that information was unknown; not the victim part, because the morgue would testify to who the dead body was; not the suspect part, because apart from me it really could have been anyone; and not the motive part as I had first-hand experience that the deceased was a bitch. So actually these were pretty good investigation notes, no filling out needed. But solving a murder was not as easy as it looked. Now that I had planted myself in the investigation, I could see that there were problems on the ground. Once you were personally involved in a case, it muddied the waters substantially.

Had I not had my friendly encounter over our different parking styles with Penelope days before she died, I might be able to now look at the photos of her on the front pages of all the papers and believe the pearly smiles. I might even agree with the media on the tragedy of such an accomplished life wasted. Penelope had annihilated key players in the limbic system of my brain that were responsible for unbiased reason and empathy that I was certain that eventually someone would have murdered Penelope simply for being her. Fait accompli, as Alex and Poppy – my new French friends – might say. If I were going to solve this case, I would have to wipe that morning from my mind. Erase it completely like it had never happened. I didn't know her. I had no opinions and no preconceived judgements. She was a mother with a child at my daughter's school. We would start there.

I looked at the time. The red numbers glared 4:54 in gaudy neon. I'd hardly slept – Rodman had seen to that. What was his deal? What did he see when he looked at me? Why couldn't I get his face out of my head? He was the first man to have come into the house since Alex had left. And what very different men they were.

Papers covered the bed with scrawled case histories of serial killers I'd seen in true crime documentaries. I imagined I could be like those people who saw patterns amongst seemingly random information, but no amount of reshuffling brought forth anything of relevance. I'd drifted in and out of less than satisfying states of REM. My pen had leaked onto the duvet. Shit. At least I was doing something constructive with all these thoughts in my head. The fuckers competed for air-time, constantly crashing around in my skull like a fast and frightening ice-hockey match and finally, they were being heard. In fact, I needed them. These fucking thoughts in my mind driving me mad had become my friends. We all needed to work together to solve the case. Before the police found out it was me and not Ava in Henrietta's car. Before the police found out that I had robbed Regina too. Before the police decided two robberies doth a murderer make.

The question was: why would anyone want to kill Penelope? The easiest answer – money. It was the big one. People had been killing people over money for centuries, since the dawn of time. It was in our blood. Money equalled power and man's desperate need for power constantly fought a bloody battle against man's spiritual consciousness.

So, as Penelope had money, the next logical question was: who stood to gain? The husband. Again, simple. It's always the people we know and trust the most. He probably gets all the money left to him in her will. The will she didn't think she'd ever need. A document that must have seemed so irrelevant when they first got married and intended on spending the rest of their lives together, their love making them immortal. An irrelevant document until the day came where he realised the sound of her voice was like nails on a chalkboard and making love to her was like fucking a corpse, and the sooner she was dead the better so he could marry someone else and start again.

Or was it the son? Xavier was a piece of work. A spoiled, entitled, Armani-clad bag of testosterone who thought that people who cleaned toilets couldn't spell toilet and that because they cleaned shit they should be treated as such. A son killing his parents for money was again not beyond the realms of imagination. Children had been taking out their parents for mercenary motives since before Cronos.

I had an in. Not one I wanted, but an in nevertheless. There was no way of finding out about the relationship between Penelope and her husband and son without Ann. Ugh. Why was good police work so damn difficult? Again my personal relationships were proving problematic. If I didn't detest Ann Donnington and her friends – the mere thought of spending time with these people made me heave – this would all be so much easier. And then there was the minor issue of having robbed two out of the three of them. There was no choice: I had to bake.

It seemed extreme, being forced to bake against my will, but I was convinced the bake sale would get me closer to the identity of the murderer. Baking had previously been a shackle of domestic life, an ode to suburban drudgery and a yellow food-colouring bricked road to hell. I saw it differently now. Through the power of self-raising flour, I would bake for my freedom, and Ava and I would emerge from the oven different people. Fuck. I'd never baked a cake before. I was out of my depth. Wattalapan. Yes, that was the answer. Wattalapan.

It had been a remarkably long time since I had set foot in a supermarket. This may have seemed odd but I tended to buy things we needed from our local corner shop from one day to the next. It was less overwhelming, took far less time and there was no chance of bumping into mothers from the school filling up extra-large shopping trolleys as if Armageddon had been announced. Everywhere I turned there were mothers and children. These women hurled in multi-packs of everything: cereal, biscuits, washing powder, soap – how much soap could one family use? But they filled up their trolleys because who knew when they'd ever get out of their bunker? Buy more multi-pack biscuits: the end of the world is nigh.

Where to park? The convenience of parking belied a definite positive prejudice towards cripples and parents with kids. If you were a parent with a disabled kid, you probably got to park inside the supermarket next to the cashier. When Papa had first come to live with us after his heart attack, the hospital had given him a disabled badge. He didn't have a car but I told him to ask for one anyway so I could use it, which I did frequently. This positive discrimination in favour of disabled people was a growing trend I'd noticed, and was not reserved for supermarkets alone. Today I found a nice place close to the doors, took the wheelie chair badge out of my handbag and threw it on the dashboard.

Trolley or basket? Neither. It was too much commitment. As soon as you chose one, they forced you onto certain tills. Started to own you, tell you what to do, where to go, who to be.

'Good morning Madam, can I interest you in a—'

'No.'

She looked crushed. I'd taken a calculated risk that she wasn't going to tempt me with £11,510 in unmarked bills and that her plastic-pot, thimble-sized samples of mulled wine flavoured tea would be of no interest.

I needed coconut milk. Where could I find coconut milk? Would it be in milk? Too easy. The supermarket had been designed to trip you up at every turn, convincing you to buy things you didn't need but now really wanted. A lanky, acne-ridden, shelf-stacker caught my eye.

'Excuse me, do you know where I can find coconut milk?' I asked.

'Umm… no. I dunno… it's not my department.'

'Someone gave you your own department?' I asked, bewildered.

'I been stacking these shelves and I know it ain't here,' said the boy, soon to grow into a man and astound the world with his powers of deduction.

'Well can you find someone who does know?'

'I don't know who would know cos I don't know what department it is. What is it again, cocoa milk? Maybe it's with the cocoa?'

I left. There was nothing more to say. It was a shame as I knew Dick sold a wonderful acne cream in the apothecary, which really hit the spot, but would this boy be any more useful with clearer skin? I didn't think so. He deserved a good beating for his incompetence but that was not my job. Somewhere, someone would see to it.

It was freezing in the milk, cream and cheese aisle and I shivered under my coat. Did it really need to be this cold? Wasn't this shit pasteurised? There was milk as far as the eye could see: full-fat cow's milk, semi-skimmed cow's milk, skimmed cow's milk, full-fat goat's milk, semi-skimmed goat's milk, soya milk, rice milk, oat milk, almond milk and butter-milk. But in a shocking twist, coconut milk was not with the other milks. Spying shiitake mushrooms I decided to move on to warmer pastures in the exotic foods section.

'I tried to tell you I was a fun guy but you didn't believe me,' said a familiar voice from behind. I turned around to see Michael. He was clearly better at commitment than me as he was carrying a basket – although, as a therapist, I would have expected a trolley. Maybe he was in a hurry.

'Fun-gi,' he said meekly, pointing to the mushrooms. I was expressionless. 'You know how to put a fun-gi down,' he continued, smiling.

'What are you doing here?' I asked.

'Like you, I enjoy the experience of seeing the products and touching the food before I buy. Online feels so clinical.'

'I don't enjoy any of this,' I corrected.

'So why are you here? He wasn't unattractive. The opposite in fact.

'I was hoping to see you.' I said, looking him straight in the eyes. Was it time for me to take a lover? Why was I even thinking such absurd thoughts?

'Really?' His eyebrows jumped up.

'No.' I wasn't progressive enough. He just didn't do it for me.

'You're teasing me?' He asked, sad.

'Yes.'

'So what are you here for, if not to shop?' he probed, disappointed. He wore a woollen waistcoat under his jacket. Men who were comfortable enough to pull off a woollen waistcoat like that had probably spent time developing their feminine side. He seemed the type to understand a woman.

'I'm baking a cake.'

'Oh.' He seemed dubious. Empathic as well as astute.

'It's for the school bake sale.'

'That's nice of you.'

'I don't give a shit about the school or their bake sale. I need to get close to the mothers to solve this murder.'

'Drea, are you sure this is wise?' He asked, full of concern that my recipe did not require.

'You're not my therapist anymore,' I reminded him.

'So what's the cake?'

'It's not really a cake, it's more of a pudding. It's called Wattalapan. It's Sri Lankan. My mother used to make…' I trailed off. I couldn't remember what I was going to say. I'd lost my train of thought because I saw… thought I saw, surely not, I was tired and my mind was playing tricks on me. No, I was right, Rodman! What was he doing here? In the supermarket. In the daytime – like an ordinary person. And he was carrying a basket! Someone who shopped for groceries, an image completely at odds with that of the giant evil troll who roared underneath the bridge and bit chunks out of women.

'That sounds interesting. I think I've heard of that before. Is it like a richer crème caramel?' asked Michael, his voice coming from somewhere in the fog that filled my mind. Why was Rodman here? This was weird. He must have been following me. First trying to intimidate me outside my house last night and now here, in the light of day, so casual, so normal. What did he think he would find? Catch me with large quantities of bleach toppling out of my arms to clean up the blood splatter from my latest victim? They'd try and pin anything on anyone. With my luck, it would turn out that Penelope had an allergy to coconut milk and then bam: Bob's your uncle. Five to ten in a women's only facility.

He was reading the back of packets. Why did he care about what his food consisted of? He was a beast ravaging on the flesh of women who found themselves in a bit of a bind. Oh my God, now he was stood next to a couple kissing at the organic juice stand. I'll show him. He thinks he can trap me. I'll show him I'm normal, just as normal as anybody else out there. Normal people kiss other normal people in supermarkets. I've seen it with my own eyes – and it'll attest to my normality, which goes to disprove homicide, your honour. Watch this. I moved into Michael to try and kiss him, but he didn't see me. As I lunged forward he sprung to the side, presumably to avoid the oncoming trolley being pushed at breakneck speed by the teenage boy. The trolley caught me at the edge of my waist and, as it knocked my feet, I tried to use it to steady myself, but it lifted me up and sent me flying into a display of coconut milk. The pyramid collapsed, sending tins everywhere and I landed at the feet of an old woman in a wheelchair.

'My dear, are you hurt?' she asked in a croaky, concerned voice. People were rushing towards me from all directions. The nearby fishmonger flapped a large salmon over his shoulder, peering to inspect any damage done to his counter. There was none, but my pride had shattered into a million tiny pieces and rolled all over the floor. Acne boy arrived with Michael.

'Did you just try and kiss me?' he gasped, out of breath, flushed and in a bit of a state, although it was me that had just gone a couple of rounds with a pyramid of tins.

'No,' I said. My ribs hurt.

'I think you did,' Michael said, more adamantly than before.

'No, I fell. Into a speeding trolley,' I said, shooting daggers at the teenage boy who was looking sheepishly at his trainers.

'It's very romantic,' croaked wheelie.

'It is not romantic because it is not what I did.' I could see Rodman watching us, me. There had been such a commotion it would have been impossible not to stare, but now that he was I couldn't bear the thought of him knowing I'd tried to kiss Michael. And failed.

'Why did you try to kiss me?' he continued.

'It's ever so romantic,' wheelie croaked again.

'I did not, so will you stop this,' I whispered sternly. Michael had bent down to help but I shook my arms out of his grasp like a sullen child and lifted myself off the floor without him.

'I don't understand,' he said, looking pathetically lost.

'People fall in supermarkets all the time Michael. And this supermarket especially is in danger of a lawsuit for an unsafe environment,' I said raising my voice. Wheelie was getting all misty-eyed from the notion that Michael and I were an affair to remember, or maybe it was her glaucoma.

'Oh, give 'im a chance, dearie,' she pleaded. I bet she was flexing those calcified calf muscles to see if she still needed a wheelchair or whether she could run to Michael herself.

'You're lying,' he said. I had one eye on Michael and one on Rodman. He was walking away from the juice stand towards us. 'You tried to deny there was anything between us and I let you, because I thought it was just me. But it can't be just me or you wouldn't have tried to kiss me,' said Michael earnestly, unbuttoning his woollen waistcoat to help make his point.

'Stop saying that!' I said, quietly screaming, my cheeks turning crimson.

'Drea, I know you think we won't work but there aren't that many reasons for kissing someone. In fact, I can only think of three. Either you want something – and, although I'm not putting it past you, I just don't think there's anything you want from me or you would have taken it already. Or you like me – and I think I can tell when a girl likes me.'

'What's the third?' I asked out of curiosity.

'What?'

'You said there were three reasons. You only gave two.'

'You're trying to make someone jealous, but number three doesn't apply in this case,' he said with a big confident smile.

And at that moment, Rodman walked past. If I had stretched out my hand, I could have touched him and, just at that moment, I found myself suck my tummy in. An involuntary physical movement birthing a terrifying realisation.

Bake Sale

'This isn't a cake,' said Henrietta, jaw long, physically repulsed as she looked inside the box at my neatly stacked plastic ramekins of Wattalapan. She quickly closed the cardboard flaps as if my puddings might crawl out and hurt someone. Henrietta looked at Regina, who looked to Ann for answers. I was in the playground, a sea of white canopy stalls. It was when I saw the bunting that I started to lose my sea legs, but I reminded myself that me and my Wattalapan were on a mission. This was covert ops, but instead of brandishing an AK 47, I had gone further, deeper, darker. I had baked.

Grabbing a stall away from the witches three, but not far enough that I couldn't hear their chanting, I pretended to look through my bag and be busy. I needed to gather intel and this was the place to do it. I hardly knew anyone, but with this many mothers in one place, the pheromones turned into truth serum after a couple of glasses of watered down Pimms, and the small talk became less banal. I just needed to deduce who was worth talking to and get myself next to the appropriate person. Everybody had placed their wares on the main table by the entrance to the playground for the PTA to divide the goods and price them.

'Who made this?' demanded Regina.

'Is there a name on the box?' Henrietta asked.

'If there was a name on the box, would I be asking who made them?' Regina seemed on edge.

'We don't have time to worry about it now,' said Ann, returning from one of the stalls where she had just arranged a sea of perfect-looking red velvet iced chocolate cupcakes on red plastic cake stands. I wondered how many parts of insects – legs, arms, heads – were in those cupcakes. People liked to think it was just certain chocolate, chocolate made in third world factories or perhaps more specifically, chocolate that they weren't eating. But all chocolate came from cocoa beans. Insect corpses in chocolate was not a secret, at least not one that anyone was trying to keep, but people saw what they wanted to see.

'Ooh, those ones look yummy,' said Ann, drooling a little. 'Just get them out, price them and put them on a table. Regina, you were meant to be here half an hour ago.' Ann had dressed up for the bake sale; her Longchamp bag was navy blue instead of black.

'I'm sorry Ann. Amelia was at the hairdresser and her lowlights ran over.' Regina's mouth downturned slightly at the corners in deference.

The playground was filling up with good samaritans; mothers who had nothing better to do than spend a day in Gatlin playground selling their baked goods. A Chinese mother trotted up to me. I wasn't sure if she bowed or dropped something.

''Allo,' she said brightly. 'Su Lee.' She stuck out her little hand to shake mine. She had jet black straight hair, making her look like a Lego doll. Her body looked prepubescent and, if it were not for her chubby, motherly cheeks, she might have been mistaken for a student.

'Drea,' I said.

'Velly nice to meet you Dray-ah,' she said. 'You have children here?'

No. I just want to spend my Saturdays at a fucking school bake sale so I can be near other people's children. 'Yes, I do.'

'You have boy or girl or both,' and she started giggling as if the thought of more than one was hilarious. Why was she laughing like that? How was that funny?

'One girl. You?'

'Four boys,' she said giggling. But this was not a funny situation. Four children. This woman must have gone mad but she was soldiering on, living through the madness, embracing it and holding madness by the balls – hence her participation in the bake sale.

'Are you alright?' I ask.

'I hungry,' she giggles. 'Maybe I no sell and eat all da cake.' She was in the eye of the storm. I could recognise a woman on the verge.

Excitable children in fancy-dress costumes were arriving with fathers in tow. A dark-haired man, in a tweed jacket and tailored trousers, walked into the playground with an identical twin holding each hand. Scanning the area, he headed over to a stall where Henrietta was bent underneath the table adjusting a gingham cloth. His voice must have surprised her as we heard her head make contact with the wood. When she crawled out, she was rubbing her scalp and her face wore a pained frown. Su Lee took out a flask and some tupperware boxes. 'I bring noodles and chicken with black bean. I no eat English food. It make me sick like dog.'

'I thought you eat dog.'

'No! No!' she giggled. 'Ah yes, Chinese eat dog but no me. I eat dog I am sick like dog. You know Enny?'

'No, I don't know her.' I was obviously staring, or Su Lee was more observant than she looked.

'Poor Enny somebody kill my dog.'

Oh for fuck's sake. 'Her dog. Somebody kill her dog. Maybe it was the Chinese,' I said.

'Ah for food! Ah yeah,' gasped Su Lee. I could see Henrietta talking to the twins, who were freaking me the fuck out. Ava hadn't mentioned Tabatha having freaky twin sisters. Tabatha herself hadn't mentioned she had freaky twin sisters, but then I suppose I wouldn't talk about them if they were my sisters. When one looked left, the other looked left. When one looked right, the other looked right. And God help anyone if they both looked at you at the same time. Henrietta didn't seem to acknowledge Henry. I could see him making attempts at conversation, but she carried on fussing over the twins – brushing their hair and adjusting their socks and skirts, as if any of that would make them look less like graveyard apparitions.

'Do you know her?'

'She velly nice lady,' said Su Lee, smiling and nodding at the same time.

'She doesn't look that nice,' I said.

'She big bitch,' said Su Lee, still smiling and nodding.

'What?' I must have misheard. She must have said she was a bit rich.

'I must careful. My mother clean for me.'

'For her. Your mother cleans for her. Really?' I felt my eyes spring open but my heart sank as Ann's bony body strode across the grounds.

'Drea,' Ann nodded to two cardboard boxes of cakes on the trestle table covered with a dainty flowered tablecloth. She always said my name as if I were the replacement act for a poorly attended show in which the main draw had cancelled.

'It's £4.50 a cake. These are bottles of isotonic water flavoured with matcha green tea – £10. And these are lemon cupcakes with vanilla frosting. This box is crème caramel.'

'£10 for water?' I asked, shocked at this abhorrent daylight robbery. It was much more refined to rob at dusk. I looked inside the box. 'It's Wattalapan,' I said.

'I don't know what will happen,' said Ann.

'I made it. It's not crème caramel, it's a Sri Lankan pudding called Wattalapan,' I explained. Ann's dead eyes were unimpressed, yet unsurprised.

'You made this?'

'Yes.'

'It's not a cake.'

'It's not a cake sale. It's a bake sale. I baked it.'

Ann tried not to breathe out too heavily, but her nostrils flared wide, despite her efforts.

'Collect all the money in this tin,' she said, bothered and itching to get away, which was fine by me. As soon as she left, I turned to Su Lee. We were meant to set up our table and arrange the cakes into neat displays like the others, but we were a dangerous combination. Su Lee gave a big yawn and started opening her tupperware and sprinkling different coloured foil sachets onto her miso soup. I needed to get back to the subject of how dirty 'Enny was.

'So your mum is Henrietta's cleaner?'

'Enny cleaner, ah yes,' she nodded determinedly.

'Maybe her husband is nicer than she is,' I said, trying some reverse psychology.

'Why you bullshit me?' said Su Lee, frowning.

'Sorry?'

'You no think he nice. Why you just say that?'

'I don't know why I said that. You're right, Su Lee, I don't think he looks very nice.'

'He o-k,' she said, elongating and deepening her voice. 'He touchy feely but all men touchy feely.'

'He's come on to you?' I couldn't see it myself. The businessman and the Lego girl. But there had been stranger partnerships.

'Not me,' she slurped.

'Your mum?' I said.

'No, my mum. She like the ladies. Her name Pusi Lee.'

'He's cheating on Henrietta?'

'Maybe. They no happy. Enny say he have affair but he say no. They fight all time and Tabatha, she cry. She cry on me. Here,' Su Lee pointed adamantly, drawing a circle on her shoulder with her finger. She was very specific about the area she was cried on.

'Ah, look so busy now.' Su Lee put her chopsticks into her handbag. I had been so engrossed in our conversation and she in her miso soup that we had missed what was happening in the playground. We had shut ourselves off from the outside world and as soon as we emerged from our little bubble, our eyes and ears thirstily soaked up the atmosphere. Children were running and playing everywhere, the lively notes of jazz reverberated from the speakers, and parents sipped alcohol from inconspicuous plastic cups whilst tapping their feet to the beat.

'Hey, that's my wand. Give it back,' said a beautiful caramel-coloured child who was dressed in a pink satin ball gown with a long muddy train.

'No,' said the older boy in blue lycra and a superman cape. Children were so much more attractive when parents sullied the gene pools and mixed things up a bit. In fact, being cursed with an unattractive mixed race child was like genetic gazzumping.

'I don't need my wand to put a spell on you,' she claimed.

'You don't know any spells,' the boy retorted.

'I hope you choke, I hope you cry, before you bleed then slowly die,' said the girl. At this, the boy's lips began to tremble before he burst into tears. I winked at the girl, who handed me a folded piece of paper.

'This is from the palace,' she said. 'They're looking for the evil queen. If you know where she is then you must go to the palace.'

'Yes, maybe a mass letter appeal will flush her out,' I said, 'somebody must know something.' I opened the letter. There was nothing on it. I liked this girl and she'd given me an idea.

'Oh sorry, you're not set up yet,' said the mother. Our cakes were still in boxes. I recognised her from the school magazine. Victoria Taylor-Singh, head of the school board. She didn't reek of the same eau de bitch perfume as Ann and co., but she played hardball just the same. She'd married one of the richest men in India. Devilishly handsome – rumour had it that he had brought over an ayah just to carry his golf clubs.

'No, no we have cake. Me stay there,' said Su Lee frantically lifting the cupcakes out of the box, dropping them onto the table and licking up the spilt icing with her finger.

'She means you stay there,' I said.

'They're meeting in the woods by the birch tree,' the girl said to me, pulling on my trousers.

'It's ok, thank you,' said Victoria as Su Lee hurriedly tried to stack the ramekins. One of them fell and the Wattalapan toppled out, brown congealed gloop when not formally contained. Victoria grabbed the Princess and Superman and headed towards any other stall.

'Su, I'm going to the toilet. I'll be back in a minute.' I wove my body left and right and in and out of the throngs of people, who failed to move an inch even when they saw you coming.

'Excuse me. Excuse me.' I put my head down when I saw the side profile of Ann chiding a table for not attaching their banner properly. Did we even have a banner? Mind you, if we did, it would be dripping in miso and lemon frosting by now. I headed into the school.

Inside the building the air was quiet, dormant. A distinct but barely audible hum from the buzz of academia. The books slept quietly, grateful for the time to rest their pages. The toilets were right by the entrance, but I slipped into one of the classrooms instead. I needed paper and a pen. The class was doing a project on religions of the world. Each poster took a major religion with photos of important buildings. On a table at the front was an assortment of holy books, and various religious artefacts had been taped to the wall. Rows of desks with empty chairs greeted me. It was odd without people. Eerie. As if the weekend was the time for all the dead children to come to class: no bodies, just souls. Those who had experienced an interrupted education from a life cut short. There was a pen lying on the table. I wrote:

Penelope Coultard found out about your affair and was going to tell your wife. Is that why you killed her?

I read it back to myself. It was good. Succinct. If the evil queen could be flushed out, why not a murderer? And we'd start with lifting the lid on Gatlin's noble-born. Get the dirt up in the air and flying, and once the shiny black cockroaches were running around, like eyeless beetles on Gatlin's nicely manicured lawns, it would be easier to see who was sniffing, who was cheating and who was killing. I folded the paper twice.

As I came out of the classroom, I heard a door bang. The twins. They were walking towards me, Lucifer's leprechauns, immersed in a private conversation without words that, I imagined, was typical of their everyday conversation. Was this serendipity or suicide? I had not been so proactive on the suicide front so I was betting on serendipity this time. Quickly I pushed open the door and ripped the Hindu devil mask off the wall. I leaped out and covered my face with it. The twins stopped, looked at each other once – all four eyes now fixed firmly on me. Utterly calm, they processed the scene with the visual mind of a crime investigation officer: a stranger wearing an even stranger mask in the school corridor. Nobody spoke. I gave the one on the right the letter.

'Give this to your father,' I said, using my 'mugging' voice. It wasn't as if they knew me at all, but they seemed scary beyond their years so I didn't want to take a chance. They were unresponsive. Not thrown in the slightest.

'Now,' I growled. Accepting the letter, they turned on the same foot towards the playground. I took the mask off and was about to toss it back into the classroom when the toilet door opened.

'Hi Drea,' said Maude.

Fuck. Had she heard? What had she heard? She was shaking droplets of water onto the floor.

'Dryer's broken.' She shook her hands and, as she spoke, the water droplets seemed to fall in slow motion. I was getting hot. I was starting to recognise the symptoms. This was the beginning. I watched the drops almost hang in the air, teasing me, knowing how much I needed them, baiting me to reach out and grab them.

'Drea, are you okay?' Maude tilted her head, concerned furrows collecting like stalactites around her eyebrows.

'Fine. Totally fine, just tired you know. I'm actually really tired and didn't sleep very well last night.' I needed to get back out there. I'd given the pyscho sisters the letter and now I wanted to watch Henry and follow him. My plan was to get in the car and follow him everywhere all day and hope I'd be there if he met up with his mystery lady. But I couldn't risk having a panic attack in front of the entire school. I felt a pain in my chest. I didn't know if this was the part of the attack or merely the weight of my disappointment at being stuck in here with Maude.

'I'm just a little overwhelmed right now Maude, to tell you the truth. Would you mind if I just sat down for a bit?'

'Course not, love. You look like you need to. Why don't you sit inside that classroom and I'll bring you some water?' Something about her unexpected kindness in my unplanned moment of panic made me want to cry. Life was so much simpler and richer without expectations. What had unstitched my emotions? I felt my good work about to be undone by my own anxiety. It was as if I had betrayed myself, a betrayal that could lead to no satisfying revenge. Maude smiled and walked towards the water fountain in her office. She hadn't even noticed I was holding a devil mask.

I went back into the classroom and was about to sit down on a small chair – much too small for my bottom – when I heard the main doors open outside. Somebody else for the toilet, no doubt. A skittish figure hurried past the windows. I caught the blur at the edge of my eye. The toilets were the other way. I went out into the corridor, but they had turned the corner and disappeared. Back in the classroom, major religions of the world shouted their wares loudly. Hinduism – Buy one get guilt free! Judaism – Three guilt for two! Islam – Half price guilt! Catholicism – Free guilt! It made no sense for them to splinter off into warring factions. They should unite under a new name: Guiltism. I sat down when the main door opened again and the recognisable figure of Henry Crosly-Burke ran past the classroom window. The letter. I was right! He was cheating – and with someone at the school.

I jumped up, prying the miniature chair off my posterior, and opened the door. Henry was running as fast as the figure I'd seen run before him. As soon as he turned the corner, I quickened my pace, thankful to be in soft-soled trainers. When I got to the end of the corridor, the door leading to the basement was slowly batting open and closed from Henry's exit, calling me in. But I needed to be careful. I waited a few moments before entering. Henry's shoes echoed in the cold concrete space. A fluorescent light panel flickered uncertainly on the wall. It smelled of bleach. The utility room must be down these steps. I wasn't safe here. If I got caught, I couldn't claim to be lost and the chances of remaining unheard now became slimmer as the only two sounds were the slow drip of a tap and the sporadic contracting of metal. Not to mention that claustrophobic areas were not the best areas for avoiding panic attacks.

Whispers. They tried to hide themselves, but the walls offered no refuge – rebuffing the soft muffled words so they slipped to the floor. I followed them. The whispers wanted me to find them, even if the whisperers did not. Slowly I strained to hear, and then they stopped. Had they heard me? Should I leave? Should I run? Then I heard a door close. They must have gone into a room. I continued forward and turned a corner. A slim dirty glass panel in the door gave them up. The couple were in the corner of the boiler room. Henry was talking, angrily – no, panicked. He had his back to me so, for a moment, I couldn't see her. Then he turned to the side, putting his hand up against the wall and, as he did so, I saw through the old yellowy glass the duplicitous face of Regina Salter.

Hate

Regina Salter and Henry Crosly-Burke. Why was I shocked? Well, there was the obvious, they were both married to different people. It's not much of an affair unless those involved are copulating with people with whom they specifically did not take their wedding vows. But it was more than that. I had the impression that they had a bond, the way the three of them – Ann, Regina and Henrietta – cavorted. Probably Penelope too in the olden days, before she was too dead to cavort. In my head, I had turned this bond of elite society high flyers into something unbreakable, impenetrable. I suppose I had coloured in the rest of the picture myself – the way people tend to do – and assumed an unshakeable loyalty between them. Unless Henrietta and Regina's husband knew all about their liaison, in which case they weren't being disloyal at all. That was an entirely different kind of bond. But secret meetings in the damp school boiler room did not seem like the behaviour of people with open marriages.

I knew I wasn't going to hear any of their conversation without risking being seen so reluctantly I tiptoed backwards until I'd turned around the corner and then ran as quickly and as quietly as I could through the concrete labyrinth until I reached the steps leading up to my unexpected salvation. How the fuck had that happened? How had this hideous bake sale suddenly become a safe place to be? This was the real crazy in the world. Those tramps who lived in the road pushing trolleys, talking in tongues and stinking of arse with their whole life in plastic bags – that wasn't crazy.

As soon as I got out of the basement and into the light, it felt as if I was on dry land again. The din of the playground pushed its way into the school from the open windows, and the sound of children laughing felt strangely comforting. I was clearly in a bad way.

'Aaggh!' I screamed.

'Drea! What's the matter?' asked a startled Maude, carrying a plastic cup of water.

'Sorry Maude. Nothing is the matter. You scared me, that's all.' We were perilously close to the door from which Henry and Regina would be emerging from any moment now.

'Let's go,' I said taking a bemused Maude firmly by the arm and leading her towards the main entrance. Dare I say it, I was dying to get back to my stall and sell some cakes.

'Where did you go? Are you feeling better? Drea, why are we walking so quickly?' asked Maude, turning around to see if she could get a glimpse of the savage tiger that must have been lurking behind us.

'Maude, I need to get back. I have responsibilities involving lemon frosted cupcakes and Wattalapan.'

'Whatwillhappen?'

'I really couldn't tell you, Maude.'

'Oh. Well we better hurry then. I'm glad you're feeling perkier,' she said smiling but confused.

The absence of life in the school corridors simply intensified the fact that Maude and I should not be there. At any point, a killer could bound up those basement steps and kill us both in a fit of fury to protect his illicit liaison with an asinine cucumber stick.

'Hurry Maude,' I said, trying to make her legs move faster by pulling on her arm, her breaths starting to quicken in short, soft puffs.

'Drea, the water,' said Maude as it spilled over its lip. I grabbed it from her fingers and drank it one gulp. When we reached the main entrance, I glanced back – nothing yet.

'Okay, Maude. Well, I'll see you out there,' I said, turning to leave. I wondered how angry Su Lee might be that I'd left her alone on the cake stall for so long. Or might she be feeling liberated by the freeing of her repressed entrepreneurial spirit.

'Drea,' said Maude.

'Yes,' I snapped, whipping my head around.

'I'm surprised to see you so... involved.'

I looked straight into her river blue eyes, leaning in just an inch. 'I don't give a shit about the bake sale, Maude.' From somewhere far along the corridor I heard the faint but regular clipping of a man's shoes. 'There's a killer out there and I think I've found him.'

Once outside, despite the autumn sun, my skin felt cooler. I threw myself into a passing crowd of families and steered myself back to my stand. The playground was heaving with cake-obsessed parents and children, and the lines to the different stands were as identifiable as the rungs and reptiles on a snakes and ladders board. I passed one line as it intersected with another and reconnected back to Su Lee. Politely I pushed forward, getting looks from people low on refined sugar reacting to queue injustice.

'It's ok, I work here,' I said. They broke into wide innocent smiles, as if they hadn't been roasting with rage just milliseconds before I cleared my name. As I approached the table, the first thing I saw was the metal tin with different coloured notes fanned out like peacock's tails. Next to the tin was a stack of cloth moneybags with black lettering denoting the type of note or coin.

'Where fuck you been?' Su Lee wiped a thick line of lemon frosting from her forehead creating a unibrow, and white streaks of icing sugar down her coat. She seemed angrily liberated.

'Sorry. Business.' I slipped in behind the table and took up position. All the Wattalapan had gone, as had the lemon cupcakes. But somehow our stock had been replenished: now we had cake stands upon which sat cakes with pink sprinkles. I didn't know we had surplus stock. Soon we could become a franchise. The Gatlin bake sale was not a small ad hoc affair by any means. There must have been a couple of hundred pounds on this table alone. I looked around the playground and, without counting them all, I could see at least ten stands. It was likely that me and Su Lee were the two least in line for employee of the month; if we had a couple of hundred on our table then everyone else would have had at least that on theirs. At some point, all this lovely money would be collected and stored somewhere. As it was school money, it would probably be kept inside the school. I needed to get my hands on it before it got to the safe. It would mean having to engage in some blunt force trauma. This wasn't ideal; given my mental state, I could do without the aggravation. But it had to be done. Life didn't always go the way we wanted it to. After one organised robbery and one disorganised robbery, I was enlightened to the riches of preparation. This could get messy, but I didn't know exactly how because of the nature of disorderly crime. From lessons learned in the kitchen I knew that, without the proper reconnaissance, I was inviting all kinds of trouble. Not sifting the flour leads to lumps in a cake, over-filling leads to over-spilling. But still, in the kitchen there is order to be found amidst the chaos. Disorderly crime led to badly planned suicides, tetanus injections and perjury. With so much activity in the playground, I would have to be vigilant.

'You do all work now. I go pee,' huffed Su Lee. Great.

'Don't be too long,' I stressed.

'You be long, I be long,' she slammed back.

How was I to stay vigilant when I was stuck behind this stand with a queue full of bulimic mothers. I mean, I could see them all eating but where did it go? Some were slimmer than their teenage daughters.

The sky had darkened from alpine blue to mechanic grey. The music had turned from sophisticated daytime jazz to a more frenetic pace of drum machines and electro beats. Bodies weren't moving to the beat, but they seemed looser, tendons limbering. People were laughing harder and louder. Women like Ann – for whom the end of the pole fixed up their arse was normally visible – were being tactile, and the usual, repressed English stiff upper lip was quivering under same-sex shoulder squeezing and non-marital waist hugging. I might be selling isotonic water but one of these stands was offering alcohol.

Su Lee was paying me back. She still hadn't returned and I was nose down in cherry-topped, nipple-looking white fondant iced cupcakes, changing money like a sex slave with nothing in front of me but a sea of people. I was about to make my own 'CLOSED' sign and hunt down Su Lee with a trapper's net when a group of women inches away from the table began a conversation worth staying for.

'A murder in Gatlin. It doesn't even make sense does it?' asked Ann.

'And it makes no sense for it to have been Penelope,' said Ann's friend in jeans and an off-the-shoulder chiffon tee.

'Lucinda, I couldn't agree more. I know it's not the thing to say, but there are so many other people we could afford to lose with less important roles in the PTA than Penelope,' said Ann. 'Do you know what I mean?'

'The truth is, it was only after she died that I realised just how much work she actually did. She certainly had her fingers in a lot of pies,' said the other, shorter, woman with a boyish figure and wrinkled, diamond-encrusted fingers.

'Ooh Davina, don't speak ill of the dead,' said Ann, frothing lubriciously.

'I jest. But apart from her obvious extra-curricular activities, she had a humanitarian side to her she never talked about,' said Davina.

'Well, why would you? It's so boring,' said Lucinda flippantly.

'So true,' agreed Davina. 'She was on a sub-committee for an exchange programme with a school in India. Can you believe it?'

'I'm in charge of all the committees and I don't know about any sub-committee,' said an outraged Ann, spilling the contents of her cup over her friend.

'I have a little charlie barley if anyone would care to follow me to the little girls' room to powder our noses,' flirted Lucinda.

'That sounds super,' said Davina.

'Who else was on this sub-committee?' pushed Ann.

'Ok, let me just make sure there's enough in this bag. I let Dahlia borrow my lip gloss the other day and since then I've been wondering whether she saw it and has been helping herself,' said Lucinda, full of parental concern.

'Kids!' said Davina, shaking her finger disagreeably.

'Forget about that. Where is the money for this sub-committee coming from and who is chairing it?' growled Ann, nose upturned like a bloodhound on the hunt.

'Ann, I think you're forgetting that Penelope was PTA treasurer,' squealed Lucinda.

'I most certainly am not! I rigged that bloody vote myself to get her that job,' Ann said furiously.

'And as treasurer, she re-appropriated funds all the time—' Lucinda went on.

'Re-appropriated funds...?'

'Penelope and Victoria did whatever they wanted – isn't

that the point of a school board? Like the India thing. The programme was all ready to go until Victoria delayed it, announcing that their Liaison Co-ordinator, Felicity Spencer, wasn't up to the job of travelling to India due to her being a bit of a nutcase,' explained Davina.

'I mean, I get them wanting to come here, but why would anyone want to go there?' said Lucinda, arching an over-plucked eyebrow. 'Anyway, there's nothing wrong with Felicity, really,' she continued.

'I know, but remember when she came back from India and her family lied and said she'd had a breakdown to explain why she'd run off and got herself an Indian boyfriend? Penelope used that. I think Vicky's niece wanted the job,' suggested Davina.

A new suspect? Sure, Henry possessed all the hallmarks of a serial killer: pompous smile, thin pursed lips, overly polite without a trace of emotion, and now a wandering cock. But I wondered if Henry was a red herring. Felicity would have done anything to go back to India, to breathe again in the place that she called home, to stop existing and start living. Gatlin had sucked the life out of her and probably caused a mental condition of sorts through a broken heart. There was nothing wrong with Felicity that a large dose of happiness couldn't have cured. She must have been over the moon to have got the job as Liaison Co-ordinator. And then to have it taken away? Could that be motive for murder? It sounded beyond preposterous but if my one true happiness seemed within my grasp and then somebody snatched it away, what would I do?

Davina and Lucinda trotted off in the direction of the toilet for some good old-fashioned nasal gazing. Ann seemed too fired up about the sub-committee to follow. Her skin was tense and her hands balled into fists as she glared at me.

'You better re-stock,' she snapped.

'With what?' I said.

She lifted up the tablecloth. There were three boxes of wine. '£5 a cup.' I obediently started opening up the boxes. 'The school's reputation has suffered terribly with this Penelope business,' she said, biting the ends of her words. 'We have to think about the consequences for our children. Which college is going to offer Catherine a place when they find out she's from—'

'Murderville,' I said.

'You know nothing. Catherine is top of her class and whatever little game your daughter thinks she's playing, messing around with her position as class president will not change that. However, Penelope's personal choices have obviously brought a defamatory spotlight on all of us and maybe if she hadn't been so... secretive she might be alive today.'

'Alive to explain her actions with the sub-committee,' I stirred.

'You know about it too! This is inexcusable. I will not stand for it! I am—' Transparent?

Su Lee appeared in the middle of Ann's rant, looking clean and relaxed like she had just returned from a spa day.

'I finish my pee,' she announced.

'Yes, it would appear you peed for England,' I said.

'Yes, I pee in England.'

'Drea, clean that money out of the tin and pick up all the money bags. You're coming with me to put the money in the safe,' said Ann. I heard the word money three times. This was not the way it was supposed to be. Disorderly crime. What was the difference between hitting someone else over the head and grabbing the money and hitting Ann? For starters, that person would not know I was there because they would not have asked me to accompany them anywhere. This was a salient point, but I did not have time to dwell on it. Secondly, this was Ann who probably had eyes in the back of her head and would see me coming. Well, I had no choice. A significant theme in my life these days.

'You no leave me again,' said a panicked Su Lee. Scared Su had replaced Spa Su.

'We need to put the money in the safe. We won't be long,' said Ann.

'No, it too busy before and now we sell happy drink,' she exclaimed, looking at the three different colours of wine I had poured into plastic cups and arranged into pyramid shapes on the table.

'What's wrong with you? We're not putting you on a boat back to Shanghai,' cursed Ann.

I had two plastic bags full of money and geared up as I followed her into the school.

'Cunt,' said Su Lee, under her breath but not really. Was it directed at me or Ann? I assumed it was at Ann and nodded sympathetically. I began to scan the crowd for Regina. For Henry. For a sign saying '£11,510 THIS WAY'. I didn't want to do what I was about to do. But as soon as we got inside and the doors closed, all the outside noise was shut out and the wheels were set in motion. I was left with this bizarre feeling of how worlds could change in an instant. My ears needed to familiarise themselves with different sounds, my eyes to different sights and how did my mind feel about all this? Maybe this is what Mother was reacting to when she took those pills. Maybe it wasn't that she hated me or even hated herself, but that she was just trying to achieve some sort of equilibrium inside her body. Was parenthood helping understand my own mother? Passing the wisdom baton in a slow motion reverse relay race.

I walked behind Ann like a lost, homicidal lamb behind a shepherd. She had sharp, small, pointy heels that pricked the atmosphere with every step. Without a plan, I'd have to rely on my environment and take whatever it had to offer. We weren't going to Maude's office as we'd turned in the other direction. When we got to the end of the corridor, Ann proceeded up the stairs, content to let me carry two heavy plastic bags of money like her lacky. As we reached the top of the stairs, I could see she was headed for the School Director's office.

The door was closed and, unless I was planning to pierce Ann in the leg with a pencil, I wasn't sure how it would help me even if it were open. As Ann put a key in the lock, a small red metal canister floated before my eyes. It was as if I had just seen water in the desert. It had been separated from its wall attachment and was lying on the floor. Deep breath. Focus. Turn disorderly crime into orderly crime – that was my assignment.

In one smooth, sweeping manoeuvre, I deposited the bags of money on the floor beside me, picked up the fire extinguisher and, taking it high above my head, brought it down upon Ann's skull. She crumpled concertina-style, folding like a worn out ballerina, and slumped to the floor. It was effortless for both of us. I would simply say the attacker ran off when I came up the stairs. The 'he' was important. Society reserved rage and violence for men and hysteria and insecurity for women. Such bias became useful in situations such as this. Now what to do with the money? I'd have to hide it somewhere and then come back and pick it up.

Stepping around Ann's lifeless body – she was so much more bearable in this state – I was en-route to collect my money bags when, through the office window, I saw a figure walk into the gym down below. It was Victoria Taylor-Singh. She headed over to the cupboard where they kept the equipment. If something caused her to look up for any reason, she'd see me in the office. I got to a corner, ready to drop if I needed to. It was at that point that something made her turn around. She looked to the door of the gym as it opened. I shot to the floor, leaving my eyes still on the window sill. She smiled a relaxed, easy smile and turned back to the cupboard.

Was this another illicit rendezvous? Were Regina and Henry merely part of a growing trend and the bake sale was the new roadside motel? A woman walked over to Victoria. A lesbian affair wasn't going to shock me any more than Regina and Henry – unless maybe it was Su Lee and Ann.

What was that in the woman's hand? It looked like a knife. Why would they need a knife? Maybe to open a new case of rackets. Or tennis balls, or... Oh my God, no! The woman extended her arm out as far back as she could and then plunged the knife into Victoria's back. Victoria stopped searching in the cupboard. She stopped reaching, her arms dropped down by her sides and she faltered. She fell back onto her assailant, who moved away letting her drop to the hard floor. I screamed, and as soon as fear convinced me screaming was not a good idea, I stopped, but then I realised it didn't matter. It was soundproof, toughened glass. I couldn't hear a thing and they couldn't hear me.

One stab wasn't enough. The killer wanted more. She leaned over Victoria and savagely rammed the knife up and down into her stomach. Victoria shuddered, as if she felt every slice. That was when the blood started pouring out of each slit the blade had made into her skin. Dark red, almost black, blood spilled from her onto the white gym floor like a blanket. The killer must have stabbed her five times at least and it was only on the last entry that the blood rushed up into the air like a fountain. I had never seen life leave a person. It was quicker than I thought. How was this possible? Who could do such a thing? I didn't really have any friends at the school so I had no way of telling, but could one mother even hate another to this extent?

There is a fine line between heroism and idiocy. Even if the killer had missed every possible artery, her blood was all over the gym floor. And blood was one of those substances, like jelly from a mould, that never went back in exactly the same way. Do I bother to set off the fire alarm and get people in there to try and save her bloodless life, or do I get the fuck out with my money? And just then, for no reason at all, the killer looked up. Felicity's eyes were motionless and fixed, like a deer milliseconds before the kill shot.

Love

She hadn't seen my face as the glass was one way. But something made her look up, and now she was startled. Maybe stabbing someone to death had her riled up. It seemed as if a gun had been cocked with the contestants poised on their starting blocks, and then bang – gone. Felicity running, trying to find me; and me, running, trying not to get caught. She seemed so much more startled now than when she was hacking into Victoria and watching the life spurt out of her – but then everyone's anxiety levels are different, and for that she'd find no judgment here.

I burst out of the office and opened the door, only to be greeted by the recumbent body of Ann – trust Ann to be the first obstacle in my way. She was curled up on the floor, murmuring. Her cold lips were warming up. I looked at the two money bags sitting there calling my name and my heart knotted. There simply wasn't enough time and, between Ann waking up and Felicity finding me, I couldn't risk it. Disorderly crime had just gone nuclear. If I had attended a few more parent–teacher meetings, I would know the layout of the school better. But this was no time for poor-man's regret. If I went back down the way Ann and I had come up, I'd be in the main corridor – which Felicity could be half way along by now. She'd know I was the one who had been in the office the moment she laid eyes on me. There was no one else about – it would all be too much of a coincidence and I wasn't that good an actress. Plus, she was looking for someone and I'd be who she'd find. Ordinarily, Felicity was not someone to be scared of, but the fact that she would be holding a weapon, potentially still dripping blood, told me I shouldn't arrive to a knife fight without a knife. She was already two bodies down, three would probably feel like the holy trinity rather than a step too far. I shuddered as I remembered the gruesome details one of the local papers had printed about Penelope's murder. I thought they were being sensationalist but after watching the ruthless way Felicity had just ended Victoria's life, I realised everything they had written was true – that sometimes life was peculiar enough all on its own without adding any drama. There was only one thing I could do to keep Felicity from coming this way.

I picked up the fire extinguisher – my new trusty friend had come in handy twice in one day – and smashed the glass box of the fire alarm. I looked at Ann, who was facing away from me. If Ann ever found out that I'd deliberately pulled the fire alarm during her precious bake sale, I was sure she'd kill me herself. I took the stairs down two at a time, just the sound of the siren made me feel safer.

Suddenly I thought of Victoria's body lying in the gym. The fire would burn her to ashes, leaving no trace of her for the police or her family and I was overcome with remorse – what had I done? And then I relaxed, I'd done nothing. It wasn't a real fire. Disorderly crime – check. Paranoia – check. Fiction and reality morphing into one – check.

I was just approaching the doors when I saw Maude running and scanning the classrooms with her eyes.

'Drea! Have you seen Felicity? She came into the school ages ago and I'm worried she hasn't come out. Can you smell smoke?' Poor Maude. She and Felicity were always so close. It broke her heart when Felicity came back from India in the state that she did. Being an only child, I could only imagine what it felt like to have a sibling. Maude had said to me once that sibling love isn't like normal love – that when you come from the same womb, it fuses people intangibly. It fuses love and hate, and everything in between.

'Come on,' I put my arm around her and ushered her out. 'I saw Felicity leave just before you came. She's fine.' Okay, so mentally she's not that fine.

The tableau of screaming children and half-drunk parents appeared like a silent movie through the main double glass doors. Like one of those comical farces where people are constantly tripping over their own shoelaces and doing fantastical somersaults in the air as they walk. I wish it had remained as amusing as in that moment. But that was not to be. I saw his large, imposing body walk towards me as if he was walking through fire. He was flanked by a uniformed and serious looking Officer Frampton; but once I'd taken her in, she vanished from the image. All I could see was Rodman, and a stupid, unlicensed part of my imagination ran riot with the worst kind of anti-feminist fairy-tale tripe sold to young girls. I imagined him lifting me up into his arms and carrying me out of my pretend fire, searing red flames lashing up around us, making us hot, making us sweat, with the fumes from the smoke causing us to breathe deeply, together, almost panting, my whole body held and supported in his oh-so-strong arms.

'Miss Peiris,' he said, jolting me back from my fantasy. The entire playground seemed to have surrounded him, walking with him like followers of Jesus in his more popular years. Rodman had never said my name before. Not like that.

'You're under arrest.' No, never like that. The fire alarm was still going strong but I could hear the audible exhale of the crowd. Judgments from inebriated parents and righteous teachers started crawling up my trouser leg and down my back. Eyes narrowing, taking me in fully for the first time, it would be hard to remember me from the bake sale where I'd sold them and their families cakes and refreshments moments ago. But they'd all remember me now – the prime suspect.

'For the murder of Penelope Coultard.' Frampton's turn; I was now officially tired of this double act. It was like Rodman couldn't even be bothered to tell me why I was under arrest – he just wanted to arrest me. Quizzically, the men and women assessed me whilst holding their children close. That was who I was. The police had decided I was guilty, so it was true. Great police work guys. Really well done. Forgive me if I'm not jumping up and down, knowing that Ava can sleep soundly in her bed tonight because the killer has been apprehended – because in fact she has not.

'Who is she,' whispered a woman.

'I don't know.'

'She works at the doctor's,' said a man.

'Oh yes.'

'Turn that music off,' Frampton shouted into the crowd and it stopped, one less noise to compete with the fire alarm. Su Lee was watching, her face devoid of emotion or expression.

'Where's the fire?' Frampton asked no-one in particular, yet everybody answered, sycophants needing to both exonerate and ingratiate themselves with these retards who couldn't solve a case if their life depended on it. Frampton appeared down to earth, with her sturdy body and rosy cheeks, but I could see the fat cat of her low self-esteem lap it up like a big saucer of milk, slurping the adulation and rubbing it all over her under-developed ego. Rodman had gone back into his caveman shell, nothing to keep him warm in the wild but his bison hide and contempt for me. Tabatha had found her way to the front of the rabble, and as soon as she saw me, her face became grave. She nodded and disappeared. Was she going to get Ava? Oh, Ava. Frampton got her handcuffs out. Arresting me at the fucking bake sale was bound to cause a landslide for the elections, and not in Ava's favour.

'Do you have to do this here?' I asked in lowered tones, but loud enough that she'd hear me above the alarm.

'Sorry?' she said.

'I said must you do this here – handcuff me. I'll come with you, but this is my daughter's school you know.'

'Nope, can't hear you,' she said. I was sure that at least three other people next to her had heard me. Was she faking it? Was she seriously that jacked up on the power of her own heist that she was choosing this moment as the most appropriate to be a complete cunt? Fucking great.

'I know you can hear me,' I said.

'Nope sorry, can't hear you.' Bitch. Frampton could have been one of the good ones, now even she had turned. I stuck my wrists out but she strong-armed me and threw me into a wall for resisting arrest. The piercing scream distracted us both. It was tinnier than the fire alarm, yet rising. It started somewhere far away and then, as she got closer and came into our view, we all saw it had erupted from Ann's mouth. Dishevelled and hysterical, Ann pushed the glass doors open and crash-landed on my back like a faulty parachute, clutching my money bags.

'She's been murdered – somebody's killed Victoria,' she mouthed.

Screams. The dusk air filled with screams, which in turn soaked into the rapturous sirens of the two fire engines pulling up outside the school. Everyone had become so used to the hideous noise of the alarm, it was as if they forgot that there might be a fire. And when the huge oppressive engines drove up, with their steel sprung ladders slowly lifting into the sky, everyone seemed shocked and introduced to their panic for the first time again.

'What's your name ma'am?' Frampton asked Ann, peeling the limpet off my back. 'Everyone calm down, please.' She looked around. 'We gotta contain this crowd,' she said to Rodman, who seemed unaffected. Did nothing phase this man?

'Blood. She's covered in blood,' Ann was shaking, eyes full of tears, with a large swollen purple lump on the top of her forehead where she had made contact with a fire extinguisher. I contained my smile and wrapped it up inside my mouth.

'Where is the body ma'am?' asked Frampton.

'She's dead. The blood. She's dead, she's deadddd,' she began screaming with a large open mouth. There'd never be a better time. I slapped her hard across her face. Cue second shocked audible gasp from the crowd.

'Miss Peiris!' Frampton scolded.

'She was hysterical,' I said. That felt good. Long overdue.

'Get her out of here, Rodman,' Frampton said, disdainfully nodding at me. Rodman shot her a look. I was sure by ordering him to do anything, Frampton had overstepped the mark.

'In the gym,' said Ann quietly, as if reciting the last poignant line of a eulogy.

'Did you see anything? Anyone?' asked Frampton. People were trying to leave. 'Stop those people,' she screamed. Rodman seemed happy to oblige that one, maybe because it wasn't a direct order.

'Hey!' He projected his booming voice and it bounced off the walls, standing out amidst the chaos.

'Excuse me, ma'am,' said the man in the uniform with a large hose wrapped around his torso. Behind him, came a troupe of firemen laden with various pieces of fire-stopping equipment. The men marched past us. I had never been completely sure about their uniforms. I know they needed to be safe and protect themselves, but the outfits seemed cumbersome – like astronauts, but unaided by the weightless atmosphere.

'We've reports of a murder,' said Frampton to the fireman.

'Do we know where? Is the assailant still at large?'

'In the gym. And yes he is.'

'Where's the gym?'

'At the end of the corridor,' said Maude, looking at me, worry staining her face. The firemen entered the building. They bounced in like an alien race in their big coloured suits and their paraphernalia. A welcome invasion, we let them pass and wanted them to save us, albeit slightly too late for Victoria.

'What is it?' asked Frampton.

'I'm worried about my sister,' answered Maude. 'She was inside and I haven't seen her since the alarm went off.' Frampton looked pensive.

'Are you having a genius moment?' I turned to Frampton. 'I don't want to interrupt, I know they're few and far between. But if it helps, I didn't kill anyone and, I'm sorry Maude, but Felicity killed Victoria. I saw her.' I felt Maude's sibling loyalty rise like a ferocious, rarely sighted monster from the deep. Her eyes turned dark and locked onto me.

'You saw her kill Victoria. Actually saw her?' asked Frampton.

'She took a knife and stuck it in her and then kept going to make sure she'd finished the job.'

'Lies,' breathed out Maude.

'Please can you turn the alarm off so I can turn this place into a crime scene!' shouted Frampton.

'Maude, I'm sorry. It's what I saw.' Steely anger held her face still. I understood. It was her sister. I didn't have a sister but I had someone close to me who I loved, and if anyone had accused Ava of such a crime I would be angry too. But first I would be shocked. Where was the shock? She had brought

Felicity's disappearance to Frampton's attention herself, she obviously had no idea where her sister was and was genuinely concerned. Worry straight to anger without the smallest stop over at shock? We'd missed a step.

'There's Felicity,' shouted a bystander. Felicity was being allowed to come forward as the crowds parted like the dead sea. A somnambulist in a long skirt that brushed down by her ankles. Her hair was tidy and her clothes were conspicuously devoid of blood. She had obviously been by the little girls' room on the way here. That was where Lucinda and Davina had been. Was that it? Was she on coke? Was this a crazy, irrevocable act committed by a junkie?

'Felicity Whitefield, could you step over here, please.'

The fire alarm finally stopped.

The silence felt weird. Our senses had been assaulted for so long that the peace felt abnormal. Like there was something wrong with us, or as if suddenly we couldn't hear ourselves in the quiet.

'My head. Ooh, my head hurts,' said Ann. 'I think… I think someone hit me over the head. Drea… you were with me?' It was Chinese whispers played by one person. We should all play. Everybody could take a turn saying something that would dramatically change the identity of the murderer and the course of Frampton and Rodman's infantile investigation.

'We need some statement rooms. Back up's here. Must have come with the fire brigade.'

'Cuff her,' said Rodman.

'Mum!' Of course, this was the moment Ava had to make her entrance.

'Ava. It's fine,' Ava knew I detested the word fine. That I thought it had two meanings and was used by people who either had nothing to say, or who couldn't bring themselves to consider what it might mean to feel otherwise.

'You're in handcuffs!'

From behind the crowd, I could hear dance music. People stepped back and made a circle. Tabatha, Amelia and two boys I didn't know filled the space.

VOTE for AVA.
The pigs tryin' to pin a crime.
But Ava's mum is in-no-cent,
don't let her do the time.
Vote for A-V-A.
She stands for justice every day.
She stands for change to lead the way!

The girls were head to toe in skimpy cheerleading outfits, all they were missing was a pole. The boys were break-dancing, swivelling their heads on the ground and bending their legs in opposite directions in a way that looked as if it should be incredibly painful. They repeated the chant, other kids started clapping and chanting Ava's name. Out of the boys' back pockets the girls pulled conveniently located leaflets about Ava and her policies. I had to hand it to Tabatha. She had a mercenary pragmatism that I was beginning to adore. Did she really want to fuck us? Maybe not. She'd turned a three ringed circus into the best thing she could and I loved her for it.

'I'll take Peiris to the portacabin,' said Rodman.

Frampton didn't answer, but I saw the blur of concern scurry across her face. She certainly couldn't have thought I'd be a threat to Rodman. She must have thought he'd be a threat to me.

'I don't want to go,' I said instinctively. Frampton looked back at Rodman. It was his call.

'Move,' he said.

Other police officers were filing into the playground. The presence of the law put a real dampener on the party spirit. As I walked in handcuffs to the gate that led into the field, Su Lee gave a glum childlike wave, four fingers down to her palm and then slowly up again.

Ava ran behind me, tears flowing. 'Mum! This makes no sense. You didn't do anything.'

'And they'll see that soon. Don't worry. I'll be home tonight.' I avoided looking at Rodman. I didn't need his judgment on why there was never a right time for a parent to lie to their child.

Once the gate had shut behind us, the school fell away almost instantly. There was something wholly demeaning about being told how to walk. How a person walked in the world was a sign of freedom. Chains and cells kept people from their liberty and, as I walked with my hands cuffed behind my back, I noticed my centre of balance had shifted.

The ground was dry, unlike the last time I had walked across it, and footsteps were harder to hear but I could sense him still.

It sneaks up on you – love. You could say the word a million times, but when love decided it was ready to show itself you needed to put on a yellow mac and hang on because Niagara Falls was nothing in comparison. The power, the force. Everything I'd done up to now, I'd done out of love. If Ava hadn't been around, this would have been nothing more than a sticky situation. But because of Ava, it was a walk through a field of shame. I couldn't bear the thought of leaving her alone, and yet everything I'd done for her had put her at risk of that. I couldn't bear to think of her sweet soul growing up hardened and defensive, showing none of the best sides of herself because she was petrified that deep down no one loved her or that she was so bad they would never be able to love her enough. Love all of her. And how would I stop her thinking there was something wrong with her? Wasn't that the natural progression? Parents don't love you the right way so it's got to mean that there's something's wrong with you. Tears ran out of my eyes. I love you Ava. I'm so sorry. I breathed in deeply so Rodman didn't hear me, but there were too many tears to control. I had to take quick shallow breaths just so I wouldn't choke. I hated sounding so pathetic, but when love wants you to feel it, you become a prisoner. Alex must have known when he left. He must have known how I felt about her before I did, despite my denying it, shunning it, trying to be in control. I'm a mother. A mess. There is no going back. It changes you forever.

Rodman walked ahead to open the door. I wondered if I should be grateful he hadn't made me open it with my teeth. Frampton had seemed so odd at the suggestion of me being alone with him. Did looking mean always result in being mean? If he hurt me, it would be my word against his. And who would believe the word of a murder suspect over a police detective? I'd probably keep it to myself. Tabatha could only turn so many scandals into triumphs. Maybe he'd hurt me so it wouldn't show? It would be the clever thing to do.

Rodman shut the door behind us. I stood awkwardly waiting. Here we go. He walked over to me and I flinched. I wished I hadn't. I didn't want to give him more power than he already had. Putting his hands in his pockets, he brought out a band of keys and, moving behind me, he undid my cuffs. 'Sit down.'

I sat. There were two chairs and a camera on a tripod. I needed to try not to antagonise him, to do what he wanted. And if I thought he was going to hurt me, to see how much I could actually take before screaming. Screaming was bound to make him angrier.

'Tabatha Crosly-Burke lied. Why?' He leaned against the wall, standing two feet away from me, arms folded.

'I don't know.'

'Why?' Same tone. It was hard to tell how thin the patience was wearing when the tone was the same.

'I really don't know. If I had to guess it's because she wants me to owe her a favour or because she genuinely likes my daughter. I don't know which.' He paused, uncrossed his arms and took off his jacket. It was cold. I kept mine on.

'Why was Ava's hair in Crosly-Burke's car?'

'Because...' Lie, go on lie. What's wrong with you? Fucking lie... 'Because I used her pink gloves that were in my car to cover up my fingerprints when I robbed Henrietta.' Bang bang. Shit. Why I had I said that?

'Why would you do that?'

'Because...I needed – need – the money to pay my daughter's school fees.' He looked at me with bright black eyes. The stubbly beard across his face reminded me of a muzzle, the kind worn by dogs who can't be controlled.

'Stand up.' I stood up. Just waiting in the middle of the room seemed stupid. Even if they knew the lion was going to catch them, the jungle animals still ran when chased. Now that he had taken his jacket off, I could see the tail of a tattoo down the middle of his inner right arm poking out from under his rolled-up shirt sleeves. Veins bulged in his wrists as if his body couldn't contain the strength of his blood. He came towards me and instinctively I backed away to the wall. There was nowhere for me to go. He came closer, so close I knew that the punch would hurt. When he kissed me I was so shocked I just stood there, motionless, waiting for the kiss to become something less than perfect, but it didn't. In the beginning, I couldn't feel his body – just his lips. He had one hand above my head and the other on my waist. He kissed hard. And then soft. And then he pushed, pinning me flat against him.

When I heard the thud, I was convinced he'd hit me. The assault I'd been expecting. His hand banged hard on the glass and the top window above us flung out just as the door opened. Frampton entered and Rodman stepped away from me smoothly like he was never there. Had I been kissed? Yes. Had I kissed back? Yes, I had.

'What's going on here?' she asked.

'She says she got a tetanus for a rusty nail,' said Rodman. He lit up a cigarette. I'd never seen him smoke. I was still up against the wall. I couldn't walk, my legs wouldn't have carried me to the chair.

Frampton surveyed the room, uncertain. Then she spoke. 'Hospital has you checked in the night after the robbery. The doc also says he urged you to stay the night, but you insisted on leaving,' Frampton said, sitting down. 'Felicity has an alibi that checks out for the Coultard murder and, apart from your testimony, there's nothing that makes her a suspect in the Taylor-Singh murder.' I said nothing. That couldn't have just happened.

'You look scared, Drea.' She turned to Rodman. 'Why isn't the camera on?' He shrugged his shoulders. 'Rodman, the camera should have been on,' she said grittily.

'I forgot.' It was dark, but inside this portacabin, I felt like I was in the twilight zone. He had kissed me. Why? Did he like me? Like me the way I liked him? Because that was it, I did like him. Or was this part of some game? Some power trip he got off on? But he just covered for me with Frampton. Why do that? Was that part of the game too?

'Drea, I'm afraid your alibi for the robbery of Mrs Crosly-Burke doesn't check out,' smiled Frampton. When I showed the self-defence teacher your picture, she said she had never seen you before. It also occurred to me that your insisting on being discharged from the hospital on the night of the Coultard's murder gave you both the time and opportunity.'

I didn't look at him. I still felt him inside my mouth. She was on to me. I didn't make sense to her. I didn't make sense to me. Why do people lie? Because they think someone else can't handle the truth. I don't think if I'd told Frampton the truth, she would have had me up against the wall and kissed me.

'Where were you on the night of Penelope's murder, Drea?'

'She was at the cemetery. Her mother's there.'

He kissed me. He lied for me. And he knew where my mother lived.

A Knock at the Door

When I got home, it was past ten o'clock. I knew because the grandfather clock in the middle of the town square chimed ten loud rings and I jumped at the sound of it, despite being in my own car. On the drive home I smoked a joint and hoped the weed would show me clarity.

My mind wandered to Alex. Alex was aware of his physical self. He was so much more tactile than me and, observing his responses to other women he encountered in his life, we often talked about just how turned on Alex was able to become given varied but indiscernible stimuli. I had never considered myself highly sexed in the same way. For me, I needed a mental connection. The neurons in my brain needed to be stimulated before anything below my waist would even wake up. I needed a story, a fantasy.

So how had this man slipped inside my mind? What was the story in my head that my loins were feeding themselves? Life had taken a turn for the bizarre since Alex left. Things with Ava had me going crazy. And after two robberies, two murders and a fucking bake sale, kissing Rodman seemed like the craziest thing I'd done. It made no sense and it scared me. Maybe all the times in my life that I had thought would count as crazy were just normal. If that were true and Rodman was realigning definitions, then it would seem that the new crazy was desperately wanting something whilst being terrified of getting it.

The lights were on in the living room and it made me smile. Since Alex had left, we'd gained a living room and it was all because of Ava and her new friends. As weird as I thought they were, we'd become a little family and it was kind of nice. Days like this made it so. I was coming home to something. Deep underneath me, the earth's tectonic plates were shifting. I could smell it.

I opened the front door and heard music and girly chatter.

'Mum!' Ava ran into my arms and for once I let her hold me like she wanted to. Public displays of affection were not my thing, but right now I could feel what all the fuss was about. I held my girl with Tabatha and Amelia smiling and clapping in the background.

'Way to go,' said Tabatha, grinning.

'Way to go,' said Amelia, clapping.

'So,' I said, kissing Ava gently on the forehead, disentangling myself and trying to regain composure. 'What's been happening since I left?'

'Ava's has a thirty-point lead in the polls. Unheard of in student election history for a new candidate to be this popular,' said Amelia, consulting a sheet of paper on a clipboard, but nothing on her face suggested she had her numbers wrong.

'Unprecedented,' echoed Tabatha.

'I hate to say it, but I think you being arrested actually helped,' said Ava sheepishly.

'Glad to be of service, darling.'

'Sorry about lying and then getting you into trouble,' said Tabatha. 'They spoke to my optician. I was having an eye test that evening and he confirmed the appointment.'

'Never apologise for bending the truth,' I said gratefully.

'I didn't know you wore glasses,' exclaimed a horrified Amelia.

'I don't,' Tabatha snarled back. 'I wear contact lenses. There's nothing wrong with my sight. It's an astigmatism.'

'Perjury is normally such a foolproof crime,' I yawned and, as I looked at the sofa, I realised how tired I was. 'I think it's time you girls went home. It's been a long day for everyone.'

'They're staying the night, Mum.'

'Ok well up to bed then, after you've picked up all this crap.' They collected their campaign posters and bowls of half-eaten cereal. I grimaced. Only teenagers could eat cereal at night. So weird.

'Mum,' said Ava, just before she left the room.

'Yes.'

'Are you okay? He didn't hurt you did he? That detective.' Did he look like he was going to? Did that mean he still could? Was I being a complete fucking idiot if even my daughter could see it?

'No. Of course not.'

I went into the kitchen and poured myself a glass of whisky. I knocked it back and poured another. The first shot of yellow liquid swilled in my throat, coating it, and then the next one just slid down fast and easy. The kitchen was a mess. It felt like a lifetime ago since I was last in it. A large ceramic bowl sat on the table with a hand whisk, a couple of spoons and a measuring jug. Dirty utensils with which I'd made the Wattalapan. Empty cartons littered the floor and wrappers from the jaggery, the round, solid, brown-coloured sugar. Why didn't shit just wash itself up after you used it?

I wondered if Papa was home or if he was with his lady friend? It felt kind of wrong that we both had these people in our lives who were making us feel things. It felt disloyal. We were fucked up, damaged misfits, not meant to be able to connect with anyone or feel anything. Existing but never living. That's what we became when Mother died. Didn't we owe it to her memory to stay that way? I'd never even visited her grave but I carried her with me. I carried her in that little bottle of pills that had lain in the bottle of my bag for years. That was my loyalty card. But what were Papa and I doing for her memory now?

A denim cloth satchel sat on the chair. Tabatha had left her bag. I lifted the flap. Purse. Cigarettes. I took one and lit it up. Hairbrush. Make-up: some sick-smelling, fruit salad scented lip gloss. Presumably to entice boys into kissing her, why they would be lured by the smell of rotten melons I could not say. A condom. Fucking whore. And a diary. I pulled out the diary and took a seat. This was what I needed after the day I'd had. Some easy trash.

Dear Diary, (Seriously. Who writes like that?)
I'm sorry I haven't written for a while. There's been a lot going on. Some of it you've heard before so I won't bore you with the details, but Dad's cheating again. This time it's with Amelia's mum and he's getting really paranoid that I'm going to tell Amelia, which I wouldn't because I'm too fucking embarrassed. Now me and Dad aren't talking. We haven't spoken for three weeks, (three weeks! How can you not talk to your daughter for three weeks?) *which ordinarily I'd be really upset about but Ava's mum has been distracting me. I mean she's really weird. She smokes weed, drinks a lot, I'm pretty sure she was the one who robbed Mum and she says stuff normal parents aren't meant to say, but she really loves Ava who isn't even her own daughter which is so weird because she didn't give birth to her and only looked after her since she was four so that made me think that maybe it's like the lottery, you know, and if you choose shit numbers you get shit parents. It's not coz I'm shit, I've just got shit numbers. Ava got good numbers. (Though Ava's Dad seems as shit as mine). Mum's ok mostly but I think she suspects Dad's up to his old tricks, which is making her go a little crazy. The dog shop rang to update their database and she found out that Dad had originally bought Miss Congeniality to give to Regina but then gave it to Mum when she found the dog by mistake. I think Mum killed the dog. I'm trying to be there for her because I know she's going through a lot, but it's more fun round Ava's house.*

I jumped out of my skin when I heard the knocking. The sound was intentionally low for the time of night but definitively persistent. Perhaps Papa had forgotten his key. I hoped so. It would mean maybe I'd catch him with his lady friend.

I opened the door and there he was. Unkempt, tired and intense black eyes. Rodman was on my doorstep. We looked at each other for a moment and then he lunged forward. He grabbed my face, kissing me, closing the door with one hand, kissing me, moving me up against the banisters, kissing me. My skin felt like electricity was running through it. Like my body was a conduit and finally someone had paid their bill and turned it on. He smelled of cigarettes and alcohol and him. A simplicity of scent that was almost baby-like. His stubble grazed my skin and the more I felt it the more I welcomed it, wanting it to tear up my cheeks.

'You ok?' he asked pulling away tenderly, stroking my face.

'Don't talk,' I said.

The hands that I'd first perceived as rough didn't feel rough anymore. He moved them all over the contours of my body, edging around my breasts then moving away. I found myself contorting in ways that I hoped would enable him to find his way back there. I kissed his neck and he caved, moaning, loving it. I wanted him everywhere. A noise upstairs startled me, not him. I guess three teenagers wasn't his idea of the worst nightmare, but it wasn't great for me. I pulled him into the kitchen where behind the kitchen door we continued, harder than before. With a new illusion of privacy, he lifted up my T-shirt, his hands took in my breasts whilst we kissed and I melted into this strange, unknown, gorgeous man. I pushed him away from me, just for a moment, just to breathe. Silence. He put his head down, looking at the floor.

'I don't why I told you the truth today,' I said, and as I said it I knew why. It was because I couldn't lie to him.

'I don't know why I lied for you,' he said, looking up slightly. 'They're working on getting some DNA from the robbery,' he said, sounding disappointed.

'I wore gloves,' I said.

'DNA from the hair around the dog's mouth. Frampton's clutching at straws, hoping that maybe the dog bit the robber.'

'The dog's dead.'

'Forensics aren't scared of dead dogs,' he moved past me and sat on the edge of the table looking around. I could see him taking it in. 'You bake?' he asked.

'Do I look like I bake?'

'I arrested you at a bake sale.'

'Are you profiling me?' I demanded suddenly. Was he here for a booty call or to audit my house? See how sharp my kitchen knives were?

'Why would you go to a bake sale if you don't bake?' he asked.

'I go to the park, but I'm not a paedophile.'

'See? Even that tells me you went to that bake sale for something and it's not because you got a kid at the school or because you want to support the PTA.' He continued to scan the kitchen. 'You reading?' he said lifting up the book which I'd placed open and face down.

'It's Ava's friend's diary.'

'You're reading her diary?'

'Ok! I went to the bake sale...' I started, but then he smiled and he threw me completely. 'Why are you smiling?'

'Carry on, I want to hear this.'

'I was trying to steal some money and figure out who killed Coultard and I think I was doing pretty well on both fronts before I got side-tracked watching Felicity Spencer stab Victoria Taylor-Singh to death in the gym.'

'Some school you people got. Steal money?'

'Do not refer to me as people.'

'Felicity's alibi for Coultard is airtight. It wasn't her.'

'But I saw her kill Victoria,' I insisted.

'Okay, so she killed Victoria. Why?'

'Because Victoria stopped her going to India with their new exchange programme.'

'So?' he asked incredulously.

'So it was her dream, to get the fuck out of here, to go back to India. Don't underestimate people who dare to dream.'

'But she didn't kill Coultard,' said Rodman.

'Then someone else did.' I said.

'You after my job? That sounds like a senior detective deduction,' he said, teasing me.

'Funny. You and Frampton were pretty sure I was your killer and she probably still is. You still might be if we hadn't, you know, done stuff.' He shuffled his feet and became shifty.

'What is it?' I asked.

'Nothing. Frampton. It's tricky. She can't know about us,' he said, looking straight at me, his jaw determined. It was impossible to look away. This was how he looked in an interrogation room. If my bare skin wasn't still warm from his hands and I hadn't still the sound of him breathing like a wounded bear in my ear when I kissed his neck, maybe I'd be scared.

'Are you saying getting involved with suspects in open murder cases isn't actively encouraged?' I asked innocently. He smiled.

'I should go.' He got up and everything felt awkward. Of course he should – he shouldn't have even been here – but that was the awkward part. I wanted him to stay and I think he wanted the same thing.

'You should.' He opened the kitchen door and I was hit by a wave of overwhelming sadness. As I walked behind him through the hall, I felt bereft. What the fuck. Could the vagaries of my emotions not remain consistent for longer than twenty-four fucking hours?

Rodman paused and then turned around when we got to the front door. 'In a town like Gatlin where crime is limited to Inheritance Tax evasion, Frampton's convinced that the robberies and the murders were committed by the same person. I can try and introduce the tall tale of a robber, a murderer and another murderer, but she's convinced that you are not all that you seem.' He looked at me. 'I guess she's got that part right.'

'So she's trying to put this all on me. That's why you mentioned my mother?'

'Yes.'

'I'm assuming you knew my mother's dead because you're a police inspector and you have access to things like that. Details.'

'Must have been tough for you. Suicide.'

'I see. All the details. We all have our parents' legacies to contend with. Mine's no different.'

He looked at me so sweetly that my body started itching, allergic to the kindness.

'I've never been to that cemetery,' I said.

'The night watchman is a friend. He'll cover. Get Frampton off your back. There aren't any suspects here, Drea. Everyone who is remotely connected has an alibi. I'm not saying someone's not lying, but right now I can't prove it. And in fairness to her sloppy detective work, she's a third right: you did rob someone.'

'She's a half right,' I said quietly.

'What do you mean?' asked Rodman. Shit, shit, shit. Just keep your mouth shut.

'I robbed Regina Salter as well but she just hasn't come forward. Yet.'

'Jesus, Drea! What the fuck is wrong with you?!'

'Ssh! Nothing! And I don't need a lecture from you. I am doing the best I can for my daughter. Maybe you don't understand what it's like because your parents gave you everything, best schools, best education—'

'My mum worked two cleaning jobs and my dad was a fisherman. I went to a perfectly good state school—'

'Well maybe that worked on fantasy island, but in the real world I can't afford to move house and live in hope that she gets into a perfectly good state school.'

'We lived in Brigham and my parents thought that Brigham High was good enough.'

'Maybe they didn't love you enough.' I couldn't take it back. Was that hurt in his eyes? I didn't mean it but it didn't matter.

'You think if you'd gone to a private school, you'd have been a different person and your mum wouldn't have topped herself?'

I moved past him and opened the door, wide.

'You're behaving like a crazy person,' he pronounced in his almighty omniscience.

'I want Ava to be happy,' I hissed.

'Maybe we have different ideas of happiness.' He took a few steps forward, looking out as if he wanted to turn back and say something, but then took whatever it was away with him and kept on walking out into the night.

I shut the door, exhaled deeply, waiting for a part of me to run out and apologise. I'd had a long day and should have been in bed. I regretted saying what I did as soon as I'd said it. On the other hand, so what if he was a good kisser. A great, amazing kisser. He had no right to say that about my mother. He knew nothing. I'd let him off lightly. I should have kneed him in the balls. He didn't look the type to take that well so it was probably good that I hadn't. But I should have. I put my hand on the banister to go up to bed and end this day when I remembered Tabatha's diary lying open on the table. I started walking back to the kitchen when there was a knock at the door. Ok, this was my chance to do things right.

I ran and pulled it open as quick as I could, talking all the while.

'I just wanted to say I'm sorry—' A sharp intake of the night air stopped me in my tracks as my mouth hurried to catch up with my eyes.

'Officer Frampton.' Rosy cheeked. On my doorstep.

'Hello Drea. I was worried you might already be in bed, but it looks like you were expecting someone.'

'Yes. My neighbour. I was just talking to my neighbour.'

'What's her name and what have you done, Drea? What are you sorry about?' she smiled.

What was her name? How was I to know what her fucking name was? She was my neighbour. 'I was just going to bed, Officer. It's late and it's been a long day.'

'Yes it has. Of course. And I don't want to keep you any longer,' she said, striding her navy blue polyester covered bottom into the house. I closed the front door, glancing up at the staircase. Just moments ago I had desperately hoped the girls would not come down and see me and Rodman together. Now I wanted them to burst in so I could apologise for waking them up and kick Frampton out. Were police calls to people's private homes even allowed at this time?

'It's a little awkward, to be honest Drea, but sometimes in life we feel compelled to behave in a way that feels a little risky if there lies the chance for a real greater good, do you know what I mean?'

'Not really.'

She sat down on the sofa. 'My partner, Rodman. He's actually not my partner, he's more of a bounty hunter. Ha! Rodman has a history. With the ladies. And I'd hate for you to involve yourself in something here, Drea. Do you know what

I mean?' This was the first time she had stopped smiling. I wasn't sure which was more disconcerting. She paused, as though she wanted to hear nothing from me, just wanted to know that I'd heard her. 'There was a sexual assault charge. It got dropped, but no smoke without fire. I'm sure a woman such as yourself can understand.' She'd used an expression without any expression. Interesting. There was a way to behave right now that would eliminate her suspicions but I was too shocked at what she was saying to know what it might be. Would my silence confirm or deny there was something going on? I should say something, but I couldn't think straight. Something about her delivery, the lack of finesse and introduction told me she spoke the truth – or a version of it at least. So it was a game with Rodman. I wasn't surprised there had been others. Us broken girls loved a good chunk of emotional sadomasochism.

'Those who sleep with dogs shall rise with fleas,' I said.

'Sorry?'

'It's an expression.'

'And what do you mean by that?'

'I'm sorry for the girl, but part of me feels like she must have known what she was getting herself into. Thanks for looking out for me, Officer Frampton. It's nice to know someone cares. Now if you don't mind I really must get some sleep. My daughter has her school elections tomorrow—'

'On a Sunday?' questioned Frampton. And I hadn't even meant to lie.

'I mean Monday. There's a lot to do and I'd like to make a better impression than I did today. Do you know what I mean?' It was rhetorical.

'I can see myself out. No long trips anywhere mind,' she said, smiling again like a clown at a children's party. I heard the door shut – louder than it needed to – and seconds later a car drove away.

I wondered who this girl was. How old she was? How he'd left her. He had some weight behind him and I imagined that if you weren't consensually allowing yourself to be pinned to a wall by his body, he could really hurt you. I felt stupid. I needed a drink. And a joint. And some pills, but I didn't have enough. I'd made a mockery of Mother's memory by allowing this man to make me feel alive, and for what? So I could be a joke. A locker room laugh. A story he told down the pub with his detective friends: 'Do you remember that stupid bitch?' it would start, and they'd laugh – not because they'd remember but because just that was enough to be a joke. Ransacking my handbag, I found the pill bottle half-full. I opened the cupboard desperately hoping to find an unopened box of paracetamol. There were bottles of flavoured oils and various types of Sri Lankan pickle, but no little white pills to make life just that little bit more bearable.

I sat down and rolled a joint. The paper made an L shape. L for loser. L for liar. L for like you have a fucking chance at being happy. It makes sense that Ava's not my real daughter. I couldn't have a child. What would grow in a barren womb like mine? One-legged freaks with oversized heads and three eyes. Not cute, just deformed. Wrong conditions. Wasteland. Conditions to thrive are nada. Nothing encouraging in the lining, just toxic gases. A belly rotting. That's why people like me are given children instead. It's actually a very sophisticated process of elimination. Earth mothers to the left and infested uteruses to the right please. To create life your own life had to mean something didn't it?

Didn't it? DIDN'T IT?? Someone fucking answer me!

There was a knock at the door. Were they serious? What the fuck. Had the powers that be sent someone to answer my question? Was Rodman back to pummel me senseless, like some insightful men just instinctively know a woman wants? Was Frampton here to arrest me? I walked through the hallway as I'd done so many times this evening. Maybe I'd just leave the front door open.

'I'm sorry,' said Papa holding a brown paper bag in his arms, 'I forgot my key.'

'No problem.' I walked back to the kitchen.

'Everything okay?' said he asked, putting his bag on the table.

'Fine.'

The trick is not to see them as your parents. The minute you do you're fucked. That's when the disappointment hits – the expectation, the resentment, the hurt. Who needs it? I had a quirky flatmate who due to similar blood work knew intimate details of my early life. That's all.

'How's Ava?' he asked, noticing his flies were undone and doing them up.

'Good.' Most men don't decide to become fathers, they just want to have sex. Some deal with the consequences of that sex better than others.

'Maybe soon we can have a movie night,' he suggested. I peered into the bag. DVDs.

'If you want.'

He looked excited.

'Shall I get some popcorn? Do you like popcorn?'

'No.'

'I'll get some for Ava?'

'Ok.'

He picked up his bag to go.

'Did Mother want me?' I was starting to shake now I'd asked the question, wishing I hadn't. I was scared of the answer.

'Drea. Why are you bringing all that business up?' he asked, instantly irritated. 'Let it go.'

L is for let it go. L is for leave it alone.

'Nothing, I… just wondered.'

'Of course she wanted you. She just didn't know how to want herself. It's two separate things and your mother could never – what do you call it – multi-task very well.'

Protests

The bed should have warmed up but it was still cold. I'd been awake for what felt like hours. I could tell I hadn't slept because my body was tired but my eyes were already open. I was scared. The feeling lay next to me in the bed. Long and thin. Quiet like a friend, but friends weren't meant to make you feel scared were they? I didn't have too much experience but I didn't think so. The feeling had its eyes open too. Watching me. Ready to do what I did. Go where I went. It came closer but I knew it wouldn't be enough. It wanted to get inside me. Be me.

Pills. I needed to refill the bottle. I searched for meaning and for the exact point where my life had become so unmanageable. It was since the pill bottle had been half emptied that events had truly escalated. The bottle needed to be empty or full, not this half-arsed, half-decided, I'm-not-sure-if-I'm-a-suicide-aid-or-a-pain-reliever arrangement. Who needs this aimless drifting through life – trying to jump over one hurdle, knowing that just when I've got into my stride there'll be another. I was too scared to come out of the bedroom, let alone from under the duvet, in case I bumped into Ava or her friends.

I brushed my teeth, avoiding the mirror. If the girls found out I wasn't here, they'd just have to make their own way to school. But if they saw me there was no way I'd get out of it. Not on election day. I grabbed my bag and edged the door open as slowly as I could manage, peering out into the deserted hallway. No one. No noise. Not even seven o' clock yet. So far so good. I edged it open a little more and put a toe on the wooden floorboards. It wasn't that I no longer thought of Alex. I thought of him now, and wished the fucker had banged a couple of nails in these boards whilst he was banging everything else. I crept on tip-toes holding on to the banister. Past Papa's room and the deep rumblings of sleep that thundered from inside. I got to the end and put my hand on the balled newel post.

'A-V-A, Vote and have your say, A-V-A

'If you want change, vote A-V-A.'

Tabatha and Amelia came kicking their way out of Ava's room in their cheerleading uniforms. Ava wore a pleated knee-length skirt and my mother's old silk blouse and looked like… like Mother.

'For luck,' she smiled, shrugging her shoulders. Only Ava would think wearing her dead step-grandmother's blouse could be lucky. I was suffocating. I couldn't do it. How were you meant to turn children into these balanced individuals when you were nothing like what you were encouraging them to be? It helped that Ava appeared to be doing a good job on her own. So then what was I doing here in this life, anyway?

'I'm nervous,' she said. Tabatha and Amelia were twirling over the banisters and heading down the stairs, practising their moves.

'There's no need.'

'Politics is quite exposing,' she said thoughtfully. 'I keep asking myself "Can I do this. Am I this person? Will people like me enough to think I can do this"?'

'You don't need people to like you, you just need them to vote for you,' I pointed out.

'But if they don't like you, they don't vote.' She bit her lip.

'Stop biting – and yes, good point, but that's not the way to think about it. You need to think about why you want to be president. Because you can do a good job. You think about that. Think about the things you want to change and then people will think about that too. Don't focus on the shit. Shit is not inspiring. You are. You are inspiring. You inspire me every day just by being you. That's why people will vote for you. People need to be inspired.' I held her in my arms and hoped to God she knew how special she was.

'I feel like that was a real Kennedy-style campaign speech,' she said tumbling out of my grasp.

'I learned from the best,' I said nodding in the direction of Papa's bedroom just as a humungous snore built to a crescendo and then tumbled down again. Ava and I laughed.

'He wants to have movie night soon,' I said.

'Movie night?'

'Yup. That was my reaction.'

'Okay sure,' Ava agreed.

'He said he's getting you popcorn.'

'Oh no, are we watching a western?'

'If you're lucky.'

The girls chatted away in the back, reminding me of busy bees at a honey pot. Being the taxi driver bestowed an anonymity I was grateful for, today of all days. The horoscope in the local paper for Aquarius read 'Life is challenging at the moment. You will want to lay low. Do it.' Genius fortune tellers or a crock of shit? Didn't help me either way. I was feeling jittery, in need of a distraction to quiet the thoughts. The thoughts were racing, screaming 'you thought he could love you. Ha.' I put the radio on. Someone else's voice. Someone else's fucking thoughts.

'You're tuned into *Abigail in the Morning* and may I be the first to say how very glad I am that you are. So what are we talking about today? What's hot and what's not. I tell you what always seems to be hot, and that's schools. Education. The controversial and provocative subject of how to school our young people. And today there is a demonstration about that very subject. We radio presenters love a good protest because it gives us lots of juicy things to talk about. But when did it all get so complicated? Has it always been so? Did Adam want to send Cain to a private school but Eve vehemently disagreed? I don't know. Does it go that far back or have we created something for ourselves that wasn't necessary for all our predecessors? Now I don't mean to ostracise other religions from this debate, far from it, it's just that I'm a lapsed Christian myself so when searching the recesses of my mind for religious figures that's where I go. But please I want to hear from Muslims, Hindus, Jews. Everyone. This is about all of us isn't it? Call in and tell us what you think. Who's on first? We've got Mercy in Hawthorn? Hello Mercy, tell me all about it.'

'Well Abigail, I don't have long because my friend will ring the doorbell any minute now. We're going on that march you were talking about against this new faith school, but I just wanted to say that we're not a religious country. We shouldn't have religious schools or other religions taking over our streets. Religion is the Devil's work. It makes us turn on each other and hate our fellow man.'

'Mercy, you do know that this particular faith school is Catholic?'

'Yes I do.'

'Just checking. So Mercy is against but no doubt they'll be people there today that are very much in favour of the new school. I'm not a million miles away from you, Mercy. I'm not a great fan of religion myself. I don't think I'd go as far as to bring the devil into the mix –that's a bit too religious for me – but aren't people at liberty to educate their children by whatever doctrine or philosophy they see fit? We like to see ourselves as a tolerant society after all.

'Tolerance and religion don't go together. They are diametrically opposed to each other and anyone that tells you different is a liar.'

'How tolerant are we being condemning people as liars because they're attempting to suggest that religion could be a positive influence. Mercy? Mercy? Ok, so I think Mercy's friend must have arrived. Who do we have next? Ezekiel. Ezekiel – a good sturdy Biblical name, what are your thoughts? For or against?'

'They named me Ezekiel in the Christian orphanage in India. I am born and brought up in Mumbai and am travelling with Doctors without Borders for the next three months. I am in UK for just few days but I heard your show and wanted to call, Abigail.'

'And call Abigail you did Ezekiel. Where does all this sit with you?'

'I'm not sitting. I'm standing.'

'What would you like to say?'

'Well, I studied at an Indian school. In the orphanage, we were lucky if we got education after age seven but I worked hard and I think if you work hard this is what makes the difference. It is the student and not always the school that is the key.'

'Ezekiel, that is a marvellous point and grossly overlooked, I think. In fact, if my days at Sunday school serve me right, the prophet Ezekiel actually wrote the eponymous book whilst being held in captivity.'

'That is correct.'

'And there's no better evidence for the "it's the student not the school" argument than that. Thank you, Ezekiel. Doing a great job, by the way, working in the marvellous charity organisation Doctors without Borders. We've got time for one more caller before we head to the news. Susanna from Herrick, you're on the air.'

'That's not my real name.'

'Ok. Well I'll just go ahead and call you Susanna anyway. What would you like to say, dear? For or against?'

'Nothing is that simple. Sometimes you have a plan and the plan changes and then you have to think about what the best thing to do is so that your children don't suffer.'

'Susanna, can you elaborate for us?'

'… A friend of mine was promised a place in a school and then the school took it back. Now she has to find her child another school.'

'Took it back? What was the reason for this?'

'It's a private school. It came down to money.'

'But surely your money and Joe Blogg's money is the same colour?'

Silence on the radio. I recognised the voice but couldn't place the face.

'Was something other than money involved?'

'… My friend was told she had a place that where the fees would be greatly reduced.'

'Like a discount, or maybe even free?'

'Yes. But then the place was given away.'

'I see. So the original terms were not honoured, leaving your friend thinking about sending her child to the new faith school.'

'Yes.'

'Because there is nowhere else?'

'Not that doesn't involve an hour commute.'

'So we need it. If there are children who are having school places promised and taken away, whatever the circumstances, then we do need another school. I suppose then the question is, does it need to be a faith school?

'I have to go now.'

'Right, uh, well ok, that seems to be a good time to go to a commercial break. Thank you to Susanna who made a valuable point. What if this school is actually necessary and not about religion, but simply education? How desperate would you be if your child didn't get into the right school and what lengths would you go to, to get them in?'

Good to know that other people had problems too. It made a difference sometimes to turn on the radio and hear that the world was just as fucked up as things were in your own head. That you were not alone.

They had closed random roads off because of the protests and helpfully put up diversion signs that would have worked if I was a squirrel and could drive my car made of nuts up a tree. I saw a group of boys pointing and giggling as the cars kept turning around when they reached the large oak. They must have moved some of the signs around as a prank. Ha ha, very funny. Cocks. Young, still-forming, adolescent cocks. If you're still pulling this shit when you're a fully formed, adult cock, I'll key your car.

I could see people moving en mass across the park. They held placards and home-made cardboard signs with slogans in capital letters: 'WE DON'T NEED DIRTY PRIESTS, WE WANT CLEANER STREETS' and 'SAVE OUR SCHOOL – HOLY CONVENT OF THE BLESSED ST MARY MAGDALENE AND OUR SACRED LORD JESUS CHRIST.' Catchy name. It seemed as if, whilst on route to the site of the new school, the for and against factions had been forced to become one – a cohesive unit walking together by order of the road diversion, with only their placards to differentiate their loyalties. I pulled up at the lights whilst a group of five or six people walked in front of the car and into the park. I was shocked to see Felicity amongst them. She waited in the middle of the crossing, waving someone to hurry along. It was Maude with a 'Save Mary' sign.

I dropped Ava and her campaign managers off at school and drove straight to the apothecary. Pushing open the door,

I saw the man-sized penis in his white coat standing behind the counter and was unpleasantly reminded that in times of intense disquietude, and despite running an apothecary, Dick was an anti-comfort. In my more reflective moments, I wondered if my detestation was born of similarity. To see someone is to acknowledge them. Dick couldn't see me and I just saw a dick.

'Maude's not here,' he boomed before the tinkle announcing the next customer had finished ringing.

'I need some paracetamol,' I said.

'Size?'

'Large, Dick.' He took a box down from the shelf and put it in a paper bag. 'I just saw Maude and Felicity.'

'You saw them?' he asked, surprised.

'Yes.'

'Where?'

'In the park.'

'Oh.' He quietened instantly.

'How much?'

'What for?' he said absentmindedly.

'The pills.'

'I don't know,' Dick answered.

'They had placards for the march. Good of Maude to give her time like that. Not sure I feel so good about Felicity roaming the park alone, and by alone I mean without handcuffs. How much?' All the time I was talking I had been looking in my bottomless bag for my purse, not looking at Dick. When I finally found it and looked up Dick was ashen. Spooked.

'Shut up,' he said. I looked behind me. 'Shut up,' he said again, puerile and reactive, even though I hadn't said anything. He appeared as if he was looking straight at me but he was looking through me. 'Shut up, shut up, SHUT UP, SHUT UP, SHUT UP!' I grabbed the pills and stuffed them into my trouser pocket with the intention of leaving the shop as fast as I could. Our relationship was acrimonious in so many ways and had been building over the years towards exactly this kind of outburst, but something told me this wasn't about me and that I was in the right apothecary at the wrong time. There was a woman on a poster by the door, smiling with gleaming teeth, advertising the new sensations she was experiencing with HRT. Come in and ask your pharmacist it said on the poster. I would have to recommend against this. The pharmacist had lost the plot. Maybe he should be taking some HRT himself. Dick was still shouting as the door tinkled, closing behind me.

I felt better now the paracetamol was stocked up again. Humans weren't good with change. Even the ones who said they were. We were creatures of habit and for most of us change signified pain. We could try and hide, stay away from possible threats and catalysts, but life found us in the end. Life was all about feeling. There was no other way out. And whilst I thought I was safe from the monsters of my childhood – from the suicidal mother who didn't love me who lurked underneath my bed and where I knew never to look – there were other monsters. The relationship monster sat in the back of the car, confident, telling jokes to the other monsters, working the crowd. 'How can someone love you if you can't love yourself?' Big guffaws. What a comedian. The shame monster rode legs akimbo in the passenger seat, audacious, brazen. A smooth talker. Listing all the times he'd talked happiness into taking a long walk off a short pier. The low self-esteem monster was a shady character, could sell ice to Eskimos, so it had no trouble in convincing confidence that she'd walked into the wrong room again. One thing they all agreed on was that the pills needed to be stocked up and within easy reach. Depleted stocks of paracetamol had caused dissent in the ranks, almost in-fighting; a danger of being monsters without purpose. After my trip to the apothecary, they were united again. We all felt calmer. Life was a morass, no getting away from the feelings but the trick was to block the fuckers out.

I had to be at the school and pick Ava up at twelve. Half-day. I wound down the window. The sign ahead pointed left for the cemetery. Sadness filled my body like sand in an egg timer, every space, every particle, right down to the ends of my eyebrows and the tips of my fingernails. I had avoided seeing Mother, and Papa never once asked me to come with him or ever made me feel guilty for not going. If I was to visit her now, what would be the reason? And did a daughter need a reason to be close to her mother? Was the fact that I needed to find one part of the problem? The cemetery was a beautiful place. I thought I'd go for a drive.

I parked the car and pushed open the large black metal gates. The trees were huge, expansive beings, some forty feet tall, three or four feet in diameter and drenched in moss. The branches were so wide they tended to touch each other, as if reaching out, arms outstretched to form a collective. Moss dripped down from them, long skeins of ash green. Some skeins were more than eight feet in length, choking at the branches with their rootless, thin and scaly stems. The trees gave the impression that, because their roots reached deep down to the many who were buried underground, that you were not alone. The place was teeming with birdsong and the lively sonata of insects. I was suddenly struck by the intense living beauty of the graveyard and wondered if that was why Papa had put her here, so she could live. Maybe it wasn't us who kept her legacy alive but the cemetery, pushing her decayed corpse to find life amongst the ancient oaks and allowing her to breathe again.

I didn't even know where she lay and the cemetery spanned out in every direction as far as the eye could see. Anything that wasn't flat stood out in a cemetery. I wandered over to a small cabin that sat on the outskirts by tall metal railings, separating the dead and the living. The door was open.

'Hello.' He didn't look up from his crossword. 'Nine letters. Begins with S and ends in E. Spend Christmas with one's family.'

'Suffocate,' I said.

'S,u,f,f,o,c,a,t,e. That's it,' he exclaimed.

He looked up. 'How did you know it was cryptic?'

'I didn't. I'm looking for someone.'

'Hope it wasn't important, love,' he chuckled. 'It's a bit late, if you know what I mean.' He had about three teeth that I could count, and by the way his gurning smile spread across his face I think I was able to count them all.

'Dorothy Peiris.'

'Dotty! Lovely lady. Quiet as a mouse. Who are you?'

'Her daughter. Drea.'

'Rodman told me about you. I bet she's sick of the sight of ya,' he said. 'Told me to tell ya to stay away. She don't wanna hear you no more. Whittling on,' he laughed, holding his belly.

'I've been busy,' I said.

'Mothers and daughters. You don't need to explain. I'm post-op meself – born Edwina and changed to Edward, Ed. After I had it tucked away, I saw the difference like you wouldn't believe – me and the old dear get on like an 'ouse on fire now, but before that, it was messy. If you want to talk to ya mum, now's the best time coz she can't answer back.'

'It wasn't like that. She died when I was young. Killed herself. I didn't know her.'

'Tortured soul was she? There's many a them walking the earth I'll tell ya that for nuffin'.' So Dotty had her demons. Well, at least this way you never became one of 'em. There's comfort to be found everywhere, you just gotta look. You see, all muvvas love in the best way they know how. It's instinctive. And wiv some muvvas, it's as much good as a chocolate teapot.

Plot E. Keep walking past the wisteria and stay on the right. You'll be reunited soon enough. And love—'

'Yes?' I said, nearly gone.

'You'll make ole' bones you will, so don't you worry 'bout following in your muvva's footsteps.'

The air clung to my face. It was cold but I took off my coat anyway and carried it in my arms. Large slabs of stone interspersed with weeds and flowers surrounded me like a patchwork quilt of death. This was what was left. After the lives had been lived, they ended here. It was a sublime cemetery, which had to be said because if it mattered – if the beauty of these large gothic oaks could be appreciated at all once we were gone – then this was the place to be. And if those left behind needed somewhere to go, to be, to spend time beside the dearly departed, then it was an especially serene setting in which to wait awhile. It was as serene as anywhere could be whilst bodies rotted in layer upon layer of decaying composition. It all made sense. What made less sense was why I was here. Why I was walking through plot C, mystifying myself by my actions, walking towards the grave of Dorothy Peiris – a woman known better by the caretaker of the cemetery in which she lay than by me. Was this all because Rodman had used her as my alibi? Was I trying to prove that I was a good daughter, or had the pernicious hand of guilt clawed its way in? Guilt telling me, 'She's your mother. You should be kneeling by her grave arranging fresh flowers. You should be in pieces amongst other devastated daughters tormented by the hole, the void that keeps getting bigger now that the one person who had the potential to think the best of you is gone.'

What was I going to say when I reached her? I'm sorry you left. I'm sorry you left without me knowing you. I'm sorry you left without you knowing me. I'm sorry you destroyed the life of a man who loved you. And what would she say?

Nothing. And if she did speak, if her ghostly gases became vapour long enough to communicate with me, what could she say? Live your life, my darling girl, to its very fullest and love yourself, my sweet child. Well fuck you – you didn't.

I turned around and found myself walking back to the car so quickly that when I looked down at my legs they were running. I heard muffled screams coming from the earth. They were calling me back, all the disgruntled, unloved souls, desperate for some attention. Some wanted to make peace, say all the things they'd been too scared to say. Others screamed louder, wanting to wreak havoc, still suffering from the pain of human injustice. It didn't matter that they did not know me, they just needed someone to listen. My coat fell and I kept on running. I saw Ed pelting out of his cabin.

'Everything okay?' he called out. 'What did she say? She didn't mean it love. I bet she's bored stiff.'

The Results

When I got to the school, part of me wondered if I should have stayed at the cemetery. It was heaving with people and there was even a van with a camera crew setting up. Although these were student elections, two unsolved murders meant the turf war between Gatlin and the Holy Convent of St Mary Magdalene and Our Sacred Lord Jesus Christ was hotting up, and nothing screamed media more than a murder at a school. I sat in the car in the school car park, rolled down the window and lit the butt of a joint. The noise of nervous political excitement filled the air and rushed into the car, but the silent screams of desperate corpses still echoed in my ears. Desperate. Desperate for redemption. Desperate for acceptance. These were corpses whose families could not or would not be there for them, so they latched onto any grief-stricken passer-by.

How desperate would you be? Abigail had asked her viewers that question just this morning. The two murders had to be connected. If Felicity had killed Victoria and everyone else had an alibi, who was desperate enough to kill Penelope that Felicity might lie for? In the sun, a shadow lingered for a moment.

'Beginning to think you're more school-spirited than I gave you credit for,' said Rodman, opening the car door. He sat down. Something about his smell was so familiar. I could smell the rain. Or rather the smell of the earth as it prepared itself to receive the rain. That's what he smelled like. He smelled like I'd known that scent my whole life. Nourishing. Trustworthy. But the earth could also swallow people up. Bury them. Was I losing myself with this man? How much of myself did I even have left that I hadn't already lost years ago?

'Big police presence at the school for today's elections. Must be because of the murder count that's racking up. Frampton's avoiding me and it's making me wonder if she's found something.' He pushed the seat back as far as it could go to accommodate his huge legs. 'Whatever she's got, she's got to share it with me and if she's not, then I'm wondering why. I don't think it's because she knows about us. There's no way she can know about us—'

'She knows about us.'

'What?' he exclaimed.

Something hit me. I jumped in my seat. 'What did you just say to me?'

'What do you mean she knows about us?' snapped Rodman.

'When you got into the car, you said something to me. About school?' What had he said? Whatever it was I'd heard it somewhere before. 'That's it. You said "That's very school-spirited of you" or something like that.'

'So?' He wasn't interested in remembering. He thought it wasn't important. How wrong he was. Maude had said that to me when I came for the police interview at the school. That was the voice on the radio. The last caller. It was Maude.

'Drea?' he demanded.

'Frampton came to my house after you left. To inform me about the sexual assault charge that was filed against you,' I said.

'Fuck.' He looked down. 'Oh. That's why the cold shoulder. I knew we were tougher than a disagreement on education,' he said cynically. 'It was never "assault".'

'She asked you to hit her?'

'It was a relationship. That I ended and that she didn't take too well.'

'A relationship. I see.'

'It's not professional and it's not something I set out to do.'

'It certainly felt like you set out to do me,' I said.

'Drea, don't be childish. It's two different things.'

'Sounds pretty similar.'

'Seriously, you're gonna do this?' He was angry and banged his fist down hard on the dashboard. I wasn't sure if it was the force of his reaction or because we were sitting in a school car park in the daytime surrounded by plenty of potential witnesses that made me feel like maybe things weren't as black and white as Frampton had led me to believe.

'She lied. I never touched her. Look if you want to pretend this is nothing, you can do that. I work long hours and sometimes shit happens with the wrong people.' He was annoyed and grunted like a hurt bull in a pen.

'I think Maude killed Penelope.'

'Maude Spencer. Felicity's sister. Why?'

'I don't know exactly. But when you're desperate, it's family who protect you. And Felicity gave Maude an alibi.'

'If you had to guess.'

'Then I'd say Gatlin promised her kid a place at the school and then took it away.'

'So what?'

'Penelope's on the board and high up in the PTA. She must have been the one who pulled the place.'

'There's a strong smell of marijuana in this car.'

'You have no idea what people will do for their kids. It's not logical. Being a parent is messy. Dick's unravelling. Yes, it makes sense—'

'It makes no sense—'

'Talk to Dick. He knows something. The sisters are giving each other alibis, aren't they?'

'Well, yes but—'

'None of this is what you think it is. People don't always feel what they should feel. Robberies and murders are not always committed by the same person, and these murders happen to have been committed, not by the abused children of Mormon sex offenders whose only light source was a bowed floor board in the ceiling of a cellar, but by nice people; good, and obviously desperate people.' We were all desperate in some way. Was that what life was really about – getting better at managing our own desperation? Maybe even being more honest about it. I got out and left Rodman sitting in my car. He was listening. He couldn't quite believe it but he had listened. No one was left in the playground. Everyone must have already moved into the hall for the election results and I suddenly felt a huge surge of pride. Ava would find out today whether she had been voted school president and I knew what an enormous amount of courage it had taken for her to put herself up there, especially in the cruel and lonely face of other people's judgements. It's certainly not an arena I'd have thought I'd ever see Ava in, and maybe I was even prouder because of this. Alex would be too. However, Catherine wasn't any old adversary. That girl's jealousy ran thick through her veins and she would fight this to the end. But Ava had wanted something and gone out there to get it. Whatever happened, good for her.

As I walked down the corridor, I heard cheering. A host of uninvited butterflies flew into the pit of my stomach. If this was what I was feeling, Ava must have been shitting herself. When I entered, I was shocked to see not just the parents of the candidates but all the other parents too. A short-haired American girl with a high-pitched, nasal voice – perfect for Crufts – was shrilly barking orders at a camera crew. An anaemic-looking Maude and gaunt Felicity stood together at the top of the hall in conversation with Ann who was pointing and gesturing. Regina and her husband Andrew were seated next to Henrietta and Henry. Regina glowing with adultery, Henrietta constipated with anger. The men were deep in conversation, oblivious. A loud, sharp crackling from a microphone boomed from the speakers, violently jolting the crowd.

'Attention everyone,' said the voice of Lady Clarissa Gatlin, a buxom lady in her mid-fifties with the wealth and connections to leave the lesser-known vagabonds of the royal family's outer circle trembling in their suede Sunday loafers. She had little to do with the school except in name but had obviously donned a corset and sheer stockings for the cameras. Nothing better to wipe away the unsightly memories of two murdered mothers than some class and refinery from a living, stately grandmother. I could see Su Lee clapping vigorously.

'Welcome everyone to what I'm sure will prove to be a most exciting election day at Gatlin. I believe,' she looked over to Felicity and Maude, 'that we're coming to the end of the third and final count. The results are imminent, so while that's happening let me take this opportunity to tell you all about some great accolades Gatlin has received in the last few months, proving that we really do need to keep growing the schools we have and putting our money and resources into existing institutions.' She began droning on about how great the school was, with constant references to their excellent accomplishments in badminton. Rodman and Frampton entered inconspicuously from the back: a policewoman in uniform and a senior detective in a cheap suit working a live murder case. The place was farcical and Ava was maybe the only real thing in it. Frampton was eyeballing me. Unashamedly and with purpose.

'I need to talk to you,' said a little voice. I turned around to see Tabatha. Another one trying to blend unseen into the crowd, in full cheerleading regalia.

'What is it?'

'My diary's missing,' she said. It didn't sound like an accusation so I didn't admit to reading it.

'I'm sure it's a page-turner. Sounds like a matter for the police rather than me. They're at the back,' I nodded.

'Yes, I'm worried it might be a matter for the police—'

'Ladies and gentlemen, I believe we are ready. Candidates please.' Tabatha disappeared into the crowd, a lithe cheerleading unicorn, as the heavy red velvet curtain pulled back and Ava and Catherine emerged from either side. Ava had her hair in plaits and was slowly turning the same shade as the curtains, whilst Catherine showed us how wide her thin lips could stretch with all the composure and confidence of a dwarf show pony.

'Voting is now closed and the ballots have been counted and verified. The president for the next school year is…' Lady Clarissa opened the folded paper and took a deep breath. She hesitated… 'Ava Thorn!'

The hall erupted into a cavernous cacophony of noisy cheering. I was stunned, and despite myself I choked on a crag of uninvited emotion. In a shameless bid for attention, said emotion managed to shoot a tear out of my eye. Quickly wiping it away, I pushed past the excited hoards and got to the front. Ava was rooted to the spot, overwhelmed and in apparent disbelief. Not a good look for a president.

Cheering became interspersed with louder jeering. Regina and Henrietta were on their feet booing. I felt blood surge into my hands and face, sizzling. Fucking bitches from hell. Such loyalty to their cult leader born out of their twisted sorority; however, Ann was clapping, smiling, and giving the most frightening and juxtaposed expression of a graceful loser.

What did she know that I didn't? Lady Clarissa looked uncomfortable. She was searching in the wings for moral support, but Maude and Felicity had vanished. Tabatha and Amelia were dancing on either side of a star-struck Ava. Reluctantly, Catherine moved off the stage, but not too far away, glaring from the steps.

'Ava,' I shouted, up to the stage. Long creamy extremities flashed perpendicular shapes whilst chanting Ava's name. Tabatha and Amelia had great bodies. Wonderfully nubile, toned flesh that was probably making it difficult for some of the fathers to concentrate on the real politics at the heart of the election.

'Ava!' I screamed, and she looked down slowly as if, were she to glance any quicker, she might fall off the narrow precipice she wavered on and into the crashing sea.

'You've won, my darling girl!! Congratulations!! Now pull yourself together. Give a speech. Thank the voters. Act like a fucking president.' She could hear me and was taking in the information to process. Her eyes began to lose their glaze. She tapped on the microphone hesitantly. My heart dropped into a restricted access area of my stomach where things were able to fall lower than they should but not fall out.

'Hello,' she said, to the microphone. Tabatha and Amelia stopped cheering. The room began to hush bringing itself to a quiet equilibrium.

'I want to thank everyone who voted for me,' she spoke, quietly at first, but with a measured gait, tentatively looking around the room. She took a moment. 'I didn't know I wanted to be school president. I assumed that the qualities you needed to be a good one were not ones that I possessed, but I was wrong. I think a good president needs to be passionate, interested and dedicated and I am all those things. I'm also a little shocked,' she smiled and the crowd murmured receptively, 'but I'll get over that. Thank you to Catherine for everything you have done for the school so far. I'm excited for my term as new school president and know that together, we're going to achieve great things. I also really want to thank everyone who voted for me, Tabatha and Amelia, and especially my mum – thank you for always believing in me.' Ava smiled at me. This must be the moment that you spend your whole life as a mother secretly waiting for. Unprompted, unexpected, public acknowledgement. She filled me up.

What happened next was quick, and changed everything. Catherine started running up the steps. Once on stage she pushed Ava hard and Ava, who was not expecting it, toppled to the floor sliding over in my direction. The crowd gasped in unison.

'What the fuck is wrong with you' I screamed at Catherine as I ran onto the stage.

Catherine cleared her throat at the microphone. Apparently even in times of high adrenalin fuelled catastrophe, having a good, clear speaking voice was paramount.

'Ava's mother robbed Mrs Crosly-Burke.' The crowd gasped again. All eyes were on me and Ava.

'It's true,' continued Catherine, 'and as the robber and the murderer are the same person, the new school president's mother is a murderer!' Another gasp from the crowd. She was a convincing orator, I'd give her that. Frampton snaked her way forward, shoulders square, chin slightly raised and on alert, hands fisted.

'Mum, what's she saying?' said Ava. 'Stop it. Stop saying those things about my mum.'

'Oh for God's sake, it's not like she's your real mum,' said Catherine, a fact that made Ava lose all reason. She jumped up and lunged at Catherine who, not expecting such demonstrative behaviour from the new school president, was floored as they both slid across the stage.

'Get off my daughter!' screamed Ann, running onto the stage pulling Ava's plaits.

'Get off my daughter!!' I screamed jumping on top of Ann. Catherine and Ava broke away from underneath us to wrestle with further freedom and, as Ann and I rolled off them, a gunshot brought us all to attention. All eyes turned to Su Lee who appeared to have fired a gun at the ceiling.

'I solly. I cally gun now. I no want to die.' I saw a police officer snaking his way through the crowd toward her.

'Miss Peiris, you're under arrest for the robbery of Mrs Crosly-Burke, and the murders of Mrs Coultard and Mrs Taylor-Singh,' Frampton called out across the room as she walked up the steps with her cuffs swinging in her hand. 'And me!' squeaked Regina.

'You're not dead. Yet!' I screamed.

'She robbed me as well and she threatened my daughter.'

'And that is why you wore a last-season Marc Jacobs coat and bag a few weeks ago,' sneered Henrietta. Shame filled Regina's face.

'Where's the evidence? I don't know anything about this,' said Rodman, asserting himself into what had clearly become Frampton's investigation.

'There's evidence,' she said, without looking at him.

'What is it?'

'A diary.'

'Fuck,' said Tabatha.

'What?' asked Ava.

'It's my fault. It's not real,' she said and I saw her exchange an agonising glance with Ava. 'I wrote some stuff in my diary, but it wasn't real,' she pleaded. 'It was just made-up shit.'

'What did you write?' asked Ava.

'You're taking a teenage girl's diary into evidence which she herself is denying,' said Rodman, pushing his body into her space.

'Yes,' said Frampton decisively.

'That's bullshit,' said Rodman.

'Why would Tabatha write in her diary that you robbed her mother if it wasn't true?' spat Ann.

'You wrote that?' Ava asked, her mouth falling open.

'Yes. But I didn't mean it. It's not true—'

'Then why would you write it—'

Ava's stared at Tabatha and her face contained so much disappointment in her new friend, it was too much to bear. I couldn't do that to Ava.

'It is true,' I said. 'I did rob Henrietta and Regina, but I did not kill anyone.' The entire time I was speaking, I felt as though my body was on fire. I couldn't look at Ava. I didn't need to. Shame consumed me. Told me exactly how she must have been feeling. Screamed it at me in fact. The people around me became blurry at the edges. I felt as if my insides were on the outside. Like a leper. Open sores of disappointment exposed on my body. I was disgusted with myself, I didn't need to look at all the people who were disgusted with me too. How could I have let her down so badly?

'We'll let a jury see about that,' replied Frampton, putting the cuffs on my wrists as if she had sentenced me already.

'Hell hath no fury like a woman scorned,' I said. Her face froze for a second and then she turned her head quickly. I thought she looked towards Rodman, but then thought better of it.

'Mum?' Ava looked imploringly at me for some kind of explanation.

'There's a chance I won't be home tonight, but you make sure you celebrate darling. There's pizza in the fridge and your Grandpa wants to watch a movie with you. I'll be home – just as soon as I can.' The crowd came together, assimilating into one thuggish personality, hurling out their condemnations. 'MURDERER,' 'LOCK HER UP,' 'DOG KILLER.'

As Frampton pushed me like a human shield through the throngs of flabbergasted teachers, parents and children, my attention was diverted by Tabatha and Amelia's pom-poms. Four heaps of fat, once shimmering, tassels had been cast away. Pom-poms, that just had to be happy and shaking all the time because if they weren't happy for a single second they'd collapse into sad balls of disillusioned apathy. Ava's big day was ruined and yet she looked confused rather than angry. A sharp stabbing pain in my heart caught me off guard and I inhaled sharply.

'You ok?' asked Frampton, as we approached the doors

'I need the toilet.' I had fifty pills in my pocket. 'It'll have to wait till we get to the station,' she said, her mouth fixed in a repugnant sneer.

'Well, it can't. You think I'd have a problem pissing in your car,' I smiled, a straight one. I wanted to try it and see what all the fuss was about. How women like Ann, Frampton and the like pulled off acting like bitches through the thin guise of a winning smile. It felt weird as I suspected it would.

'Make it quick,' said Frampton when we got outside the student toilets.' You're going to need to undo these,' I said. How she wanted to say no, acting as if, in undoing my handcuffs, she was doing me the greatest favour. I felt her hot, angry breath on my neck. She wanted a version of this with Rodman, but maybe with her in handcuffs and his breath on her neck. I felt sorry for her. Coming to my house in the dead of night like a desperate alley cat, looking for love in all the wrong places. She just wasn't his type. He liked them fucked up, morally ambiguous, broken. Frampton could lose weight, put on a pretty dress, but she'd never be broken. Lucky old Frampton.

All the cubicles were empty and had turned into time machines. I was transported to my high school where I spent so much of that period in the toilets: formative early years hiding from the bullies – the mean girls who ruled the school and everyone in it, including the teachers. I remembered pushing my hair forward into a fringe to cover up the latest bruise I'd received from not ducking quickly enough when a book was chucked at my head. I'd eat my lunch sat on the toilet seat because in the canteen they'd throw food at me to see if they could hit my open mouth. Who needed the park, a steak, a glass of wine? This was a much more fitting tribute. I'd returned to the safety of the school toilets for my swansong. Well done, all you parents who home school. I mean that. Really, well done.

I reached into my pocket and pulled out the bottle. The cap came off like butter in my hands. Everyone was ready. It's not like it was a spur of the moment decision. There were five sinks and I stood in front of the one farthest to the back by the window. I looked in the mirror. Nothing to see. I opened the tap and stuck my head under the faucet and took two. There was plenty of space in my mouth and as time was very much of the essence I'd take four on the next go. The water ran down my face and onto my neck as I held my head to the side. I lifted it up chucking the pills to the back of my throat. Four. I was glad Papa had a girlfriend. He needed someone to talk to. Four more. Even if what they were saying to each other was unspeakable, at least he wasn't on his own anymore. Another four. My room was a mess. I hadn't even made my bed this morning. Ava would do it. I shook my head. Don't want to think about Ava.

Four. That was a good Wattalapan I made if I do say so myself. I wonder what will happen to Felicity? Four more. And to Maude. Another four. And the weird thing is I can understand it now. Four. I did things for Ava I'd never imagined I'd do for anyone. Four. Would I have killed for her? Four. Yes? Would I have lied for her if she'd killed someone? Four. Yes. Loving anyone was a risk. It's a relief at least I don't love myself. Where was the time? Four. Imagine what I'd do if I did. Last four. Live? Probably. I dropped the empty pill bottle in the sink and it rolled around on its side until it eventually found solace in the drain.

Climax

I had never been inside a police cell before and what they saved on interior design I was hoping they had spent on heating: under floor, over floor, not picky. I'd assumed my cell would be made of stone, but maybe I was thinking of the Romans with their law and order. As people of today were choosing stone as a luxury material for their bathrooms, instead I had a stud wall with a metal chair, and steel bars to look through and reflect on how I'd reached such lofty heights.

However, I wasn't in the mood for reflecting.

'Hey. I want to call someone. I get a telephone call don't I?' Frampton strolled up to the bars with jangling keys, a pasted grin on her face that I was now all too familiar with. The calling card of a bunny boiler. A woman who pretended to be sweet, fat and law-abiding, but was really a jealous, grudge-harbouring, penal-twisted, nut job. Okay, she wasn't pretending to be fat.

'Let's have a little chat, Drea.' She unlocked the cell. 'I hope you weren't waiting long. Police business can be so time-consuming. I find I just never have enough hours in the day.' She led me out of the cell and down the hall into a room.

'Let's pop in here where we can be more comfortable, shall we?' The room held a large metal desk and two chairs on either side. She sat me down in the chair furthest from the door. Was I cold from fear? Was my fear of being locked up and someone else deciding when I should be allowed to see the sky literally chilling my blood? Or was it from the fear that my life wouldn't be my own to end anymore?

'Can you uncuff me at least? My wrists hurt,' I said.

'No.' She sat down herself. 'We know you robbed Mrs Crosly-Burke and Mrs Salter and we have obtained indisputable evidence from eBay to support this. We also know you lied about your whereabouts on the nights of both robberies. Be clever, Drea. Tell me why you killed Mrs Coultard and Mrs Taylor-Singh and this will go a lot easier.'

'Will it? So if I admit to two murders, you'll reduce my ten-year sentence for robbery to a traffic fine.'

'Ten years sounds a bit lenient for a double murder, don't you think?' Her brow mock-furrowed. 'I was thinking more along the lines of putting in a good word for you to work a couple of hours in the library. You were a physics teacher, right? And your husband was a teacher too? Before he ran off with his younger mistress?'

'Wrong. If you're trying to rattle me, Alex isn't the way to do it.'

'Okay, Drea. Where should I go instead? Shall I start with your dead mother who killed herself or your step-daughter's aiding and abetting?'

'Ava knew nothing. Stay the fuck away from her.'

'Knew nothing about the murders?' said Frampton.

'Yes.'

'So you did murder those women!' she screamed, banging hard on the table.

'What? No! I'm saying Ava had nothing to do with anything! You're twisting what I'm saying.' She was manipulative as fuck. She threw a firework onto the table and then stepped back to watch it burn. Those tablets were kicking in. I could feel them now. Things were slowing down around me, inside me.

'Am I muddling the thoughts of a cold-blooded killer?' continued Frampton, sarcastically. 'I'm sorry. Let's rewind. Where were you on the night of—'

'Doesn't matter,' announced Rodman, bursting into the room. He looked as dishevelled as he had the first time I'd seen him but his eyes were bright. Like he'd been doing some police work and was fit to burst with newly acquired information, his face tense having tried hard to piece it all together instead of arresting the most obvious suspect in this cockamamie roadshow Frampton was running.

'What are you talking about?' she snapped, tersely.

'The victims of the robberies aren't pressing charges,' he said to my great disbelief. Frampton and I both thought we'd heard wrong and leaned in further.

'What?' said Frampton.

'What do you mean they're not pressing charges?' I said.

'They've recanted. Salter is stating she had a migraine that day and didn't know what she was saying. Apparently she asked Drea to put the clothes on eBay herself. Crosly-Burke has said that after witnessing a stranger kill her dog she became upset and delusional. Therefore, she too has withdrawn her original statement.'

'Stated?' Frampton said, confused.

'I first interviewed Dick Spencer,' said Rodman, looking over at me and then quickly back at Frampton.

'Why?' she asked, annoyed.

'He confessed,' said Rodman.

'To what?' said a confused Frampton.

'To his wife murdering Penelope. She was promised a place at the school for her daughter. It's the reason she took the job as school secretary in the first place. She's been working there for the past five years thinking her kid was in for free.'

'Really?' said Frampton and I in unison.

'Penelope Coultard pulled the place reserved for Maude Spencer's daughter, giving it to a fee-paying student instead. And Felicity Whitefield murdered Victoria Taylor-Singh after Taylor-Singh gave evidence to the school board regarding Felicity's apparent breakdown. The board promptly withdrew their offer of co-ordinator for their exchange programme to India. Maude's husband, Dick Spencer, reckons there were medical issues, HRT or something.'

It was unclear who was more shocked, me or Frampton. We both stared at Rodman, almost waiting for the punchline, but there wasn't one. And as the relief startled to trickle its way over me, I felt small white circles dissolve in my bloodstream.

'Therefore, Drea, Ms Peiris, is free to go,' announced Rodman.

There was silence in the room. It was the kind of silence that I felt would not have been ruined by a string quartet playing Debussy.

'I'll take her home,' said Rodman. Frampton's round eyes shrank into the oval of a jealous feline. She stood up, walked out and slammed the door so hard the table shook beneath my fingers.

I did not expect that. Any of it. Sometimes it's the things that happen that you don't expect that can shock more than any of your worst nightmares. I thought I was done for sure. Handcuffs can do that to a person. It must have had something to do with Tabatha and Amelia. Who else could possibly have had leverage to make Regina and Henrietta keep their mouths shut? No one else would have had any incentive. The girls must have done it for Ava. Did she ask them too? Did that mean that she'd forgiven me? But it was too late now, the pills had started to kick in.

I remember saying little in the car on the way home but thinking about poor Maude and Felicity. How one wrong move had changed their lives forever. How many wrong moves had I made? The stench of leather overpowered me. The sun-dried flesh of animal hide and chemical tannins found its way out of the smooth factory bleached blue head rest and into my dying nostrils.

'Can you open your window please,' I asked, after rolling mine down all the way.

'Sure,' Rodman answered, his large hands and fingers eager and dextrously obliging. His voice had changed. It was lighter, freer.

'This, uh… it must have been tough for you… right? You okay?' He was understandably struggling. I'd been publicly defamed at my daughter's private school elections and released from prison without charge. Rodman was used to finding dead body parts wrapped in plastic sacks. He might be experiencing difficulty pinpointing the exact trauma of this morning's events, but it was sweet of him to try. It's all relative anyway.

'Maybe there'll be another murder and you'll have an iron-clad alibi for once. Gotta look on the bright side you know. Chin up.' I said nothing. I found the expression 'chin up' truly insufferable and yet hearing it from Rodman it somehow sounded endearing. He seemed unchallenged by my silence. Perhaps he put it down to the shock of my near incarceration.

'I mean Frampton seemed like a dog with a bone on this case. I don't know why, but I'm sure it didn't make it easier for you. When a detective wants to see you go down for something, it can feel intense. I should know cos I've been her, the one to make the suspect feel that intensity. I did my best you know, to fend her off. I tried,' he said apologetically, supporting his head as he drove with one hand on the steering wheel. His naivety was astounding, or maybe it was simply that if a man didn't have an interest in fucking a woman he assumed that was where the interest ended. Such confidence in one's penis. Never occurring to him for one moment that maybe Frampton was interested in him.

'Look I know things have happened that were kinda weird for us but now it's all over – now that the case is over. Uggh, look, I'm shit at this. But I gotta eat, you gotta eat. Maybe when you feel like it we can go somewhere and eat. Together.' We pulled up at the kerb by the house. The neighbours' ceanothus had exploded into full bloom, swaying over our doorway like a magnificent hanging basket of bright pink flowers. I was free and I think maybe my daughter loved me. I was free and I had this guy – this intense and intoxicating guy – who liked me. What irony. All this time, life had been emerging around me and now that I was on my way out through a slim crack in the fortress I could see it. My life? Since when was my life worth looking at?

'I'm not going to come in. I mean, if you want me to I can. Do you want me to?' Rodman said, turning the engine off just in case. I shook my head.

'Of course. Didn't think so. Family time. Ok then, well, here's the thing. I've never met anyone like you, Drea. You're different. You don't try and be anything else but you. I don't think you could if you wanted to and it's… well it's really fucking refreshing. Beautiful. You are.' I opened the car door without looking back at him. It wasn't intentional but my body had started to dissolve into milk and slow all the way down so that I couldn't move my neck to turn. Luckily for me. Rodman jumped out and ran round to the other side of the car. I stepped out and as the air hit me. I felt a wave of resignation brush through my hair. It was all going to be fine. It was good I'd gone to the toilet when I'd had the chance. Good I'd had the pills in my pocket and not in my bag. Now this was serendipity. I'd been brought the opportunity and had been equipped with what I needed.

As I got to the step, I faltered and held onto the fence to steady myself. Rodman flew up the path to assist me as the front door opened wide.

'Mum! You're back!' Ava ran to me with gangly legs in her school uniform. The strong, wide reach of Rodman across my waist fell away and was replaced by Ava's willowy arm as she pushed him and he let her.

'You! How dare you arrest my mum like that? It's lies and rubbish and you've got no case at all. Furthermore, my father is a lawyer and he will be—' If she was using Alex to bail me out, I could expect a disturbing defence of adulterous adjectives and passive-aggressive pronouns. Sweet of her to lie though. Looks like I'd done something right.

'Ava – they dropped the charges,' I said, before she dug herself a deeper hole.

'Have they?' she asked, sighing deeply and gratefully. 'Tabatha and Amelia promised they'd—' she stopped talking, looking like she'd swallowed her tongue as she made the astute deduction that Rodman probably wasn't the best person to be privy to that particular disclosure.

'Promised they'd come by and see how you were,' she continued moving her head to the side and looking into the distance, 'because they are concerned. About you…' She trailed off, biting her lips.

'I should go,' said Rodman. As he turned away, I wondered how it was possible that I should meet a man who made me feel as though my tragedy could be beautiful. Like my self-fragmentation might be complexity and my pain was perhaps there to show me where I was going rather than hold me back to where I'd come from. And that if I didn't like such things as parks, people, conventions of niceties and anything with the remotest maternal affiliations, I was still worthy. And he used another word to describe me. What was it? I couldn't remember now. But he made me feel like I still mattered despite all the things I wasn't. How should it be that I was to meet this individual as I neared my forty-first birthday, a day for which I already had a very important date?

'Okay, so Grandpa is home and has popcorn. I know! He's ridiculously excited and I promised I'd watch some movie he's got. He didn't even get sweet and salty he bought cheese flavour. Ugh, rank. Anyway, let's just watch ten minutes of John Wayne trotting up to the OK Corral, then you say you're tired and I'll say I'll take you up to bed and we can talk!' I nodded, allowing her to deposit me on the sofa. She didn't seem angry. I was sure I'd read shame. Had it been and gone. Can shame be escorted to the door so quickly? Wouldn't true shame kick up a fuss, create a ruckus, stage a coup and just do whatever it took to stay? Maybe I had read it wrong. As a self-diagnosed paranoid, it was true I could never be sure. But what else could it be? She fluffed up the cushions and arranged them around me. I lay back, my head heavy. My mouth opened and I couldn't feel my lips.

'Is everyone ready?' said Papa.

'Yes,' answered Ava. She snuggled up to me on the sofa and dropped her head onto my shoulder. 'I love you, Mum.'

The television flickered, arranging pixels for our passive viewing pleasure. When I imagined the last things I might lay my eyes on when I died, seeing Papa naked on an old grandma in a paddy field, thrusting himself up and down in the long grass was not high on my list. It was not in fact on my list at all. Yet there he was. The camera pulled in close on his seventy-five-year-old face and her varicose veins. On her wrinkled hands, hoisting up her sari, as they huffed and puffed together. As if taking their last geriatric breaths and making the oldest sound in the world, the horror dawned on me and Ava that they were, in fact, climaxing.

'Grandpa – what the fuck?' exclaimed Ava jumping up from the sofa to point at the screen.

'It's me,' Papa beamed proudly.

'I can see that. Grandpa, why are you...why would you... look we all know you have a new girlfriend. We hear you. And if you want to film yourselves, fine. But why would you ever think we'd want to watch this? Grandpa, I'm a child!'

'Girlfriend? What? I don't have... Ohhh. No, I was rehearsing. She's my co-star. Lovely lady. Five grandchildren and she volunteers part-time in the children's playroom at the hospital.' My eyelids were within millimetres of closing. They let in a strip of light, as if someone had turned down a dial in the editing suite reducing Ava and Papa into short, scrunched up accordion images.

'Rehearsing? For what?' said Ava, hands on her hips.

'For a movie. It's not finished yet and the editor says there are some scenes that might not even make the cut.'

'Like this one, hopefully,' said Ava. Her voice had become far away now. Distant like an echo.

'Maybe, but it's okay because there are plenty more like this. It's called Anal Chutney. It's porn for the over sixties. It's a very specialist market. And, sorry Drea, but I borrowed some things from your cupboard. Props and clothes for the movie.'

'A specialist market is kangaroo fillets! This... this is disgusting.'

'Well I'm sorry you feel that way. I realise it's not everybody's cup of tea, but I bet you'll think differently when you see my payslip. It's an advance for two more movies and I want you and your mum to have it. All of it. For school. I know you don't talk to me about this sort of thing Drea, but I got the feeling maybe you were struggling a bit with Alex gone.'

'Oh my God! £15,000 pounds. Grandpa, you're serious. This isn't a joke?'

'No it certainly is not, my dear, although it is very funny that in the twilight of my years I seem to have found a renewed zest for life. It's true what they say, it's never too late.'

'Mum, are you hearing this?' All I could do was hear. My eyelids couldn't open and neither could my mouth. 'Look at this cheque Grandpa's got.' Pathways were beginning to melt away, I could feel it. Roads that connected organs were becoming unusable and not merely for maintenance, simply road closed.

'Mum. Mum. Are you sleeping? Grandpa, I think she's asleep. She must be so tired. Mum?'

'Ava. Ava call an ambulance. Tell them that your mother has taken an overdose.'

'What?'

'JUST DO IT, AVA. NOW!'

'What? But, but why?'

'Because the stupid idiot thinks it's her fucking legacy.'

Family Therapy

A white sofa with some cream cushions. It screamed impractical. Blood was notoriously difficult to remove from anything, let alone white home furnishings. I appreciated that the design team had been in communications with the medical team. Departments rarely spoke to one another anymore. It took too long and who cares if the results were better as long as there were results. No one did a job properly. But the white and cream was to create a neutral underpinning. A calm and relaxed state.

Flowers in a vase. Gerberas. Also white. Stilling the mind into the abyss of absence. A chair. Someone was expected. No windows. I would have liked windows. What better way to de-stress than with a tranquil view. Maybe there was no view to be had. And no pictures. Nothing we could talk about whilst not talking. Minimalism to the extreme. She came in, sat down on the chair and started reading her notes. She wore a knee-length white lab coat with white vintage-looking court shoes. It wasn't the most prepared entrance, but she seemed like the concerned type so I reserved judgement. I don't know how I could tell she was concerned, but I could smell the rain again.

'Drea.'

'Yes.'

'Do you know why you're here?'

'I can guess.'

'How are you feeling?'

'You really want to know?'

'Yes I do.' I believed her.

'Clearly my latest attempt at suicide didn't work and I'm a little pissed off.'

'A little?'

'I'm really fucking pissed off.'

'And what does that look like?'

'What does what look like?'

'Anger. For you. What does your anger look like? Where do you put it? How do you show it?'

'Well, I, don't really get that angry.'

'Really?' she asked in disbelief, and when her eyes rose up she looked familiar.

'Yes.'

'If my mother had committed suicide and left me all alone as a young child, I think I would have been very angry.' She could have been smug as that was critical information she pulled from up her sleeve but she wasn't, she was kind. I felt kindness. Dare I say, apologetic.

'How do you know that?'

'We're here to talk about your suicide attempt Drea. But is it so strange that I should know that?'

'Did my father tell you that?'

'I think you do get angry Drea. I think you have a lot of rage and I think you turn it on yourself. I think that's where your anger goes.'

'Where's Ava?' I asked.

'You just wanted someone to celebrate you Drea, that's all. It's not a big ask of your mother, really. Someone to gaze lovingly at your wondrousness. It's what we all want Drea. And you should have had it. You didn't but you should have.' Despite all my best intentions, I started to cry. It started off slow, just one tear. It moved to two, one from each eye and then multiple, until both sockets threw out water like mini waterfalls running down my face and my chest heaved from the agony, the pain that this woman was unearthing that had laid like volcanic black rock at the bottom of my infant heart for years.

'That's right, Drea. Let it all out, darling. What a weight you've been carrying Drea, all alone, all by yourself, the weight of being unlovable. But you see Drea, that you are not. You are not unlovable by any means; the opposite in fact. You are strong, funny, intelligent, creative, loving and incredibly lovable and it's all from you Drea. That's who you are really.' My tears came out hot from the burning emotional lava that Dr What's Her Name was stirring up. I suddenly had a flashback to myself as a child and saw my child self asking my adult self, 'Is this how you pictured your life when you were younger?' I realised that I had never pictured my future life when I was younger. I was so busy trying to survive and get through each day that one day my adult life just arrived.

'I don't know your name,' I sobbed.

'Dorothy. Dorothy Peiris.'

'My mother. That's my mother. Are you... are you my mother?'

'Do you need me to be?'

'Just answer the fucking question,' I roared, half-crying, half-screaming.

'We all need our mothers, Drea. Our mothers are our mirrors for where we go to discover how special we are. And sometimes mirrors break. Why do you think it's bad luck to break a mirror? But you didn't break it, sweetheart. Children can't break mirrors. Not these ones. They break because they do. They just do.'

'Open your coat.'

'Excuse me?'

'Open your coat.'

'Drea.'

'Please.' With a peculiar type of excited resignation, her fingers began to move, slowly, carefully, and, as she released each button, a knee-length white bridal dress began to emerge. It had three-quarter length sleeves and a gold brooch in the shape of a flower pinned to her chest. My mother's brooch. The photo on Papa's desk.

'Where did you get that from?'

'Do you like it?' she asked, smiling down at the only piece of jewellery that I'd ever known my mother to have owned.

'My mother had a dress and brooch exactly like that.'

'Did she?' She said with fondness.

'I… didn't know her.'

'But you wanted to,' she repeated with a childlike smile. 'You wanted her to know you?'

I could hear voices. Indecipherable and indistinct.

'Are you cold? It is cold in here,' I said. I heard Ava. She was calling me.

'My daughter is calling me. I need to go. Is this one of those evaluations where unless you certify me sane and not a danger to myself then I can't go home?'

'There's nothing wrong with you, darling. Nothing at all. You're wonderful. Do you want to go home?'

'Yes.'

'Is that right? You want to go home, Drea?'

'I think so.'

'No, Drea. Once they've sent you here, to me, you need to really want to go back for me to send you back.'

And all at once my body seemed almost hostile. I was pulled away, detached from it with such a pull, such a centrifugal force, and yet bound to it so hard that it hurt. Hurt everywhere but mostly in my gut, my arms, my legs and everywhere. I stretched out both hands to Dorothy in an effort to stay with her but she was already too far away. Only a belief in something bigger than what I could see with my eyes, a creator, a God-like figure, could explain or have the capacity to make what was happening possible. And although I didn't believe in a benevolent God, the pain from the wrenching of me and my body suggested the existence of some other type and thus I found myself believing for the first time ever in a deity I could not see.

'Goodbye, my darling Drea, goodbye,' called Dorothy, on her feet waving furiously at me, smiling proudly. Suddenly, I was hit with the most terrible pain in and around and behind my eyes. People composed of angles and colours began flittering into focus. I saw them before I heard them.

Ava was crying, and Papa and a nurse were trying to restrain her. Her arms reached out like desperate tentacles around them, trying to break free, and the nurse was a hazy blur of blue and white trying to hold her back.

Bleeps. Staccato. People in white coats hovered over a bed. A hospital. No one could see me looking at them but I could see everyone. Where was I? I tried to touch Ava but the thought of moving my hands fell into a dark void. I tried to call out to her but the thought of a sound emanating from my throat also fell, plunging into the deep. The staccato bleeps lengthened, elongating into one continuous stretch of sound which seemed to stretch far beyond that of the hospital room and into far-off lands and places still unseen. Ava was screaming, shaking. Papa was sobbing, collapsed. For the briefest second, I felt connected to everyone and everything and then it all stopped. The pain, the people. Just stopped. And I waited. And I waited. And I waited for a really long time. Time is actually a lot more perspicacious than I realised because in all that time when I thought nothing happened, I came back.

Glendale School for Girls
4 Ruans Lane
Lauriston

81 Barlow Road
Lauriston

15th January 1971

Dear Anand Peiris,

It is with regret that I am writing to you at this time. I understand that you and Drea are still suffering after the tragic loss of Mrs Peiris. However, after a recent poetry class, I feel that Drea may be struggling more than any of us realise. The class was asked to pick their favourite food and write a poem.

Jam
Jam is inside me.
It waits until I sleep to speak to me.
My jam isn't like the others.
It has no sisters and no brothers.
It isn't sweet and doesn't spread.
It bites the inside of my head.
I don't like jam, I NEVER WILL
Jam puts me on the window sill
I'm scared up there, it's really high
Jam says I'll sleep longer if I die.

by Drea Peiris, aged 9

'She's waking up.'

Ava?

'Doc, get over here, she's waking up.'

Papa?

'Drea? How are you feeling?' The doctor came into view. I nodded. 'Okay,' he smiled, 'I can work with that. You're here to get better. Understand?' Yeah, I got it doc. I really do.

'She must be starving,' said Papa.

'I imagine she is. I'll get the nurse to bring her something,' said the doctor.

'aaaam,' I mouthed.

'What did she say?' said the doctor.

'What do you want, Drea,' asked Papa.

'Jam,' I whispered.

'Jam?' said the doc.

'She hates jam.' said Papa.

'Jam,' I said.

'Not anymore. Nurse, get this patient some jam, please.'

One Year Later

'Mum! Where are my campaign posters?' shouted Ava from her bedroom.

It was a fact. A mother was an important cog in the family machine. Maybe even the most important. Over the last year, I had witnessed the effects of what happens to a family when the mother isn't 'fully present,' as the professionals liked to put it.

'Dad?'

'Ask your mother!' shouted Alex from the kitchen.

I was having a 'me moment', out of the window, puffing on a cigarette and staring out at my street – which seemed so different from a year ago. New neighbours for a start. The newlyweds had left. The divorce wasn't particularly costly but had still meant they'd both had to move back in with their respective parents. There were more street lights. It had first started with security around the park being tightened up but had then been extended to certain streets deemed more at risk. Ironically, mine was one.

I'd been in group therapy for three months, family therapy for six months and individual therapy for a year. The pamphlets said the effects of suicide were 'tragic' for children and the more right-wing literature said it was 'the selfish and cruel act of an adult'. This made it easy to know what to say to make the facilitators think I'd reformed. Seen the error of my ways and repented. At first I cried on cue and nodded regretfully when appropriate. Talked about God here and there, they loved that. Between you and me, suicide is a personal decision. I'm not saying people won't shed a tear, but it's like abortion; my body, my business. But I did learn things. Things I worked out for myself in the spaces in between all the therapy. I learned that suicide is a lifestyle choice, and not a lifestyle I necessarily wanted but one I sought out for safety. To keep from being shocked by sadness, I chose to live with the sadness of the inevitable. My sadness, my terms.

I didn't drink or smoke weed the way I used to. I hated the righteous way the doctors campaigned against it, but over the year I found I relied on it less than I used to. I would use them like an anaesthetic; to numb the area. These days I survive in a different way. Turns out that when I wasn't trying so hard to escape my life, I actually preferred peppermint tea.

Ava took a while to accept the suicide concept. There was anger there. She felt abandoned by her biological mother and then again by me. It was unfortunate. It hadn't been my intention. My needs and hers had simply clashed. It happens. It happens all the time in families actually and I suppose that's also what life's about. Alex had understood more, but then he was more practised at disappointing people. Things hadn't worked out between him and Poppy so he'd returned, a little more mature and with a lot of smelly cheese. Due to his own flexible moral stance, he was that much more open-minded about the failings of others. He'd been unflinchingly supportive and, whilst Ava and I struggled, Alex and I got closer. Alex brought Ava back to me – I lost her for a little while. As a resident dignitary of extreme moral virtues, her expectations of others were high and for me the fall from those heights felt very lonely.

After six weeks, the government cut the free therapy. They probably thought that if you were still feeling that bad, just go ahead and do it because the country is over-populated anyway.

As Papa was still paying Ava's school fees and Alex was back teaching, we were doing alright. Who knew there'd be such a market for over-sixties' porn?

I talked about Mother. More in the last year than I ever had before. About the mother I wish I'd had. The mother I thought I deserved. About the mother I'd actually had. And how not getting what I needed as a child led me to create fantasy mother figures. There was the punishing mother and then the genuine mother. Both had fused into a belief that embodied an idea of the only mother I could ever hope to be. The mother that was never good enough. It was all very interesting, extremely painful, but enlightening in a way I had honestly never expected. I had assumed these talking therapies were exclusively for other groups; refugees, gluten frees, minorities. I was pleasantly surprised to find that there were those just as fucked up as I was – and they were the ones who admitted it.

Today was I smoking a celebratory cigarette to mark the end of my individual therapy. I was all grown up. We had been working towards it for the last couple of months. I made some jam doughnuts to give my therapist. I knew she'd appreciate the symbolism. Fucking complicated, doughnuts. I should have just bought them and said I made them. I was a bit sad to say goodbye and she said she felt the same. Who knew a suicide junkie would have a problem with goodbyes? I'd also enrolled in a Masters in Psychological Criminology. Over the past year, I'd started wondering about people and everything we're capable of and it had got me thinking. It wasn't necessarily supposed to lead to a job but I decided to go wild and study something I found interesting just for the hell of it. Regina Salter was actually the one who gave me the idea. After Henry decided to go back to Henrietta and try make the marriage work, Regina hit the bottle hard. One day she lured him to her house for a last goodbye. She tied him up and cut off his penis.

It shocked the town, naturally. Gatlin didn't think it was that sort of town – although after two murders it was exactly that sort of town.

Regina has a lot of time to think whilst she does time in a women's facility. It's been tough for Amelia with Regina away but she's a strong girl. She's been spending a lot of time in our house and I think she's contemplating a career in medicine with a possible specialism in penile reconstruction. It's not as uncommon as one thinks, apparently.

Maude and Felicity are in the same corrective institution as Regina but in a different wing. I visit both sisters once a week. Dick's been a lot less of a dick over the last year. It came out later that he was prescribing the sisters himself with HRT treatments as they were both enduring terrible mood swings from the peri-menopause. He testified to how much better they had both been feeling but that Gatlin withdrawing his and Maude's daughter's place and Victoria pulling the plug on Felicity's job had set them back somewhat.

I see Ann from time to time and she looks tired. Catherine caught her in bed with Xavier and is blackmailing her. She's turned her mother into her personal slave until further notice. Tabatha and Amelia say she's got a bell and demands Ann come to her bedroom when she rings it. I feel sorry for her, but it does make me smile.

I look at the clock and head downstairs. Ava's running for re-election today. How time flies. It's a sure-fire win but she doesn't want to act complacent. Alex joked about whether she was sure that she wanted me there after what happened at the last one, but on the other hand how did she expect to win without two murders and two robberies?

'Mum! Door. It's for you.' I arrived downstairs barefoot, in my dressing gown, no make-up. He had his back to me at first and turned around when I got there. He was the one thing I really regretted and I just expected I'd never see him again. He hadn't changed a bit. My stomach flipped and then I remembered I hadn't even brushed my teeth.

'Hi,' said Rodman.

'You,' I stammered. I couldn't believe it. How many times had I dreamed of opening the door and finding him there? I'd called the station and they said he'd transferred to another branch but they had no other details. I'd assumed he'd come to his senses. Wanted nothing to do with me. Birds cheeped around us – it was that early. I wondered if he thought I'd changed. Got older. He looked the same. No softer. What was I thinking? He wasn't here for me. It must be a police-related matter. It had to be.

'I knew you were in hospital.' I didn't answer. What was there to say?

'I heard you took a load of pills but I didn't think I could help. Figured you needed to work through some stuff.' Loved that about Rodman. Hated the small talk as much as I did. I held my dressing gown tightly around my chest. It was in no danger of falling, yet I was naked underneath and Rodman was standing on my doorstep so it was as if I had no dressing gown on at all. The sun shined on my face and I moved an inch to the left. Scared to move too much and change how things were right at this very second.

'Darling, shall I put some toast on for you?' Alex marched outside in his boxer shorts and my stomach flipped again the other way.

'Alex, this is Detective Rodman.'

'Oh. Is there a problem?'

'No, uh, no problem,' said Rodman.

'Detective Rodman worked the case a year ago.'

'Okay. But the case is closed right?'

'Yes,' stalled Rodman. I didn't know what to say. I hated leaving him out there alone like this but I was struck dumb.

'So why are you here, Detective?' asked Alex.

'I think he wants to ask Mum out,' called Ava from inside.

'Really?' said Alex. 'Is this true, Detective?'

'Look I'm sorry, I didn't mean to. I thought you… Drea, I'm sorry,' and he took a step back.

'Oh I see,' mused Alex, 'you think. Well, I can see why you would. How dare you?' he roared. 'How dare you come to my house and try to break up a home, a family!' Rodman turned to go as his face sunk into his cheekbones.

'Mum and Dad aren't 'together' together,' shouted Ava. 'They just live together because they love me.'

Rodman looked surprised. I'd never seen him shocked before. It was funny. He was so composed and sure of himself that when he looked shocked he almost looked scared.

'Oh, I had to,' laughed Alex, holding his stomach. 'It was too good an opportunity to miss.'

'Is that true?' he said, looking at me with the deepest and sincerest eyes.

'Come in, Detective,' said Alex, stepping aside. 'Drea and I have an 'avant-garde' relationship, although something tells me I don't have to educate you in the wonder of Drea. Come and have some breakfast with us.' I smiled and nodded, goosebumps all over my deliriously happy arms. Rodman followed me into the house.

'So tell me the story from the beginning,' urged Alex, 'I do love a good love story.' As the front door closed we heard Ava scream, 'Well then who's gonna do the fucking school run?'